MAGE DISSOLUTION

Christopher George

Mage Dissolution 1st Edition

This novel is entirely a work of fiction. Any resemblance
to actual persons living or dead, is entirely coincidental.

Cover design by Christopher George
Cover photography by Ian Harding Photography
& Trace Hudson
Cover artwork by Megan Owenson
Editing by Lu Sexton – A Story to Tell
Typesetting by Odyssey Books

ISBN: 648578406
ISBN-13: 978-0-6485784-0-6

DEDICATION

This book is dedicated to Michelle Culling, my high school art and theatre teacher. School was never one of my favourite things in the world, in fact I was a lousy student until you found a way to get through to me. In going through my experiences in writing *Mage Catalyst* and reliving my own experiences in high school through Devon's eyes it has become apparent to me that you are in no small part responsible for the person that I have become.

Thank you.

ACKNOWLEDGMENTS

This book represents a turning point in my writing, when I had taken that foolish step into thinking that I knew what I was doing. I would like to especially acknowledge Rebecca Truong for her subtle (but effective) way of telling me that I was on the wrong path. The massive rewrite that you prompted changed the story and made it so much better than I had thought it could have been. Thank you.

I'd like to thank Ian Harding once again for his work on the cover. He must be getting sick of taking photos of various people's hands by now. Megan Owenson for her digital work for the cover. You bring my characters to life in your artwork.

Also I'd like to thank Trace Hudson for his amazing photo of the Grand Teton Mountain Range that was used on the cover. You can check out more of his work at www.tracehudson.com.

To Rebecca and Imogen for once again being patient and understanding with me during this process.

Dissolution

/dɪsə'luːʃ(ə)n/

- The action of formally ending or dismissing an assembly, partnership or official body.

- debauched living; dissipation

PROLOGUE

Hatred is a poor pathway to power. It does not seem like it would be, but it is. Hatred leads only to stagnation and loss. I had thought myself all-powerful, but that was not the case. I was not stronger; I was simply out of control.

My name is Devon Wills and I have been consumed by my hatred. It burns like a fire within my mind and keeps me locked into the worst moments of my life. I see the death of my father every time I close my eyes. I feel bile rise in my throat as I again remember my helplessness over my inability to protect Allie.

I had thought that I could protect them from those who sought me harm. I knew that my actions would cost, yet I thought that I was somehow above the consequences. I was not. And those I loved were the ones who paid the price for my arrogance.

In a foolish move I attempted to use my hatred to make myself powerful enough to overcome my enemies, only to learn that there is a more powerful thing than hate – regret. Hatred is a shackle that binds you to the past. Regret destroys that past. Everything is tainted by your regret and your guilt until it is all you see. Every action you took, no matter how noble, is twisted into a parody of its former glory. My hatred changed me; then my regret destroyed me.

I cast aside the vows I'd sworn to hide the magic from the real world. I conducted a guerrilla war as I sought to punish those who had wronged me. Yes, I am guilty and perhaps tonight I shall pay the price.

I flex my fingers and feel the power arch across them. A small shiver of pleasure passes through me. This is the only thing that I can still feel. My eyes cast over the horizon and I feel nothing for my home. The light that once shone so brightly in my eyes has been dulled and the laugh in my voice quietened. I no longer care for those around me. I no longer feel empathy or joy, sorrow or grief. I simply am.

Enjoy what solace you find in this life, for it is fleeting. Treasure the time you share with your loved ones and remember it takes only but a moment of weakness before they are gone. There is no power on this earth that can stop it. We live in a lie. There is no safety and salvation for those we love. No, there is only eventual death and loss.

A spectacular explosion lights up the skies as a skyscraper comes tumbling to the ground. I notice it only as a passing interest. The noise is deafening and a wave of fresh smoke and dust washes over me like water. I can feel small shards of concrete and rubble impacting my shield. If I were a normal man, I would be dead now. But I am not a normal man. I am a Mage. Such a small thing could not bring me harm. I am above such things and yet here I stand on this building ready to face the one foe who could bring me death.

I do not need to name him; it must be obvious of whom I speak. I once called him Master and revered him. He appeared to be everything that I wanted for myself. So powerful and in control. He taught me what it meant to be strong. He put me on the path that led to this, and for that he shall be punished as I have been.

He is here, in this city. I have finally found him and I finally have the knowledge necessary to bring an end to him. I have broken every law our kind has to bring forth this confrontation. I have brought war and destruction to those I love to bring him down. Tonight I will end this.

Tonight Victor Whittlesea shall die or I will. This I swear. There is no escape. We pay for the injustice of our actions.

CHAPTER ONE

I glanced around the crowded barroom as I nursed a near empty glass. A large crowd of men appeared to be only seconds away from a riot as they watched the television in the corner. The TV had been muted but was broadcasting some sports event, soccer, I think. I'm not good with sports.

I wasn't concerned by the impending uprising from the soccer hooligans. For one I knew it was just the way they were about their sports and secondly, I knew that I was by far the most dangerous person in this room.

I checked the clock. My target wasn't here yet. I was in a small bar in Berlin. My travels had brought me here several weeks ago. It had taken me some time to locate this particular bar. A person who frequented it regularly was someone that I very much wanted to talk to. He was the final link in a long and arduous search. A search that I hoped was nearing completion. This man was going to lead me straight to my missing cousin, Allie, and my former Master. He didn't know he was going to do these things yet, but he was. He wouldn't have a choice.

I'd spent three years travelling from city to city, hunting for my cousin and the man who took her – Victor.

I searched Singapore and found that Victor had already withdrawn his interests from that city. I futilely extended my search northwards into other Asian cities and deeper into mainland China. It was obvious though – he wasn't in Asia. So I moved west and entered Europe.

I occasionally met others of my kind, but I kept my distance. Most nodded amicably and moved on, some I am sure would have reported my location instantly had they known who I was. I passed through towns as no more than a ghost, completely off the grid. I'd long since lost any form of identification or personal documents. I no longer needed such things.

I would do anything to release my cousin from Victor's influence. I would kill this man if I had to, although I hoped that it wouldn't come to that. I wasn't squeamish about the killing, but it wouldn't serve my ends and would create an unnecessary commotion. It was possible that I'd grown a touch callous.

I glanced around the bar again in frustration. He was late. Or maybe he wasn't coming tonight. That had happened to me yesterday. If this was the case again, I would return tomorrow. It had taken me a long time to locate this man and I wasn't going to return empty handed. He was one of Victor's many accountants and I knew that he would know where my former Master could be found. If anyone could lead me to Victor it was this man. No, I wasn't going to give up. I would return to this bar every night this month if I had to.

The bar tender nodded at me and pushed another

drink in my direction. I reached down into my pockets and leaned back onto the stool. My fingers curled around a fifty Eurodollar note curled up into a tight roll in my right pocket. I closed my eyes and began to concentrate. The Mana flowed down my arms and into my other hand.

I knew that no one else would be able to see the Mana flowing down my arms in single particles of power, but I felt self-conscious none the less. It was an automatic response when I drew upon my power. The tingling down my arm indicated the Mana was performing its required task.

I hadn't mastered this technique yet, but I was getting better. It was something that Victor had shown me once, and although I was nowhere near as proficient as he had been, I had gained a rudimentary understanding of the magic required. It had taken me some time to figure out the theory behind it and I had been quite amazed when I had first successfully completed the spell.

I gently crinkled the texture of the Eurodollar note between my fingers as I let the Mana do its work. I felt the familiar tingling in my left hand as the Mana reached completion. This wasn't a basic technique, it required a lot of energy and concentration, and it still took me a lot of time. The bar tender coughed impatiently as he waited for me to produce payment.

He made some comment in German, which I grunted at and ignored. He obviously didn't know that I could speak German. I must have screamed out-of-towner to him when I had first walked in the door yesterday. I didn't mind – let him think me a tourist if he was going to remember me at all. Which I'd rather he didn't.

Perhaps I was a tourist in some ways I had after all travelled across Asia and Europe in my search for Victor. The only counter to my frustration was that I discovered I had a gift for languages. I was able to lightly converse after a few weeks of exploring whatever country I travelled. This isn't to say that I was fluent, but I could make myself be understood and could understand most of what was said to me. That was all that was important.

I chalked this new skill up to Victor's teachings. I certainly hadn't shown any aptitude for language in high school. Victor's training regime had shown me how easy it was to teach yourself something new without guidance. Victor had shown me how to analyse a concept without applying my own prejudices, and to come to understand the truth of the concept quickly and easily. There wasn't anything magical about this, it was simply a mindset that allowed a greater aptitude for learning. It was more a discipline than a trick and it had served me well over the past few years.

The bartender grunted impatiently, bringing me back to the present. I feigned trying to fetch a coin from within my pocket. In way this was kind of the truth, except that I wasn't looking for payment. I was creating it.

I felt the usual feeling of release as the Mana completed its task and pulled a newly minted 50 Eurodollar bill from my left pocket and placed it on the bar. I flexed my fingers and released the original bill in my right pocket and leaned forward.

"Danke," I muttered as I pulled the drink to my lips.

I'd pulled this trick more times than I could care to name. I'd probably slightly devalued whatever currency I was using several times over during my exploits, but I didn't care. I hadn't been caught out yet. It wasn't likely that I was going to be either. The counterfeit currency that I was creating was identical to the original, right down to the serial number on the note. Almost impossible to identify as a fraud unless someone compared the two serial numbers, side by side. But that wasn't very likely as I rarely needed to use more than one note at a time. I kept my original in a separate compartment in my wallet so that it didn't get mixed up with any change. My expenses were minimal anyway and I had other ways of procuring what I needed if things got difficult. I could get by and that was all that was important. I had almost reached the point where I could do away with money entirely – almost.

I carried around a diamond worth approximately half a million dollars that been created by Victor without the need for a template, so I knew that it could be done. I had thought about off-loading it, but found that I didn't want to part with it. I could of course have copied it, but I would have then had the same trouble offloading the copies. You can't simply drop a diamond of that quality into a market without raising eyebrows. This was okay however as it wasn't like I really needed the money.

I could easily continue the way I was going, unless I needed to settle down and I wasn't going to do that until I had dealt with Victor.

My former master had been able to create items from memory, but this feat was beyond my poor skills so far. It was a pity as this would have been incredibly handy. I still needed to be physically holding the item that I was attempting to clone. No doubt Victor would have claimed that this was a weakness caused by lack of understanding or discipline. I that didn't bother me, I could perform the technique and I was getting quicker. That was all that mattered. Mastery would come in time.

When I had left Victor's care in Singapore, I had taken with me enough field notes and journals to continue my training. I had not been lax in my studies and my powers had increased tenfold from where I had been when I had left Singapore. Although I had learned much, I knew that I still had far to go if I was going to seriously challenge Victor.

I didn't make any long term plans or even contemplate what I would do after all this was over. I was starting to doubt that it would ever be over. I had a horrible thought that I would spend the rest of my life chasing Victor around the world until I finally died of old age.

* * * * * *

Teleportation allowed me to move freely without the need for mundane transport. If I wanted to be somewhere

I could simply move myself there. There were issues though, Teleportation wasn't easy and could be dangerous. I hadn't experienced any problems so far, but the theories that I had learned from had warned of the dangers. There was the danger of accidently teleporting into a space that was currently occupied by another object. This would be resolved in the fatal way of atomic meshing. This charming phrase was used to describe the process of where the atomic components of both the teleporter and the teleportee were merged. This was almost always fatal.

Fortunately, this was an unlikely risk. The Teleport spell required you to be able to see where you were teleporting to and as you couldn't usually see inside solid objects this was not often a problem. It could, of course, be done accidently by not scoping your jump properly. The real danger was merging with the ground upon which you're standing. A few measly centimetres too low and you've lost most of your foot. Most Mages teleporting will allow a slight discrepancy in height and fall a few centimetres to the ground after the jump rather than risk becoming enmeshed with the ground.

The Scry spell greatly increased the range of teleportation as it allowed me to see a far greater distance than I would be have been able to do with my eyes alone. Teleporting across the use of a Scry thread was much more difficult, but far more useful. For one, it meant that mundane travel quickly became redundant. I could travel in a few seconds what would have taken me an hour by car. It was definitely worth the risk.

The first time I had attempted to teleport from a Scry spell I nearly bungled the effect. I was able to correct myself at the last minute, but I had no idea what would have happened if I had not been able to fix the problem. In all likelihood the thread would have collapsed and I would have remained where I was standing. That didn't seem too bad. The other option was that some of my 'corporeal matter' as the text books phrased it would have been transported and some would not have been. This would of course have resulted in the rather quick and messy death.

I had no wish to distribute my corporeal matter across the city so I was very careful with my experimentation. My first test via a Scry thread had been very simple. It had been from one room to an adjacent one. The distance didn't really matter much though, it was more about the concept. The arrival room could have easily been on the other side of the city, but I wanted to be somewhere safe should something go wrong.

After several tentative tests I quickly became confident that I had the technique down. Once I had that confidence the next step was simple practice. As I used the technique more, I found that my range increased and I could teleport quicker. My limit at the moment was around fifty kilometres, but I was improving quickly. I knew it wouldn't be long before I would be able to scry 100 kilometres in distance and then even perhaps a thousand.

I still wasn't anywhere near as skilled as Victor who could teleport himself from Singapore to Melbourne - a distance of a little over six thousand kilometres. I had no idea if that was his maximum distance, but I doubted it. I was beginning to think that there was no upper limit to our abilities. Every time I thought I had reached the full extent of my powers I was forced to exceed them and found that my powers had increased.

This wasn't the only thing that made me powerful though. The more I understood about a technique or theory that I was drawing upon the more I found that I could use less and less raw power to achieve the same effect. This in turn meant that when I did use more power the effect was greater.

I travelled alone for the most part of my search for Victor. Renee had expressed some reluctance in assisting me as she had no desire to face down her grandfather. She did assist me from time to time. She was able to still walk amongst our kind and was able to keep me abreast of what was going on in our world.

This was a luxury that I wasn't afforded. I had been declared an outcast and to assist me was to invite death. This was one of the reasons why I kept a wide berth between myself and other Mages.

Renee was the one who often gave me hints on where to continue my search. I don't know how she was able to obtain this intelligence but I was very grateful. Renee had actually been the one who had highlighted the accountant's importance to me.

Through Renee I learned that the Primea, the leader of our kind, had fallen sick and had retreated from social appearances. In her absence the fight between my former Master and Marcus, Renee's father had escalated. This wasn't surprising. It had long been presumed that the only thing preventing all out Mage War between the two had been the Primea.

This would be a war that would be felt in the real world. I didn't even care much about that, as long as I got my cousin out of it before the shells starting raining down. I had no interest in a Mage war between Marcus and Victor and I definitely had no interest in choosing a side. Due to the conflict Victor had also withdrawn from the Mage society and had become a recluse, but to hear Renee talk about it, it was easy to see his hand in the political actions of his allies.

He was still pulling the strings, but no one could figure out from where. This was the crux of my problem. If I could find where he was hiding, I was sure that my cousin would be with him. I should have perhaps come to Germany first in my search, I knew that Victor was German by birth, but I foolishly thought he would move further north from Singapore.

He hadn't, I'd wasted much of my time searching the Asian continent for some sign of Victor.

I kept in regular contact with both Renee and Marcus during my travels, more so with Renee. Marcus was too embroiled in political infighting to be of much help, and I was loath to call upon him as I knew that there would be a cost for his aid. I never fully trusted Marcus, I suspected his assistance was nothing more than a helping hand to someone who could potentially damage his rival.

Marcus was adamant that I join him in his fight against Victor and had tried to recruit me to his cause several times. I refused, I wasn't going to be drawn into his fight. If truth be told, I suspected it was a losing cause anyway. Of the two of them, Victor was the more powerful and the more likely to win in the long run.

My relationship with Marcus had soured after he had tried to physically force me to join him during his last attempt to recruit me. Harsh words had been exchanged at my reluctance to sign up to his cause and he had lost his temper. I had always known him as a dangerous man, but I do not think I've ever been closer to death than when he had faced me down. It had gotten messy and I still count myself lucky to have gotten away with my life.

I refused several more invitations to meet with him after that confrontation. I sensed another trap and wasn't prepared to take the risk of another meeting between us. Renee had accepted my decision, although she had made comments that Marcus could help me. I never really understood the relationship between Renee and her father. She had been raised by Victor, her grandfather, and had only discovered that Marcus was her biological father a few years ago. She seemed that have adjusted to this news well, but I could tell that there was tension between the two. Unfortunately Renee would never discuss so sensitive a subject with me. In some ways she was even more close mouthed about her feelings than I was.

* * * * * *

A small bell clanged as the door opened and brought me back from my reverie. My prey was here. I didn't turn to look at him, but I could feel that it was him. There was no possible way that I should have heard the bell over the sound of the barroom, yet I swear that I did.

I waited until the accountant made his way through the crowd to get to the bar. He didn't look over at me as he sat down, but I hadn't expected him to. He simply sat at the bar and mechanically pulled his drink to his lips. After a few sips he appeared to sigh slightly. He glanced around the barroom warily, but quickly returned his focus to his drink.

"You seem nervous," I whispered to him in my stilted German. He snorted into his drink and ignored me. He might not have heard me though as he didn't respond.

"You should be nervous," I continued, switching to English.

He turned to look at me. I could see him inspecting my face looking for something familiar. I was a little surprised when His face went white with recognition.

"You!" he gasped. I couldn't tell if he was getting ready to flee or not, but he must have been considering it.

"If you run for it, you won't make it to the door," I commented darkly.

He nodded briefly and I could see him scanning the room for a possible rescue. I could tell by the dropping of his shoulders and the slouch that he realised that he was trapped. The crowded bar room would actually count against him here. If he should move away from the bar and into the crowd it was unlikely that anyone would see what would happen to him. At least here he was in the open and unlikely to be attacked.

His hand slipped down to what I presumed was a mobile phone in his pocket. I could tell he was trying to be subtle about it, but he was obviously terrified and it's hard to be subtle under those circumstances.

"I wouldn't do that if I were you," I advised softly.

His hand jerked away from his pocket and hurriedly placed it upon the bar between us.

"That's good," I said gently. "There's a good chance that nothing is going to happen to you…" I let my tone go a little darker, "…if you co-operate."

"What do you want?" I asked me timidly as he tentatively took another sip of his drink. His hand was shaking so much that he hand trouble bringing the glass to his lips.

"I want to know where Miss Burton is." I said, referring to my cousin by her surname.

"I do not know who that is," he replied in German.

"There is no point lying to me." I snapped back in German as I slipped a photo from my inside pocket and passed it across the bench top.

It was a photo of Victor and Allie, and he was standing

right behind them as they walked from his office building. It had been taken a month ago, I wasn't sure by whom, but Renee had passed it on to me. It was what had led me to Berlin. To his credit he didn't try to lie any further.

"You cannot blame me for trying," he mumbled.

"No," I agreed readily, "in your place I would have attempted the same."

"What happens now?" he whispered.

"That depends." I shrugged. I wasn't really sure what he hoped I was going to say here. There wasn't much to say.

"I cannot betray Master Whittlesea."

"Yes, you can. You have no choice."

"No, I cannot." He sighed, "he has seen to this."

Damnit. Victor's compulsions. I should have foreseen this. Victor had the ability to compel people to do his bidding. He had obviously compelled the man to remain silent, which was infuriating as I had no ability to counter the compel effect. I had scoured through the training documents that I had stolen from Victor but this was the one piece of his sorcery that I was unable to find any reference to. I did not have access to his full suite of books on Mana, but I had hoped to find at least some reference to it.

I had once spoken to Master Marcus on the subject but he didn't seem to understand the spell any better than I did. We couldn't duplicate the effect, but we could protect ourselves from it. This had been enough up until now.

"This is going to be unpleasant then." I whispered

softly, "Finish your drink. We will need to go somewhere quieter."

"Why would I go with you?" he scoffed as he took another sip of his drink. He made no move to get up.

"Because I will kill you if you do not." I replied casually as I got to my feet.

"And lose your information?" he smirked.

"If need be," I shrugged, "you're nothing more than a means to an end for me. I have other avenues, you were merely the easiest."

It was a lie, but I wasn't going to let him know that. My statement made him rethink things though. I casually looped a Mana thread around his hand resting on the table. I caused the loop to tighten around his little finger on his left hand. He looked up at me in shock and tried to pull his hand away. Unfortunately for him, a Mana thread is a powerful force. He was unable to break free.

"Listen to me," I sneered as I leaned in, "I don't care for you, and I don't care for your laws. This crowd of people does not make you safe. If I wanted to I could leave you broken and bleeding on the floor and no one in here would know any better, until I left."

He had gone white. This wasn't unexpected as I had been gradually increasing the level of pressure around his little finger. It must have hurt horribly, but to his credit he remained silent and stared at me balefully. I could see what it was costing him though. I could see the pain behind his eyes, he would break soon. Unfortunately for him, his finger broke before he did.

There was a surprisingly loud cracking noise as his finger caved in. I had placed my loop just above his knuckle and I could see the digit twist as it collapsed in on itself. He bit back a shriek. The barman looked over at us, but was unable to see anything out of the ordinary.

"You should co-operate now," I said darkly. "If you're quick enough you might even have enough time to get to a hospital in time to save that finger."

He gasped as he looked down at his mangled hand and nodded quickly as he got to his feet. I followed him through the crowd at a leisurely pace. I was certain that he would make a break for it at some point, but I could handle that when it happened. I was surprised when he didn't. Perhaps I had finally gotten through to him. There was no point in resisting.

Once we got outside he tucked his hand inside his pockets, nursing his shattered finger from the cold. I surveyed the street and assessed my next move. It wasn't that late so there was a still lot of people about, making their way home from work. It was a pity that it wasn't less crowded.

"Where to now?" He asked.

"The alley," I grunted, gesturing across the street. Once I got him into the alley I could safely teleport us both away.

"No," he stated loudly. "I will not go with you."

"It seems a little late for heroics now, don't you think?" I commented wryly.

He kept glancing nervously about. In hindsight I really should have picked up on it sooner: he had used my temporary distraction to ring for help on his phone. Mana threads arched across the skyline and ended in the alley. The very alley that I had been going to use to escape. That was annoyingly ironic.

A loud shattering bang heralded their arrival. Three Mages emerged from the alley.

I smiled, stretched my shoulders and flexed my fingers feeling the power flow out as I drew upon my Mana, "Don't go anywhere," I said casually as assessed my enemies.

I could tell from the complexity of their Scry threads that they weren't very powerful Mages, but they were skilled enough to pull off a Scry thread and a teleport spell so they must have had some skill. Also, there were three of them. This could be challenging.

They would already know who I was and where I was. They would have seen me through their Scry thread on the way in. They would have seen how powerful I was, but they were young and to judge from their expressions they were very obviously over confident. I grinned to myself in spite of the danger.

Once they got closer I could see that my assessment was correct. They weren't as powerful as I was in sheer strength, but then again few were. I doubted that they were apprentices of Victor, it was more likely that they were trained by one of his allies. None of this made my difference in the long run though, there were three of them and one of me.

"You may surrender now," the one in the lead called

once he got within speaking range.

"And if I choose not to."

He balked a little at this, I suspected that he was under the impression that I would be cowed by his superiority in numbers. He was in for a surprise.

"We can't fight here on the street," he stammered.

"You can't, maybe," I said as I let the Mana flow down my arms and formed powerful Mana threads to each side of me. With a slight flick of my wrist I raised a Mana shield over me. I could see them visibly gulp as they pulled shields over themselves.

The one on the right looked for confirmation from the leader. He obviously wasn't sure that they should be doing this. He was probably right, they shouldn't be. This was against the rules. Mages can't fight in the open street like this, but I could. I'd already been kicked out the order. I could see the emotions battle across his face. He very much wanted to attack me, but every fibre of his being was screaming against it.

His conflict proved to be to my benefit. I didn't wait for them to strike, in fact I was pretty sure that they weren't going to. They were still too worried about the people walking down the street around us. This placed the advantage of the first attack in my court.

I launched both threads around in a swinging motion, scissoring between them. The two Mages on each side wisely decided to leap over my strike, but the leader arrogantly thought he could endure my attack on his shield unscathed. To be fair, he almost did. Almost.

There was a devastating cracking noise as my threads impacted with his shield and brought it down. The thread tore through his body and brought him face first to the ground.

He didn't get up. It must have looked pretty strange to everyone else. To those without Mana sight it would have appeared that I had waved my hands at him and he fell down. I could see several passers-by look on in horror. It must have been obvious that this wasn't street performance. This led to several shouts of terror as people fled in all directions.

I didn't have to examine my fallen foe to know that he was horribly hurt. He was definitely still alive as I could see his chest slowly rising and falling, but he didn't look like he was going to regain consciousness anytime soon. I could see the Mana still surging through his body in reaction to the threat. The flow of Mana ebbed and faded as his body grew weaker. It wasn't a certainty that he would survive this. I didn't feel any pity for him, his own arrogance and stupidity had led him to his fate. He had deserved it.

My head jerked around as a thread impacted onto the side of my shield. The blow wasn't that strong, but it was enough to send me staggering back several steps. A second impact spun me round from the other side. I was amazed that I managed to keep myself on my feet after the power of that strike. My opponent obviously felt the same way as I could see his surprise on his face through our shields.

They had obviously expected to have dropped my shield by now. I lurched forward and out of the way of another one of their attacks. They were relentless in their pursuit. I glanced around for the accountant, but he must have taken the opportunity to flee. I didn't much blame him. This was only a minor problem, I'd simply collect him later.

I retreated down a busy side street beside the bar in an attempt to bring the odds more into my favour. They couldn't attack me from both sides if we were in a crowd. I could also hear the sound of police sirens in the background, so it probably wasn't a bad idea to move off the main street. The last thing I needed were cops getting involved.

A short and savage flurry of blows forced me to defend myself as I drew them deeper into the street. To be honest though, I didn't have much choice. Now that they were prepared for my attack it was hard to pierce through their defence. They weren't as powerful as I was, but they were still well trained. It would take some time to break through their defences. I just couldn't get a decent shot through with any strength to make a difference to the outcome.

I used a break in the attack to vault backwards over the wall behind me and found myself in a narrow courtyard. It appeared to be the back of a factory or something. It was deserted. I tried to catch my breath back as the two vaulted as one over the wall.

I used the opportunity to attack. A short sharp shout

of pain indicated that I had been successful as I knocked one of them savagely back against the wall. He slid down the wall and fell into a heap at the base. I knew he was still alive from his Mana signature, but he certainly was out of the fight, for the moment at least.

His companion landed with grace and launched several strikes at my chest level but his shot went wide and I was able to side step around him. He rose into the air swinging.

Unfortunately for him, without his companion to assist him he was no match for me and the tide of battle quickly turned to my favour. He must have realised very that he was over matched as his strategy altered towards the defensive.

"You should run," I grunted at him between strikes. He looked at me uncomprehendingly and I repeated my advice in German. He didn't respond but launched another attack at me, which I easily defended and countered knocking him backwards. He stumbled and fell and scrambled away from me. I let him regain his feet.

"You can't win." I said, not bothering to switch to German.

"I don't have to win," he snarled in halting English, "I only need to keep you busy."

If he had timed that statement, he couldn't have timed it any better. As soon as he had finished speaking the gates to the factory burst open and a plain black van charged into the clearing. It screeched to a halt and black suited soldiers in riot gear issued forth from the rear doors and panned out forming a rough circle around me, pointing assault rifles in my direction.

"You should surrender!" my opponent said, mocking my previous statement.

I smiled wryly at him as I allowed the assault team to complete their circle around me. They kept a healthy distance from me; they obviously knew what I was capable of.

"You think this is the first time I've had a gun pointed at me?" I enquired. My response and the grin plastered across my face must have unnerved him as he glanced nervously about and was obviously reassessing the odds.

"When you're ready." I offered.

"Place your hands on your head!" one of the soldiers behind me ordered in gruff German.

"I wasn't talking to you," I casually replied to the soldier without taking my attention away from the other Mage.

"You're crazy!" the other Mage said, "Your shield won't last long against this!"

"It'll last long enough." I said as I looked over the soldiers surrounding me. They clearly had no doubts, they wanted to do this, which meant that they had been horribly unprepared for the consequences of what they were about to attempt. I strengthened my shield around myself, which seemed to signal to my opposite that it was time to begin.

"Fire!" The Mage ordered gruffly. I could tell from his tone that he now wasn't so sure he was doing the right thing. I felt the sharp staccato of gunfire bounce off my shield. I wasn't concerned though, I barely even noticed it through the power I was pouring into my defence. The noise the shots were making against my shield was incredible. They obviously weren't worried about the local police interfering or investigating the noise. I waited, as they piled more bullets against my powers.

"You waste your ammunition, "I said as they ran through their first clip of ammo.

I had hoped that they'd get the hint that gunfire wasn't going to win this fight, but this didn't seem to do the trick. They hurriedly reloaded. My opponent was looking at me in horror, obviously amazed that I was able to absorb such a punishment. What he didn't know was I had been subject to this kind of abuse before. About two years ago I had been involved in an altercation in my home city of Melbourne. Police and swat teams had shot at me with very similar rifles. It hadn't been a problem then and it wasn't a problem now.

Actually that wasn't quite right – It wasn't a problem just yet. My opponent was right about one thing – my shield couldn't hold forever. I could feel myself weakening and the impacts from the bullets getting closer and closer to pain. My shielding skills were probably my most advanced techniques. I could now raise a shield more powerful than even Renee who had been my teacher at one point. Every time I was forced into a scenario where I was required to utilise my powers past what I had considered to be my limits, I found that the magic adapted, and the next time I used those techniques they were greatly enhanced.

The more magic I used, the more powerful I became. The counter balance to that was, the more magic I used the more I craved to use. It wasn't just a psychological need, I went through actual withdrawal symptoms if I didn't use for a few days. It was like a drug. A drug I could use every time I flexed my fingers.

I was beginning to feel the bullets now. They impacted against me like tiny little pin pricks of pain. I'd have to do something soon.

The look of shock and disbelief on the Mage's face as he saw the amount of gunfire that my shield was taking made him very easy to predict. I could tell the moment that he had determined that he should intervene. It was obvious from his facial features. I didn't need to see the tell-tale rise of Mana down his arms as he formed the telekinetic thread.

I leapt into the air over his thread and launched an attack of my own. With trained precision the soldiers altered their shots to follow me. The gunfire ricocheted off my shield as the soldiers struggled to keep pace with me. My attack smacked down on my opponent and sent him stumbling into the middle of the ring of soldiers.

My opponent shrieked as my strike impacted with his shield. The combined strength of the ricocheted gunfire and my strike penetrated his shield. He twitched several times and red blotches appeared on his chest. Weak idiot, I'd all but guaranteed him what would happen should he choose to stand against me. One of the soldiers, obviously the leader, called out and gunfire ceased.

"Take your wounded and leave while you can," I grunted gesturing towards the fallen Mage.

"I cannot do that!" he replied in crisp military German.

"It will mean your deaths if you don't."

"I cannot do that!" he repeated, sticking to his rhetoric. You almost had to admire the stupidity of it.

"Your call," I shrugged as I raised the thread that would end his life. I didn't have much choice here, even if I pulled my strike, a Mana thread at this range would still probably be fatal to someone without protection. But I never got the chance to launch my attack.

A loud bang and an explosion of white light rocked through my shield. The pain tore through my brain like a needle through my vision and I gasped and threw my hands over my eyes.

I fell back onto my side and attempted to scurry away, my shield fell and I waited for the inevitable gunfire that would finish me. I had been lured into a trap. One of the other Mages must have hit me with something while I was distracted, perhaps the Mage I thought I'd taken out as he'd jumped over the wall. I had no idea what he'd hit me with though, it must have been powerful to get through my shield. If I wasn't in so much pain I would have shouted out my rage. It was the height of stupidity that I had allowed this to happen. My fury rose to compete with my pain as my mind struggled to regain the necessary control to utilise my powers.

My eyes were blinded by the imprint of the light and a ringing resounded in my ears. I could hear, but everything sounded like it was coming from a long way away. I couldn't hear gunfire, but that didn't mean that I wasn't about to.

I shook my head to clear it. I needed to see! My desperation lent me strength and allowed me the necessary power to throw off a quick Scry spell. What I saw surprised me.

The soldiers were all in varied states similar to mine. Only the captain of the group remained standing and he was calmly advancing on me. He appeared to have been yelling something, but I couldn't hear it. He looked pissed off and was pulling out a side arm from his holster.

I quickly attempted a shield spell, but the effort of that along with the Scry spell was too much. I could barely maintain the focus for the Scry, and only the deep seated terror of not being able to see allowed me to summon the necessary strength for that, a shield was definitely beyond my skills right now.

I raised a thread to knock the gun from his hand and hoped that I'd be able to get out of there before his comrades came around properly. It was probably a moot issue anyway, as the Mage who had brought me down would probably finish me off soon anyway.

I latched a thread onto the gun and pulled, but it

didn't move, I was simply too weak. The captain grunted at the effort of retaining his weapon and stood over me.

This was it.

"You should have surrendered." He sneered.

"I couldn't do that." I gasped in pain as the motion of my jaw moving sent pain rocketing through my skull. I could almost make out the Mana signature of the Mage who had finished me, they were coming from some distance away, but they were moving quickly. I couldn't quite see them properly without moving the Scry, but they were powerful. No wonder I had fallen to them.

"You shouldn't have come alone." The soldier grunted, as he flicked his finger across the pistol to remove the safety.

The Mage became visible to my Scry, and they were indeed powerful. There was no shame in falling to them. I breathed out. It was over.

"Who says I was alone?" I whispered.

The captain's face screwed up in confusion at my statement. His confusion turned to shock as the pistol was rocketed from his hand. Unfortunately, he squeezed his finger during the attack and a round went off.

I caught the bullet on the left cheek. All in all I was pretty lucky actually. If the gun had not been moved it would have been an execution shot straight to the centre of my forehead – game over.

As it was a small spray of blood covered my vision and I fell back again in time to see the captain's body shudder as an impact sent him flying across the clearing. He landed with a sickening thump against the far wall, not far from where one of the Mages had fallen.

The newcomer casually walked past several soldiers who were attempting to recover their weapons. They didn't seem at all concerned by the soldiers. This wasn't overly surprising as they were protected by a powerful shield. The interloper leaned down over me and smiled.

"Twitch."

"Renee" I whispered gratefully. I hadn't seen Renee in about four months. I didn't even know she was in Berlin.

"You got yourself into some trouble this time," she commented as she pulled me to my feet. She extended her shield to surround me. She needn't have worried though as none of the soldiers who had regained their weapons looked interested in pursuing the fight. One soldier actively threw his weapon to the ground and backed away slowly.

"I always seem to find the best trouble," I grinned as Renee looped one of my arms over her shoulders. I hurt everywhere.

"We should go," she muttered. "You're in no condition to continue this."

"I agree."

The soldiers seemed to agree too, at least as far as I could tell.

* * * * * *

"What the hell hit me?" I grumbled as I probed my damaged cheek.

It was several hours after the fight and Renee and I had retreated to her hotel room. I still had a soft ringing in my ears, but my vision had returned and was able to function relatively normally. I really didn't want to have to go to hospital. That would be really inconvenient. I'd been fortunate in the past that I'd never been seriously injured enough that I required medical attention. However it was obvious from today's effort that my opponents were escalating things.

"A Flash-Bang," Renee replied.

"Flash bang?"

"Yeah, a grenade that sets off bright light and noise, used to disable combatants," She dabbed antiseptic on my cheek. "One of the soldiers threw it at you."

"Oh, that explains why my shield didn't help." Shields don't stop light or sound. They only stopped physical or mana based attacks. This was worth considering. I wondered if I would be able to alter my shield to protect me from this in the future?

"Though it probably affected you far less than it did the soldiers, it was pretty funny to see actually. He threw it and pretty much everyone fell down. I get the impression they're not supposed to be used at that close range."

"Probably not, no," I smiled wryly, "I'm glad you enjoyed yourself though."

"If you weren't so busy show boating, it wouldn't have happened," Renee replied crisply as she finished patching me up. "Well, it's not pretty, but it will do the trick and you do seem to heal quick. I think you'll be fine."

"Thanks"

"Don't mention it," She smiled and kissed me on the forehead, "I'm glad you're okay. You're getting pretty scratched up. You're not so much of a pretty boy anymore."

"Oh? You're going to trade me in for a younger model? Someone less banged up?" I tentatively probed the wound on my face.

"Oh, definitely," Renee smirked. "I like them young and pretty."

"I'm sorry to be such a disappointment," I said playfully.

Renee wrapped her arms around me and pulled me in close. She was obviously through playing. I hadn't seen her in such a long time and if truth were told I had missed her horribly. I had no idea what the 'status' of our relationship was and to be honest I was a little scared to ask at this point.

Every time I broached the subject Renee would wave me off. I knew that she loved me, but I was wondering if that was enough. Is it ever enough? I knew I loved her, but that didn't stop me from gallivanting around the world trying to kill her grandfather and rescue my cousin.

Was love enough for me? I had my doubts. Something else always got in the way. Renee pulled me down onto the bed, her legs wrapped around me and rolled me over onto my back. Her eyes blazed with need as she loomed over me and pulled her blouse over her head. I kissed her stomach as she arched her back against me, grinding herself into my lap. I wrapped my arms around her and felt her lean back against me. I playfully peppered a trail of kisses across the curvature of her stomach until I reached her neck. She growled as my hands played across her back and undid the clasp to her bra, letting it fall free. My hands slid down her back grasping her buttocks as I rolled myself forward on top of her. She writhed beneath me, my weight pressing down onto her. I could see the annoyance flash across her face as I assumed a dominant position. I knew she didn't like that. Several kisses across the arch of her neck stilled her complaints. She wrapped her arms around me and held me against her. With her trademark devilish smile her hands reached down for the clasp of my belt. I leaned back to allow her access and with a deft movement she launched herself forward, pushing me onto my back.

I couldn't help but grin at the triumphant expression on her face as she leaned into me and kissed me deeply while her fingers finally unclasped my belt buckle.

Our lovemaking wasn't hurried. We took all the time in the world. All our cares and the concerns were brushed away. For one shining moment we were simply two people in love, two people in the act of love. My injuries were forgotten in the heat of our passion and my doubts and fears were washed away. I wasn't a Mage anymore; she wasn't gifted. I was a man and she a woman. All else was foam on the waves.

When we were done, Renee lay in my arms, her

breathing slowly returned to normal. As her breathing slowed the real world intruded. I knew that this brief respite, however pleasant it was, was merely a diversion. As Renee rose the flow of Mana across her body reminded me that there was no escape from who we are and what we are capable of. We were Mages, we weren't meant to have a normal life.

Seeing the tell-tale flare of a Mana particle on my lover's naked hip made my worries and doubts return.

The sound of Renee in the shower filtered through the room and I briefly thought about joining her, but that would simply lead to more lovemaking and I wasn't in the mood anymore. The Mana particle on her hip bothered me more than I cared to admit. In the split second that I had seen it my body had reacted with caution. My initial reaction had been to a raise a shield. It was horrifying. The act of lovemaking is one of the most tender and vulnerable moments in the human experience and the Mana had taken all that from me. In that one moment my lover had become an enemy – someone to be feared, to protect myself from. It was sick. It was truly abhorrent. Had others of my kind managed to find true love in each other's arms without the sense that their lover represented a threat? How can you truly love someone if your subconscious secretly thinks them a danger to you? Can any love overcome that?

Renee returned to the bed and nestled in as I wrapped my arms around her. She seemed blissfully unaware of my earlier moment of panic. If she had sensed that something was wrong she gave no indication.

"You realise I'm going to have to go after that damned accountant tomorrow. I can't let this go." I said. Renee stiffened in my arms.

"I know," she said softly after several seconds, "He's going to be locked down in his offices pretty tight though, it's going to be difficult for us to get to him".

"Us?"

Renee hadn't yet taken any active part in my obsession as she called it. This was definitely new.

"My Grandfather is definitely out of the country and I'm not going to let you march in there and make a mess of things again."

"So you're going to march in with me and help with the mess?" I teased gently.

"Only if things go badly," she replied primly, tucking a pillow under her head and pulling my arm more firmly across her body.

"Trust me, they always go badly. Always."

I didn't sleep for quite some time that night. I suspect that Renee didn't either.

CHAPTER TWO

I grunted as I hit the ground at some force. My knee gave way and forced me into a forward roll. I came back to my feet with force and rose in fury.

"That was graceful," Renee commented as she landed behind me elegantly.

"Shuddap," I grinned, "it was a long jump."

I glanced around nervously as I assessed our position. We were standing on the roof of one of the main accountancy firms in Berlin. I hadn't wanted to do this. Assaulting a building in the CBD sector risked attracting unwanted attention, but I was sure that my quarry would be locked away inside. If we did this right we'd be in and out before anyone was the wiser, unless things went wrong.

If things did go wrong, I'd have a suitably large audience for my screw up, but I could deal with that.

After the events of yesterday I was sure that the accountant would be bunkered down in his offices. They wouldn't be expecting us to assault a whole building to get what we came for. Fools! Truly they had underestimated my stupidity.

We had just leapt from a larger building onto the

top of this one. It had been quite a jump, but Renee was right. It had been nothing that I shouldn't have been able to cope with. I was getting sloppy.

A security camera swivelled to face us. I could only hope that no one was monitoring the security system right now and the camera movement had been automated. Either way it didn't much matter as I turned and knocked the security camera from its mounting, sending it sliding across the roof. Renee shrugged and smashed in the door to the fire exit.

"Seems funny, breaking into your own firm," she said wryly.

"Your own firm?"

"I have been here before you know."

"What? On the roof?" I asked with mock innocence.

Renee flashed me a cheeky grin as we both entered the fire escape. We were heading down to level seventeen. We were pretty sure that's where he would be hiding out.

"Explain to me again. Why we didn't just teleport into the building?" I asked as we descended our fourth flight of stairs. The stairs were lined up in a very tight format, which didn't allow us to simply soar down the centre of the column.

"What and announce our presence to every Mage in the building?"

"How many Mages do you think are in here?"

"I don't know," she snapped, "I'd much rather make as little disruption as possible."

"Like smashing that fire door on the roof?"

"I don't want to create a disturbance big enough to bring *him* back here." Renee retorted angrily.

She didn't need to elaborate on who "him" was – her grandfather, Victor. I felt differently: I relished the chance to face him, but I wasn't going to have that argument with her now.

Renee squinted at me, her features twisted in indecision. My face had obviously given me away. I was a terrible poker player.

"You're not going to do anything stupid here are you?"

"No," I assured her quickly," well, no more stupid than usual, I guess."

Renee rolled her eyes at me.

It didn't take too long to get to the right exit. We had to break it down to get into the building. I assumed that we were setting off alarms all over the place, but I didn't want to mention that fact to Renee.

I smashed in the door and sent it flying across the room. The sudden violence of my attack would have caught anyone lurking behind the door by surprise. A door hitting someone full speed in the face is usually the best kind of distraction. To my surprise however there was no one there. I had expected another swat team like before, but I was looking at an empty office block.

I glanced nervously at Renee, "Are you sure this is the right level?"

Renee nodded grimly. We fanned out and entered the

office block. The office was divided into smaller cubicles, which made it hard to see. People could be lurking just below the divider level. I wasn't worried about the swat team, they wouldn't be able to penetrate my shield. Well, no, that wasn't exactly true. The flash bang they had used earlier had done a very effective job of neutralising me. I'd have to be more careful. I was getting careless and like before it would be my undoing. I consciously strengthened my shield around me. I could tell Renee was feeling a little worried too as her expression had taken on a mild form of annoyance, which I knew to be her only outward sign of fear.

"It should be just through those double doors." Renee whispered as she gestured towards the far side of the room.

"Tell me again why we didn't just Scry in and see if he's here?" I whispered sarcastically.

"You know why." Renee snapped caustically.

I did. The Scry spell could possibly give away our position and we didn't really know how many people we were facing here. It was best to have surprise on our side. I didn't particularly want to be jumped by more Mages.

By the time I'd reached the end of the cubicles I was beginning to feel really nervous about the whole endeavour. I nodded briefly to Renee before I smashed open the door that led into a small corridor. Small chunks of wood imbedded themselves into the wall on the far side of the door. The release of energy helped somewhat with my nerves.

There was no one on the other side. This was getting frustrating. Renee gestured towards the far end of the corridor at another set of doors.

"It's too quiet," Renee whispered as she moved forward, "I don't like it."

"It's late, all the people have gone home."

Renee gave me a look that indicted just how much of a stupid statement that was. I shrugged and grinned sheepishly at her.

Renee smacked open the last door that I presumed led into the main office. The office was empty. Renee glanced around the room in disbelief.

"Shit," I cursed loudly.

"Not what you were expecting?" a voice called in crisp English from behind us. I wasn't sure how someone had gotten behind us, but they were clearly standing in the corridor that we had just passed through.

I turned around slowly. It was a single man standing at the end of the corridor. He was right this wasn't what I expected. I'd expected armed guards and swat teams. This guy didn't seem to be much of a threat, but this could just be the calm before the storm.

"It seems we were expected," I said grimly as I let the Mana run down my arms in preparation for an attack.

The man didn't seem alarmed by this move. Was it possible that he couldn't' see the Mana? He didn't appear to be a Mage, at least as far as I couldn't see any Mana on his skin. However I wasn't going to make that mistake and lower my guard.

"Of course you were expected," the man continued, "you're not a subtle man Mr Wills."

"You know who I am?" I replied readying myself for a strike. If I could keep him talking he'd never see it coming.

"Oh yes," he replied disarmingly, "and Miss Whittle-sea, we weren't sure if you would come. This makes it a bonus for us of course. Your grandfather would much like to be reunited with you."

"Well, I don't want to be reunited with him," Renee snapped, biting off each word. I could see the Mana flow along her arms too. She obviously had the same idea as I had. It never ceased to amaze me how alike we were. I smiled grimly as I turned my attention back to our conversationalist.

The more I thought about this situation the more wrong it seemed. He was just standing there looking way too unconcerned, and yet he knew who we were. He had to know what we were capable of. He should be looking at least a little worried. Between Renee and me, we were powerful enough to easily pull this building down around his ears.

And yet he was just standing there – not moving. He wasn't even moving a little bit. He wasn't even breathing, or at least he didn't appear to be. Was it possible that he was a Drone?

I'd encountered them before. They were dead men that had been re-animated by dark sorcery. I had seen a drone take a full clip of rifle fire straight in the chest and be unfazed by it.

They would make perfect soldiers. Unfortunately they hadn't been that effective against Victor. Marcus had used them in a direct assault against him and Victor had simply assumed control of the Drones and turned them against their former Master. Marcus was lucky to have escaped with his life.

No, this definitely wasn't a Drone. For one – Drones don't talk and this person was clearly talking, or at least seemed to be. Actually, something was wrong there too. His lips weren't quite lining up with his words. It was like watching a movie where the voice track was out of synch with the film. It was close, but it wasn't quite right. There was only one explanation – illusion!

It must have been a bad one at that for me to have seen through it so easily. If I had cast this illusion I wouldn't have been so careless with the details. That at least explained how we'd walked straight past him without seeing anything untoward. An illusion had cloaked the whole area. It was possible that I was surrounded by armed troops and wouldn't see them. This was unlikely however as due to the nature of the illusion they wouldn't be able to see each other either. No, it was probably only one person or a small group hidden at the far end of the corridor.

I smiled grimly and let the Mana slide from my arms. A direct attack wouldn't help me here. I'd have to try to be clever about this. I hated that – clever just wasn't my forte.

"Where is the accountant then?" I snarled, as if I had just lost my temper.

"He is far from your reach, Mr Wills" The man responded evenly. He didn't appear to be cowed by my apparent temper.

"Nowhere is out of my reach," I snapped.

"Even now he is boarding a plane that will take him to safety." The voice continued. It sounded amused as if stating a fact beyond my control.

Bingo! He'd just played his hand. I nodded to Renee, who answered with a grin. She closed her eyes and I could see her Scry arching out from her body. There weren't that many airports in Berlin. It wouldn't be that hard for Renee to locate him.

"That's all very well and good for him," I grunted, "it doesn't save you though."

"If you were going to attack me, you would have already done so by now," the voice responded quickly. Too quickly – as if he was trying to persuade me of the fact rather than simply state it.

"You might be right," I replied thoughtfully as I allowed the Mana to build into my palms, then sent a pulse of energy barrelling down the corridor. As I expected it hit the illusion field about a metre or so past the door we had used.

When it hit the illusion field the true nature of the pulse became apparent. It had taken me some time to figure out how to use this technique, but I had mastered it some time ago. Its effect was a curious one – it unravelled Mana Threads or fields. It was a Mana disruption pulse.

I had been struck by one of these previously and I knew just how much it hurt. Had the pulse hit my opponent he would have found himself without the ability to summon Mana and in no small amount of discomfort. Fortunately for my opponent the pulse flew past him. Unfortunately for him as it passed it unravelled the illusion field surrounding him. As the field came tumbling down around him it revealed where he had actually been standing. His illusionary counterpart disappeared in a haze of Mana, revealing a smaller man at the far end of the corridor.

My opponent was easily in his late forties. He was hunched over and if the Mana pattern sliding across his flesh were to be believed he was quite powerful. I couldn't quite validate how I knew this, but I guessed that he was the Master of the three whom I had fought earlier.

"Very clever, Mr Wills," he said, showing the first sign of fear since our conversation had begun, "I hadn't expected that."

It was obvious from his placement that he had expected a Mana thread against the illusion where he could counter and take me down easily.

"I had hoped to avoid any unnecessary violence," the Mage continued, "but I can see you're going to be stubborn about this."

Now that I could see him I could assess his power. He was powerful. This wasn't going to be easy. It would have been nice if the disrupt pulse had hit him. I glanced nervously at Renee, but she was still Scrying, looking for our wayward aircraft. She wasn't going to be any help.

My opponent raised his hands and smiled as he stepped forward, Mana flowing down his arms towards his wrists. As the Mana reached his wrists they began to glow into a flickering blue spark. Within seconds small sparks of electricity jumped from finger to finger and across the palm of his hand. Soon small currents of electricity were jumping between his hands as he threw sparks from one hand to the other.

Electricity – I had no idea if my shield would protect me from that. No one had ever tried to electrocute me before. There was a good chance that it would, but I wasn't sure and I didn't think right now was a good time to test it out.

My opponent obviously picked up on my indecision as he smiled broadly and began to lurch forward, cackling softly to himself.

"It's such a simple spell," he smirked, "and yet the applications are numerous."

He was covered in at least a dozen currents of electrical sparks now. They roamed across his body and jumped between arcs, creating a sparking flickering entity of electricity bearing down on me. It was amazing that he wasn't being affected by it; he must have taken some precaution against electrocuting himself. I couldn't see through the buzz to see if he had a shield around him, but I assumed it was there.

"Sparks will burn through a shield in no time," the

figure intoned, "even one as powerful as yours."

He had closed about the half the distance between us and it wouldn't be long before he would be in range to throw one of those sparks in my direction. My lips twisted in indecision, I could engage him with a telekinetic thread, but I wasn't sure what the outcome would be. Besides, I needed to keep him at a distance to protect Renee while she was Scrying.

"It's quite debilitating, being hit with one of these babies, " he said as he threw a spark at me. It fizzled out before it reached me, he obviously wasn't close enough, he was simply playing with me, flinging sparks at me for affect. I had no choice now; I'd have to engage.

I smiled darkly as a thought took me. I did have other options, it was risky, but it was worth a shot. I raised my hand and gestured towards the roof. My gesture seemed to confuse him as he took a quick step back as if expecting an attack. I summoned the Mana to me and sent a burst of flame from my fingertips and hit the roof and leaving a visible scorch mark on the ceiling. I didn't particularly like using flame, but I had become very proficient at the spell.

"If you're intending to intimidate me, you'll find that I'm not so easily scared by pitiful displays of power." He cackled as I sent several more volleys of flame at the ceiling.

His laughter stopped as he finally realised what I was doing. I hadn't been aiming indiscriminately at the roof; I'd been aiming at the fire detector. An ear-piercing alarm echoed throughout the floor as a small torrent of water cascaded over us. For me it was quite refreshing as the water poured across my shield, but I hadn't surrounded myself with arcs of electricity. The currents of electricity intensified across his body as the water showered down across him.

He jerked suddenly as the electricity reacted with the water. I heard a loud crackling noise that I come to associate with a shield failing. My opponent jerked again and this time called out in pain. His calls quickly turned to shrieks as he fell to the ground.

His body eventually jerked to a standstill, broken only by the occasional leg twitch. I didn't stop to inspect him, but I could tell from his Mana pattern that he was still alive, but I didn't know for how long. Small tendrils of smoke were coming off him at an alarming rate.

"Why… am I wet?" A disgruntled voice called from behind me.

I turned to see a very soggy Renee, glaring daggers at me. Her hair was plastered to her head and water was dripping down the side of her face and down the curve of her neck.

"It seemed quicker," I shrugged. "Did you get the location?"

Renee nodded quickly, "Yeah, before I was rudely interrupted with a sudden shower."

"Where is it?"

"It's in the air."

"Ah." That was more difficult. Teleporting onto a

moving object was a challenge I'd never tried before. It would be interesting, especially teleporting onto something travelling at that speed. I didn't know exactly how far planes flew, but I knew it would be fast.

"That'll be fun," I nodded dryly.

"Let's go then!" Renee grinned.

"Ladies first." I replied with a bow.

"Very gentlemanly of you".

"Not really, I don't know where I'm going," I grinned cheekily.

"Fair enough," Renee smiled as she closed her eyes and summoned her Mana.

* * * * * *

I followed Renee's Scry thread high into the Berlin skyline. We approached the plane at top speed and zoomed down behind it. It looked like a military craft, one of those cargo planes that you see in the movies.

I forced my thread to pierce through the iron shell of the aircraft and into the cabin. I flexed my fingers as I began the technique that would allow me to teleport. I needed to calm myself. If I fucked this up, I'd find myself free falling down out of German airspace, or worse.

Not only did I need to move myself the distance required, I'd also have to control the speed at which I was travelling when I appeared. I was stationary now, if I arrived stationary on the plane, I'd probably end up smeared across the back of the aircraft.

The trick with teleportation was visualization. You had to completely focus yourself into the new location. You had to convert yourself into Mana and then send yourself along the Scry thread to your destination. This wasn't easy as the body doesn't like being converted into Mana.

It's like a little death, the body doesn't know what's happening and unconsciously thinks that it's the end, so it fights you on it. The cellular decay caused by the reaction isn't painful, but the anticipation is frightening. You never know for sure if you're going to appear where you want to.

I glanced to my left and saw Renee lurch forward as she materialised; she'd obviously under compensated the speed. She fell to her knees but quickly recovered. I took a mental note of this – more speed. It almost looked like a perfect landing, but I had seen her stumble. She would be fuming at her mishap. I grinned wryly; it was my turn. I had yet to see if I would fare any better.

I breathed in. The process begins as a tingling, kind of like when your leg goes to sleep. It's not painful, but it's definitely uncomfortable. The loss of sensation across your extremities is alarming, but can be ignored. There is then a sensation of speed as you travel along the Scry thread. It only takes a few seconds, but it feels much longer. It's strange that when you're travelling along the Scry thread you still have the sensation of movement. Even though it's not possible I always swear I can feel the air rush past my face and through my hair, but in that state you have no senses to register this sensation, nor hair, nor face. This has always confused me.

The arrival is always the worst part – it begins with a slight moment of paralysis as the body's cellular structure rebuilds itself. The body goes into shock for several seconds as nerve endings scream in protest and the stomach churns and nausea rises in your chest. Then just as suddenly as it begins it stops, ending with the same pins and needles that you feel before departure.

When I first began teleporting a sickly feeling would remain in my stomach for the remainder of the day, but the more I utilised the technique the less ill I felt. I never found out if it had to do with my skill at teleportation or if my body simply became accustomed to the abuse.

I breathed out. The tingling stopped and my feet fell to the ground. I was immediately thrown back into some crates; I'd used way too much speed. Physics is a harsh bitch.

My shield sprang around me almost instantly and probably saved my life. I hit the crates at full speed, reducing them to splinters. Without my shield I would have probably broken my back. I had no wish to be a paraplegic for the rest of my life because of a stupid miscalculation.

"Smooth," Renee called over the noise of the engine. I regained my feet tentatively and shrugged off the impact. I was a little winded but I'd fared worse.

"Actually, that wasn't bad for a first try," she said.

I nodded to her as I assessed the situation. We were in the cargo pit of the aircraft. If movies were to be believed, then the cockpit would probably be through the curtained off doorway at the other end of the bay.

"I'll do better next time." I grunted as I made my way to the front.

Our conversation was cut short as a soldier emerged from behind the curtain, perhaps to investigate the smashing of cargo boxes. He immediately pulled a gun. A second soldier appeared behind him. Both raised their firearms in our direction with grim looks on their faces.

"You really don't want to fire that in here," I said.

They didn't appear to be giving my suggestion much thought. I could see from this distance their fingers clamped over the triggers of their pistols.

"Look," I called, "you obviously know who we are and what we're here for."

This had no effect, other than making their frowns grow grimmer. I still had my shield up from my less than graceful landing and fortunately they couldn't get a clean shot at Renee with me in the way. Renee none the less took the opportunity to raise a shield herself.

That was probably a good move, just in case this got out of hand. Though I didn't think they'd fire a gun up here. Surely they were worried about hitting a fuel tank or something. Airplane fuel was supposed to be highly explosive right?

"You don't seriously think you can stand against us do you?" Renee called out as she pushed her way past me, "Game over boys, throw your guns down and we'll let you go unharmed."

"That won't work," I scoffed.

"Do you have a better idea?" she said, turning her back on the soldiers to face me.

"No," I admitted, "I just know from experience that that won't work."

"It might work now," Renee suggested icily, "Give it a chance."

A bullet grazed off the side of Renee's head. The shield protected her from the worst of it, but I could see her shudder at the impact against it.

"Don't even say a word!" she snarled waving a finger in my direction as she spun around to face our opponents.

"Which one of you shot me?" She demanded storming up the length of the cargo hold.

The soldiers exchanged glances, obviously unsure of how to proceed. Dealing with furious and highly dangerous women who are bullet resistant can't be commonly taught at military schools. I could tell by their expressions that they knew this wasn't going to end well for them. To the soldiers credit though, neither of them tried to fire again. This was wise – it probably would have just made Renee angrier.

"It was the one on the left." I said.

"I don't need your help!" Renee called back sarcastically without taking her eyes from her targets.

I wasn't sure what happened next, but both pistols ended up sliding along the floor of the cargo hold towards my feet. There were several more thumps as the soldiers hit the ground.

"Don't say a word," Renee said as we walked past the bodies. I took a quick look at our fallen adversaries. I couldn't tell if they were alive or dead. In the end, I don't suppose it matters much either way. They weren't going to cause us any trouble now.

I nodded briefly and moved through the curtain into the cabin. There was a row of seats along each wall. The accountant was there with two more soldiers. He had a resigned look on his face as he saw us walk through the doorway. He knew it was over.

One of the soldiers rose to his feet and drew his pistol.

"That won't do you any good," I said, "the last guys tried that."

He quickly swivelled the pistol so it was facing the accountant. The accountant's eyes balked as he stared down the barrel of the firearm. The soldier looked cautiously at Renee, myself and the accountant. Shit. The other guys hadn't tried that.

"Okay, let's all calm down here," Renee said nervously. She obviously hadn't anticipated this move either.

"I'm calm," the soldier replied with a blank look, "I'm simply following protocol."

"So, the protocol is, when you see us, you shoot him in the head?" I inquired dryly.

He didn't respond.

"Wouldn't want to be around for the long term strategy meeting," I added under my breath.

"You're not helping!" Renee snapped.

"I'm not trying to," I grinned in way of reply, "he's

not going to shoot him. He would have done so by now."

I saw the soldiers arm tense in response and had to rethink things. I could have been wrong about this.

"Please," the accountant whispered, "don't."

"Don't worry he won't." I reassured him with a forced grin. It was taking some effort to remain so chipper about this. The situation was starting to get out of hand.

Fortunately my showmanship had had its desired effect of moving the soldiers' attention to me. I watched out the corner of my eye as Renee flicked a Mana thread around the pistol, I heard a slight click as she switched the safety on.

The soldier glanced down and tried to pull the gun away, but Renee was ready. She flicked the gun from his fingers and sent it trailing along the floor.

The second soldier reacted swiftly but I hit him with a Mana thread to the chest, knocking him down before he could raise his weapon. The first soldier backed away slowly looking for something, anything that would help him now. I could have told him that there was nothing that could save him.

"End it," he hissed, bowing his head in shame.

"Don't be dramatic," I scoffed, gesturing towards the seats on the other side of the plane, "sit down in the corner and shut up."

Renee raised an eyebrow at my statement, but I simply shrugged. We'd got what we had wanted here, there was no need to escalate this further. Renee roughly pulled the accountant to his feet and directed him back into the cargo hold. I gestured towards the soldier with a cut-throat motion to stay put. He nodded. Clever man – he knew when he was beaten.

"What's your plan now?" Renee said once we reached the cargo hold, "I'm not sure I can teleport at this speed with two people."

"Me either. We'll have to do it old school."

Renee nodded grimly.

"Who takes Hugo?" Renee asked, gesturing towards the accountant.

"Doesn't matter," I shrugged quickly, "I can take him, if you like."

"Fine."

Renee flicked the switch to open the cargo doors at the rear of the plane.

"I'll go first," I said grabbing Hugo around the collar and pulling him towards the gap.

It was a long way down. I'd never, ever, ever attempted a jump from this far up before. Hugo visibly shuddered as he saw the drop and began to pull back.

"Don't we need parachutes?" he looked terrified.

"Don't struggle," I snarled, "I'll end up dropping you."

"I don't want to go," he whimpered.

"You don't have a choice," I replied as I pushed him and jumped after him. "You should have come with me without a struggle at the bar," I called to his falling figure. I doubt he heard me.

* * * * * *

I wrapped a Mana thread around Hugo and attempted to pull him in close. I had to revise this plan as I realised that he was flailing around too much, I didn't want to him to accidently hit me in the face with a wild swing.

The wind tore at my clothes and my hair, pulling against my face and forcing the air from my lungs. My eyes watered as they were buffeted by the force of the air against my fall. This was going to be difficult. I don't think I'd ever travelled this fast before. The wind was almost like a physical barrier against me. It felt like I was almost lying on something. It was only the sight of the ground rushing towards me that ruined that illusion.

I must admit that against all common sense, I was actually having fun doing this. Hugo was not doing quite so well. He appeared to have gone catatonic and was gazing at the ground in morbid fascination. The streets of Berlin eventually began to take shape as we free fell towards them at terminal velocity. The buildings gained detail and texture as they grew closer. I couldn't quite make out people yet, but I could make out the vehicles passing by on the roads below. They looked so small.

A Mana thread shot past me and latched onto a building rooftop. Renee had selected a landing site, I suppose I should do the same. We were still some height above the building, but I'd much rather be able to control my descent now rather than wait until later and then find out that I couldn't.

I sent a thread plummeting down to the top of the building, using it to slow my speed. I jerked violently as the thread took hold sending me into a tight spin. That wasn't good. That wasn't my desired effect at all. The Mana thread dissolved into shreds as my concentration broke and it took me several seconds before I was able to right myself to try again.

My thread connection to Hugo had also been broken in the tumble and it took me several critical seconds before I could locate him again. My head was spinning and I felt sick to my stomach. I quickly latched a new thread around Hugo and sent another plummeting to the ground.

I was more careful this time using far less force and began to slowly decrease my speed. Unlike my last attempt this didn't send me into a spin and I felt the pressure from the fall lessen.

The building was getting awfully close though. It was difficult to notice anything except that hard concrete surface slowly getting closer and closer. The closer I got the closer I came to realising one simple fact. I wasn't going to make it in time.

I'm not sure how hard I would have hit the roof, but the fact of the matter is the human body is mostly made up of water and isn't very impact resistant. With a shield around me I might survive the impact, probably by cannoning straight through the roof and into the building below, but I couldn't raise a strong enough shield around both myself and Hugo and I needed us both to survive the fall. So that wasn't going to work. Besides, Renee would never let me live it down if I ended up destroying the building in my landing. She had given me enough grief over my landing on the plane.

Hugo was screaming unintelligibly as the ground loomed closer. This wasn't going to be pretty. If I didn't need what was in that bastard's head so much I would have just saved myself.

I pulled our connecting thread in tight, raising the flailing Hugo towards me. I grabbed him firmly from behind and knocked him savagely over the head in an attempt to stop the flailing. I'd heard that this is what you're supposed to do if you're grappling with a hysterical drowning man. This was kind of like drowning right? It didn't work. The movies made it look so easy. You simply knock someone on the head and they go down. That's the way it was supposed to work. I cursed my luck and cursed a now angry and hysterical Hugo and got to work. There was only one way we were going to survive this. Teleportation.

If I had any other option there was no way in a million years I'd attempt this. I could see the rooftop I wanted to land on, it was getting closer by the second.

I took a quick breath to prepare and forced myself to find focus. I tightened the thread around Hugo and pulled him in closer. I somehow managed to wrap my arms around his flailing limbs, then wrapped the teleport field around us.

The felt the immediate screams of protest from my body and felt Hugo go stiff. The rooftop was frighteningly close and now I could even make out the cracks between the panels of concrete.

It was going to be a race. Which would come first? The completion of the teleport Mana field or a sudden and very violent impact?

I breathed a sigh of relief as my vision distorted into the blurry haze that comes with teleportation. I knew I could remain in this state for a few seconds before my structure began to break down and I wouldn't be able to re-corporate. I had done it.

A savage thump preceded my re-corporation. It hurt, but it hurt a lot less had I not teleported to the rooftop. My shoulder was jarred and Hugo was lying across my body. I pushed him off and got to my feet in time to see Renee make her landing. She came in hard, but then she had just jumped from a plane.

She fell to one knee as she landed, but that was the only indication of the difficulty of her jump. She had aced it. Show off. She didn't comment on it, but I could see it in her eyes. She was pretty impressed with herself.

"I've never done that before," she breathed as she rose, "it was more fun than I thought."

I didn't particularly want to ever do that again.

I moved to check on Hugo. He'd passed out. I suppose that was to be expected. This must have been a little outside of his normal daily routine. I checked his pulse, which was fine and then looked around. I didn't really know where we were, but I could make out the massive bulk of Berlin central station in the distance, which gave me a rough idea.

"What's the time?"

Renee checked her watch. "About eleven."

I never wore watches. It had been a point of contention between us. I was always asking her for the time. In my old life I had simply used my mobile phone. Now I no longer kept one. I didn't like the concept of my location being tracked by an electronic device. It wasn't paranoia – it had happened to me once before. I wasn't going to take the chance again.

"We need to find somewhere safe," I said.

"Duh," Renee replied.

She closed her eyes and I saw a Scry thread lance out from the building and into the city below. I knew she was looking for a hotel room, preferably from a large chain. Something with a lot of rooms that wouldn't all be booked out. Given how late it was, it would be relatively safe that any empty room we selected wouldn't be booked that night.

Renee eventually nodded and blinked as her vision returned to the rooftop.

"Found one."

"Where?"

"Four Seasons."

"Nice, I've always wanted to stay at a Four Seasons."

I followed her Scry thread back to the hotel room. The room was dark, but I could see well enough by the light through the window to send Hugo and myself into the room. Hugo didn't even twitch as I pulled him roughly to his feet and teleported him into the hotel room.

"We've got almost the whole floor to ourselves," Renee commented as she joined us.

I glanced at her in the darkness. She always looked especially attractive in shadow. I could see her glittering eyes peering at me.

"You just gonna stand there gaping at me?" Renee smirked. "We've got work to do."

"No." I let off a glow spell, illuminating the room in the soft glow of Mana.

That was the problem with these high-end hotel chains. They used a form of key in the door to activate the electronics. No lights, no power, no TV. That didn't really bother me all that much as all I was normally looking for was a warm bed and running water for a shower. I never stayed more than one night and was at least courteous enough to clean up after myself. If I did my job well enough, the only thing that would give away my visit would be a few missing toiletries and a less than pristinely made bed.

"We'll need some supplies," Renee said as she pulled Hugo roughly into a chair.

I nodded and sent out my own Scry thread. I quickly located the necessary items. I didn't much like it, but there was nothing for it.

My shopping list was a little unusual – a set of hand-cuffs, some fabric for a gag and something that we could use to threaten Hugo with. I selected a nasty looking hunting knife from a hardware store. It looked suitably threatening. I didn't like the necessity of torture, the whole idea left a bad taste in my mouth, but I just didn't see how we were going to get past the conditioning that Victor had placed on him. Even under the threat of pain there was still a good chance we'd fail. Even if he wanted to talk, he mightn't be able to – I knew, I'd been under one of those compulsions myself. I knew how potent they were.

At the last minute and cursing my own lack of fore-sight I grabbed a first aid kit. We'd need to patch him up afterwards.

I sat wearily down in one of the kitchen chairs as I teleported the required items onto the table. I had discovered early that I could teleport objects to me. It was this combined with my ability to clone items that allowed me to live like I did.

"Fluffy handcuffs?" Renee queried as she glanced at my haul.

"It was all I could find."

This wasn't exactly true, the hardware store had had handcuffs too, but I liked the look on Renee's face when she found something that she could tease me about.

Her gaze flickered across the hunting knife and her expression hardened. We could have used Mana to threaten Hugo, but we both knew that we'd need some form of visible threat. Mana alone wouldn't do the trick. The compulsion wouldn't allow anything less than total terror to break its hold over him.

"Do you really think you can do this?" Renee whis-pered as she gestured towards Hugo.

"I have no choice." I didn't like it any more than she did. I applied the handcuffs to Hugo's limp wrists and bound him securely to the chair.

I slapped Hugo lightly around the cheeks until he came around. He spluttered and coughed as he regained consciousness. He glanced frantically around the room and then his face dropped as he saw us. He went white.

"I can tell you nothing," he stated in stoic German, "You know this. Why do you do this?"

I didn't answer him, instead I gestured towards the knife on the table. Hugo's eyes flicked at the knife and then back to me.

"You will tell me everything I ask you." I reached for the hunting knife. Hugo's eyes followed every movement of my hand. He watched as my fingers trailed across the hilt of the blade and closed around it. He could see my arm muscles as they tensed as my fingers curled around the knife. I moved slowly, letting the tension build. If I moved slowly enough maybe I wouldn't have to do this. Maybe I wouldn't' need to, I'd see a blink or a slackness of expression that would lead me to believe that Hugo had broken the compulsion on his own.

I hoped Hugo didn't notice the slight twitch in my hand as I forced myself to continue. I silently begged that he wouldn't see the doubt in my eyes and the weaknesses of my conviction. If he even suspected that I had doubts about this then it would undermine my work.

This had to be done. This man was my only link to finding Victor and my lost cousin. Nothing could stand in the way of that. Nothing. I'd done things in the past that I wasn't proud of. I'd killed people, but only in the heat of battle. This was something new. I'd never had to torture before. I wasn't sure if I was up to it – I only knew that this had to be done. Silence filled the air, until I heard it. A sound I hadn't expected. The silence was almost a fourth person in the room with us. I could hear the small gasps of breaths that Hugo was taking. I could hear the pounding of my heart, my own breath being forced from my lungs, and then the noise. The noise a phone makes when it's dialling a number.

I hadn't noticed, but Renee had quietly backed away behind me. It wasn't until I heard her phone dial that I realised something was amiss. I turned around to face her in amazement. She said three words into the phone, "We've got him."

She hung up the phone and slipped it back into her pocket. What had she done? The look on her face was one of betrayal. The shock of it hit me like a fist to the face.

Who had she called?

Renee couldn't look at me. I turned back to Hugo who shared my amazement and then back to Renee. She had taken several steps back against the wall and kept her eyes focused warily on me. What did she think I was going to do? Attack her? She was acting almost as if she thought I might.

What the hell was going on?

I didn't jump when the Scry thread arched into the

room. I already had a feeling that someone was coming. The only question was who. The Scry thread was horribly complex. They'd done things in a way I wouldn't have thought was possible. Whoever was coming was incredibly skilled – an undisputed master of our craft.

This narrowed it down to two people. It didn't really matter which one it was, although I suspected I already knew the answer. It explained why Renee had assisted me tonight when she had previously declined. It explained why she had been willing to take the risk of running into her grandfather. She knew for certain that he wouldn't be there. I wasn't surprised when the man arrived behind the Mana. Marcus Deveraux – Renee's father.

He was the lesser of the two evils, but still not how I wanted to do this. He was just as manipulative and as ruthless as my former Master.

I nodded my head darkly to Marcus in way of greeting and flashed Renee a warning look. She didn't return my glance.

"Hugo Kurtz, it's a pleasure to see you once again." Marcus intoned as he surveyed the room. There was no warmth in his voice.

If Hugo had looked scared of the hunting knife he was terrified of Marcus. I didn't blame him. He radiated power.

I hadn't seen him since our last encounter. An encounter that had almost cost me my life. He was not a man to cross. To those with Mana sight he was a figure of terror. He was almost power defined. The Mana seemed to sit up and beg at his command. It flowed across his flesh in waves of power.

He glanced at me as he moved towards Hugo. Hugo gave a whimpered gasp and attempted to pull away, but he was firmly bound to the chair.

"I shall be quick," he announced as he leant over Hugo. "My journey over the Atlantic will have been noticed."

The Mana in Marcus's body rose as he turned and blocked my view of Hugo. All I could see was Marcus's hand forcefully clamped around Hugo's head, pulling his neck to one side. I could hear Hugo straining against the grip, but failing to match the Mage's strength. I couldn't see what Marcus was doing, but I could hear gasps of pain from Hugo. This lasted several seconds, followed by a soft sigh.

"The compulsion is now broken," Marcus announced with satisfaction as he stepped back. When had he learned to do that? I gazed at him in amazement. I cursed myself for not paying more attention to what he had been doing.

Hugo looked like a completely different man. His pose had been defiant and stalwart in the face of almost certain death, he now looked frightened and weak. His eyes searched the room frantically as if seeking an escape. He knew that it wasn't over yet. Marcus may have broken the compulsion, but he didn't have what he wanted yet.

"Where is Victor hiding?" Marcus asked softly.

"I don't know," the accountant begged, his voice cracking under the strain. "He comes and goes, I don't know from where."

"You're lying!" Marcus snarled as if his anger had suddenly got the better of him. I wasn't surprised by the sudden mood shift, he'd displayed that characteristic before. It made him unpredictable and dangerous. I backed away several steps.

I couldn't look any longer. I turned and sidled over to Renee. She glanced at me nervously as I approached, but said nothing. We could hear Marcus's demands getting more insistent. For what it's worth I didn't think Hugo was lying, but I wasn't going to interfere with Marcus. Not now and most definitely not over Hugo.

"Marcus told you about the accountant didn't he?" I whispered. I wasn't looking at her; I was still facing Hugo.

"Yes." I could barely hear her.

Renee was the one who had told me about Hugo. Renee was the one who led me to Berlin. I had once told Marcus that I wouldn't become another one of his agents. I had stated again and again that I wanted nothing to do with his war against Victor. Through Renee he had turned me into just that.

I grimaced as I let my anger settle. This was the exact position I didn't want to be in. War was coming. It was obvious to anyone who cared to look that it was coming. Our kind were at each other's throats and I didn't need to be told that once the dust settled there would only be a few of us remaining. It was obvious. I had been involved in several Mage fights and I knew from experience that they were short and they were vicious. There would be no quarter, there would be no surrender. One side would emerge victorious or both sides would be destroyed. And now thanks to Renee I was squarely in the middle of it. All I wanted was to get Allie and get the hell away from our kind before the fighting started.

I hadn't thought to question her when she had arrived to tell me about the accountant. I hadn't questioned her motives. I hadn't even thought to check her facts. Hugo wasn't going to lead me to Allie. He probably had no idea who the hell Allie even was, other than the fact that she was an associate of Victor's.

"You should have told me," I whispered.

"I had to call him, I wasn't going to let you do…" she trailed off, "…what you needed to do to get information out of Hugo."

"I'm not talking about that," I whispered a little more harshly. "I'm talking about sending me after Hugo in the first place."

Renee's face fell, "You were getting nowhere and you were getting more desperate. I feared you might do something stupid."

That was true – for the most part. I had even thought about going to see the Primea and forcing a confrontation, to see if she could lead me to my cousin. I knew where she lived in Paris. I had spoken to her once. It would have been had been a risky long shot, by even the most optimistic of odds. It was unlikely that she would help me, I was an outcast after all, and it could have led to my death, but I needed to something. My inability to find Allie plagued me. The longer she remained with my former Master, the longer he would have to corrupt her and turn her into the very monster he had sought to turn me into.

"You realise this is a betrayal right?" I whispered.

"I know."

"You were the one person I trusted explicitly, pretty much the only one left."

"More fool you," she whispered sadly. I turned to look at her, she wouldn't return my gaze. She was watching her father mentally torturing a man handcuffed to a chair. I didn't like to think what was going through her head.

"So it seems." I finished.

I didn't care to watch any more. This was a dead end for me. Hugo had no idea where Victor was hiding. He probably never did. He was probably telling the truth when he said that he didn't know who Allie was. The only reason he was cuffed to that chair was because Marcus had deemed it necessary and he'd used me to achieve his ends. I'd been played for a fool.

A direct attack by Marcus against Victor would have resulted in a war immediately. An attack by me, could be explained away. I had been less than subtle in my pursuit of my cousin, which wasn't exactly out of character. Marcus could even claim the whole attack had been my idea and that he hadn't been involved at all. He could wash his hands of it.

I knew without doubt that he would eradicate me if I became a threat to him. He'd already proved that he was quite capable of such cold-blooded practicality.

I vaguely thought about teleporting away, but I doubted that he would allow it and I had no interest in being hit with a disrupt field half way through dis-corporation. That would be fatal, and so I waited like a good little lap boy to be dismissed by the master. I cursed myself for my own stupidity.

Hugo's interrogation took about three quarters of an hour, I spent the majority of it on the balcony looking over the city. Renee didn't join me, I think we both felt that we needed some time alone. When I had first arrived in Berlin I had thought the city stunning. There was a functional practicality to it that spoke of old tradition and grandeur. It wasn't a beautiful city, but it had a charm to it that spoke to me. Tonight, the city suddenly didn't look so appealing. I wanted out of it. I wanted to get as far away from here as possible, but I was sure that Marcus would have words to say to me once he was done with Hugo.

I would do what I always did, politely listen and refuse to assist. Short of killing me there wasn't much more he could do. Marcus couldn't use the same compulsions that Victor used on Hugo with me as he himself had shown me how to resist them. This led to a stalemate – a no score loss for both sides.

It appeared that Marcus was done, Hugo seemed to

be sleeping in his chair, but I knew better. He was probably in a coma. Marcus would not have been gentle. Marcus gestured towards me through the glass and directed me to take a seat.

"This man was the final link in a long hunt for me." Marcus began, "I'd like to thank you for your assistance. I couldn't have obtained him without your help."

"Happy to," I replied dryly. The sarcasm was obvious, but Marcus ignored it.

"Aren't you interested in what I was after?" Marcus raised an eyebrow.

"Not particularly." I lied. In truth I was intrigued, whatever Marcus had been after was sure to have been something that would enable him to bring Victor down. Once Victor was disposed of, I was sure that I'd be able to convince Allie to return to Australia with me. Assuming of course that Victor didn't drag Allie down with him.

At one point I'd thought that assisting Marcus in Victor's downfall would be a good tactic. But I rejected the idea because I realised that it didn't really matter who took the dominant role amongst our kind – Victor or Marcus – neither would allow me my independence. Once one had devoured the other, they would come for me.

I looked at Marcus thoughtfully. He looked positively giddy, I had never seen him so animated. Whatever he had found must have been good. I wasn't fooled though; the outside was an illusion – carefully crafted one. Behind his eyes I could see his scheming, the plans being considered and rejected, the pieces moving across the board. He was obviously moving in for checkmate. That was the trick though, who was he trying to checkmate, me or Victor?

"What did you find?" I asked.

"Something that will allow me to expose Victor as the immoral bastard that he is," Marcus replied.

I briefly wondered if such information existed to expose Marcus in a similar way.

He continued, "I think I've found his laboratory."

"And this is important why?"

"Because it's where he devised his studies into Necromancy and if it contains what I think it contains I can go to the Primea and the council can have him exiled."

"The Primea won't do that. She can't – he's too influential."

"If you find what I think you'll find, she will have no choice."

"If I find?" I repeated shrilly.

Marcus just nodded as if this decision had already been made. I hated that about him. He always appeared to be so in control, as if nothing could possibly go wrong.

"I'm not going," I said, "Go yourself."

"Can't afford to, I'm afraid, I'll need to remain visible for the next few days."

"No, I'm not going," I repeated angrily, "Send Renee, I'm not getting any more mixed up in this."

Marcus raised an eyebrow at me.

"You'll go," he said eventually, "because I can help you. I know where your cousin is living."

"What?"

"I know where Alisha Burton is," Marcus repeated.

"And you've kept this information to yourself all this time?"

"I've only recently acquired this information."

Renee was looking at Marcus with distrust. It was reassuring to see her face echoing my thoughts.

"Bring me back what I want, and I'll tell you." Marcus said, "I'll even assist you."

"Where am I going?" I sighed. There was no point in delaying this any longer. He knew as well as I did that I was going now. I could keep searching the Earth forever with little chance of finding her. I needed help and Marcus damned well knew it.

"In southern Poland lies a range of Mountains," Marcus began, "The Tatras Range."

"Poland? Why would it be in Poland?"

"Because that area was once controlled by Germany," Marcus explained slowly. It was almost as if he was talking to a child. I didn't need the sarcasm.

"Where exactly am I going?" I didn't particularly want to discuss this any longer than I needed to.

"Hugo didn't know exactly. All he knows is that Victor has over the past few years spent quite lot of his resources keeping the resorts from up there encroaching into a specific area of the mountain range."

"So I'm what, running around the mountain looking for something?"

"I can give you a general area."

"It's still very sketchy."

"When you find it, it will be obvious."

I shook my head – this was a fool's chase.

"I don't even know what I'm looking for."

"It'll be old and it will be underground. I've been there once before, but I had no idea where it was at the time."

"You've been there?"

"Yes, Victor took me there when I was his apprentice, many many years ago."

"Fine, I'll go." I muttered reluctantly.

"I'll come too." Renee said.

"No," I snapped. "I'll go alone."

Renee flashed me a hurt look, but I didn't care. She'd already betrayed me once today, I wasn't in the mood to give her another chance.

CHAPTER THREE

I'd never felt cold such as this before in my life. My fingers were clasped firmly against the heavy jacket I'd procured before I made the trip south.

The Tatras mountains were part of the massive Carpathian range that had once separated Poland from the old Ottoman Empire. Although not a very large mountain range in themselves they were treacherous with deep pitfalls and sheer cliffs. It wasn't the best idea I'd ever had to come here during winter. My first journey up the mountain had been an unmitigated failure, without cold weather gear I almost froze to death.

I'd never really had that much experience with snow apart from a couple of family trips to the Victorian snow fields, but that was nothing like this. Those visits had been to a ski resort with maintained grounds and carefully marked out safe areas.

Marcus had given me a general area to search out, but it was still like I was looking for a needle in a haystack and it was a lot of distance to cover. Fortunately I didn't have to physically move all that often. Using Scry I was able to comb through the mountain ranges. The only issue with this was that it required me to sit still for long periods of time whilst my Scry thread searched out my target. This wasn't a good idea while you're in the middle of a snowfield. The inactivity coupled with the intense cold caused cramps up and down my legs, and my knees were getting stiff and painful to move. I felt like I was about seventy years old and I moved like I was crippled. I couldn't keep this up for much longer.

I came to hate the very concept of snow. It's supposed to be soft and fluffy right? Wrong, it's brittle and its course. It gets into the gap between my gloves and my coat and it burns. I had already turned my ankle twice on snow-drifts that looked stable, but gave way once I put weight on them. It was painful and it was infuriating.

I would have liked to have used the ski resorts as a base of operations, but they were full to capacity. So I was teleporting daily from a small Polish town at the foot of the mountains. The only problem was that this severely limited my search-range as I had to make sure that I was able to teleport back to the town with some degree of surety. I didn't want to mess up a teleportation in the middle of nowhere. That would lead to certain death.

Today I may have left my return a little late. As I attempted my first landing I found myself sliding down the side of the mountain. I slammed against a fallen branch. The impact tore through my knee joint and sent tremors up to my hip. Even through my shield it hurt. Without the shield it probably would have torn my knee into fragments. I carefully pulled myself back up to my feet and immediately fell back down. My knee just couldn't take the weight. Great. This was just perfect.

I telekinetically pulled myself out of the snow-drift that I had managed to lodge myself in while I considered matters. I was about three more jumps away from my base camp, but with the way I was feeling I doubted that I had it in me. This didn't look good and to make matters worse, it looked like it might snow again.

I needed to get somewhere secure for a few hours so that I could rest and recover my strength. I still had my survival gear, so if I could find somewhere sheltered I would be alright. The only problem was that this area didn't look too habitable.

I was halfway down a sheer cliff face. What I needed to find was a cave or at the very least an outcropping of rock I could camp under. I couldn't see anywhere from this vantage point, but that wasn't surprising. For one my main view was the side of a mountain and for two the damned snow covered everything.

I sighed as I sent out a Scry thread and began to search the cliff face. There had to be something, a cave or anything. What kind of cliff face doesn't have nooks and crannies? This one obviously.

I had just about given up when I found it. It was half luck and half logical deduction that I found what I was looking for. The small avalanche that I'd created when I'd come tumbling down the mountain had cleared away much of the snow and I could now see the rocks and cliff face behind it.

To the far right of where I had attempted to land was a small entrance into the bedrock. It didn't look like more than a metre wide, but it would be enough to crawl into. I wouldn't even need to teleport – things were finally looking up.

I telekinetically pulled myself up the side of the mountain and with some complaint from my bruised and battered legs crawled into the opening. I had no way of knowing what was inside or even if it would be large enough to house me as it had been pitch black inside when my Scry thread had found it.

It turned out that someone up there must like me. The cave was larger than it looked. I crawled a little deeper in. It was cold in here, but it was far warmer than outside. I considered creating some light, but I thought better of it. Who knows what might inhabit this cave that might be drawn to the light. I was in no condition to go looking for trouble.

The floor was uncomfortable, but at least it was flat. I lay down on my back and attempted to stretch my legs and take some of the weight off my injured knee. This actually helped a little. There was an alarming click and a jolt as my knee fully extended, but the relief was immediate. I scavenged through my backpack and pulled out a muesli bar. I couldn't understand the label on the packet when I had grabbed them, but assumed that they were at least some kind of fruit.

Apricot – damn. I hate Apricots and they were no better in bar form. Hopefully it was a variety pack and there were different flavours. I grudgingly finished off the bar as I pondered the plan from here. I assumed from the silence outside that it was snowing again. In a few hours I'd probably be snowed in. This wasn't really a problem; I could easily teleport out from here once I was ready to go. Hopefully once the opening was covered it might warm up in here a little. I didn't have an exact plan as such, but I figured that I'd spend the night here and then head back to town in the morning.

Then I'd need to determine what to do next. I was half tempted to just return to Berlin empty handed. This was becoming too much work for not enough chance of success. Maybe I could return in the summer when conditions were better. That would make sense, that's what we should have done in the first place. Had I known what I know now that's definitely what I would have done.

I sighed deeply and pulled my snow glasses from my face to rub my eyes. I was beginning to be able to see a little better in here now that my eyes had adjusted to the darkness. I still couldn't see much, but I at least was getting some indication of space. I couldn't determine where the far end of the cave finished, but it looked relatively evenly spaced on both sides.

I was just pondering the implications of this when I placed my hand on the ground next to me and instantly pulled it back. I had accidently placed my hand on something sharp. I hadn't cut myself through the gloves but had heard the fabric rip as I had placed my hand down.

Yep, I'd definitely torn a hole in the glove, right next

to the middle index finger. I groped my hand back down trying to figure out what had caused this. At first I thought it was a rock, but no – that wasn't right. The object was too smooth to be a rock.

It was metal. I slowly slid my fingers across it trying to ascertain what it was. It was a small metal bar with one end broken and hacked off. The top of the bar was smooth and tapered off at both edges.

Curious. There was nothing for it now; I needed light. I threw up a glow spell and blinked as my eyes adjusted. I had thought that I was in a natural cave. I was wrong. The walls, with the notable exception of the one that I was leaning against, were made out of hewn stone. I wasn't in a cave – I was in a tunnel.

The object that I had cut my glove appeared to be a railway track segment. The end that I had touched had been smashed, probably when the rocks had come tumbling down from above when the tunnel mouth had been closed.

I was in an old railway tunnel. I had no idea how old it was, but it looked ancient. I wondered where the railway originally led or how much of it remained intact. Perhaps there was once a bridge across the pass to the other side of the mountain. I could make out broken pieces of wood under the rail. They had been mostly smashed into kindling in the tunnel collapse. The wood looked old and brittle – yeah, this railway had definitely been here for some time.

A low growl from the other end of the tunnel snapped

back to the present. The growl was deep – far deeper than a human could make. I knew there was a reason that I shouldn't have made that light. I wasn't alone in this cave.

I heard it approach before I could see it. It sounded big. The sound of its paws striking the ground echoed throughout the narrow chamber.

The lumbering form as it shambled closer. My heart caught in my mouth. I flicked a shield around myself. This wasn't going to be fun. I'd never faced anything like this before. My new cave companion was a very large bear.

I'd obviously intruded into its lair and it looked very angry about this. I shuffled back slowly, attempting to get a little further away from the light. Maybe it wouldn't see me if I crouched in the shadows. Wrong! The bear reared up onto its hind legs and let out a growl. Okay, moving had been a bad idea.

There was nothing for it, I'd have to somehow try to chase it off. The only problem was I had no idea how. Do I scream at it? Shout at it? Wave my hands around like I'm crazy? I remembered hearing something about punching a shark in the nose to get it to lose interest in you.

That sounded like a good idea. Bears are like sharks right? Land Sharks. I grinned somewhat dryly at the thought. It wasn't that helpful.

The bear had dropped down onto all fours again and was approaching, still growling at me. It didn't look any less threatening once it entered into the light. It was a brute.

The bear reared up in front of me and roared at me. Then it dropped back down and charged. What did it want me to do – run maybe? I'd heard that running from bears was a bad idea. I braced myself as the bear got close and the inevitable swipe connected with the right side of the shield.

I staggered under the impact and felt my left side go numb. Okay, that wasn't any harder than a bullet – but it covered a lot more area. The bear seemed confused that I hadn't fallen down and quickly swiped again.

I attempted to side step, but wasn't fast enough. This bear was damned fast. How comes bears were so fast? I thought they were slow and lumbering.

The impact sent me spinning and sprawling to the ground. I immediately got back to my feet in fury. The bear was still blocking my path through and I really needed it to move on. Hopefully I could scare it off with a show of strength, as I didn't particularly relish killing the beast.

'Okay Yogey – you're getting punched in the snout.' Hopefully this would work. My fist impacted with the bear's nose and it let out a loud growl and fell forward, its paws reaching out and pulling me in a crushing embrace. The smell of the bear was over powering as my face was smooshed into its fur.

I've learnt many things over the past few years. One of the more important things I've learned is – Don't punch Bears. I can't stress this enough – They don't like it and it won't intimidate them. It took me several seconds to extricate myself. The bear had a look of confusion on its face it had obviously never fought someone like me before. It growled again and launched itself in for another attack.

I wasn't going to let that happen again. I whipped a Mana thread catching it across the side of the head. It shook its head angrily and shrugged off the attack. Shit – that should have floored him.

The bear launched another strike, I narrowly avoided it by teleporting several metres behind the bear. The bear roared in shock at the explosion of light and sound. I think its first impulse may have been to flee but as it turned it me and its eyes narrowed and it prepared itself to charge again. I didn't really want to give the bear another chance to maul me again. I turned and ran. My legs screamed at the abuse and with my swollen knee it felt like I was running across shards of glass.

The second thing I learned that day was that it's almost impossible to outrun a bear. They're big and they look slow – they're not. True, I wasn't exactly running at my full speed, but the bear had absolutely no trouble catching me. I felt its massive paws thunder down onto my back and force me onto the ground. Its stunning weight pressed down and I felt its powerful jaws attempt to close on the back of my neck.

My shield cackled in response sending a cascade of sparks off in all directions. I felt the bear rear up in shock and anger. I managed to turn onto my side just as the bear brought its paws smashing down onto me. I felt my shield buckle and truthfully I had no idea how it held through this punishment.

I now had a face first view of the gnarled claws of the bear scratching against my shield's surface. I don't claim to be an expert in discerning bear emotions, but this bear looked pissed off. I'd hoped to avoid this – but it looked like I didn't have a choice now. I really didn't want to do any serious harm to the bear, but it was looking like it was coming down to him or me.

"Okay Boo Boo," I whispered, "this ain't no picnic basket."

I managed to raise my hand and flexed my fingers into a tight fist. The bear snarled and moved to bite my forearm. From the force of its jaws I was sure it could have cleaved straight through my arm. Fortunately I didn't give the bear enough to time test my theory.

A jet of flame burst from my fist and into the bear's face. It was only a short burst, intended to scare it off. The bear reared back. I'm sure he was reacting more to the shock of the blast than actual pain.

It backed up several steps and roared at me again. I fired off several volleys of flame before it growled and began to back away. It was fortunate that it was backing away from the direction I wanted to go. I let it go. It didn't look too badly burned as it skulked off into the shadows. Just a little scorching on the hair on its head and chest.

I set off several more glow spells to navigate my way through the railway tunnel until eventually I staggered up to another cave. Whatever had closed this tunnel had done a good job. Too good a job.

Unfortunately, this end of the tunnel didn't have any entrances through the rock fall. I sighed and shook my head as I summoned my powers. I hit the fallen rocks with the most powerful telekinetic threads that I could and watched with satisfaction as several rocks exploded from the mountainside.

Light poured in as a cascade of smaller rocks and boulders rained down into the newly created entrance into the chamber. I grinned to myself. While that had been quite impressive, it had also been a little reckless. There was a good possibility I could have collapsed the whole tunnel down upon me.

I hadn't thought about that until I noticed a small avalanche of rocks sliding into the tunnel mouth. I tentatively made my way out into the daylight.

The mouth of the tunnel on the other side of the canyon looked like a wound upon the mountain face, grey rock slid down the silky white snow sheathed cliff face and the gaping hole of the tunnel looked almost like a bullet hole in the side of a pristine mountain.

* * * * * *

Now that I knew what I was looking for it was easy to spot the locations on the cliff face where a railway bridge had been secured. I was confident that should I look amongst the rubble at the base of the cliff I would find railway rails and smashed wood.

I teleported across to a clearing and was gratified to see bolted metal plates mounted into the cliff face. This had definitely been the structure of a cliff side railway bridge. I was definitely onto something here.

I sent my Scry thread further down the smashed railway line until I came to a second series of tunnels. I would need to find entry into the tunnels the old fashioned way. I couldn't dare teleport into that dark – who knew what I would be teleporting into?

I teleported as near as I dared and examined the rocks. I had suspected whoever had closed these tunnels had been systematic and effective. It took me several tries before I was able to gain access to them.

A small landside of rocks later I was inspecting another smashed railway line. I ventured deeply into the tunnels and found that the air quickly grew cold and stale. It was old air – it had been stagnant too long. I was sure I was in the right place.

This tunnel was far more extensive and seemed almost to worm its way deeper into the mountain. A set of wooden doors had barred the railway lines at one point, but this secure barrier had long since decayed through age and neglect.

I had set off a series of glow spells to light my way. The light they created was eerie and caused shadows to dance across the chamber walls. It set my teeth on edge and by the time I reached the end of the line I was already in a heightened state of agitation.

The end of the line wasn't what I expected. It was simply a long concrete platform that led into a larger subterranean yard. The yard was segregated from the train platform by a high wire fence. It would have been quite adequate security if the wire were not hanging loose and broken from the poles.

A sign above the concrete platform identified the place as 'Stolibor'. I didn't recognise the name. This complex was old. I carefully moved through a gap in the wire fence and into the main compound yard. The floor of this cavern was concreted and was riddled with cracks and craters. Small boulders littered the compound. I couldn't see the roof of the cavern, but I assumed from the lack of light that we were still completely underground.

I shivered as I glanced around the complex. The whole place had a ghost town feeling. I could make out large wooden towers at each end of the cavern, with large flood-lights attached to them. The whole place screamed prison.

At the far side of the cavern I could make out a set of steel double doors that led into the cliff face on one side. The doors looked ominously heavy. On the far side of the compound there were several dozen small cordoned off areas. Each cordon was only about ten by ten metres wide and had a small gate that faced towards the doors.

It was obvious what they were. They were animal pens. They had to be – what else would you use such a structure for? Obviously they'd been used to store pigs or sheep or something. Maybe this was an elaborate abattoir? Unlikely, but I couldn't immediately think of any other reason for the pens.

I went over to inspect them, but couldn't really see anything more up close. They were simply as they looked, small caged off areas for the animals. As with the exterior fence, the wire here was hanging loose from the poles and presented no barrier. Each pole was approximately two metres tall, which seemed a little excessive for animals. The whole place just felt wrong.

Behind the pens were the remains of some kind of wooden building. It was mostly ruins and ash. The frame of the building rose from a throne of charred beams and broken panels. I couldn't tell what the original use of the building had been but it looked like it had been one long room.

Maybe a hall of some kind, that didn't make much sense though. In fact nothing about this place was making any sense. Why had Marcus sent me here? What did he want me to find? There was only one place that I hadn't fully explored – whatever lay behind those iron doors.

I had a deep sense of foreboding as I pried my fingers behind the door and pulled. The door didn't budge, either because it was locked or because it was simply so damned heavy. I wrapped a telekinetic thread behind it and pulled. The creaking of the hinges resounded throughout the cavern. It obviously hadn't been opened in a long, long time.

The door had been leaning slightly into the mountain face, which meant that its entire weight was resting against the frame. It would have been impossible to move without magic. Whoever had built this place had wanted this room to be secure.

I peered inside nervously. As I had expected it was dark, what I hadn't expected to find though was a corridor that led deeper into the mountain. I set off a glow spell and wished that I'd thought to bring a torch. I was chewing through all my power with repetitive use of these glow spells. I could already feel a tingling on the sides of my head that would foretell the arrival of a headache caused by too much use of Mana.

I gently massaged my temples and ran my fingers across my eyes before I entered into the corridor. The corridor was about ten metres deep and ended in another set of double doors. These were more traditional interior doors though and opened easily when I pushed them. They led into a much larger chamber.

I was now standing on a catwalk that looked down over what must have been some form of operations centre. Crude machines lined the far side of the room. They looked just like the pictures that'd I'd seen in high school of punch card terminals. Very primitive computing machines. Small lamps hung from the ceiling. A thick layer of dust covered everything. This room hadn't been visited in years. I sent out another glow spell into the centre of the room.

I gripped the catwalk railing firmly as I gazed across

the room. This wasn't just an operations centre – this was a war room. The thought sent shivers down my spine, but the evidence was insurmountable. I was looking at the evidence right now. It hung almost right before my eyes. A flag.

The flag hung from the far wall at eye level. It was a simple flag, two bent lines crossed over one other, but the symbol sent chills down my spine. A swastika. This place was a Nazi army base. How old was this complex? Had it been left unused since the end of the war? It certainly looked that way. I walked down the catwalk stairs and onto the main floor. The dust was palpable and my movement caused it to be picked up and hang in the air.

It may have just been my imagination, but the dust almost appeared to be forming human figures. It was only dust hanging in the air, but with the refracted light from my glow spell it wasn't hard to see faces in the dust.

What spirits lingered here? I grimly let my mind cast back to the holding pens I had seen on the way in, but didn't particularly want to investigate that line of thought further. The conclusion was unappealing.

I don't know what happens when you pass on and I've never seen anything that would lead me to believe in life after death. In all my years and with all the strange fucked up stuff I've seen I've never found any evidence to support the theory of ghosts or spirits from beyond the grave, and yet standing there in that place I couldn't help but feel that I was an intruder in a place left for the dead.

I shivered slightly as I looked around the control

room. It looked as if no one had stood in this room for at least half a century. It was hard not to be cowed by this simple fact: Victor had once stood here. This was what Marcus had sent me here to find.

The realisation hit me like a truck. Victor had been alive during the Second World War. The wealth of knowledge and wisdom he must have accrued during that period of time must have been staggering. Was I a fool to stand against him? For the first time since I decided to leave his teachings I began to feel the cold clamour of real fear. I must seem like an insignificant speck to him, one that he could easy swat aside should I become too troublesome. I shook my head angrily. No, I was more than just an irritation. His actions thus far hadn't been the actions of a man who could remove me at any point. He had refused to directly confront me though it would have been simple for him to find me. He had done everything in his power not to face me. What did that mean?

I wandered throughout the control room trying to shake off the creepy feeling of the place. I found a series of offices on the far side of the room. The offices were even more creepy than the control room. At least in the control room I could see around me. In the offices my field of vision was limited. It wasn't too hard to imagine someone sneaking up on me while my back was turned. Shadows from the glow spell in the main room played across the walls creating movements of light that couldn't help but draw the eye.

The offices didn't yield much in the way of anything

interesting until I got onto the second floor offices. These offices were a little more elaborate and grand. I went through them not really expecting to find much when I found something.

It was obviously the office of the Commandant of the complex. It was larger and more luxurious than the others. It too was covered in the thick layer of dust but it was obvious that some care had been put into selecting the furniture. A small chill came over me as I noticed the violin displayed in the corner. This had been Victor's office – I was sure of it.

I set off a glow spell in the room to be sure. Now that I could see with clarity I was certain. This was definitely Victor's office. Fortunately like everything else in the complex it didn't look like he'd used it in a long, long time. There was a picture on the desk and I went over to it and wiped the glass. To my surprise a familiar face peered back at me. Renee!

The woman in the photo was Renee. What the hell? From the look of the photo and the way she was dressed it had been taken sometime during the war. I staggered back slightly as the revelation overtook me. I knew that Victor was far older than he looked, but I hadn't considered that Renee could have been.

When I had first met Renee she had looked like she was in her mid-twenties. True, it didn't look as though she had aged much in the six years since we had first met, but people don't age that quickly, it was possible that I just hadn't noticed.

What did this mean? That Renee was also using the same sorcery that Victor did to extend his life? It just didn't add up. I knew Renee, surely I'd know if she was doing something like that. No, it was impossible – the woman in the photo couldn't possibly be Renee. The more I looked at the photo, the more I convinced myself that it wasn't Renee. The lines around her eyes were different and that smile definitely wasn't Renee's. No – this woman wasn't Renee, but she sure looked a lot like her.

I sat down in the office chair and pondered my next move. This led to another dust demon rising vengefully from the cushioned seat and dissipating into the still air. On the far side of Victor's office was a series of bookshelves. I hadn't noticed them when I had come in. I quickly got to my feet and moved over to inspect them.

It was what I had expected – tomes on Mana. In fact as I pulled the first one off the shelf I realised that I had already read these ones. The only difference was – I had read copies of these books. These were the originals.

They were hand written pieces and loosely bound. To the right collector they would have been worth a fortune. I glanced around tentatively, I suppose they were well stored here. It looked dry and wasn't likely to ever been affected by direct sunlight. They were as secure and safe as they could be made. Only a Mage could have gotten in here without some serious lifting machinery. They had been stored in what had been the perfect hiding place, at least up until now.

I had read some of these books during my time under

Victor's tutorage. They had been written by his master sometime around the turn of the nineteenth century. I had only read a couple of them. Here was a whole bookcase. I wondered what secrets these tomes contained.

I knew that Victor had skewed my training towards the skills and powers he would find useful for me. I knew that he had attempted to turn me into nothing more than a violent thug and personal assassin. What knowledge had he hidden from me?

I thought about taking the books, but I wasn't sure that I could get them all out of here in one piece. It was a long way back down the mountain. Once I was finished in this complex I'd return here and choose a couple to take with me.

There were many to choose from. Many of them appeared to be simple bindings of hand written notes while others were properly printed books. As interesting as these were this wasn't what Marcus had sent me here to retrieve. There had to be something else.

It didn't take me long to find it. It was another series of books. I pulled one of them from the shelf and checked the title. They were much different from the others. They were a lot newer for a start. Crisp gold lettering adorned their spines and the swastika adorned the top of each volume. As I opened the first book I immediately recognised Victor's precise handwriting. I turned the cover over and inspected the title – 'Die Lehre des Lebens durch Tod'. The study of life through death. I shuddered.

This was what Marcus had sent me to recover. I was

sure of it. Victor had documented his experiments and bound his conclusions, just like any other proper scientist. It would be his undoing. As I flipped through the book I was presented with Victor's neat writing, diagrams and even photos.

It was macabre to say the least and left a bad taste in my mouth. The novel detailed experiments being done on living people or 'subjects' as it referred to them. The writing was clinical, detached and thoroughly unethical. There were hundreds of experiments being documented in this book alone, and there were five of these books.

Towards the back the book I saw photos of what was obviously this compound and discovered that my search of this complex hadn't been as complete as I had thought. There was a whole wing I had missed.

There was a trapdoor in the main parade ground that led into this wing. It wasn't easy to see and I wasn't surprised that I had missed it when I passed through that area. I remembered a pile of wood that I had assumed was the remains of a structure. The trapdoor was most likely underneath it. The photo showed the parade ground and the trapdoor. A small frame of wood held a sign over the door that stated 'Krankenstation'. It was an infirmary. Why the hell was it beneath the main parade ground? This didn't make any sense. I put the books back on the shelf and made my way back into the parade ground.

I would return after I was done to recover the books and be on my way. I didn't particularly want to linger here any longer than I needed to, but I felt that this was important.

* * * * * *

I found the entrance to the infirmary easily enough. I pulled away several beams of wood to reveal the iron door beneath. It was covered by a thick layer of dust and dirt and was relatively indistinguishable from the rest of the parade ground floor except for the two metal handles on the doors and an iron chain looping them together. Someone had gone to a lot of effort to ensure that no one got in here. The sign that had once been displayed over the entrance had been broken in two and now simply said 'Kranke'.

As I snapped the iron chain in two I had the sudden feeling that perhaps the lock hadn't been put in place to prevent someone getting in, it may have been to prevent someone getting out. I shivered slightly and pulled on the right hand side door. It eventually gave, with a tremendous creak that echoed throughout the cavern. This didn't help my nerves any.

The doorway yielded a small ramp that headed down to a set of double doors. I cautiously crept down the ramp. As I got closer to the doors I could see that the frames to each door had been smashed almost to splinters. There was no way of securing the doors now, they had been completely destroyed. Something had come through here and hit this door with great force. I could only attribute this type of damage to one thing. Mana.

One of the doors hung freely from its frame and the other had fallen down as the weight of time took its toll. I could only see several metres behind the corridor that lay beyond. A thick shade of darkness veiled the whole place. It was almost as if the light from my glow didn't dare illuminate that corridor.

That was crazy talk. I was getting myself all stirred up for no good reason. I shivered again as I passed through the shattered doorway and into the corridor beyond. I set off another glow spell and sent it a fair way down the corridor before detonating.

It revealed a standard looking corridor. There was nothing creepy about it at all. Each wall was adorned with sterile white paint and the floors were a crisp white tile. It reminded me of somewhere I'd been before, but I couldn't place where.

A medical gurney stood against the wall just round the corner. A tingling sense of dread rose in my throat. I'd been somewhere like this before. It had been one of Marcus's warehouses in Singapore were he had performed unnatural and evil practices – practices he claimed that he had learned from Victor. Had Victor used this facility to research and develop those very same dark arts? If so what evils were left behind after Victor had perfected his techniques?

I shivered and gritted my teeth as I battled with my fear. I raised a shield around myself to steady my nerves. It actually helped a lot – it gave me a sense of invulnerability that helped calm me and allowed me to proceed. I am a Mage – short of another Mage I am the most dangerous person in this complex. I had to remind myself of this several times before I could continue.

The sign at the end of the corridor marked that the way left led to the operating theatre. This seemed as good as any place to start. I made my way into a large circular room. Surrounding the room were several circles of chairs facing inwards. I went down a series of small steps onto the theatre floor. The chairs were covered in the usual thick layer of dust that everything else was covered in. No, wait. The floor wasn't completely covered in dust. There were noticeable footprints in the dust – footprints that didn't belong to me. They were easily visible even in this poor light. I couldn't tell how long ago the prints had been left, but someone had been in here, and the dust had not yet settled.

As I looked around the room I kept catching glimpses of something right in the corner of my vision. It kind of looked man shaped. It was beginning to freak me out. I wasn't one hundred per cent sure if it was just my imagination going nuts or if I was being stalked.

I knew for certain that it wasn't invisibility. If I were being hunted by another Mage I would see their Mana aura – in fact the invisibility spell would make them all the more visible to my eyes. No, there was no one else in this room with me. It took me several seconds to reassure myself of this fact.

I gritted my teeth again and shook my head. It's

funny how you can build yourself up into a state of hysteria. I would have felt more at ease if the threat were revealed and someone were physically assaulting me. At least then I would have known what the threat was and could have dealt with it.

Part of me wanted to just get the hell out of here. Perhaps I should go back up to the parade ground get some air. The whole atmosphere down here was stifling. It wasn't that I was running away – It was just a rest. I'd come back down here in a few minutes to finish searching this place. I'm so full of it sometimes.

I made my way back into the corridor and was heading back to the trapdoor when I heard it. It began so softly at first that I wasn't sure that I had heard anything. It was a kind of shuffling. At first I thought it was noise that I was creating – but that wasn't the case.

Eventually I saw it. It was human shaped and I couldn't believe what I was seeing. It was shambling down the corridor towards me. If it had noticed me, it didn't give any indication. It reached the corridor T-intersection where the glow spell was in effect and it suddenly gave out a shrieking wail.

I took several steps back – the voice wasn't human. It may perhaps once have been human, but it didn't sound human now. The thing was still shrieking as it attempted to cover its head. It looked like it was beating itself savagely over the head repeatedly.

Now that I could see it better I revised my opinion that it was human shaped. A better term would have been that it had once been human shaped. I took another step back. This was exactly the wrong thing to do. My movement attracted its attention. It screamed again as it raised its head and looked at me. Its grimy face twisted in rage as it charged me.

As quick as I was, I must admit this thing took me by surprise. Its fists impacted twice against my shield before I was able to react. The dull thumps of its strike all but unfelt through my shield. Its rage wasn't spent by its apparent inability to hurt me though. It just kept throwing punches.

They weren't exactly punches either, they were more like it was throwing its fists in my general direction. In most cases it was the underside of its forearm that actually impacted. I took several steps back to get a better view of it.

It had definitely been human at one stage, but it had shrunk into a tight wasted shell of a man. Its body was twisted with knots and blisters and grime. It shrieked at me and leaped to attack me again. This time however I didn't let it strike.

I aimed a telekinetic thread at its chest and flicked it away. The thread impacted solidly and sent it reeling. It landed further down the corridor with a thump, but shrugged off the strike and leapt to attack again. What the hell? That attack at that range should have broken every one of its ribs. It was tougher than it looked.

As the wretch charged again, I could see that this was indeed the case. Its chest cavity had collapsed. Its unceremonious landing and scraped off some of the grime and dust and I could make out the tell-tale glow of a Mana signature. A Mana signature? This thing had a Mana signature? This thing was a Mage? Or at least had once been one. Why the hell wasn't it attacking me with Mana? It didn't make any sense.

I hadn't been able to see it earlier under the collected filth on the thing, but now that it was visible it was obvious. I could see the Mana ebb sluggishly across its flesh, its path occasionally blocked by areas of grime too thick for it to be seen through.

This didn't make any sense, if it was a Mage it should have been attacking me with something far stronger than its fists.

I looped a Mana thread around its torso and forced it back to the ground. Its whole body shook as it struggled, but it was unable to break free. I forced it firmly against the ground as a dark thought took me. I moved forward and tentatively scraped some more of the grime from its chest. Its skin was tough and leathery and felt more like wood than flesh. Stomaching away my distaste at the texture of his flesh to my dread I found what I was looking for. A small series of scars leading up to the centre of its chest.

They were difficult to find, especially with the thing flailing beneath me, but they were definitely there. I'd seen these before. The only thing was the last time I had seen them they had been on a corpse. No, that wasn't quite right. The scars had been on a Drone.

I'd seen them in Marcus's laboratory, on a corpse that Marcus was reanimating. But this didn't add up. From what I knew of Drone's they weren't supposed to attack you. They waited like marionettes to be given orders.

Maybe this thing's last orders had been to defend this place? I wasn't sure about that. It just didn't seem right. The thing beneath howled with impotent rage as I pondered what to do with it. It was old, very old. Was it possible that this is what happens to Drones if left unattended for long periods of time? If so what did that mean?

Marcus had claimed that the personality and will of the departed was gone. Yet this thing clearly was able to make some, if not warped, decisions. I don't think it could reason or think rationally, but I could see it attempting to tear at the Mana bands that held it immobile. If it were completely mindless it wouldn't do that.

What had Victor discovered in these Drones? I put the thought from my mind. I couldn't imagine a worse hell than being trapped in a body not under my control for eternity. Marcus had claimed that there was no intellect and that the personality that had once owned the shell was long gone. What if he was wrong? Dear god. What had been done to this poor man?

I looked into the things eyes as it struggled against me. Its eyes were glazed and milky white. It wouldn't be able to see through those – at least not conventionally. Was this, as Marcus put it, just a machine made out of flesh? Or was it something more?

This left me with a conundrum. What should I do with this thing now. It didn't seem right to kill it. I wasn't even sure that I could. All I'd be able to do was dismember it so that it wasn't mobile and I didn't have the stomach to do that.

No, I'd have to find somewhere to secure it. I remembered that the operating theatre had had secure bonds on the operating table. I lifted my captive into the air and carried him into the operating theatre.

I looped a second Mana band around the restraints and locked them into place. I breathed a nervous sigh then released him from the Mana. This table was quite old – it wasn't out of the realms of possibility that the bonds had fatigued with age. The instant the Mana bands left it, the thing on the table raged against its bindings. I could hear the complaint of twisted leather and metal being strained. Fortunately for me – it held.

I closed the door to the operating theatre hoping that this would mollify it, but I could still hear it groaning and clawing at the table through the doors. The noise didn't do much to improve the atmosphere of the place.

Trying my best to ignore the shrieks I made my way deeper into the underground complex in the direction that the thing had come. This led into a small series of offices and then to a cell block. I kept my shield at full strength expecting to find another one of those things at any moment.

I crept into the cell block. Each of the cells was secured by a small iron door and a series of bars, which fortunately allowed me to see into each cell without entering. I had cast a glow spell at the end of the cell block so I was pretty sure that there was nothing in the cells, but it paid to be safe. I certainly couldn't hear the same type of racket that the other Drone had made upon discovery.

It wasn't until I got to the second last cell on the left that I found something interesting. It appeared to be a prisoner. Or at least it had once been a prisoner. I assumed that it was now a Drone. It wasn't acting like the other one though; it was simply standing facing the wall. It seemed to be completely unaware of my presence.

"Hello?" I said softly. My voice sounded too loud to my ears. It echoed throughout the cell block. The thing didn't even budge.

"Are you okay?" This seemed like a redundant question.

The Drone's head shook slightly as if to clear it and it tilted its head to one side as if listening. Maybe it had heard me.

"Hello?" I repeated again.

"… Ist da… Jemand?" a voice uttered in stuttered German. It spoke? What the hell? Drones don't speak! The voice had been garbled and hoarse but it had definitely come from the figure in the cell. I quickly checked the lock on the cell door and noted with some degree of relief that it was secure. There was quite a bit of damage to the doorframe, but it too was still intact.

"I'm here," I replied back in German. It had asked if anyone was there.

The figure slowly turned its head. I couldn't imagine how much effort it took. Dust seemed to fall from its frame as it moved. It took the figure a long time to move.

"Who are you? It's been so long since anyone came here." The figure gasped as it slowly managed to turn its frame to face me. "You're a Mage," he accused in a croak before I could answer.

I nodded. There wasn't much point in denying it. What the hell was going on? This thing could see Mana?

"How long have you been in here?"

"I... don't... know."

"Do you have a name?"

"I... think so. I don't remember," came the eventual reply.

This wasn't getting us anywhere. I wasn't going to take chances though. This thing was a Mage and that meant that it was dangerous.

"What's... the number... on the door?" the thing croaked.

It took me several seconds for me to locate the sign as the door had been fairly badly damaged. I found a small square of paper with some faded words on the ground surrounded by some shards of broken glass.

"Patient 616." I informed the thing.

"Oh," was the thing's only response.

"I... think... my name... is... Karl." He continued slowly. He didn't sound too sure, but Karl was as good a name as any.

"When were you put in here Karl?"

"I… don't know… I remember… a camp… being… arrested… Doctors?"

Karl's wizzened face took on a curious expression. It was obvious that he was having trouble remembering. I didn't blame him. I was well and truly ready to believe that he had been in that cell since the Second World War. There was something definitely off about him. When I had studied with Victor he had spoken about a technique that allowed him to regenerate his body at a cellular level. It was possible that this is what they had been researching here?

"Do you want me to let you out?" I ventured tentatively. I wasn't sure I wanted to let him out, but at least he didn't appear to be that much of a threat… at least yet.

"No!" Karl's voice whipped out far quicker than his previous responses, "Randall is out there! He keeps trying to get in, but I can't let him."

"Randall?"

Karl didn't answer, but he didn't have to. It was obvious who had been referring to – the Drone I had managed to incarcerate earlier.

"I've locked him away."

"He goes away for some time – he always comes back."

"How long has he been trying to get in here for?"

"I don't know." Karl replied somewhat irritably. I'd heard that asking the same question in different ways could jog the memory of someone with amnesia. Maybe this was the same?

"I remember... a camp... I think." Karl continued, "...I thought I was going to die there."

Karl's voice, which was already difficult to hear, cracked and for the first time I thought I heard a glimmer of the man beneath.

"But... someone came... a man... a soldier.... He was like us... he pulled me from the crowd and... took me somewhere... Here... I think."

Karl's story took several hours to unfold completely. He was Polish Jewish by birth on his mother's side and when the Nazis had invaded Poland, Karl had been rounded up with other Jewish people and sent into concentration camps. He hadn't known for sure at the time, but the rumours were that they were being taken somewhere safe out of the country. Karl hadn't believed them at the time, but couldn't have guessed what the truth actually was. They'd had suspicions though.

I didn't have the heart to tell him that those camps had been death camps where the Nazis had executed close to two million people. Had Karl been sent to in one it was unlikely he would have left. I don't know what kind of hell that Karl had been forced to endure here, but looking at his twisted and desiccated body it was quite clear that death would have been preferable.

Karl continued with his story and it wasn't difficult to see what had happened if you read between the lines. A German officer had removed him from the rest of the prisoners and brought him here. The German officer had been a Mage. Karl had known about our kind, but was unable to make much use of our powers. He wasn't that powerful. His mother had been a Mage too, but she had died before the war. Karl had been quite sure that the fact that he was a Mage was why he had been removed from the camp, although he did say that other non-Mages had been selected as well.

I was almost certain that this officer had been Victor. I wasn't surprised that Victor had once been a Nazi – it seemed obvious given his past. Marcus had mentioned that there was a black mark against Victor that had prevented him from being elected as Primea. Involvement with the Nazi party seemed like a fairly serious breach of our kinds laws. We weren't supposed to overthrow governments or invade other countries. The Nazi party had done both.

I vaguely wondered why Victor hadn't been put to death. Our kind had harsh punishments for those of us who broke our laws so flagrantly.

Karl had said that there were hundreds if not thousands of people who came through this research facility. The death rate was catastrophic with prisoners undergoing surgery and experimentation according to some unknown roster. Periodic trains of new prisoners would come and the body bags of the victims would be sent back. Prison labour had been used to ferry the bodies from the facility onto the trains.

Karl was lucky in that he had managed to avoid most of the surgery and had survived longer than most. He had mostly been questioned about his heritage and any others of our kind that he had met. The German officer had been most persistent in trying to trace Karl's lineage as he had refused to believe that someone of Jewish descent could be a Mage. It hadn't complied with the concept of Arian superiority.

This didn't surprised me very much either. During my stay with Victor he had on numerous occasions indicated that our powers were passed down through bloodline. He had also stated that our bloodline appeared to be Romani in nature – gypsy. He hadn't sounded very happy about that at the time, but I hadn't thought to query it until now. Karl's memory had been vague at best and I had to piece together pieces of information from what I already knew, but one thing was certain – human experimentation had occurred on this site.

Karl had only undergone one experiment and it had been in the final days of the facility. He had surmised this because most of the officers and other prisoners had already left the camp. There only remained one other prisoner – Randall. He had been in the cell across the walkway from Karl. They had spoken briefly before they had dragged Randall away.

When they had returned Randall he was a changed person – in that he wasn't a person any longer. He simply followed his captors and did as instructed. When no instructions were given Randall stood still and simply waited. The most frightening thing about it was though, Randall now had a Mana signature. Karl had tried to talk to Randall to find out what had been done, but Randall remained mute.

They came for Karl the very next day. He remembered trying to fight his captors, but being forced onto a surgical gurney. In vain he tried to use the Mana, but it was as ineffectual as his fists. His captors were simply too strong and he was too weak. Months of inactivity and poor diet had taken its toll. They brought the gurney into an operating room and forced a mask over his face. That was the last thing Karl remembered of that day.

He wasn't sure how long he was out for, but when he awoke he was in a small room with the German officer that had pulled him out of the prison camp. He was surprised to find that the officer was actually the Commandant of the complex.

The conversation was short and sharp with the Commandant simply inquiring how he felt and Karl was surprised to note that he didn't feel any different. He searched in vain for surgical scars but couldn't find any. The Commandant then asked Karl to draw upon his powers, to simply lift a small object from the table.

Karl hadn't been the most powerful among our kind, but simple levitation was well within his capabilities. At least it would have normally been. That day he was unable to draw the necessary strength to even lift a teacup. It jittered and rocked slightly, but didn't overly rise. They had removed his powers.

Karl would have assumed that this had been the point of the exercise except that the Commandant had been furious demanding again and again that Karl try to lift the cup. They had even resorted to beatings and punishments, but his threats were ultimately unsuccessful. Karl could see the Mana in his body and it appeared to be doing something, but not what he was trying to get it to do. It was as if the Mana was already being used elsewhere and nothing was left for anything else.

The Commandant was eventually forced to admit that the experiment had been a failure, but hadn't specified how or why. He hadn't even bothered to tell Karl what they had been trying to achieve. The facility was completely abandoned the next day with the notable exceptions of Karl and Randall.

Karl wasn't sure how long he had waited in the dark until he had thought of escape. The rumbling of his stomach eventually shook him into action, but he found that he was unable to break out of the cell – the bars were simply too strong. He had managed to survive for some time using water from the cistern from the toilet, but eventually that ran dry and he was forced to go without.

It must have been at least three weeks before he realised that something was wrong. There was no way for him to accurately measure the amount of time that had passed. With nothing to eat or drink his body was wracked with starvation and was beginning to succumb to death. Starvation is a horrible way to die, but being in a cell Karl was unable to do much about it. He had tried unsuccessfully on several occasions to take his life, but had also been unable to complete the task. It was as if his body just refused to damn well die.

Karl didn't know how long it had been when he realised that something wasn't right – that he should be long dead. It seemed like months since food had last passed his mouth and his body had become shrunken and weak. He went through fits of delirium, and hallucinations were common. He finally came to the conclusion that he simply wasn't going to die.

Some unknown agent was keeping him alive. There was only one explanation – it was the Mana. Somehow the experiment had caused the Mana to sustain him past when he should have died. His body had twisted in on itself as its usual source of nourishment had been removed and it was forced to subsist on Mana, but he was still alive.

The knowledge sent him crazy. He had no way of knowing how long he spent in the dark, in the cold, surviving on magical powers he could neither control nor cease. His next memory was that of a noise bringing him out of a stupor.

It was coming from the other cell. At first it was a low groaning. Randall was making noises. Karl couldn't see him, but he could see the Mana signature and was shocked to see how shrivelled the frame of Randall's body was. It was skeletal. Leathered flesh, pulled taunt over a skeletal frame. Karl didn't need to be told that his own frame mirrored Randall's. In truth Karl wasn't as bad as Randall, he at least had maintained a muscle structure and frame – albeit incredibly frail.

Karl had come to the grim conclusion after what must have been months that of the two of them, Randall had been the luckier as he didn't appear to understand or care what had happened to him. That is at least up until now. The noise Randall was making was getting worse. It was nothing more than a rumble in his throat, but it was getting louder over the days, weeks, months or years. Karl had no way of knowing.

Karl tried to placate Randall, and his soothing seemed to calm him down a little. Karl had no idea how long this went on for as he himself dropped in and out of stupors. One day it came to the point when Karl had tried to quieten Randall and it hadn't worked.

Previously Randall would respond to his name and the groaning would stop. But this day the groaning got louder and louder and Karl was unable to make it stop. Then something new happened.

Randall took a hesitant step forward, turned and screamed. He screamed and screamed until his voice turned hoarse. He took a second step and fell forward onto his knees. It took him several tries before he was able to recover his footing. Karl couldn't see this of course, but could determine what was happening by the noises being made. He kept calling to Randall to attempt to calm him, but nothing appeared to be working.

Then the beating began. It was the sound of pulped flesh hitting solid metal over and over again. Randall had started bashing against the inside of his cell. Karl didn't know if it was a break for freedom or merely another symptom of the madness that had overtaken Randall.

Karl can't remember how long it took for Randall to break out from his cell, but it must have taken ages. Eventually there was a metallic shriek and the door swung open with a grinding chirp.

Karl had been happy for his friend to have finally achieved his freedom, but soon learned the truth. Although free from the cell – Randall was far from free. When Karl had called to him, Randall responded with a groan and stumbled over to Karl's cell, The sound of mashed beatings began again.

He was trying to break into Karl's cell. Now that Randall was closer Karl could make out his appearance. There was nothing of his cell-mate left. The 'thing' trying to break into his cell was a monster and Karl knew without a doubt that his own appearance was similar.

Eventually Randall became distracted and had wandered off. He would return periodically to resume his assault on Karl's cell, but so far Karl's cell had proved stronger.

Still Karl knew that it was only a matter of time – after all Randall had broken out of his own cell, it stood to reason that he would eventually break into Karl's.

Karl soon found that he was looking forward to it. He knew that once Randall broke in that he would finally die. Only a sliver of doubt remained in Karl's mind. What if he didn't? What if he remained trapped in this shell of a body after Randall had beaten it senseless?

I shuddered at the thought. The longer Karl spoke

the more eloquent and knowledgeable he became. It was almost as if he was waking up from a long sleep, which I suppose in a very real sense he was. After he finished his story, he begged me to kill him.

The only problem was, I wasn't sure that I could.

CHAPTER FOUR

"Over seventy years?" Karl repeated incredulous.

"As best I can tell, given that we don't know exactly when you were put in here," I said.

Karl remained silent for a long while and slowly moved to sit on the bed. Movement seemed painful for him. His arms shook as he moved them, his feet didn't quite walk as much as shuffle from place to place and the effort seemed enormous.

"Does it hurt?"

"No," Karl replied softly, "I stopped feeling pain pretty quickly... at least it seemed pretty quickly," he finished wryly.

That made sense I guess. If he could still feel pain then it would feel that his body was screaming at him. It was obvious that while the Mana was keeping him alive, it wasn't providing enough nourishment to keep him healthy and the body was suffering and had been for a very long time. Unable to die and unable to nourish itself, Karl's body had fallen into a kind of state of continual shock.

I sighed. I wasn't sure if there was anything I could do about that. Could I end this poor wretch's existence with the Mana sustaining him like this? I had no idea where to begin. With some experimentation I might be able to figure out how this all worked, but that wasn't sure thing.

He was never going to be able to live a normal life after this. He was mentally, physically and emotionally scarred by this experience. Even if it were possible to nurse him back to health I doubted that this body would be able to digest nourishment any longer. It seemed cruel to deny him an ending and force him to endure this longer.

Karl was reluctant to step out of the cell, despite my frequent assurances that Randall had been secured. I didn't blame him as this small cell had been his whole world for so long. I had no idea what the sight of daylight might do to him. His eyes certainly hadn't registered natural light in over half a century.

I toyed with the idea of ending his existence by incineration, but to be honest I wasn't one hundred per cent sure that this would work and I really didn't want to make his plight any worse. I couldn't imagine how the Mana would react to that. Would it simply fade away as the body was consumed? Or would it slowly continue its work and bring the poor man back from the dead? If he was damaged now – I couldn't even imagine what that would do to him.

No, external damage wouldn't help here. The only solution that had any chance of working would be to attempt to disrupt the Mana powering the regeneration and end the process at the source. This would be difficult as Karl himself was powering the process unconsciously.

I wasn't sure how long it would take. I wasn't even sure if once I had finished and Karl had died, if the process might begin anew. I was swinging wildly back and forth between theories when a distant explosion of sound echoed throughout the complex.

At first I had worried that Randall had broken free, but I quickly rejected that Idea. I'd knew that sound. It was caused by teleportation. Someone had teleported into the complex, probably onto the parade ground above. The enclosed area had made the sound seem louder than it should have. I steeled myself. There weren't too many people that knew of this complex and none of them were people I wanted to run into now.

"Karl, if I don't come back. Stay in the dark and don't do anything." I said as fear began to rise in my throat. Karl didn't respond. He appeared to have dropped off into a stupor again. He had done that several times throughout his story.

"I promise I'll come back for you," I called as I headed back down the cell corridor. I took the opportunity to relock his cell, should I be unable to return. That at least would provide him so protection should Randall get free again.

It was getting harder and harder to force myself to walk down the corridor. There was one of two people at the other end of the corridor and I couldn't decide which one I wanted to see least. I made it past the smashed doorway and began to climb the steps.

My glow spells from earlier were still lighting the parade ground illuminating a solitary figure standing at the far end. I saw him as soon as I emerged. I breathed a desolate sigh; it didn't look likely that I would be coming back for Karl. He didn't appear to be on the defence – he hadn't even raised a shield. I moved across to talk to my old master.

"I'm surprised to see you," Victor commented as I got close enough, "I had expected only Marcus would have been bold enough to intrude here."

"He sent me," I replied dryly. There didn't seem to be much point lying about it.

"So, you're his errand boy now?"

"No," I snapped, "and I'm not going to discuss this with a Nazi!"

"That's a part of my life I'm not proud of," Victor immediately cut me off, "and I will not discuss it with you."

"I don't give a damn if you're proud or not!" I snarled, "how many people did you murder here?"

Victor didn't answer immediately. He had a strange expression on his face. On anyone else I would have attributed it to regret – but I doubted that Victor had the capacity for guilt or regret. The look passed quickly across his face and was replaced by his usual look of benign indifference.

"Too many," he said quietly, "but their legacy has not been for naught."

"Yeah," I scoffed, "they died so you could make yourself immortal!"

Victor just nodded.

"You found my experiments did you?"

"I don't know how you live with yourself."

"I said, I'm not going to discuss it with you," Victor snapped, his eyes growing dark with rage.

I'd never seen Victor this angry before and I couldn't help but be cowed by the sight. This wasn't an explosive rage kind of anger, no this was worse – this was a cold calculated anger. What little warmth and humanity he had vanished from his features and was replaced with a cold glare of the monster within. Victor's irises expanded, making the effect even more intimidating as he drew upon the Mana. His face took on a dark smile as the euphoria of spell-use came upon him.

His face looked devilish in the half-light of my glow spell. This must have been the face that my father had seen when Victor had killed him. I used that thought to draw upon my powers and make me strong. I vibrated as my rage, and power that flowed with it, worked its way through me. This man had killed my father, he had taken my cousin and he had tried to have me killed. The power caused through me and I was lost in the euphoria that the Mana brought. I was going to avenge my father and finally bring an end to this monster.

This needed to end now! I screamed in fury as I launched myself into the air. I immediately surrounded myself with as strong a shield as I could form. I doubted that it would be strong enough to fully protect me, but it was better than nothing.

I didn't wait until I'd landed to attack. I struck out in mid-flight sending three threads arching towards my former teacher. They struck across a shield that had instantly sprung to life around him. He didn't even flinch at the impact. I sent several more threads his way before I landed, they had about the same effect as the first ones. This wasn't looking good.

Victor's shield was incredibly strong, far stronger than it should have been. There was something unusual about it, but I couldn't place what it was. It had been built using a technique that I wasn't familiar with, but I didn't have time to study it properly. I launched myself back into the air again using my momentum and speed to make my threads hit harder.

"You've learnt too much from Master Chen!" Victor called, referencing a former student of his, "I could never convince him that there is only strength from solid ground. Keeping yourself in the air is a weakness. One that can be easily exploited."

A thread arched out from his hand and impacted into the side of my shield and sent me reeling. I landed badly, but regained my footing almost immediately. The shield had absorbed the attack for the most part, but even so I was winded by the impact. I shook my head and looked around, Victor was still standing waiting for me to recover my strength.

"You have grown in power," Victor commented as I made my way cautiously back to him. I wanted to keep a distance, but it was obvious that he, being the quicker would have the advantage at a further distance. I had to get in close.

"…And you're not as powerful as I remember." I quipped back. Victor didn't respond, instead he launched an attack against me that I was easily able to intercept and block with a thread of my own.

"There, you see. On the ground you are stronger." Victor said. The fact that he was still attempting to give me lessons enraged me further. How dare he presume to lecture me now!

My counter struck with all my fury, but again I wasn't surprised to see Victor easily parry my attack and return it. I was slowly being forced back, but this was okay. I tend to fight a little better on the defensive.

We covered the parade ground and Victor was slowly forcing me back towards the animal pens. Human pens I quickly corrected myself. These pens had once contained humans.

"You cannot win!" Victor intoned as his threads thundered against my shield. "I have studied the techniques you're using for half a century! You're going to fall, and when you do I'm going to destroy you."

Victor thought he was in control of the melee, forcing me to respond to his strikes. What he hadn't noticed was that I had allowed him to fall into a pattern of attacks. Perhaps it had been too long since the last time he had actually sparred with someone. His power level was impressive and his speed inscrutable but his melee technique had become predictable. I waited until he was just about to close in for the kill when I did something he didn't expect.

I ducked rather than block, and allowed his thread to sail harmlessly over my head. I heard Victor curse and try to bring the thread back around, but it was too late. My thread impacted solidly in an overarm strike down on him. The impact of my thread on his shield resounded throughout the cavern.

He cursed and was forced down onto one knee by the weight of the strike, but he rose quickly with fury in his eyes. My attack hadn't made much impact on his shield, but it had allowed me to glimpse an important fact that I hadn't seen earlier. I wasn't sure how I could use this to my advantage yet, but it might give me an opening I could exploit and possibly save my life. It was a long shot though.

"Impressive!" Victor snarled angrily and I saw the power run down his arms towards his outstretched thread, "but not enough I'm afraid!"

Victor's thread immediately burst into flame. It didn't look like normal flame. I sucked my breath in when I realised it was a flame of super charged Mana. Blue pulses ran up and down the thread as the Mana was constantly renewed. It was beautiful to gaze upon, as the Mana was super-heated until it exploded and then was consumed only to be replaced anew. I couldn't tell how much energy Victor was expending doing this, but this was far outside my abilities. This was truly how masters of Mana fight.

Victor was right, I was outclassed and I was going to lose. Victor had taken this fight to a level that I couldn't possibly compete in, let alone survive. I'd read about this technique in my studies. There had been mention of it in several of the books that I'd stolen from Victor when I left his apartments in Singapore, but I'd never seen it performed or managed to figure out how it was done. The effect was called Mana Nova and it was as deadly as it was beautiful.

Victor swiped at me with his usual level of speed and I knew that I had to get out of there. I didn't even attempt to block. I knew the Mana Nova thread would consume any Mana I brought to my defence in an instant and then burn through my shield in seconds. I had no choice but to launch myself into the air and hope that I was fast enough. I was – just barely.

I used my momentum to throw myself backwards and land on the other side of the pens. This didn't seem to faze Victor though as he brought his thread around again and swiped at me straight through the pens. There was a screech of burning metal as the poles from the pens were sheered through and tumbled to the ground. The noise echoed throughout out the chamber and the distraction almost led to my death.

It was only luck that had saved me as I hurriedly threw myself to one side. I felt my shield crackle and buckle as the Mana Nova passed over it. That had been too close! The nerves on my shoulder burned like fire and I could see that my clothes were burned from where the Mana Nova had grazed my shield. It hadn't even touched my shield for longer than a second! I definitely didn't want to get hit with one of those directly.

I glanced down at the poles on the ground. The ends that had been cleanly cut through were still glowing red and smoking slightly. Victor's attack had opened up an opportunity. If I was smart I could exploit it and turn it into an advantage.

I threw everything I had into an attack, which Victor promptly blocked with his Mana Nova thread. As I had predicted it hadn't had much effect. I felt a shudder as my thread collapsed as it collided with the Mana Nova, its whole structure was consumed in mere seconds. It had stopped Victor's thread though, at least for a little time, enough to be used defensively. I could block with it – that was at least nice to know. The effort of re-summoning my thread each time would really begin to draw upon my reserves, but it could be done.

I quickly went on the offensive again, forcing Victor to keep his thread close to protect himself. I had to cast the thread again and again and again as previous threads collapsed through the strain of colliding with the Mana Nova thread, but it was working. I was chewing through what remained of my strength at a staggering rate, but Victor didn't have time to go onto the offensive.

I summoned two threads and sent them against my former Master. I hadn't expected them to strike, but that was okay. They weren't supposed to. They were supposed to keep him busy and prevent him from attacking back. Victor didn't have much choice. If he allowed these threads to hit him it would surely cause him to stumble and fall again and he didn't want that. Besides, he had a better option. He could wait me out. He knew I couldn't keep this level of aggression up for long.

He was right, but the thing was, I didn't need to. This was only a distraction. My attacks had kept Victor so busy that he didn't notice the third thread I had sent arching out behind me and looping around one of the fallen poles from the prison pen. It was perhaps ironic that I was going to use one of these to bring him down. Perhaps the fates do indeed have a sense of poetic justice.

I used everything I had to sweep his thread away and give my strike a chance to impact. I had one shot at this so I had to make it count. I swept to the side and arched two threads away leaving him open for the third. Victor's eyes widened as he saw the severed pole heading like a spear towards him. His head dropped in shock as the pole passed straight through his shield and into his stomach.

The pole had cut through his shield as if it had been butter! It had taken me a little while after I had first noticed the peculiarities with Victor's shield to realise what he had done. His shield had been optimised to stop Mana attacks and not physical. He hadn't bothered to concern himself with the physical as it was unlikely that any Mage would ever think to do that. This is why his shield had been so strong. The technique was worth remembering, but so too were the consequences.

I fell to my knees in exhaustion as I watched Victor's shield and threads fail and frizzle into nothing. The pole had passed straight through his stomach and he took several staggered steps back before he reached down and pulled the pole from his flesh with a strangled gasp. He grunted and gurgled and his eyes rolled back into his head as he collapsed onto the ground. I didn't move closer to inspect him but from this distance his stomach looked like a mess. There was blood everywhere.

I could see him staring at me from his fallen position. He looked so small now, almost helpless. This was a far cry from the figure of power that he had presented only moments early. Somehow he was still conscious and I could see his lips grimacing as he fought to overcome the pain.

He looked over at me with a look of intense hatred and then his head lolled forward and he closed his eyes. He appeared to have at last lost consciousness. I could tell that he wasn't dead yet, there was still too much Mana activity in his body for that, but it was fading fast. He probably only had a few minutes before death would take him. I breathed a sigh of relief. I had done it – Allie was free now and my father was now avenged.

I waited and watched as the monster in front of me died. I felt no sympathy as the Mana slowly left his body. He had tortured and murdered thousands of people. It was perhaps fitting that he died here amongst the ruins of his experiments, brought down by someone that he had tried to manipulate and control.

I moved in to inspect the corpse. Something was wrong. He should have been long dead by now, but the Mana in his body was still flowing. It was weak but it was still there. It should have faded into nothing by now.

I edged closer to him. He wasn't dying! To my amazement, I could see the Mana pooling into the wound, wrapping around the edge of it. I could see new flesh being created as the skin around the wound regenerated itself. It was happening at an incredible rate. He was healing himself!

I tried to summon my powers to finish him off but I was on the edge of complete mental and physical exhaustion. I could already feel the beginnings of the pounding headache that came when I used too much Mana. I knew from experience that once that started I wouldn't be able to focus enough to summon my powers with any strength. Still, I had to do something. I raised my powers and went to strike him down.

A shield immediately sprang up around him and my thread impacted against it. Victor's eyes opened and he gritted his teeth as he coughed up blood.

"You can't kill me," he coughed, "No one can."

I watched in horror as the wound on his side closed and the Mana began to pulse from the newly created pinkish skin on his side. He coughed several times before slowly attempting to rise to his feet.

I needed to get out of here! There was absolutely nothing I could do against this. In a few seconds he would be back to his former strength and then I would be finished. I had expended too much energy to have any hope of victory and I doubted that Victor would fall for another trick so easily. Even if I did strike him down – he would eventually regenerate again anyway. I had lost.

I tried to send out a Scry thread but it took me several tries before I was could summon the necessary strength. I was just about to attempt to teleport when the spell fizzled and my left side exploded in pain. The bastard had hit me with a disrupt spell. Already I could feel my side go numb and the remaining Mana in my body go nuts. There was no way I'd be able to escape now. I fell to the ground and turned to face him as he walked towards me. I wasn't sure what he hit me with next I just saw a burst of Mana and then I blacked out before he got to me. I suppose that was a small mercy – If I was lucky I wouldn't wake up.

* * * * * *

I wasn't lucky. When I came around I was restrained on a medical gurney in a familiar room. I was in the damned operating theatre. A bolt of fear shot through my body.

Randall was standing mute and immobile on the far side of the room. I glanced carefully at him looking for any sign of the insanity that had gripped him before but he seemed perfectly placid now, just like the other Drones that I'd seen Marcus that had made. Victor had obviously reasserted his control over him.

I tried to draw upon my powers but felt the familiar numbing ache down my arm that let me know that I was still being messed up by the disrupt spell. I couldn't say how long it would be until I was back to normal but for the moment I was helpless.

I strained against the bonds, but for leather straps that were about three times my age they had been well preserved. I couldn't see Victor but I knew that he wouldn't be far. He wouldn't take the chance that I'd regain my powers and be able to escape. Whatever he had planned for me wouldn't be long in coming.

It seemed about twenty minutes before the door opened and Victor stomped in. He had a strange expression on his face as he surveyed the room. He gestured towards Randall who came over and gripped both sides of my head and forced my head back down onto the cushion with his talon-like fingers.

"I never thought I'd stand in this room again." He said conversationally as he moved over to the head of the table. He appeared to be having trouble walking and I could see that he'd changed his shirt. He was now wearing what appeared to be an army officer's uniform. There was a swastika on the collar. This didn't help him look any less intimidating.

He placed a strap over my forehead, restricting my movement.

"You have joined a very select group today." Victor continued in his conversational tone. "There are few people who can say that they have bested me. Not even

135

your friend Marcus can make that claim, you should consider yourself honoured."

I gritted my teeth. I wasn't going to give him the satisfaction of conversing with him. Whatever he planned for me he could do without my input.

"I should add though, everyone else in that group is already dead." He finished ominously. "I had planned to simply kill you, but I've had a change of heart. It would be a waste to kill you, and you know how I despise waste."

"Whatever you're going to do, just do it." I grunted, hoping I sounded more sure of myself than I felt.

"All in good time Master Wills," Victor continued, brushing some hair from my brow. "You should consider this my final lesson to you." I didn't answer, I just gritted my teeth and wished he'd get this over and done with.

"I would normally make you forget the procedure, but in this case I want you to know what I've done and that you're powerless to prevent it. I think that's a suitable reward for your efforts today."

Victor's eyes loomed into me as he stood over me. I vainly tried to summon some Mana, but it just wouldn't cooperate. I needed to try something, anything to get out of this.

"No, no... you won't be able to generate Mana just yet," Victor chuckled as he moved around to my side.

Victor flourished his hand like a bad stage magician and drew forth a Mana thread. It was small, only about thirty centimetres in length. It was horrendously complex – there was no way in a million years that I'd be able to figure out what the hell it was doing.

"What you're looking at is a compulsion thread."

I shivered slightly as confusion hit me. I was supposed to be immune to these now, Marcus had apparently taught me how to defend myself against them. This wasn't making sense – Victor wouldn't be doing this if he knew I was immune and he definitely knew I'd shaken off the last compulsion he had placed over me.

"Now, I know what you're thinking, that you're immune." Victor chuckled. I'd forgotten how good Victor was at being able to discern what I was thinking. I didn't know if this was caused by sorcery or if he was just an excellent judge of character. My fear must have been quite plain to see on my face.

"The fact is, you're not immune as such, you're just highly resistant," Victor whispered, "and I for one am quite interested to learn how resistant. This will not be pleasant."

I tried to remain calm, but my mind was awash with doubts and fears. Renee had once told me she was terrified of being confronted by her grandfather. I now understood why.

"As you probably know, your brain is made up of electrical impulses and signals. Everything you are, everything you remember is simply nothing more than motor neurons firing wildly in the void of your mind.

"Everything you see is nothing more than an interpretation of electrical signals as it passes across your brain. In a very real way there is no external reality."

"You should just kill me." I snapped, "You killed the father, why not the son?"

Victor looked perplexed, "I did not kill your father."

"Bullshit."

"No," Victor pressed, "you're mistaken. Your father was already dying by the time I got to him."

"You admit you were there then!" I snarled as I strained against my bonds.

"Yes, I was there, but I wasn't responsible."

"I don't believe you!" I hissed.

"Your sister was the one who struck your father down." Victor's words were cold.

"I don't have a sister!"

I knew he was referring to Allie, as he'd mentioned this theory before, but I refused to even give the idea any credence. There was no way that Allie was the one responsible. He was lying. Of course he was lying!

"Don't be stupid boy; of course you have a sister. The odds of you both being Mages without being related are astronomical."

"She's not my sister," I repeated.

"Half-sister at least."

Could he be right? My father's eyes as he lay dying came back to me. I hadn't been able to be there physically, but I was able to Scry to be with him when he passed. He had gone on about apologising to someone – a girl. He could have been talking about Allie? I had assumed at the time he was apologising for being unable to protect her. Could it have been more? Could Victor be telling the truth? Could she actually be my sister?

The more I thought about it, the more I didn't want to believe it was true, but the more it made a strange kind of sense. Mum and Dad had broken up shortly before Allie had been born. Allie's parents were less than vocal on their feelings about my father. It was obvious that they had taken Mum's side in the divorce. I had never thought to question why? What if he was Allie's father? What if?

"Okay, so she may be my sister?" I grunted sourly, "That doesn't mean that she's responsible for Dad."

"She struck him down in anger as she was unable to control her powers adequately. In many ways that's your doing. You brought her to power. You left her with just enough knowledge to be dangerous. You are responsible for that at least."

Victor's words cut into me like a knife. He was right, and I knew it.

"I wanted to keep her safe and away from you!".

"I was the one person who could train her properly. Had you turned her over to me first we could have avoided this whole situation. Your father would still be alive."

"No!" I cried as I pulled against the bonds again. The leather creaked loudly and Victor gestured to Randall to hold me down. Randall's clamp like hands closed over my wrists and forced my arms down. How had he gotten so strong? He hadn't been this strong when we had last fought.

"You're lying!" I screamed in inert rage. "I'll fucking

kill you! I'm going to fucking tear you apart so bad it will take you a fucking year to regrow!"

"Believe what you want," Victor waved me off, "In a few minutes it won't matter."

Victor didn't seem concerned at all at my rant. It was as if my anger simply didn't matter to him. I gritted my teeth as I strained against Randall, I knew it wouldn't make a difference, but I had to do something. I wasn't going to submit to this without a fight.

Victor walked back to the head of the table and I had to tilt my head to face him as far as the straps would allow me. He appeared to be ready to do whatever he was planning to do. I could see the Mana working its way down his arms and into his fingers.

"The brain is an exceptional creation." He announced. "It allows its owner to rationalise any number of contradictions. Any manner of hypocrisy is made acceptable through the way your brain processes memories and external input."

Great, I was in for another lecture. Why didn't he just kill me outside? Victor reached down and placed his fingers against my forehead, with his forefinger and little finger against each of my temples.

"The ability to manipulate this external input is simplicity itself," he continued. "The brain processes unfortunately are much more difficult."

I could see the Mana building in his hand literally centimetres from my face. I had no idea what he was doing, but it looked complex.

"Fortunately I don't have to manipulate those, I simply introduce an idea." He finished as he removed his fingers from my flesh. I saw the thread build in his fingers and felt a jerk as Victor's thread arched down and rested gently on my forehead.

It didn't hurt as such, though I felt a weight upon my forehead. This was impossible – I shouldn't be feeling any weight from the thread. It was far too lightweight for it to have produced such a sensation.

"It took me many years to master this. The active mind will actually support any new concept introduced once properly stimulated. I simply need to deactivate the part of the brain that rejects the new stimulus."

I felt sharp pain behind my eyes and saw a bright flash of light in front of my face as Victor continued his work. He made a slight grunting motion and the pain lanced through my head once again.

"You have become most resilient," he commented sourly, "still, we seem to have plenty of time."

I don't know how many times he tried it must have been a dozen or so before I felt a crack in my head followed by immediate relief as the pain went away. I glanced frantically from side to side as Victor nodded approvingly.

"Now you are in a receptive state," he said softly, "we shall begin. And once we are finished you yourself will complete the work. Cognitive dissonance will ensure that the idea takes hold and you become a willing advocate of the process."

"Cognitive dissonance is the ability for the mind to deal with two opposing concepts and find a rational that explains the two." He explained with a dark smile as if educating an exceedingly stupid student.

"It's quite clever really, I simply implant the compulsion into your mind and your brain rationalises it and will in fact support and defend it with every fibre of your being."

"I'm going to kill you," I whispered softly.

"You can't, I thought we established that." Victor chuckled.

"I'll find a way."

"I'm really quite curious as to what will happen here," Victor continued. "You'll be unable to understand why you're supporting your decision but will continue to do so against your direct will. In fact the harder you struggle to deny the compulsion the more you will be compelled by it – all with the knowledge that the compulsion exists and memory of its implanting."

"Somehow, someday I'm going to find you and end you." I whispered again.

"No, you're not." Victor replied, "You're going to kill Marcus."

What? My mind was screaming in outrage? I had no intention of killing Marcus, but funnily enough I couldn't seem to voice my concerns. Thoughts kept passing through my mind that this seemed like a perfectly logical thing to do.

"You will return back to Marcus as quickly as you

can. When he is at his most vulnerable you will kill him. You see, you gave me the idea. If you can best me – then you can surely best him."

The idea rolled through my consciousness like a shockwave. Yes! It would solve all my problems. Once Marcus was out of the way I would be able to continue my quest to recover Allie without his interference. He had been the one that had been slowing me down and delaying me. He had it coming to him, really.

"No! That's not right! I will not be used like this!" My subconscious screamed, but it was a distant voice in the void of my mind. It was easy to ignore. I gritted my teeth as the compulsion took hold. Once I destroyed Marcus this would all make sense. No! That wasn't right either. I will NOT become an instrument of another's will! Victor made a clucking sound as he moved around to examine the thread.

"Interesting, very interesting. You might end up in psychosis. I hadn't considered that. That would be disappointing.

"Oh, well," he shrugged, "either you go insane, you kill Marcus, or he kills you – either way. I am content."

I glared at Victor as he finished his work. A strange buzzing sensation settled over me. It felt like someone had thrown cotton wool around my head. Everything sounded distant and distorted.

"In a few hours you should be able to remove yourself from your bonds, I'll leave the Drone here as company." Victor gestured towards Randall.

He turned and left the room. The glow spell fizzled out long before I regained use of my powers.

* * * * * *

The darkness was like a cloak thrown over my eyes. Randall's presence in the room didn't help much with my nerves. Nor did the pounding headache from excessive Mana use, and the frantic sense of frustration over my inactivity and inability to get to Marcus.

After what seemed like an eternity, but couldn't have been more than a few minutes, my eyes adjusted. I could vaguely make out an unmoving shape standing in the darkness. I couldn't see any details, just the dull throb of the Mana as it passed across the flesh of his withered and broken frame.

Knowing that Randall was there and knowing what he had been like before Victor had regained control of him was wreaking havoc on my nerves. Would he revert back to his previous state before I regained my powers? He could beat me to a pulp and there wasn't a damned thing I would be able to do about it.

After an hour or so the numbness of the disruption spell faded and the Mana began to regulate properly throughout my body.

I set off a glow spell and a telekinetic thread to unhook myself from the table. Randall was still standing there staring off into space completely unfazed by anything I was doing.

It was kind of creepy actually. I kept a wide gap between us as I left the room. The vaguely thought about locking the door on my way out, but quickly realised there wasn't much point. The wooden door wouldn't survive long against his attempts to break free.

I'd had plenty of time in the dark to think about what Victor had told me about Allie. I wasn't quite ready to believe him yet, I'd need to talk to her myself for that. The idea that she was my sister kept taunting me and riddling me with guilt.

I knew with a certainty that I couldn't define that Victor was lying to me. I just couldn't figure out how or why. I rejected outright that Allie was responsible for Dad's death. I clung to my original theory that Dad had tried to prevent Victor from taking Allie, but Victor's words kept coming back to me.

I was the one who had initially taught Allie. I knew just how easy it was to lose control over your powers when you were learning. I was a testament to that fact; my own training hadn't exactly gone to plan. Was it possible that I was the one ultimately responsible for my father's death?

It was fortunate that I didn't have a lot of time to ponder this as the compulsion that Victor had placed upon me kept me moving. I made my way out from the infirmary and out onto the parade ground. I had to recast the glow spells as I made my way through the complex as my previous ones had long fizzled out.

I felt bad about my promise to come back for Karl,

but Victor's orders were pounding my head by this stage. With each step I took they seemed to become more demanding. I needed to meet up with Renee and Marcus, wherever they were. But before that there was something I needed to recover.

I stormed into the main building and through the Nazi control room and into Victor's old office. With each step the voices in my head screamed that this was an unnecessary waste of time and that I should be trying to track down Marcus. It wasn't easy to ignore Victor's voice, but I managed to do so with the thought that I would need these books to lure Marcus into a false sense of ease that would allow me to strike him down.

It was strange, even though I knew I was lying. My original intentions for recovering the books had nothing to do with Marcus. Once I had voiced my intentions the voices seemed to accept the lie and I found that I was even finding reasons why this was in fact a good idea.

I grabbed a backpack that had been left in one of the storage rooms and threw the five Necromancy books into it. I also quickly selected several other books that looked interesting. There wasn't much time to make an informed choice, but I grabbed several volumes that I hadn't heard of before. I'd be able to get a chance to review them properly once I had killed Marcus.

I lingered in the complex for as long as I was able. In truth I didn't particularly want to make the trek back through the snow and wilderness just yet. I had expended more Mana in the past few hours than I had in quite some time and my temples were throbbing painfully already. I knew that if I kept this up for much longer I would be doing myself some serious damage.

I had heard of cases of Mages who had suffered from internal haemorrhaging caused by the pressure placed on their bodies by the excess of Mana use. The stories never made it seem pleasant. I had no idea if I even had it in me for the extended use of teleport spells that would be required to get back to civilisation. I could do with about three days of sleep, unfortunately the compulsion had no intention of letting me have it. I suspect that may have been Victor's intention. Either I die through Mana fatigue or Marcus or I kill the other. Either way – he wins. I gritted my teeth as I summoned the power to teleport back into the snow-drift and then from the Tatras mountains.

It didn't take me long to get back to civilisation. I survived the three teleports to get back to the closest small town where I could make a call. I planned on moving quickly as I didn't know if they were still in Berlin or had moved on. It was likely that they wouldn't have lingered long in Germany. It had been almost a week since I left Berlin. They could be anywhere – hopefully they're still in Europe.

My last teleport was a little wonky and I felt a sharp pain in my left wrist as the Mana field dissolved around me. I pulled the phone Marcus had given me shakily from my pocket, turned it on and dialled Renee's number.

"Where are you?" I demanded when Renee picked up.

"Devon?"

"Yeah."

"I'm in Paris."

"Is Marcus with you?"

"Yes."

"Ok, I'm coming to you." I said, immediately cursing myself. Paris was within teleporting distance, but it would be about six jumps. There was a good chance I was going to do myself some serious damage here.

"No! Devon! Not here! We'll meet you somewhere else – somewhere safe."

"No, no time. I'll come to you." I hung up.

I didn't have time to waste setting up a rendezvous it would be simpler to meet in Paris. Sure, it was a touch dangerous as Paris was the city that the Primea lived in. There were many of our kind in residence. An outcast going there would be quickly discovered. I had previously avoided Paris for this reason, but this seemed worth the risk. Surely I'd be able to get in and out without creating too much of a scene. Besides, it would be something that Marcus wouldn't expect.

The journey to Paris was uneventful other than the fact that I was well and truly running on fumes. I really wanted to stop and rest for a few days, but I simply didn't have the time. I could rest once this was done.

I reached Paris the next day on the verge of complete exhaustion. My temples were on fire and it felt like my veins were about to explode. I staggered as the final teleport dropped me onto the top of a building on the outskirts of the city. I almost passed out as the teleportation finished, but I had done it. I could barely lift my hands I was so exhausted, but I was in Paris and that was all that mattered. All I needed to do now was to locate Marcus. That shouldn't prove too difficult. All that was required was to sneak into the city with the most Mages on the planet, track down and assassinate an Arch Mage whose power was far in excess of my own and get out with my ass intact. No – this wouldn't be difficult at all.

CHAPTER FIVE

My arrival in Paris hadn't yet been noticed by the resident Mages, but it would be. Teleporting, while requiring a lot of power was at least quick. It was like a lightning strike. If you weren't looking directly at it you wouldn't have known where or what it was other than a flash of power. I'm sure that some of the Mages of Paris were aware that something had happened, but just didn't know exactly what. The more academic of my kind may have recognised a teleport spell, but that can't have been uncommon here. No, for the moment I was safe. The question was – for how long?

Unfortunately, I was somewhat of a celebrity in my infamy amongst my kind. It wasn't out of the realms of possibility that I would be recognised. This would lead to disaster. I wasn't in any condition to adequately protect myself from even an apprentice. No, I would need to be quick here. My only hope was to get in, meet with Marcus, catch him by surprise and then get out as quickly as possible. If my first shot didn't kill him I was unlikely to get a second.

I called Renee again to arrange to meet up with her and Marcus. Renee sounded worried on the phone but agreed to meet me at a small bar. She gave me the address and rough directions. Unfortunately, as French wasn't one of the languages that I had learned to speak, I was having some trouble navigating. Paris is a warren of boulevards and side streets.

I saw several others of my kind as I moved through the crowded streets. I kept my collar pulled tight and nodded briefly to them as I moved on. To ignore them completely would be to draw suspicion. Our community wasn't so small that they would recognise me by sight, but there were few enough that my passing could draw attention if I were discovered. Fortunately, those I passed weren't curious enough to investigate.

The bar that Renee had selected was quite open and in a very crowded street. I think she'd intentionally chosen a public address in the hope of keeping it relatively civil. She had obviously guessed that something was wrong. There was small chance of keeping things friendly though – Victor had seen to that. The compulsion ran through my mind like wildfire burning my senses and fuming at the delay.

"Kill him," it whispered. "Kill him now!" The constant distraction of my subconscious making demands coupled with the fact that I managed to circle back on myself several times meant that I was seriously late. I gritted my teeth and cursed my luck.

There were only a few customers inside. I suppose that this was for the best. I didn't particularly want an audience for what I was about to do. Marcus and Renee were seated at the table on the far side of the room.

Renee looked up as I entered. She looked worried, far more worried than she should be. As I made my way to them, the barman gestured towards me in greeting and said something. I assumed he was asking if I wanted a drink. I shook my head. His face wrinkled in confusion. Maybe I'd assumed incorrectly. He let me pass without further comment.

Renee glanced nervously at me as I approached the table. She tried to hold my gaze, but I wouldn't let her. I had a job to do and I wasn't going to be distracted now.

"I'm glad you're okay," she murmured as I sat down opposite them. Marcus looked at me; his face was unreadable.

"Kill him!" The voices in my head screamed! "Kill him now!"

My fingers itched within my coat and the Mana ran down my arms to pool at my hands. I would have done it too! I was just about to, when a second voice bombarded into my head. I didn't recognise it at first. It was my own. I knew that there was an above average chance that I was going to die here and there was nothing I could do about it, the best I'd be able to do would be to take Marcus with me.

I shook my head to shake off that thought. It was too soon! Another voice in my head cautioned me to wait, that I still needed him, that now wasn't the right time. Victor had said strike at his most vulnerable! I latched on to this idea. Yes, I could wait. Wait until it was the right time.

"No! Kill him now!" the first voice thundered back in response. The argument went back and forth, back and forth.

"He knows where Allie is!" the second voice urged frantically.

That did it. We wait. I nodded and breathed out. I could wait for that much at least. Once he had told me, then I would kill him.

My prolonged silence had obviously created some discomfort in Renee and Marcus. Hopefully they it attributed to my obvious exhaustion.

"I'm pleased to see that you survived your ordeal." Marcus commented. The sound of his voice made the urge to strike him down to rise within me once again.

"Victor was there." I replied darkly.

Renee and Marcus exchanged glances. Marcus seemed to be telling Renee to be quiet, but she shook her head firmly.

"He knew Victor would be there." Renee whispered. "Marcus led Victor to believe that he would be going there himself."

Renee's eyes expressed conflicting emotions. She was obviously upset with her father for the betrayal and guilty about her own involvement in the deception, but there was something else there. She was nervous about something. She knew something and couldn't tell me with Marcus present. It didn't matter much in the long run though, after tonight either he or I would be dead.

An icy feeling of anger rose in my stomach, I glanced

at Marcus, my eyes narrowed with rage. He'd lured me into a trap. He had wanted Victor to finish me. He had intentionally placed me in a position to die, but he would not get the opportunity to do so again.

"You tried to have me killed?"

"No," Marcus said softly, "I needed to ensure that you were fully aware of the consequences of your actions and how futile attempting to engage Victor would be if you weren't properly prepared."

"Lies! I've become a liability to you now."

"Liability?" Marcus smiled disarmingly. "Maybe, but you also could become a powerful ally. You simply had to be tempered. You had to understand why your assaults against Victor could never achieve your desired goals."

"I've told you, I'm not in this for your war. I don't want to become any more embroiled in this than I need to be," I said.

"Like it or not, you're involved," Marcus said curtly.

"No, I'm not. I'm going to rescue my cousin and then we're out of this."

"Don't be naïve," Marcus sneered, "Victor won't allow you or your cousin to walk away from this. You're both among the most powerful Mages in the world. Victor can't afford to let you be unaligned, and neither can I."

"So sending me to be killed by Victor was a recruitment tactic?"

"No, it was to open your damned eyes boy. He's evil – anyone can see that. He needs to be stopped. The problem is he can't be stopped and now you realise that!"

"Then he's the more powerful amongst us and deserves to be Primea." I retorted angrily, "We only respect power and the truth of the matter is he has the most."

The argument in my head was still raging and playing havoc on my nerves. The power kept rushing to my fingers and a thread was just itching to be launched at the man across the table, but my mind kept whispering not now. Now's not the right time. Wait for it – wait for it.

My finger-nails had gouged small holes into my palms as I clenched and unclenched my fingers. The pain was a good distraction from the argument in my head and the conversation going on across the table.

"You can't possibly believe that!" Renee said, aghast.

"No," I amended. I had only said it for shock value, "I just don't see why I should be the one to do something about it."

"He tried to kill you." Marcus said irritably, "Doesn't that mean anything to you?"

"No," I replied, "he doesn't want me dead. He could have killed me yesterday, but he didn't."

"I wasn't talking about that! Do you remember my aide?" Marcus asked. "When we first met in that car in Singapore?"

"Winters? Yeah?" I nodded.

"Winters worked for Victor, I'm quite sure that he shot you on Victor's orders. He was a double agent designed to keep an eye on me. When I found out I had him fired."

"I know. Winters told me, just before I killed him."

"Victor thought you were a risk to Renee and therefore needed to be removed." Marcus continued. I could tell that he was a little thrown off that I'd already known about Winters.

"Sounds like someone else I know," I muttered.

"I didn't send you to Victor to kill you," Marcus said, "I sent you there to make you realise the monster you face."

"You're just as much of a monster as he is," I snapped.

"Devon, you know that's not true," Marcus said.

That was just the point. I didn't know it. As far as I was concerned Marcus was every bit as manipulative and cruel as Victor. As much as I didn't want to be, I was now wedged firmly between them. Either of them would take me down in a second if it meant achieving their goals. The only sane thing to do here would be to run. But I couldn't.

There were two reasons. One was screaming for blood in my head and the second was sitting on the other side of the table from me. Renee had already signed on to Marcus's side. I'm not exactly sure what he had shown her or what he had told her. But she was a willing advocate of his, despite all this. I sighed deeply and pulled the books that I had taken from Victor's complex.

"I took these," I threw the books down on the table. The Nazi emblem gleamed in the light from the candle. "I'm assuming they were what you wanted me to recover?"

Marcus stared at the books as if I had just thrown an angry snake onto the table.

"No," he breathed, shaking his head, "I didn't expect you to bring back anything. I assumed that you'd confront Victor and then escape once you realised you were over matched."

"I wasn't over matched. I won." I hissed.

For the first time the stern façade of Marcus's expression broke and I caught a glimpse of the man beneath. He didn't like my statement. Didn't like it one bit. The lapse only lasted for a moment, but it revealed the depths of ambition and cruelty within the man. I finally saw the monster in Marcus that I always knew was there.

"You won?" Renee said.

"The battle at least," I continued. "Your father is right. There's no way to kill Victor. I beat him and he damn well regenerated. He's immortal."

"That's not entirely true," Marcus interjected.

"We need to nullify the magic sustaining him." I said before Marcus could continue.

He nodded briskly.

"Do you know how to do so?" I asked.

"No, but the answer will lie within those books." Marcus said, his eyes eager as his fingers ran across one of the book covers. "I hadn't expected you to ever find them. I had wondered what had happened to them. I had assumed that Victor had had them destroyed."

"He wouldn't have destroyed them," Renee whispered, "they're a part of the magic and he couldn't knowingly destroy them. No matter how evil they are."

Renee and I exchanged glances. I knew that Renee disapproved of her father's forays into Necromancy and it seems that by giving him these books I hadn't helped matters. With Marcus so distracted by the books it would be a perfect time to attack, but I couldn't do that yet. He still hadn't told me where Allie was.

"Okay," I nodded, "I've done what you asked. You've now got your weapon against Victor. It's time to give me what you promised."

Marcus didn't respond. I could feel him trying to delay. He obviously didn't want me going after Allie right now. His eyes flicked between me and Renee. Renee looked at her father in annoyance. It was obvious that she knew what he was thinking and that she disapproved. Maybe their relationship wasn't as harmonious as I had thought?

"Where is my cousin?" I prompted again. There was no way around this. Marcus was going to tell me and he was going to tell me now.

Marcus sighed as he came to his decision. He obviously couldn't see any way of out of this either. He was at least a man of his word.

"She's in the last place you would think to look. Somewhere you searched years ago."

I coughed impatiently as I waited for him to get to the point.

"She's in Melbourne." He said eventually . "Melbourne is the site of the next Occursus."

I closed my eyes. It made a strange kind of sense – if I'd stopped to think about it. I'd been chasing her all over the world and she'd been put in the one place I'd ruled out. Besides it was likely that Victor would keep her close to her parents.

"Why was Melbourne selected from the next Occursus?" Renee asked. "There's almost nothing there for our kind."

"The Primea thinks that the rise of such powerful Mages from Australia bears investigation. It is an area that we have long avoided. Devon's rise and subsequent fall has led her to believe that we need to keep a closer eye on those who find their powers without our guidance."

I was only half listening to his explanation. I didn't care. I just cared that Marcus and Renee were distracted in conversation with each other. It meant that they weren't focusing on me. I was slowly and quietly building the Mana down towards my fist. One strike – that was all I needed. He didn't have a shield up; he was defenceless.

The effort of drawing more Mana was almost more than I could manage. Pain lanced through my temples and ran down my arms, but it would be enough. I shivered as the usual wave of euphoria overtook me and washed away the pain.

I knew the pain would return once the Mana left me, but for now I was in a state of peace. A delicate balance between the pain of over-use and the ecstasy of its consumption. There would be payment required for this later. I was consumed by the Mana and sustained by it as it flowed down towards my wrists. The process was taking far too long, if I were refreshed this would have happened almost instantly, now it seemed to be taking eons to summon my powers. I glanced up, Renee and Marcus were still distracted. When I was ready I didn't shout out, I didn't even stand up. I made no effort to announce my actions.

I simply raised my hand and sent the thread arcing towards my foe. Maybe it was my exhaustion, or the fact that I truly didn't want to do this, but the movement of the thread seemed woefully slow as it lanced towards Marcus.

The smug façade of condescension dropped from Marcus's face as his death approached. As slow as the thread was, he wouldn't be able to get a shield up fast enough.

Time seemed to slow down. Marcus attempted to throw himself from the chair to get out of the way, his body literally glowing with power as he sought to raise his shield, but it was too late. He wouldn't be able to get away in time. This was done, or at least I thought it was.

The blow never landed. A second thread arced out and collided with mine out of nowhere. Time immediately sped back up again as my thread was brushed aside. The force of it caused both threads to slam into the table, smashing it into splinters.

I had failed. I threw myself to one side expecting an attack, but no attack came. I turned to see who had thrown up the thread in defence of Marcus and wasn't overly surprised to see Renee readying herself for a second attack. I didn't want to fight Renee, but it she was standing between me and Marcus. This couldn't be allowed; Marcus must die. The voices in my head demanded it. That order couldn't be ignored, but I didn't want to fight Renee.

I couldn't hurt Renee. Something snapped inside of me as a thread launched from my fingers. The thread was aimed at Marcus, but Renee easily intercepted it as Marcus got back to his feet. My thread smashed harmlessly into the wall behind her. I pulled it back and brought it around for another strike.

"I don't want to fight you." Renee warned as she readied her thread again.

"Then get out of my way," I growled as I readied myself.

"No. If you want to get to him, you're going to have to go through me!"

I didn't want to fight Renee. The words kept repeating themselves in my head like a mantra. I blinked several times as I realised the silence around me was deafening. The whole bar was staring at me in horror. I looked around warily as I backed away from the table. Marcus and Renee both took steps forward in pursuit. It was obvious that they weren't going to let me just walk away from this. But that was, okay. I wasn't going to go anywhere while Marcus still lived.

An impasse of sorts settled over the bar as the three of us stared each other down. The Mana was starting to throb down the left side of my body and my head was pounding. I couldn't keep this up for much longer. I clenched my fists and prepared myself. I needed to do something while I still had the strength.

"Don't!" Renee hissed. But it was too late I was already on the move.

I leapt backwards to give myself a little bit of space then let my thread swing wide to shatter the windows behind me. This caused panic, shouts and screams and a rush of people for the door. My feeble plan was that the chaos that I had created would distract Renee and give me a chance to strike Marcus down.

Well, that plan had failed. Now that Marcus was prepared he had raised a shield. It was a strong one and it would be unlikely that I would be able to break through it in my current condition.

Renee leapt forward and a thread arced towards me. It took everything I had to bring my thread around in defence. My own shield was beginning to waver and I knew it wouldn't last long against this kind of abuse.

I had to get Renee out of the way so I could deal with her father who had yet to act in his own defence. He was staring at me strangely as if trying to figure something out. The look on his face brought another bout of rage to me and caused me to throw caution to the wind and launch a string of savage attacks at him.

My attacks went wide as I inevitably reached the end of my strength. My last thread impacted against Marcus's shield, but it was horribly weak. There was a slight flicker as it absorbed the assault, but otherwise there was notice-able effect. If I were at my peak I would have been able to tear that shield down around him. It was powerful, but I had seen stronger – perhaps Marcus himself wasn't as powerful as I had once thought. Unfortunately I wasn't exactly able to draw upon my full powers. There was no way that I could win this, but the voices in my head insisted I continue with this fool's folly. I had no choice.

I felt Renee's thread smash against my shield, but for some reason the shield held. That was impossible. I knew for a fact just how weak my shield was right now. It should have shattered instantly. Renee obviously wasn't striking to kill.

Part of me was glad about this. It meant that I might survive this ordeal. A deeper part of me anguished at the fact that it would drag this out. More than anything I wanted this to be over. Why wasn't she ending this? The pain in my head and the pressure pulsing throughout my body as I forced the Mana to my will was almost overpowering.

The feeling of my pulse pounding throughout my body overtook me as my blood slammed against my veins. At this point I wasn't thinking clearly any longer, my actions were primal and uncontrolled.

Why hadn't someone ended this yet? Was it because they couldn't? Although Renee was much stronger than me right now, the ferocity of my attack kept her on the back foot, she seemed unwilling to take the offensive. This led to a balance of powers: Renee could strike me down, but refused to do so for risk of killing me, and I refused to strike her as my target was her father.

Marcus stood by and watched impassively. This was infuriating! Why hadn't he intervened? He could end this farce now and yet he was allowing it to continue. My subconscious screamed at him to kill me while Victor's voice in my head ordered me to kill him. A cacophony of voices demanded things in the confines of my head and I was rapidly becoming too dazed and exhausted to pay much attention to them.

I needed to do something and I needed to do it now before my strength finally gave way. I swung a Mana thread at Renee hoping to knock her out of the way to allow me a clear shot at her father. But she easily blocked it and sent another arcing toward me. I gritted my teeth as I awaited the impact of her thread. There was very little I'd be able to do to stop it anyway.

I tried in vain to increase the strength of my shield, but my remaining reserves had been depleted. There was nothing left – I was drained. The impact rocked my shield and caused me to fall to my knees. Somehow my shield survived the impact and remained around me. It was weak, but it was still there. I pulled myself together as I rose in fury and attempted to draw forth more strength that I didn't have.

My whole body tensed at the effort and I closed my eyes and gritted my teeth as the pain increased with vengeance. Then all of a sudden it was gone. The respite only lasted for a second before it returned threefold. My wrists felt like they were on fire.

My will dissolved under the increased assault and the Mana finally fled and my world became pain. I pulled my wrists up in front of me and watched, incredulous, as purple bruising spread rapidly across them. The pain was almost more than I could stand.

I fell to my knees as I grasped my right wrist. The bruising caused by internal bleeding was spreading rapidly. The pressure of my Mana use had finally become too much and I had ruptured the arteries in my arm. I was now freely bleeding internally.

My vision went blurry and the noise around me echoed and reverberated through my skull. I could see Renee and Marcus closing in. With any luck they'd end it for me. The pain was almost more than I could bear.

I fell forward but Renee managed to get to me before I hit the floor. I felt her wrap her arms around me as she pulled me to her. She was talking to me, but her words were lost in the chaos in my mind. She seemed to be calling my name, but I couldn't actually make out the sounds. My eyes glazed over and darkness overtook me. For the second time in the past few days I hoped that I wouldn't awaken.

* * * * * *

For the second time in the past few days I woke up when I didn't want to. Someone up there hates me, I'm sure of it. I woke up in a soft bed in a room I didn't recognise. It took me several seconds to fully regain consciousness. As I brought my hands up I noticed that someone had bandaged my wrists. It took me several seconds to remember why they required bandaging. The pain that I felt now was but a grim shadow of the agony that I had felt before I lost consciousness. As the details of the past few days came flooding back, I glanced around the room to see if I could find who had bandaged me, but I was alone.

The room wasn't very large and was nicely if sparsely decorated. I sat up and was able to see out onto the street below. It was a good bet that I was still in Paris. The street outside certainly looked Parisian.

I couldn't tell if this was a good thing or not. There was a chance that I was about to be executed for my crimes against the order. I could only hope that whoever had placed me here had seen to that and that I was safe – at least for the moment. It was a good bet that Renee or Marcus was responsible for my recuperation and obvious medical treatment. No one else knew where I was and this didn't look like a hospital room. That didn't mean that people weren't still hunting for me. I must have made quite a mess before I had been brought down. That would have been hard to hide that from the general populace, especially considering the number of people that had fled the scene during the fight.

It was possible that I was going to get into quite a bit of trouble for that. Oh well, I already had one death sentence – what more could they do?

I gently ran my fingers across the bandages. It didn't

feel too bad, it was slightly stiff and throbbed slightly, but that may have had more to do with my experience over the past few days. I slowly lifted the bandages to reveal an ugly purple and blue bruise that ran from the bottom of my hand to half way to my elbow. There wasn't any pain, which I took to be a good thing. I'd had enough pain in the past few days to last me the next three years. I flexed my fingers slightly as winced as pain lanced through my wrists.

I was actually lucky to be alive. I had no idea how many arteries I'd managed to rupture in my wrists, but the cases I'd found of people suffering rupturing from excessive Mana use hadn't been pretty. Most had been fatal. It seems that someone up there wasn't done with me yet.

I contemplated getting to my feet and getting out of here, but couldn't muster the effort required. My head fell back into the pillows as I reflected that this was the most comfortable that I'd been in quite some time. I might as well enjoy it while it lasted.

I must have dozed off because the next thing I remember was being roused by the sound of a door opening. I blinked several times as I groggily came of my senses. It was much later in the day as the streetlights were on. It took me a moment to recognise who had entered the room. It was Renee, but she looked different, I couldn't place why though. It was obviously her, but I'd never seen her like this before. She had a softness to her that I'd never noticed before. She'd never seemed more beautiful. I couldn't explain it I couldn't quite see her properly in this poor light, but something was definitely off here.

"How are you feeling?" she asked softly as she moved closer. She was carrying a tray, which she placed on the bedside table.

"Better than I should," I replied with a grin as I leaned forward in the bed to inspect the bowl. It looked like tomato soup. I hate tomatoes, I was hungry – but not that hungry. I carefully reached out and tentatively wrapped my fingers around the glass. It hurt a little but I was able to bring it to my lips with minimal effort.

Renee scooped a chair and brought it to the side of the bed and nodded grimly, "You're lucky to be alive."

I couldn't argue with her. Whatever was wrong with her? Was it possible that this wasn't Renee? No, I was sure that this was Renee or someone had really, really done their homework.

"I'm a little surprised to be alive. I did try to kill your father."

Renee nodded briskly, "I can see why you'd think that. Marcus thought it would be a waste and a little unfair considering that you were under a compulsion."

I nodded grimly. Renee wasn't looking at me squarely in the eyes.

"He tried to remove the compulsion but wasn't sure how successful he's been," she continued softly. "He said it was quite different from anything he's seen before."

"He's obviously done some good," I replied, "my subconscious isn't screaming at me to kill him."

"Well that's something at least," Renee smiled

relieved. "He thought it best to keep some distance. You were in pretty poor shape and he wasn't sure you could endure any further strain."

"Hard to argue with that."

"Do you need me to feed you?" Renee asked softly, gesturing towards the soup.

"Okay, what's going on?" I grumbled irritably. Renee would never play nursemaid unless something was really wrong.

"What? Nothing?" Renee's eyes flared with their usual fire.

"Why are you being so... so... nice?"

"I'm not!" she said curtly, still not looking at me directly.

"What's going on? Am I about to be executed?"

"No, fortunately that problem seems to have been resolved – at least for now."

Renee was talking in riddles and it wasn't helping.

"Renee, tell me what's going on." I begged.

"Marcus asked me not to. He said—"

"I don't give a fuck what he said! Just tell me."

Renee held up her hand and looked at me. There was a deep sadness in her eyes as she said her next words.

"What do you see?"

I peered at her hand. Nothing was out of the ordinary. She flexed her fingers and the room was bathed in light. I blinked several times as the sudden burst of light hurt a little. What the fuck? Why did she do that? Who lets off a glow spell in a well-lit room?

Then it dawned upon me and my stomach went cold.

I hadn't seen the Mana she'd used to create that glow. I glanced up – I couldn't even see the Mana flickering and burning as it interacted with the air. All I could see was the light generated by the reaction.

I blinked several times and attempted to force my vision to change. It didn't. I turned to Renee who was looking at me with that same look of sorrow.

"I'm sorry, Devon." She whispered.

I threw back the covers to inspect my chest. There was no Mana there either. Zip, nada – nothing. I looked normal!

"Who did this to me?" I got to my feet. Renee leaped forward to help me as I stumbled but I pushed her away as I made my way to the mirror. I looked at my reflection in and didn't recognise myself without the Mana. I looked so weak and so… human.

"No one did this to you," Renee replied sadly from behind me. "You burnt yourself out. You did this to yourself."

I glanced briefly at her trying to detect if there was a hint of a rebuke in her words, but she seemed genuine. I stared at her for several seconds as the ramifications of this sunk in. I had failed. There was no way I would be able to rescue Allie like this. Victor would sweep me aside as easily as I would brush a fly from my shoulder. Renee endured my scrutiny with good graces, until I turned back to face my reflection in the mirror.

My normal, round irises seemed to scream accusation as they stared back into my depths. I had once hated the eyes of my former kind, they marked me as different when I wanted to be normal. I had once intentionally cast off my powers and tried to live that lie. Now I had no choice. I was normal and I hated it. The irony was sickening.

I closed my eyes and rested my head against the cold surface of the mirror. I felt Renee's hand rest gently on my shoulder.

"I know you don't want to hear this now," Renee began, "but this might be for the best."

"Get out."

Renee didn't argue.

I spent the majority of the night staring into that god-forsaken mirror cursing my fate. The rest of the time I spent staring into my outstretched hands attempting to will the Mana to flow down to my fingertips. The sensation was so tantalisingly familiar. I could almost feel it. The shiver and the rush of excitement as the Mana arced down my wrists to do my bidding.

I would flex my fingers and await the inevitable hit of endorphins – a hit that never came. After several minutes of this I would return to the damned mirror and examine my normal face. Without the Mana my features looked different, softer, weaker and much more vulnerable.

This wasn't the face that Vin had seen when I had cast him down. Had he seen this face he would have justifiably ended my pitiful existence. I hated this face. It wasn't mine. It was like staring into a stranger's face.

I had once thought like this about the Mana. I had

called the eyes of my former kind "stranger's eyes", but that was what I was staring into now – stranger's eyes. It was made all the more worse that they stared back at me with disdain.

"You're going to get past this," Renee said from the door. How long had she had been standing there? I resented the intrusion and only grunted in response. Renee came in and put a small of piles of clothes on the bed.

"I would have given everything for this when I was a teenager," Renee said, sitting on the bed.

"... and what about now?"

"I don't know," she mused, "maybe. The Mana hasn't exactly meant I've had a happy life so far."

I nodded. "Yes, but that would be your choice. This wasn't mine."

"No," Renee smiled sadly, "but you play the cards you're given."

"What am I going to do now?" I whispered. I wasn't sure if Renee had even heard me.

"I've left you some clean clothes. You should at least make an attempt to leave the room today." Renee said lightly as she made her way to the door. "And as for what to do. You can do anything you like, you're finally free. Get dressed, breakfast is waiting for you in the dining room."

She shut the door behind her.

* * * * * *

They say what doesn't kill you makes you stronger, but I didn't feel any stronger. In fact, I felt weaker, diminished and wholly terrified of the whole prospect. I did as I was instructed, putting on the clothes that Renee had left for me. I toyed with the idea of ignoring Renee's suggestion, but the grumbling of my stomach convinced me otherwise. As I came out into the corridor a woman walking past my door nodded at me. I quickly discovered that there were many people staying here – wherever here was. I passed several people in the hall, going about their morning routines.

Any one of them could be a Mage, at any minute they could strike me down with a telekinetic thread and there would be nothing I could do to stop them. I couldn't even see their Mana signatures as warning. To walk amongst them without knowledge of their reality was one thing, but to do so forewarned was simply terrifying.

I found my way to a small dining room. There were about a dozen people already in there. Renee pushed a jar of cereal in my direction as I took a seat.

"Glad to see you're up and about."

"Where are we?"

"My grandmother's house," she replied flippantly as if this weren't amongst the most dangerous place I could be.

I had met Renee's paternal grandmother only once – Victor had introduced me to her in Singapore. She had seemed nice enough, if a little distant. The only problem was that she was the current Primea and the official leader of our kind. Great, this meant that I was probably in the only place on earth with a larger Mage to human ratio. Furthermore it was almost assured that someone here would recognise me. I did have a death sentence on my head after all.

"Where is your father?" I asked nervously, if this was going to get unpleasant I was sure that Marcus would be able to get me out of here.

"I'm not sure. He's been busy for the past few days."

"How long was I asleep for?"

"About a week." Renee shrugged with a grin. "You looked like you were pretty tired."

I snickered a little at that.

"What is this place? Why so many people?"

"I suppose you could call it a school of sorts. One of the duties of the Primea is instruction."

"So everyone in here is of our ki— " I began, going to say the word "kind" but quickly switched to "Mage" instead. I was no longer of their kind.

"Mostly," Renee replied softly, "it's okay though, most people wouldn't recognise you now."

"I recognise you though," a third voice cut in as they pulled out a chair to join us.

My head snapped around to see who had invited themselves into our conversation. He was the last person I had expected to see here. He was a former enemy turned friend – Master Gabriel Tychus. We had fought briefly when I had been working for Victor – a fight that I had proved the stronger. I'd met the guy several times since then, but it had always been a little awkward, neither of us could seem to forget that the other had been an enemy. This distrust aside I quite liked the man. Although powerful, he was much more relaxed and easy going than the other Masters that I'd had the displeasure to associate with.

"Glad to see you on your feet." He said in way of greeting.

"Master Tychus," I bowed my head.

"Please, call me Gabe," he waved me off, "I never much like the whole Master title thing. That was always Whittlesea's thing."

Tychus spun the chair around and straddled it. You wouldn't know it to look at him, but he was probably the third most powerful Mage that I'd encountered behind, Master Victor and Marcus.

"I was sorry to hear about your burn out," Tychus murmured softly. "Bad news, always unfortunate when it happens. Usually only happens to apprentices. Can't imagine how that feels now."

"Feels great, thanks for asking," I grunted dryly.

Tychus laughed amicably, "Okay, that was stupid."

I nodded in agreement.

"What are you going to do now?" Tychus asked.

Renee coughed into her breakfast and flashed Tychus a warning look.

Tychus just laughed the look off with a wave and whistle, "She's certainly protective of you."

"I have no idea what I'm going to do now." I replied

bitterly. "I hadn't exactly prepared for this."

"Yeah," Tychus nodded, "damn shame none the less. You were quite promising there for a while."

"Promising? How?"

"Thought you might be the one to actually do it there for a while," Tychus continued.

"Do what?"

"Kill the Big Man. Knock the old kraut down." Tychus made a throat slashing motion with his finger. It was obvious to whom he had been referring – Master Victor. "A lot of us were secretly rooting for you."

"Can't be done." I said sourly, "trust me I know."

"Where there's a will there's a way."

"Someone else will have to find a way now."

"Never know." Tychus smiled as he got to his feet. "Burn outs aren't always permanent. I'll catch you later – we'll talk when your nursemaid ain't glaring at me. "

This condition isn't permanent? I turned to Renee. She was staring with annoyance at Tychus's retreating form.

"Why didn't you tell me?" I said softly.

"It's not a given. Some apprentices do recover – it's true, but more often than not the powers never return. Or if they do they're greatly weakened."

"But it happens," I pressed.

"Yes it does!" Renee said sharply. "But I wouldn't hold out on it."

"Why didn't you tell me?"

"Because I wanted you out of this! You were out of

control! It's better this way. Better where I can keep you safe."

"What?" I stormed, getting to my feet.

"Sit down! You're making a scene!

"You had lost control," she said, keeping her voice down. "You were throwing yourself against my grandfather again and again. You were taking risk after risk without cause or concern for the consequences. For crying out loud you were going to torture Hugo in Berlin! That's not you! That's not the man I fell in love with!

"I couldn't bear to see you become the monster you had to be," she whispered. "I wanted the boy who blushed when I talked about my breasts the first time we met. The man I know you are meant to be!"

"That man died with the boy when I was forced to kill Vin." I shot back as I sat down. Vin had been the first person I had ever had to kill, he'd been another Mage who had sought my death. It hadn't exactly worked out as he had expected.

"No he didn't." Renee whispered, "I could see him still in that small country town I rescued you from. I saw him when you chose to stand against my grandfather to rescue your cousin. You were determined but you hadn't let it consume you."

"Very well, then he died when my father died," I said.

"People die! It's how you live that matters," Renee pleaded, "surely he wouldn't have wanted that life for you."

"He's dead!" I snapped. "What he wanted doesn't matter any longer!"

"Of course it matters. It's all that matters now."

"I'm not going to discuss this with you any longer. He's dead and somehow I'm going to take my revenge on the one who took his life. I promise you that."

"I hope you never recover from this burn out," she said sadly, "I don't think I could bear to see the person you'll have to become to do that."

"You'd better hope I never do recover my powers," I whispered ominously as I stood up to leave.

I suddenly wasn't hungry anymore.

* * * * * *

The burn out wasn't always permanent. This brought me some glimmer of hope. It was slim, but it was better than nothing. I returned to my room in fury. How dare Renee keep this from me? How dare she presume to say what was best for me? She should have told me! I deserved to know!

I was nothing without the Mana! What other skills did I have to fall back on? Nothing! The moment I discovered the Mana the rest of my skills atrophied. This was a conscious decision on my part as I could envision no future where the Mana wasn't a part of my life. I was a fool.

This realisation did little to help me now though. All I could do was simply wait and hope that one day I would see the tell-tale spark of Mana as it flared across my flesh and know that my powers had returned. Until that day I had no idea what I was going to do.

Tracking down Victor and having my revenge would be impossible. Or would it? If I could sneak up on him unbeknownst. He would never expect an attack from a norm. He might not even recognise me without my powers. It was possible. I could take a job as a security guard or something at one of his firms. I knew of several firms that he owned where I could possibly set my trap.

I would wait and bide my time, until he showed himself and then put a bullet in the back of his brain. If I was quick and managed to fire before he raised his shield, it was possible. Then I would have my revenge.

This didn't of course help me with my cousin. I hadn't taken the time to process the lies that Victor had told me. Allie had killed my father? Preposterous! Victor was a master of deceit and this was merely another twist of the knife. Not content in the knowledge that my former Master had killed my father, Victor had sought to lay the blame on my cousin.

Was she even my cousin? Was Victor lying about that also? It was hard to say. My gut instinct said he was telling the truth, but my brain was saying that it was impossible. There is no way that she is my half-sister, that this was another of Victors lies.

The look in my father's dying eyes as he was trying to tell me something kept coming back to me. He had been so insistent. Was it merely the delusion caused by drugs and impending death? I didn't think so.

"Tell her… please…" My father's last words haunted me as they went round and round in my head. Was it possible that he was trying to tell me that I had a sister? I hadn't been present for all of his dying words. Maybe I'd missed something important. I was being beaten half to death myself at the time.

The more I thought about it the more I came to the conclusion that only one person could answer this question – Allie herself.

A knock at the door distracted me from my thoughts. Probably Renee coming to tell me again how wonderful this whole thing was. I didn't want to hear it. When I opened the door however I was surprised to see a small Asian girl. She seemed familiar, but I couldn't place where I'd met her before.

Her eyes narrowed as she scanned my face. Then her face twisted in anger. "It IS you!" she hissed as she took a step back. The hairs on the back of my neck stood up. I had no doubt that she was summoning Mana. I took several steps back from the door and contemplated slamming it, but realised it would make no difference.

"Do... do I know you?" I stammered. This woman hated me? Why did she hate me? I can't recall having done anything that would provoke this kind of venomous reaction.

"No!" she snapped, "but I know you!"

I wished I could see her Mana signature, it was hard to recognise a Mage without it. The pattern and flow of the Mana across the body was a big give away. I tried to mentally picture her, but for some reason the only thing I kept coming back to was Singapore. No, wait.

It wasn't just Singapore that she reminded me of; it was the Occursus in Singapore. She had been there. Once I realised that the rest came easily.

"You were guarding the Primea in Singapore," I ventured tentatively, unsure if I was about to be struck down in telekinetically assisted rage.

"That's my job you idiot!"

"Have I offended you in some way?" I asked as delicately as I could. I didn't like this. Didn't like it one bit. If I had my powers there's no way this shrimp of a girl would be talking to me like this.

"Only that you killed my husband."

''I'm sorry I—''

"My name is May Chen. Aaron was my husband. You killed him!"

Aaron had a wife? I didn't know that. He didn't seem old enough. I suppose he was in his mid-twenties. Now that I came to think on it, Aaron had said that he was married when I had first met Aaron in Singapore. He had gone by the name Degs at the time and he had helped me get safely to Renee's grandfather. The reality of the situation was however that Renee's grandfather wasn't the haven of safety that he had assumed. I tried to break away and Degs was sent after me.

"I didn't kill Degs," I said softly. "I fought him, but I didn't kill him."

"Bullshit."

"Your husband was shot by a man named Winters who worked for Victor."

"He was killed by a norm?" she sneered. "You're lying! You must have been involved somehow!"

"Why would I lie?"

"Because you're a fucking coward!" May shrieked, raising her hands in anger. It may have been my imagination, but I could almost make out the blue halo of Mana particles surrounding her fingers.

"Is there a problem here?" A voice cut in from behind May. I was ashamed to admit but I was actually quite glad to see the familiar shape of Tychus coming down the corridor at high speed. I hated that.

"No, no problem," May snarled turning to face the new comer, "I'm going to execute the outcast."

"No, you're not. That's already been decided."

In any other circumstances it would have been incredibly funny. May measured somewhere up near Tychus's sternum, yet the small woman was holding her own against the far larger man. Eventually she obviously realised that arguing with Tychus wasn't going to achieve anything and she turned to me.

"I'm going to kill you one day outcast. I don't know when, but you can count on it," she snarled, then turned on her heel and stormed off down the corridor. "One day Outcast! One day!"

"I think you've made an impression there." Tychus said dryly. "Did you kill her husband?"

"No."

"Most people seem to think that you did."

"I didn't"

"You were the only one around."

"I didn't," I repeated more firmly. "If I'd killed him I wouldn't have used a bullet."

"Fair point," Tychus conceded, "I've always wondered though, I had thought you two were friends."

"We were."

"What happened?"

"What do you think? I realised what Victor was and Aaron didn't."

Tychus nodded sombrely. "Whittlesea can be like that. He can be charming and influential when he needs to be – even without his compulsions."

I didn't bother answering.

"It's a good thing that I happened to be by." Tychus grinned.

"Let's not fool each other," I sighed wearily, "I'm sure Marcus asked you to keep an eye on me."

"You're not as dumb as you look. If you're not doing anything this evening, I thought I'd invite you out."

"Out? Where?"

"There's a bar I know. Pretty good, for a French place."

"I'm not sure I'm up for hanging out at a bar."

"Sure, brood in your room. At least until May comes back to kill you. I'll be at the bar."

"You make an excellent point." I said wryly.

* * * * * *

"I've never much liked French wine." Tychus said as he

swirled the glass in front of him. The bar that Tychus had chosen was actually more of a club. It was quiet and it was discreet. We had been here for about three hours so far with Tychus talking about everything other than the weather.

"Okay," I sighed, "get on with it."

"Get on with what?" Tychus raised an eyebrow.

"Whatever it is that you wanted to say to me without anyone else knowing we talked."

Tychus grinned at me from behind his glass. He leaned back into the couch and flicked the edge of his glass a finger.

"Ever wonder why both Marcus and Victor are so hell bent on recruiting you to their causes?"

"No," I grunted, "I haven't thought about it."

"You should have. Both you and your cousin are amongst the most potentially powerful members of our kind.

"Well at least up until recently," he finished, tipping his glass in my direction.

"So each side wants the strongest Mages to support them? I'm not seeing the point." I grunted, ignoring the gesture.

"It's not about support, it's about controlling the gene pool."

I raised an eyebrow. I hadn't expected that.

"Each generation our kind gets the potential for more power, more control over the Mana. Assuming they don't burn themselves out. Each generation is more powerful than the last."

"Right? Is that so?"

"Added to the fact that the age of enlightenment and science did much to dispel the archaic ideas that surrounded our kind. It did much to remove the rituals and the bullshit from our art. The last hundred years or so has seen a dramatic increase in our understanding of Mana and how it can be used. We can do things now that would have humbled our predecessors."

"I'm assuming you're going to get to the point sometime soon."

"It means that our children are more powerful than we are, and thanks to our learning, are better able to utilise their powers."

"Sounds like a natural evolution. I'm not seeing the problem."

"The problem is that our growth was held in check for hundreds of years and that kept us weak and well within the abilities of the rest of society to control us."

"Sure," I nodded.

"This is no longer the case."

"Let's assume that I agree with that. Why is that a problem?"

"Use your brains boy. If you wanted to destroy a city, was there anyone other than another Mage who could have stopped you?"

"A whole city? That's a big ask," I mused, "but I suppose… eventually… maybe."

"Now think like a terrorist. Only you're a terrorist that can only be stopped with overwhelming force. Force that would do more collateral damage than is acceptable and you're totally unrelenting unless your demands are met."

"You're saying we're dangerous?" The statement seems a little redundant.

"It's more than we're just dangerous – it's that we're a ticking time bomb. Every generation is more powerful than the last. In every generation there is the potential for one of us with a messiah complex to attempt to overthrow everything and setup themselves up as an emperor."

"Maybe we should. We couldn't do a worse job than the norms are doing. It might even be better for them in the long run."

"Ahh, now you've reached the crux of the matter. Both Victor and Marcus believe that civilisation needs to be protected, but both had vastly different ideas of how this should be done.

"Marcus believes that integration with civilisation is our only choice. Eventually the risk of us not being able to control our numbers without collateral damage is too high."

"Yeah," I nodded, "Victor talked about it – he believes that the disturbance our discovery would make would be cataclysmic. There'd be very little left to save."

Tychus nodded. "He's probably right, but I believe that the alternative is worse. That's why I'm signed on with Marcus and not Victor. It only takes one of us to lose the plot and we're all fucked. Look at yourself as an example – in your hunt for Victor you did more damage to our cause than if you were actively attempting to bring our order down."

"Not intentionally."

"Doesn't matter, every time you flaunted your powers in public you exposed us. That's why you've got a death sentence."

"So why aren't I dead now?"

"You're not a Mage now. Our laws are clear – we don't execute norms."

"So you're saying I got off on a technicality."

"No, not as such. We don't know how to handle this. Many think you should still pay for your transgressions, others think you have already paid."

"Why are you telling me this?"

"Because it's time for you to choose sides. You can't keep acting as a free agent. You're going to play a very important role in our kind's future. You'd be an idiot not to see that, and neither Marcus nor Victor are idiots. It's time for you to grow up."

"I don't think that's true anymore. I have no powers." I said bitterly.

"I wouldn't say that," Tychus said, "No one of your potential has ever burned themselves out before. We really don't know what happens. If I were a betting man I wouldn't count you out yet."

"Here's hoping," I raised my glass. It turns out I don't much like French wine either.

CHAPTER SIX

I didn't feel well the next morning, in fact I felt like crap. At first I thought it was a reaction to the wine, but as it got worse and the fever took hold, I realised what it was. This was no hangover – it was the start of withdrawal symptoms from lack of Mana use. This wasn't fair.

My stomach churned as my body simultaneously tried to force out every ounce of liquid out of my body in sweat. Small hammers took turns pounding my head as I cursed my existence, the Mana and the world in general. This wasn't a good way to start to the day.

Renee came to check on me about mid-morning.

"So it's begun." She brushed back a lock of hair that had been plastered to my brow with sweat.

"It's not fair," I groaned. The room spun around in protest to my attempted speech.

"Lie still. I'll be back."

She returned shortly with a cool damp cloth, which she placed over my brow. The coolness brought the only relief I'd had felt all morning.

"Thank you," I murmured, sending the room spinning off in another direction.

Renee was patient and considerate, even when I was

less than grateful to her. She had given me the time I needed to cope with this without complaint or comment. You don't realise how much someone loves you until you see how they treat you when you know you're being unreasonable back. I was lucky she was here.

I knew from experience that the next few days would be the worst until the withdrawal symptoms subsided. Once the fever had broken I could just look forward to the shakes and the odd bout of headaches.

Excellent. This was just what I needed right now. At least last time the whole process was worth something. Now it was simply something that was happening to me for no good cause. It was just another cruel punishment that the fates had cast upon me. I vaguely wondered what I had done in another life to be forced to endure such indignities.

I had gone through several bouts of withdrawals before though, so at least I knew what to expect. The hardest part is the psychological torment. The craving never goes away. It's like a hand held up in front of your face. It dominates everything and prevents you from seeing anything else.

Previously it had taken everything I had had not to cave in and begin using the Mana. Now I couldn't even if I wanted to. I couldn't say which fate was worse – to be able to use but choose not to, or to be unable to use but want to.

Renee patiently remained by my side and nursed me through the worst of it. By the time the fever finally broke we were both on the verge of complete exhaustion. My recovery was slow and it was days before I felt comfortable on my feet and outside of my room. When I did leave my room it was normally only late at night, and I didn't linger. I didn't particularly want to advertise my current state. I knew that any sign of weakness would be exploited and I was sure that there were others out there, like May who were howling for my blood. I wasn't sure that the ruling that I was no longer a Mage would protect me, should they decide to take matters into their own hands.

Truth be told, I was also hiding because I was ashamed. I had once been a beacon of magical might and power. Now I was a bitter and broken thing that deserved to be cast aside with the other broken things.

It was a full week and half before I felt more like my body wasn't trying to turn itself inside out anymore. After the fever had broken Renee no longer spent every moment by my side. I didn't begrudge her this; in fact I was actually kind of grateful. It allowed me to brood in peace.

A knock at my door brought me from my depression. Probably Renee with dinner. But when she came in she didn't have a tray of food. This was different from the routine. Different wasn't good.

"Get dressed," she said briskly.

"Why?"

"You're being brought before the Primea."

Renee went to the cupboard and selected several

formal shirts and threw them on the bed. She narrowed her eyes as she tried to decide on pants. She selected a pair and they joined the shirts on the bed. Apparently I didn't get a choice with the pants.

"Can't turn up in track pants huh?" I commented as I retrieved a pair of socks and slipped them inside the formal shoes that Renee had just passed me.

"No," Renee snapped, "take this seriously."

A pulled a shirt on and noticed with some degree of amusement that it was loose on my frame – I'd lost weight. I slipped the pants on and needed to pull the belt tight as I turned to Renee for her inspection.

"No," she murmured curtly, "not the red shirt, the green one. Red is too confrontational."

"You didn't think to tell me that before I put it on?" I grumbled as I removed the offending shirt.

Renee gestured towards the door. "When you're ready."

"As ready as I'll ever be." I murmured.

I wasn't ready.

* * * * * *

As we passed through the house everyone stopped to look at me. I got a distinct dead-man-walking vibe. It wasn't pleasant. I'd never been in this part of the complex before. We were heading towards a set of double doors. There were several people waiting outside, some had the look of guards others had the look of onlookers annoyed at being unable to gain entry. Renee gestured towards one of the guards who nodded and opened the door. Before we entered Renee turned to me, looked me up and down and straightened my collar. Once she was satisfied that I looked presentable she kissed me on the forehead.

"Be careful."

There were a lot of people in this room, most of them blurred into the background though. The whole vibe of the room had the feel of one of those TV law shows. This looked just like a court-room with the Primea sitting in the vaunted position of judge.

The Primea had aged horribly since the last I had seen her. She was leaning forward in a gurney with a host of tubes connected to her and an oxygen mask lying to one side. She had already been old when I had last met her, but she seemed to have aged at least ten years in the three years since our last encounter. She was dressed in a high-collared black blouse and had blankets over her lap. The broach that proclaimed her the Primea was displayed high on her chest where it could not be ignored.

May was standing in the centre of the room facing the Primea. I wasn't surprised to see her there, as she was obviously the reason that I was here in the first place. She turned to me with a look of pure hatred on her face. What did surprise me though, was that standing right beside her was Victor.

Renee's fingers tightened around my arm. She obviously hadn't been expecting to see him here either. My lips tightened into a sneer as I looked at the man. If I had my powers I know I would have struck him down, nothing could have stopped me. Fortunately for him I didn't have my powers. Victor for his part didn't appear to be paying me any attention at all. He face was unreadable. I couldn't decipher what he was doing here or even if he wanted to be here at all.

A small hush fell over the assembly as they become aware of my presence.

"Ah, it is the man – Devon Wills," Victor intoned as I reached the centre of the room. He had intentionally placed emphasis on the word "man". Now that I was no longer a Mage I was of no concern to him. He used the word "man" as others would use the word "vermin".

The Primea coughed as she struggled to lean forward. Her ancient face scrunched up as she examined me. She didn't make a comment, but she kept my gaze for several seconds before apparently coming to a decision.

May looked frantically between Victor and the Primea as she realised this might not go the way she had anticipated. She had obviously counted on Victor's support and his choice of the word "man" had clearly rattled her.

"He's a murderer! He killed my husband!" she shrieked. "How can you deny me my justice?"

"Your husband was slain by a bullet wound to the back of his head. I examined his corpse myself," Victor said. "Had your husband been more adept this would not have downed him. The fault is his own."

"He broke our laws!" she insisted, pointing at me.

"Silence girl!" The Primea's cracked voice was no more than a whisper, but it reverberated throughout the room like a thunderclap. No doubt the she was using the whisper spell to increase her volume.

I almost felt sorry for May. I really did. She stood alone in the centre of the room facing down the most powerful Mage of our kind.

"You have served me well," the Primea continued curtly, "and for that I grant you much leniency, but I will not allow you to dictate who lives and who dies."

May looked as if the Primea had physically struck her, she looked to Victor for help, but his face was impassive.

"Now, everyone – leave us!" The Primea ordered. "I wish to talk to Master Wills alone."

Master Wills? What the hell did that signify? Did it mean that she still considered that I was subject to her rule?

As the crowd dispersed, I noticed that Victor hadn't left. He had gently, but forcefully directed May to the door and returned to his position in the court. May had stared daggers at me as she passed by me and hissed, "This isn't over Outcast!"

Once the crowd had left, four people remained the room. The Primea, Victor, Renee and myself. The Primea looked irritably at Victor.

"You too, old one," she ordered.

"I prefer to remain." Victor's reply was cold.

"No! Either strike me down and take the damned broach, or do as I order."

I almost thought Victor would do it too, his face remained cold and hard but I could see in his eyes the anger brimming over. He crisply bowed and uttered, "As you wish.

"Granddaughter," he said in acknowledgement as he brushed past us. Renee's fingers tightened into claws around my arm. She stared at the man who had once been her sole provider and carer and said nothing. The message was clear. He meant nothing to her now.

Her response seemed to go unnoticed by Victor, but I could tell that he wasn't as calm as he appeared. Inside he was seething.

The rough slam of the door indicated that he had gone. I had noticed with some degree of wry awe that as he walked there was no limp or unbalance in his step. It was almost as if a ten-foot metal pole had never been plunged through his hip.

"You too child," the Primea said to Renee.

"I'd like to stay please," Renee answered meekly.

"If I'm going to order your grandfather, what makes you think I won't do the same to you?" the Primea barked.

"No, I don't mean it like that. I'd just rather not go outside just now," Renee murmured, "not while he's out there."

"I'd prefer she remain also," I tentatively added.

"What you want is of no consequence." The Primea glared at me. "Now come closer so I don't have to shout. Renee may remain if she wishes."

I hesitantly moved closer to the side of the bed. The Primea looked so fragile and frail. It was obvious that she wasn't a well woman, but I hadn't realised just how unwell she was. Clearly a lot of expense and effort had been put into keeping her alive. The Primea must have seen the pity in my eyes as her expression went steely as I approached.

"If I had known what chaos you would cause after our last meeting I would have taken your life when I had had the chance," she growled.

"If I had known, I might have asked you to," I replied darkly.

The Primea chuckled, which turned into a strangled cough. "And again, it seems that I have to decide between your life and death."

"So it seems."

The Primea's eyes bored into me as if she was searching for something. I had experienced her piercing stare before and didn't allow it to unnerve me. The truth of the matter was that I simply didn't care. Should she choose to execute me it would almost be a relief.

"Care you so little about your life?" she prompted.

"Without the Mana, it seems to matter little," I replied lightly, which led to an angry glance from Renee. She seemed like she was about to interject, but was cut off by the Primea.

"I allowed you to remain child, but you will be silent if you wish to stay."

Renee glared fiercely at me but kept her mouth shut.

"You have changed," the Primea announced. "No longer are you the brash young man who stood before me at the Occursus. Ready to take on the world."

"People change," I muttered.

"Not as often as people think they do," the Primea snapped. "True change is painful, and not as common as people believe. You are less than you once were. It is sad to see."

"We are defined by the Mana," I began,

"Not so. The Mana does not define who a person is, if it did we would all be alike."

I didn't particularly want to argue the subject with this old woman.

"It is sad to see one so full of life so ready to throw it away," she continued, "especially hard to see for one at the end of their own."

"Are you going to execute me or not?" I was sick of being lectured by the old crone.

"Ahh, there's the old fire, it seems that you're not so different after all." The Primea chortled, "I do not know what I will do. I am loath to side with Victor in anything and he does not wish you killed."

"Victor doesn't care enough to see me killed," I grunted. "There's a difference."

"Do not be so quick to presume what that one wants," the Primea said. "Many have fallen into that trap and paid the price, my son among them."

"I don't care what Victor wants. All I cared about was rescuing my cousin."

"Are you sure that she wants to be rescued?"

"No," I whispered, "but that's not her call."

The Primea snorted, "If memory recalls you didn't do an impressive job in teaching her. Are you sure you would be a better mentor?"

"I had other concerns, I was being hunted by your son at the time."

"Teaching our kind is the most serious of tasks. There can be no other concerns. This is a failure that both of you are guilty of. Had Renee deferred to others of her kind rather than attempting to train you, this whole mess might have been avoided."

"I'm not interested in teaching Allie. I'm interested in getting her away from Victor."

"At what cost?"

"What do you mean?" I raised an eyebrow.

"What cost are you willing to pay to rescue your cousin?" the Primea pressed.

"It doesn't really matter now. Whatever plans I had, died with the Mana in me."

"Of course it matters," she hissed, "it is a reflection of the man you are. You disregarded our laws, you revealed your powers to the world at large. You broke our most sacrosanct rules. I would know why you did this?"

"I didn't think they applied to me," I muttered. I was aware how weak this sounded.

"And yet during the last Occursus swore to me that you would obey them."

I nodded sadly, "Once my Master tried to have me

killed I didn't think the rules counted for much."

"You're wrong. They're the only thing preventing total chaos."

"Hard to see that when you've got a gun pointed at you."

"Bah," the Primea waved off, "I wouldn't imagine that a gun matters that much do you."

"No, but he did send Master Chen after me."

"Did he now? He claims that Master Chen acted alone."

"If you believe that, then you're deluding yourself."

"Let's say that I'm willing to concede the possibility that Chen was acting under orders, even so the end result was the same. A massive assault over Melbourne with hundreds of spectators, Mages using their powers in full view of witnesses and a stupid child who pulled an entire car park complex down on top of himself."

I couldn't help but grin at that, that car park stunt had been more effective that I had anticipated. It certainly had made a mess. That hadn't really been the purpose of the exercise though. My father had just died and it was entirely possible that I wasn't thinking too clearly.

"You smile, but do you know how much fear you created that day?"

"Our kind should be afraid," I said, "it will keep us in check."

"Not amongst our kind, amongst everyone else. They saw that day a power that they cannot understand and cannot stand against. Humans are a shallow species that will not allow anything to stand greater than them. You just issued a challenge to the world. They will respond."

"That wasn't my intention," my words sounded lame even to me.

"Intention or not boy! That is what you did," the Primea hissed. "There are those amongst the governments that search for you still. I wonder what would happen should they find you now.'"

"They would probably be very disappointed," I murmured dryly.

"As am I," the Primea shot back. "You have taken your gifts and abused them. Perhaps this punishment is a fitting reward."

"This is not a reward," I snapped. "This is a consequence."

"Is that so?" The Primea raised an eyebrow.

"Yes, this is a consequence of Victor's work and my own choice. When he compelled me to kill your son, I made a choice. It's a choice I now regret, but one I would probably make again."

"I did not know Victor ordered you to do this."

"Didn't you? Well, he did and I knew there was no way to resist the compulsion. It burned like a fire in my mind. It was all I could focus on. It dominated my thinking. I knew that should I strike Marcus down there would be nothing to stand against Victor."

Renee looked at me, her face twisted with a mixture of curiosity and guilt. She was the one partially responsible for sending me after Victor. In a way this was a consequence of her decision to bring me before Marcus.

"I knew that there was a possibility that I could kill Marcus and I didn't want to do that," I continued, "so I pushed myself. I kept myself going. The Compulsion did not force me to act with the speed and urgency that I kept up. I did that! I made the compulsion work for me.

"I pushed myself to the brink of complete exhaustion, thinking that when I confronted your son I would be too weak to be a threat. And it worked! When I did finally confront your son my powers were weak. I knew that should it come to fight I would be easily overcome and I assumed that Marcus would not destroy me.

"What I didn't realise of course was the possibility of this." I finished, waving my cold Mana-dead hand in front of my face. "Had I known my fate I probably would have rethought things.

"No, probably not," I reflected grimly, "my fate was sealed the moment I stepped foot into that prison camp."

The Primea nodded in agreement, "You weren't ready for the task that my son assigned you. Still we needed to do something."

"We?"

"If you think my son does anything without my knowledge you're sadly mistaken."

"You did this to me?"

"No." The Primea coughed, "I saw the potential in you, but first we had to find you. You were moving from city to city searching for god knows what, creating havoc and chaos as you went."

"I was searching for my cousin. You know this."

"Victor had hidden her well, you were never going to find her that way."

"What other choice did I have?"

"You could have worked with us," she said sternly.

"What? With the very same people who had me named Outcast and threatened death?"

"That was Victor's doing," the Primea snapped. "You accomplished one thing with your crusade, you kept his eyes focused firmly on you and not on what we were doing. He even tried to have you killed."

How could I forget. Six Mages had ambushed me in Shanghai. This was when I still thought that Victor was operating out of southern China and I was moving north from Singapore, attempting to reach the mainland. I was travelling through a night market contemplating where to search next. I knew something was wrong when the street quickly cleared itself. I looked up and there they were, three of them, standing at the end of the road. The other three didn't show themselves until the battle had already started.

I originally thought that they had been sent by order of the Primea. Then they stated outright that Victor had pronounced my death. It hadn't been a pleasant fight, but they hadn't been strong enough to carry out his decree.

"When you killed three of his number," the Primea continued," I think you brought fear to him at last. He hadn't expected that and he didn't like it."

"You knew about that attack?" Renee queried, "and you didn't do anything?"

"How could we have helped him if we didn't know where he was?" she scolded her granddaughter. "It wasn't until you led us to him in Berlin that we were able to become involved directly.

"You are just as much at guilt here as I," she continued. "Had you trusted us, we could have prevented this."

Renee shook her head, "I don't believe that, I don't think you had our best interests at heart."

"Foolish child," the Primea snapped. "What do you know of such things? Your path has only led to ruination, first for your man, and now your cause."

Renee didn't reply, but I could tell that she wanted to, she really wanted to.

"Are you going to execute me?" I asked again, the old bat hadn't answered me last time.

"I have only one question further," she said. "Aaron Chen. Did you kill him?"

"No, he was killed by one of Victor's henchmen who sought revenge upon me. Aaron wouldn't allow it and so he was attacked from behind. He was killed before he knew what was happening."

"I thought as much," the Primea mused softly. "Leave me now, I have much to think about."

"You haven't given me an answer yet."

"No, I suppose I haven't" the Primea's voice was losing power. "I am tired. Leave me."

"Primea," I said, "if you're going to have me executed

I deserve to know."

The Primea sighed. "The last time that question was before me I chose poorly. My instinct now is to have you killed and be done with you, but I was wrong last time. This time I need to be more careful."

"Then I have my answer," I whispered darkly as I turned to leave. The Primea didn't say anything further. She simply let us go. It wasn't a good sign.

Once the door was shut behind us Renee turned on me in fury.

"We can't just sit here and wait for her to come to her decision," she snarled.

"What do you propose we do?"

"Let's go! Just you and me! We'll find somewhere safe and just wait it out." Renee whispered urgently.

"Where could we go that we could not be found? The only reason they had trouble tracking me down before was because I was constantly on the move."

"Then we'll do that."

"Do you think I could really live that life without my powers?"

"You keep coming back to that point!" Renee hissed angrily.

"It's a rather important point don't you think? I used my powers for food, comfort, shelter. Without them I would be dead within a week. No. It might be better to just end it here."

"Don't you say that!" Renee slapped me.

"I'm tired," I whispered as I rubbed the bridge of my

nose. "I'm so fucking tired of this."

"Fuck you Devon! Fine! Go off and die then! Just don't expect me to wait around to see it!"

She stormed off.

"Trouble Mister Wills?" a snide voice shot in from behind, placing extra emphasis on the word "Mister". Victor.

"I keep you alive, because you bring my granddaughter happiness. The moment that is no longer the case, my protection withdraws."

"Don't lie," I sneered, "you've been trying to kill me for three years and I don't believe for a second that you're acting out of any moral imperative now."

"Perhaps I merely wish to express gratitude. You did remove one of my more dangerous enemies."

What the hell was he talking about? I had no idea what that meant but I wasn't going to give Victor the satisfaction of seeing me stumped. I merely nodded and attempted to move on. I had no interest in talking to him.

"I was surprised that you actually survived, I had expected Master Marcus would kill you. You have always been resourceful though."

He thinks Marcus is dead? Wait a minute. Is Marcus dead? I don't remember killing him, but it was possible that I couldn't remember everything from that day. Renee had brushed me off when I had asked after Marcus. Was it possible he was actually dead?

"Burning yourself out in the process was a delightful

extra," Victor continued smugly, "I couldn't have planned it better if I'd tried."

I didn't even look back. I just kept walking. So what if Marcus is dead? Let Victor join him. I'm sure they'll both end up in hell. I don't care anymore. I just want out.

* * * * * *

The sound of my door opening and closing brought me out of my slumber. At first I thought they'd finally come to put me to death, but quickly rejected that idea. Surely they'd at least wait until morning for that. As I blearily opened my eyes, the light flicked on, flooding the room with bright searing light.

"What the hell?" I grumbled, rubbing my eyes. Renee was throwing some clothes into a bag while Tychus stood guard by the door.

"What's going on?" I asked.

"The Primea has fallen into a coma. She's not expected to awake," Tychus informed me from the door. "She hadn't made an announcement about your execution, so we're moving you to a more secure location."

"Just in case," Renee said, throwing some clothes at me. I'd need to talk to Renee about this at some point; I was capable of choosing my own clothing. I threw the clothes on and joined Tychus by the door.

"What's the plan," I whispered.

Tychus grinned, "Plan?"

Right, this was going to go well then.

We moved through the house at a rapid pace. There were a surprising number of people active for this time of night, but no one paid us any attention.

Two identical cars had been parked by the front door. Both had darkened glass.

"You go with Tychus," Renee motioned towards one of the cars, "I'll draw them off."

"Are you sure?" I whispered. "Remember what happened last time we tried that plan?"

We had been trying to escape from Renee's father. The plan hadn't exactly worked out that well. True, I had gotten away, but Renee had been captured and it was several months before we saw each other again. Actually, come to think of it, the Mage we'd been running from had been Tychus. There was a strange irony to that.

Renee grinned and kissed me on the cheek, "Second time's the charm."

"This won't keep anyone serious about searching from finding him," Tychus warned as he threw himself into the driver's seat of the first car. Renee grinned and raised her hand. She flexed her fingers and I knew without doubt that she was calling upon the Mana.

"That'd just about do it," Tychus commented dryly.

Suddenly all the hairs on the back of my neck stood up and I had a strong feeling that someone was right behind me. Well, that was good news at least. It meant that I was still sensitive to Mana. When Renee had been training me she had explained that many people could sense the flow of Mana, but were unable to utilise it. Most of them went through their life without ever knowing what was causing the tingly sensation – I envied those people.

"Shading?" I guessed. Without being able to see the Mana I was forced to make an educated guess.

The shading Spell was designed to prevent people from Scrying on an area. It threw up so much magical noise that it was like looking at static on your TV. I'd tried to peer through a Shading veil once and knew just how futile it would be.

"Go, I'll see you soon," Renee whispered. I smiled back at her and headed towards the passenger seat of the car.

"Get in the back you idiot," Renee called as she moved towards the second car.

Tychus took off at high speed as soon as I got in.

"Where are we going?"

"Business district," Tychus said. "Called in a favour, going to get you air lifted out by helicopter. That'll get you to the airport, then you're going to chill in New York for a while until this all cools down."

"New York?"

I'd never been to America. I'd always wanted to though. As a kid growing up in Australia, America had seemed like an amazing place to live. All the movies and TV shows made it seem like the centre of culture and entertainment. I hoped that the reality would prove as exciting as my younger self had believed.

"Just sit back and relax," Tychus advised, "We'll be there soon."

We were moving through the streets of Paris at a good clip. I could see the central business district in the distance. The Primea's manor had obviously been some distance from the centre of Paris. That made sense I guess, you wouldn't want too many Mages that close to the hustle and bustle of the city where someone could accidently see something they shouldn't.

After about fifteen minutes Tychus brought the car up front of a building. Someone jumped in the driver's seat as soon as we got out. I was ushered through the front doors of the building and towards the elevator. This had been really well organised.

Tychus kept clenching and unclenching his fists, but neither of us commented on it. The elevator took its sweet time getting to the ground level and seemed to take an inordinate amount of time to get to our destination.

The building was only five stories or so. When we got to the top floor, we had another flight of stairs to climb to get the rooftop, where we were greeted with the panoramic view of the Parisian night sky. Paris really was a beautiful city.

Tychus cursed when he saw the helipad was clear, but was assured by one of the attendants that the chopper would be here soon. Tychus paced up and down the length of the rooftop, obviously annoyed at the delay. We were a little exposed up here. A Mage on top of a building would be visible from even the most cursory Scry spell.

A tingling sensation down my spine was the first alert that something was wrong. I turned to Tychus and saw his mouth drop open in shock. The next clue was the feeling of all my atoms in my body fizzling as they were bombarded with Mana.

I knew this feeling. This had happened to me before. This was the product of a teleport spell! Tychus cursed as he ran towards me. I could have told him not to bother; there was nothing he could do now. Should he attempt to disrupt the effect it would merely result in him scattering my molecules across the distance between here and where ever I was being teleported to.

Teleportation when you're in control is scary enough, but when you're not the one calling the shots it's terrifying. I knew from experience just how difficult this was, one mistake and your body is trying to be in two places.

The last thing I saw before the teleport spell took hold was Tychus's trying to tell me something. It may have been that he was promising to find me, or maybe it was simply that he was apologising. It didn't matter much now. Whoever had done this probably had a plan to deal with Tychus. I was on my own. For the moment at least.

It took a few moments for my eyes to adjust to my new location. It was large, dark room. From the pipes and cables run across the ceiling I guessed it was a sub-basement level of a large building. I couldn't see who had teleported me, but I knew that they wouldn't be far away. It would be even more difficult to teleport a target from one location but send them to a third. There was only one person I knew for a fact who could accomplish that feat.

Victor.

I glanced around nervously. The only light source was a series of lights hanging from one of the ducts on the ceiling, but most of them were out, creating pockets of darkness in the room.

"Okay," I said, "why have you brought me here?"

Silence. If my captor was hoping to freak me out they were succeeding. I called out several more times, eventually concluding that I was alone down here, wherever here was. I wasn't sure if this made me feel better or worse.

In the half-light I made my way to one end of the room hoping for a door or something, but only found some crates and storage barrels. The other end of the room yielded a better result – a set of double doors. Unfortunately for me there was a chain link locking them together. There was no way I was going to be able to get through that.

Maybe I could find some bolt cutters. Maybe there was a toolbox or something down here? It wasn't out of the realms of possibility. It took me about fifteen minutes poking around in the darkness before I came upon a locker bay. Most of the lockers were locked, but one of them at the far end swung open freely. Sitting inside the locker was a small flathead screwdriver.

It wasn't ideal, but it was a start. Maybe I could

leverage the lock off the chain with the screwdriver. No, probably not – the chain links were thicker than the screwdriver. Still if nothing else the screwdriver might serve as a weapon should I need it. Bah, who was I kidding? A Mage had brought me here. A screwdriver wasn't going to be of any help.

A more thorough exploration of the room confirmed that I was underground. There were no windows, only large vents periodically lining the walls. I wondered if I could use the screwdriver to pry open one of the vents. I supposed it was possible, but I wasn't too keen on the idea of crawling around a duct system. Knowing my luck, I'd crawl into the vent and end up scorched by hot air and pass out in the vent and die. That didn't seem like a pleasant way to go.

No, for the moment I was probably better off here. I had found a jacket in one of the lockers, which I pulled over myself. For a supposedly temperature controlled room it was certainly getting cold. My best option at this point was probably waiting until whoever had nabbed me came to collect their prize.

My money was on Victor. I just didn't know why he had brought me here. Was it simply to keep me out of contact for a few hours while he did whatever he needed to do? Or did he have a darker purpose in mind? He had claimed that he would leave me my life, but I didn't believe him. He'd lied to me before and I was sure he would do so again.

Worrying about it wasn't going to help me, but there

was very little else to do in this room. It would have been nice if he'd left me a book or something. Hell even a deck of cards would have been nice. It had been some time since I'd last played solitaire, but I was sure once I figured out how it was dealt out I could remember the rules.

I pulled up a mangled office chair that had been thrown into the corner and tried my best to make myself comfortable on it.

I must have nodded off as the next thing I knew I was jolted awake by a loud explosion of sound rocketing through the room. I jumped to my feet. I recognised that noise. Someone was teleporting into the room.

I quickly slipped the screwdriver up into the sleeve of my jacket. I knew it would be no good, but it made me feel a little better to have it resting against my wrist.

"Hello?" I called out.

"Hello Outcast!" a voice sneered back. I recognised that voice. It wasn't Victor. It was May Chen. I couldn't decide if that was better or worse.

Victor was more powerful, but he didn't seem to want to harm me. May had claimed on several occasions that she was going to kill me. No, this was definitely worse I concluded grimly. I was going to die in this room. I just knew it.

It seemed like such a waste, after everything I had been through, to go out like this – it seemed almost ironic. I turned towards the sound of May's voice.

"You're here to answer for your crimes," she announced.

"What crimes?" I scoffed, "the Primea never pronounced judgement."

"She was going to!" May hissed.

"But she didn't! Let's not pretend this is anything, but what it is. This is you taking revenge for your husband."

"No! This is an execution of an outcast from our order."

"I'm not a member of your order anymore," I reminded her.

"Doesn't matter, you need to pay for your crimes."

"Like the death of your husband?"

"Like that."

"I didn't kill your husband."

"You were his friend, then you turned on him and joined his enemies."

"No! Listen!" I begged, "I didn't turn on Degs, Victor ordered him to come after me."

I could tell that this wasn't going to do any good. May was slowly working herself up into a state where she could do this. It would take her some time, but I had no doubt that she would strike me down, and when she did the small screwdriver in my pocket would be no defence. My goose was as good as cooked.

"He trusted you! He helped you!" she said, almost on the verge of tears, "and you let him die! Why did you do that? Why? Make me understand!"

The hair began to rise on the back of my neck. May was drawing upon Mana. It would happen soon.

"Why? Why did you live and he have to be the one

who died?" She sobbed as she stepped towards me. I took several steps back, even though it was useless. There was nowhere else to go.

"May! Don't do this," I whispered, "you're not a murderer!"

"This isn't murder," May hissed, "this is an execution!"

"No, no it's not!" It was going to happen soon.

"Devon Wills!" May announced, her voice taking on an official tone, "for your crimes against the order, I sentence you to death. Do you have any last words?"

"This is murder May!" I said. As far as last words go they lacked a certain something, but I couldn't really think of anything better.

"Very well," May finished, "I will now deliver the sentence. Kneel down and receive your judgment!"

"I'm not going to kneel down before you!" I grunted angrily, "If you're going to kill me you're going to have to do it without that nicety. You're going to have to murder me while I'm standing before you."

The hairs on the back of my neck were going crazy. I wasn't sure how much Mana she was generating, but my senses were going wild. I needed to do something and I needed to do it now. I took a deep breath and readied myself to leap forward. If I took her by surprise, it's possible that she didn't have a shield raised, my little screwdriver might just allow me to end this. Who was I kidding? But I didn't have any other choice. I leapt forward.

That leap probably saved my life. The thread that was

going to end my life, clipped me on the side rather than hitting me full on. The impact still sent me reeling and sliding off away from her. It may have been the shock of the strike or maybe my nerves were just playing havoc with me, but I swear I saw the thread for a few seconds as it arced away from me.

May screamed in frustration and tried to bring the thread around again, but I was on my feet and moving.

"Stand still!" she shrieked as the thread passed over my head. I'd gotten lucky, I'd managed to dodge a thread without being able to see it. So far I'd done better than I had thought. It didn't matter much though – she almost certainly had a shield up now. Again it may have been my vision playing tricks, but I thought I make out a faint distortion surrounding her where her shield would be.

The distraction proved to be detrimental as May brought the thread around and hit me square in the chest. I felt a crunch and pain lanced through me. The impact knocked me back off my feet and sent me sliding across the floor.

I tried to get to my feet, but the pain in my chest was too much. She'd definitely broken some of my ribs, I'd felt this pain before. It took me several tries before I was able to pull myself roughly onto my knees. The pain was excruciating, but I'd learnt to deal with pain. I wasn't going to simply roll over and let her finish this.

May closed in and readied herself. I could see it in her eyes and the sharp grimace of her lips. I was going to die. I briefly wondered if it would hurt, if I would feel it, or would it be quick and I'd simply just find myself in the darkness. I sighed deeply, ignoring the pain in my chest and awaited the strike that would finish me.

May took a deep breath. I could see her eyes steel over – it was coming. Then it didn't. May's eyes widened in shock and she took several steps back.

"No, no no!" she repeated like a mantra, "no!"

What the hell was she going on about? The Mana in her body reacted frantically to her state and her shield wavered. The thread that she had been going to use to end my life backed off as she readied to defend herself.

I glanced around, who else had arrived? Had Tychus or Renee arrived to rescue me? If so their timing was amazing. I hadn't heard the noise of their teleportation, but that could easily be explained away.

Then I realised what had happened and just how wrong I had been. I could see her thread! I could see her Mana! In the stress of the situation I hadn't realised it, but I was seeing Mana! I glanced down at my chest and saw with hysterical joy the pulse of the Mana on my own flesh.

"NO!" May snarled as her thread arced down.

Time seemed to slow down for me as I sought to raise a shield. Pain lanced through my body from my wrists and deep down into my core. My whole body twisted in agony as I sought to draw upon my power. A primal explosion of power erupted from me as the magic finally took me. I wasn't able to raise a shield – nothing so elegant. It was simply an explosion of telekinetic energy that burst from me like a thunderclap. Everything surrounding me was thrown away. The blast hit May and impacted against her shield sending her stumbling backwards.

In the inferno of pain released in the explosion the pain from my ribs didn't seem so bad anymore. I took a step up and got back onto my feet. May rose in fury too sending a thread arcing towards me. I sent a thread of my own to block it.

The thread was slow and weak, far below my norm, but it was sufficient to deflect May's strike. A flood of endorphins swam into my body as the euphoria of Mana use overtook me. May's next strike went wild and I took the opportunity to raise a shield. I had no doubts about the shield – it would not survive more than one direct hit, but it felt good to have something protecting me, shielding me. I no longer felt vulnerable and weak. I was in control and I was getting stronger, I could feel it.

May charged towards me in fury and her thread lashed against me. I was able to hold my own, but just barely. May wasn't the most powerful Mage I'd ever encountered, but she bristled with energy. The Mana burst from her like wild fire and hammered against my defences again and again. She had been well trained and would have been a challenge to my previous power level. She was stronger than I was, but was unbalanced and emotional. I was weaker, but had greater motivation. No, the outcome wasn't assured at all.

I stumbled backwards under the weight of her onslaught and then responded with a strike of my own.

It landed impotently against her shield, but the impact caused her to take several steps back in shock. She hadn't expected to get hit; I went on the offensive.

With each step forward my thread got stronger. I hammered against her again and again. With each strike the Mana flared in me to a new level. The shield pulsed around me as the energy flowed from me. The Mana came quicker now and I was able to reinforce my weakened shield. I howled in joy as the shield surrounded me in my precious Mana.

A wild thread hammered the locker bay into a misshapen wreck and a second brought the ducts down from the roof. May was in full retreat now only barely able to keep up with the speed and ferocity of my attack.

With each step my power increased tenfold. The Mana literally sizzled from me in a fiery hue of power. The Mana responded to me quicker than before and with more power. It was intoxicating. I turned on May in fury and hammered my power down upon her, her thread was cast aside in the ferocity of my attack and her core laid bare.

May's eyes widened in fear as I stood over her, with a contemptuous flick of my wrist I shattered her shield and brought her to her knees. She looked up at me resolute, her face twisted in hatred and grief. There was nothing more she could do, she was now over matched and she knew it.

"Kill me!" she snarled, "Kill me the way you killed my husband and be done with this!"

"I'm not going to kill you," I intoned darkly, "I never wanted that."

"This doesn't change anything," she hissed, "I'm going to keep coming for you. You should kill me!"

May shuddered as I raised my hand, she obviously thought that I was about to change my mind and end her. Her look changed to confusion as the awareness spell swept across the room. The spell burst from my fingers like a supernova and easily consumed the room. I wasn't sure just how large I had made the effect, but it served my purposes.

It didn't take too long before I heard the explosions of two people teleporting into the room. I didn't have to turn to see who they were. May sighed in defeat and hung her head as Renee and Tychus approached from behind me.

"Take her some place safe," I growled to Tychus.

"What am I going to do with her? Tychus shrugged back.

"I don't know," I sighed, "just take her away."

"Maybe we should finish this," Tychus murmured, "She did start it."

"No!" Both Renee and I said in unison.

"Just asking," Tychus grunted, "I doubt she's going to stop coming after you."

"I'll deal with it as it becomes a problem."

Both Renee and Tychus gave me a look of disapproval but said nothing. My head was beginning to throb painfully. This was normally a sign that I'd over indulged in Mana use, but after the last few days the pain was a delightful reminder that things were back to normal.

* * * * * *

"I've got May locked away in a store room," Tychus announced gruffly, "I hit her with a disrupt spell, she's not going anywhere for a while."

We had teleported out of the basement and were holed up on the top level of the building that I was supposed to take the helicopter from.

"So what happened?" Renee asked, looking critically at Tychus. "How did she manage to grab Devon?"

"She teleported him," Tychus said.

"I guessed that," she said dryly.

"Then hit the whole roof with a shading spell. By the time I got out of range she was long gone. I had no way of tracking her." He turned to me, "If you hadn't set off that awareness blast I never would have found you."

"Effective trick," I said.

"She was one of the Primea's key operatives," he said sourly, "I should have expected it."

"Primea's operatives?" I queried.

"Used to hunt down and negate rogue Mages," Tychus explained.

"Why wasn't she sent after me earlier?"

"The Primea wouldn't allow it."

It was becoming increasingly clear that there was one hell of a lot of internal politics going on and the Primea hadn't remained as impartial as she should have been. She obviously had been supporting her son in some of his goals, or at least attempting to thwart Victor's.

"The question still remains, what are we going to do with her?" Renee said.

"Nothing," I replied, "we're going to let her go."

"Let her go?" Both Renee and Tychus were incredulous.

"Sure, why not?"

"Because she tried to kill you?" Tychus replied sarcastically.

"...and she now knows that she can't." I finished.

"That's beside the point," Renee said, "She's not going to stop coming after you."

"She can't hurt me."

"That's not the point either!" Renee snapped, "...and not necessarily true!"

"So... what do we do? Kill her?".

"No, of course not!"

"Then what? Keep her imprisoned for the rest of her life? Ask her nicely not to kill me please?"

Renee didn't answer. My sarcasm obviously wasn't appreciated; I'd pay for that later. But clearly she couldn't think of a better solution.

"That's a conversation for another day," Tychus said firmly. "Now we need to determine what we're going to do next."

"Do about what?" Renee asked.

"About the Primeacy. With the position now likely to be open soon we're going to have a war on our hands."

Renee nodded. "We're going to need to move fast. My grandfather is probably already rallying his votes."

"How does this work? Who votes? How do they vote?" I normally didn't pay attention to politics, in truth I really didn't care who the Primea was, provided that it wasn't Victor. But he was the most likely candidate now that Marcus had disappeared.

"Only the senior Masters vote," Renee said.

"And who determines who a Master is?"

"We don't have a rigid structure around that," Tychus said, "You're a Master if no one is willing to stand against the claim."

"So I could claim to be a Master and vote for myself?"

"Probably," Renee said. "What's your point? You thinking of running?"

"You can't," said Tychus, "you're an outcast."

"Don't worry, I'm not planning on running," I grinned, "Renee is."

"What?" It's not often I get the honour of seeing Renee stumped. "Why me?"

"Because you're a more moderate choice," Tychus cut in excitedly. "As much as I admire Marcus, there are those that would not follow him because of his talk about revealing ourselves to the norms."

"I'm not a Master." Renee said. "My studies have all but atrophied."

"That's not the point, neither Marcus nor Victor would challenge that point and you would draw votes from Victor's camp."

"Forget it!" she said angrily, "I'm not doing it!"

"Then we have no choice," Tychus announced ominously.

"Once my father comes back, he can sort this out."

"Where is Marcus?" I asked. Victor had thought that I had killed him. I had been pretty sure that hadn't been the case.

"I don't know," Tychus said.

"I know." Renee said softly. "He let everyone believe that he had fallen to you, but he actually had something else in mind. I'm assuming it had to do with those books you gave him. He called them a game changer."

The books on Necromancy. That didn't bode well, I'd intended to use those books to expose Victor for the murdering megalomaniac that he was, not for Marcus to disappear with them. I didn't trust Marcus enough to hope that he had the noblest of intentions with them.

"We need him back," Tychus grunted, stating the obvious.

As much as it pained me to admit it, Marcus did have a plan for how to deal with Victor and was probably the most capable among us of standing against him. I had no wish to stand against Victor again until I could counter the magic that was sustaining him. Last time we had fought he had been secure in the knowledge of his superiority, should I face him now he would strike me down and strike me down quickly.

"So what do we do?" Renee asked.

"We wait," Tychus said.

"For what?"

"The Primea to die," he stated darkly.

"Very well," I nodded, "I'm going to go to Melbourne."

"Melbourne?" Tychus snorted. "What the hell is in Melbourne?"

"My cousin. I can use this situation to my advantage and pull my cousin away from Victor, while he is distracted."

"We could use you here," Tychus murmured.

"I'm an outcast," I reminded him, "I can't do anything here. I return with my powers and my head is on the block."

Tychus wasn't happy, but he couldn't exactly fault me either. I was right. If any of the others saw that I had regained my powers they would be clamouring for my death. I had no part in the order any longer. He eventually stopped arguing and returned to take charge at the Manor whilst the Primea was incapacitated.

And for the first time in a long while I contemplated my future.

* * * * * *

"Don't go!" Renee whispered as her lips left mine.

She had thrown me against the wall the moment that Tychus had left.

"I have to."

"No you don't!" she murmured, "you want to."

"Allie needs me."

"No, she doesn't." Renee scoffed, "She's what sixteen? Seventeen now? Old enough to take care of herself."

"Maybe even eighteen," I had always had trouble keeping track of her age. To me she was my little cousin that I used to see at Christmas and Easter. I wondered about the kind of woman that she had become. The woman that Victor had made her into. What was she like? Did she still resemble the girl I once knew? I had no idea.

"I can't go with you," Renee said.

"I know." I put my arms around her.

She leaned in close. "We could just disappear." She whispered. "Now, tonight. They'll never find us."

The idea had some appeal. Find somewhere safe, somewhere far away from all this and just be with the woman I loved. I was sorely tempted to just leave it all behind, the pain, the fighting. Let others do it. There are others as capable.

"I need you," Renee urged, "I can't do this by myself."

"Then help me!"

"I can't." she said sadly.

"Why not?"

"Because there is no good ending for this." Renee replied darkly, "I can see only your death in this. Either at my father or grandfather's hand. I don't want that. You don't want that."

"Of course not, but Allie deserves to make the choice herself."

"She's made her choice. You need to make yours!"

I didn't answer her.

"You've already made your choice haven't you." Her eyes narrowed, "Go on then, leave me."

"I'll be back," I promised.

"No, you won't," she sighed. "And I'll already be gone."

I often wondered what would have happened had I taken Renee up on her offer. Would we have lived happily ever after as husband and wife? Would we have had children? In my quieter moments I often dream of this. It brings me peace and solace to think of a life that I cast away.

"Devon…please." Renee whispered.

Regret is a powerful emotion, more powerful than hate, sometimes even more powerful than love. It is the knife that slips between the plates of your armour and brings you down. Regret will cause you to do things that you do not wish to do. To think things that you don't want to think about. Regret is the bane of mankind, it brings discord when there should be peace and it brings pain when the wound has long since healed.

"I can't…" I whispered, "I just can't."

"Devon, I'm…" Renee started, but I cut her off. I often wonder what she would have told me had I not. She looked and me strangely as if she was judging something. Her expression went dark and the she wouldn't look me directly in the eyes.

"Then go. "Go off and find your place to die. I don't care anymore. I don't need you. I can do this on my own."

My decision not to run away with Renee still haunts

me. Did I make the right choice? Did I even have a choice or are we merely following our predestined fate? I chose to go after Allie and that choice may very well have led to the end of civilisation as we know it. Mine is the hand that casts down mankind, not in anger, nor in hate, but in love – misplaced though it had been. And I will be forever cursed by it.

CHAPTER SEVEN

The journey to Melbourne would not be difficult. I was far more powerful now than when I had made my original trek north. What had previously taken me four or five teleport jumps I could now do in one. I hadn't measured my range yet, but the outer limits of my Scry range were impressive.

I hadn't seen Renee since our last conversation. She had left Paris and hadn't told me where she was going, but it was obvious that she had chosen to remove herself from the whole situation. I couldn't blame her. This was a family matter for her and despite her vocal hatred of her grandfather I knew that deep down she was conflicted – the man had raised her after all.

I packed lightly, just a small backpack. Hopefully wouldn't be on the road for that long. Most of my belongings had been stored by Renee when I had returned from Poland. I was able to find my laptop and other personal effects. Against my better judgement I kept the mobile phone that Renee had given me so I could be contacted should she so desire.

I didn't linger long in Paris. I couldn't risk being seen by another of our kind. Now that my powers had returned I assumed that the death sentence also had returned with it.

I passed through Europe and into India with just three jumps. I was unable to make the jump directly across the bay of Bengal, so I deviated southwards into Sri Lanka. From Colombo I jumped straight onto the mainland of Malaysia and helped myself to a hotel room in Jakarta. From there I knew it wouldn't be too difficult to get back into Australia. Three or four jumps later I would be home.

On my original journey north I had been forced to island hop between Broome and Jakarta as I didn't have the range. Where I was unable to find an island that suited my needs, I used a commercial fishing boat or ocean liner to jump to. Now, none of that would be necessary. I could make the jump directly from Jakarta to Broome and from there I could make my way south to Melbourne.

While my new Scrying abilities were impressive I still doubted that they were at the same level as Victor. I could not yet teleport straight from Singapore to Melbourne, but it wasn't that far from it. Maybe with enough time. I wasn't sure if my new strength had been caused by my burnout or if I had achieved this level prior, but had never needed to test it. In the end it didn't matter. I was becoming more powerful and that was all that mattered.

The actual jump into Australia was uneventful. I didn't feel a sense of relief as I walked once again on my homeland. It was just another place to me now. I made my way across the deserts of central Australia and down into central New South Wales. I didn't particularly want to teleport straight into Melbourne. I was sure that my arrival would be noticed and didn't want that just yet.

Victor would have left someone watching over his prize. Stealing Allie from under his nose would be difficult. The only advantage I had was surprise. I was trusting that the news of my recovery hadn't reached him yet. Or if it had, that he would be too busy facilitating the exchange of the Primeaship over to himself to care.

I found a cargo truck heading into Melbourne and stowed away in the back. This way I could sneak into Melbourne without anyone detecting me. Teleporting myself into the cramped confines of the rear of the truck proved easier than I had anticipated. There was a great deal of space available on top of the cargo and all I needed to lie flat on top of them. My skills with teleport had obviously improved much since the last I had tried to teleport into a moving object. Then again, this truck wasn't moving anywhere near as fast as the plane had been.

My arrival into Melbourne wasn't the cause of celebration. I did not arrive in my hometown in splendour and triumph. I sneaked into it like a thief in the night, hiding under the cloak of darkness and the deceit of my powers. I was careful to limit the use of my powers once inside the city limits. Nothing that would draw attention to myself.

A quick teleport out of the truck and into an empty

street off the highway gave me my first glance of my beloved city. It had been almost three years since I had last seen it. It hadn't changed much.

It wasn't until I reached the city centre that I realised just how much I had missed my home. It was a part of who I was and would be forever dear to me. It was perhaps fitting that my quest would end in the very same place that it had begun. I glanced around the street outside my father's old apartment with detached interest. I didn't linger here, my search was not yet over and I didn't have the luxury of self-indulgence in memory. That wouldn't be healthy anyway. Some things are better left in the past.

I pondered where to begin my search. Allie could be anywhere, but something told me she would be in the city. I procured a vacant hotel room and began my surveillance. I decided to use a slender Scry thread to do my searching. This would mean that my vision would be impaired, but the thread would be harder to detect, especially over distances.

Locating Allie didn't actually prove that difficult. She was in the last place I would have expected to find her, and yet once I found it was the most obvious place I should have looked. It was a small unassuming apartment in Carlton. It was an apartment I knew well. It had been Renee's.

It was difficult to get a feel of my cousin through the Scry thread. She seemed so different from the young girl that I had known, but I knew from experience how a Scry spell could warp your perception. When we gaze upon our kind we don't exactly see their features. We see their Mana signature, and the more powerful the Mage the more we see their power, and not them. Allie was powerful, very powerful indeed. And she wasn't alone.

Her companion was one of our kind. It was difficult to get a good read on him. He was obviously there as a body guard and certainly seemed powerful enough to fit the role. I was sure that Victor would only have placed his most trusted underling to protect his cherished prize. He would be difficult to deal with, and what's more I couldn't rely on the situation not getting out of hand with Allie. I would need to rely on my subtlety. This was unfortunate; subtlety isn't my strong suit.

* * * * * *

It took several days of surveillance and three swaps of hotel rooms before I was able to find a chance to talk to Allie. I had learned that she was attending Melbourne University, which meant that she was almost never alone. What time she spent away from the university she spent with her bodyguard.

There was something that wasn't quite right about him, but I couldn't place my finger on it. I was sure that I'd met him before but for the life of me I couldn't place where. I just had this nagging feeling that something was very wrong. I would need to be cautious. If I could just get Allie alone, I was sure I could convince her to come with me.

It wasn't until late Thursday night that I was able to get my opportunity. Allie appeared to have had a late class that day. There were many parks and nooks throughout the campus. During her travels between the buildings it would be possible to talk to her somewhat privately. If Allie followed her usual route she would pass through a park area on her way to the tramline she used to get home.

I teleported onto one of the campus buildings and dropped down to road level, lurking behind a series of trees to remain out of sight. Allie would emerge through a set of double doors and make her way across the park any second now.

This was the first time that I had seen her directly since I arrived. The last time I had seen her I had been involved in a fire-fight with the Melbourne police department and Aaron Chen. She had been confused and frightened and so very, very young.

She didn't look so young now. She looked tired and had a tightness around her features that hadn't been there before. Her eyes were dark and cold. It's possible that the scowl on her face could have been caused by her studies, but I got the impression that it was more than that. It looked permanent.

She made her way across the road and into the park. I walked out from behind the trees and fell into step behind her, letting out a slight flair in my Mana signature to alert her to my presence. She reacted with predictable speed but an unexpected level of power. A shield sprang around her instantly and she spun around to face the threat. Her eyes narrowed down as she scanned the environment looking for whatever had spooked her.

Her shield was very strong. It radiated power and was very, very complex. Victor had obviously trained her well in the three years that he had her under his tutelage. Her eyes widened as she spotted me. I wasn't sure what I must have looked like now or if she actually recognised me, but her face immediately lost colour and I thought for a second that she was going to make a run for it.

I didn't want to scare her any further so I slowly walked towards her with my hands held before me. I hadn't raised a shield or made any move to protect myself. This may have been a mistake. With the speed at which she was able to raise a shield, she would easily be able to strike me down before I could raise my own.

Allie trembled as I got closer and her face fell into a mask of indecision and fear. She was looking at me as if I were death itself coming for her. Something had seriously scared the poor girl. What the hell had Victor done to this woman?

"Allie," I whispered.

"No, no... no, " Allie murmured, taking a hesitant step back.

"Wait, please!" I begged. She looked poised for flight and whilst I could probably stop her, I didn't want to do anything that might scare her off.

Unfortunately I didn't get a chance to say much further as a shout from across the plaza interrupted us.

Allie's face fell as she realised who had called. It was her damned bodyguard. Where the hell had he come from? He had obviously been waiting for her and had been alerted by the use of Mana. Damn! I'd missed my opportunity.

He was running towards us with a shield raised. The shield didn't appear to be very well constructed. This didn't count for much though, on occasion I'd used a roughshod shield as a form of deception to lure my opponents into a hasty action. I wasn't going to fall for such an obvious trick.

"Leave her alone!" he yelled as he barrelled through the park.

A shield sprang up around me in response to the implied threat and I turned to Allie looking for confirmation. Allie was still staring at me as if I was a ghost. Her bodyguard appeared to be on a collision course with me. I think he intended to tackle me to the ground. A thread lanced out from him.

With a flick of my wrist I sent a thread to intercept his. My thread easily knocked his aside and barrelled through to strike against his shield. The flare of my Mana thread impacting against his shield caused Allie to physically flinch. To my surprise the shield collapsed as if it were made of butter and my thread hit the guy on the side of the neck.

It had happened so fast. I hadn't meant to actually down the guy, merely to keep him from crashing into me. I'd known his shield was weak, but I had never expected it to be that weak! What kind of guard was he?

Allie's eyes narrowed in rage. She took a step towards me as if she was going to attack me. I glanced from her to the man I had just taken down in disbelief.

Allie let out a shriek accompanied by a burst of Mana. The primal blast hit my shield buffering it. She took another step towards me. I couldn't help but take a step back in the face of her anger. Power was flowing from her in waves. I wasn't sure I'd be able to defend myself against her should she attack.

Just when I thought a thread was about to come in my direction a strangled sob escaped Allie's lips. She turned from me and ran over to the fallen man. She gathered him up in her arms and cradled his head against her chest. Tears were pouring down her cheeks as she looked at me.

"Is this my punishment?" she sobbed at me, spitting her words at me, "I killed our father, so you kill him! It's not fair! You should have taken it out on me!"

"What are you talking about? Victor lied to you. You didn't kill my Dad!"

"No! Our dad! He was my dad too and I killed him!"

"Allie, please!" I stammered, "you didn't do it. You don't know what you're saying! You weren't responsible! It's not your fault!"

"Yes!" Allie hissed. "Yes it is! I confronted him about it! I went to him and asked him. I asked him directly if he was my father and he said no!"

Her face twisted with hate as she looked at me as

her tears ran dry. The man in her arms wasn't moving. I couldn't tell if he was still even alive. A small trail of blood ran down from the corner of his mouth. I couldn't see if his chest was moving or not. It didn't look good though; the Mana in his body was gone.

"He lied to me!" she snarled, "he said no! That he wasn't my father! But I could tell. I could tell he was lying! Why did he have to lie?"

The sound of sirens rang out in the distance. Someone must have called the cops. The sound was getting closer, but I didn't care. I wasn't going to leave Allie like this. Let them come, I'd deal with them later.

"I didn't mean to do it!" She wailed, "it just... happened... and I didn't know what to do. I didn't want to do it. It just happened."

I didn't want to hear this. This just couldn't be true, but staring into her hateful eyes I recognised truth when I heard it. I didn't want to believe it, but Allie obviously did. She believed it with every fibre of her soul. In my darkest dreams I had never thought that my reunion with my cousin would go like this. How had this gone so wrong?

"I killed your Dad!" Allie snarled, "... and now you've taken your revenge!

"Justin had nothing to do with this," she continued as she rose from the now still body. "You should have taken it out on me! I'm the one responsible. Justin had nothing to do with anything!"

She took several steps towards me and my shield

unconsciously strengthened itself in response to the threat. I didn't have much time to get out of the way though. Allie shrieked at me and a thread arced out from her raised hands and hammered against my shield.

The impact knocked the breath out of me. She was so powerful! I was amazed that my shield had been able to absorb the shock without sending me tumbling to my knees. Several more blows rang out and impacted against my shield. This was all going wrong, and it was going wrong very quickly.

So far my shield was holding up but I was expending more and more energy to keep it held. Allie appeared to be getting angrier and angrier by the second that my shield hadn't failed. For my part I was still reeling, I couldn't comprehend that the one inflicting this damage was my cousin… or my sister or whatever she was to me.

I deflected her next strike more on impulse than design and sent her thread careening into one of the trees that lined the park. The impact uprooted the tree and sent it tumbling down onto the side road and into a series of parked cars. Due to the laws of comedic timing a car alarm went off several seconds after the tree hit the ground.

"Allie, wait!" I called out, but I wasn't sure that she had even heard me over her fury. She swung her thread back with another primal shriek and if I hadn't blocked it would have smashed my shield into pieces. I hadn't counter attacked yet, I just didn't want to hurt her. She obviously had no such restrictions.

All reason and all conscious thought had left her. I could see she was intent on only one goal – my complete destruction. I stood amazed as she looped a thread through a car and lifted it easily from the ground to pummel me. My shield was barely able to absorb the concussive force of a car hammering against me again and again. The weight of the car added extra power to her strike. My shield sparked as the impact of the car glanced off me and the shock sent me reeling. I wouldn't be able to absorb this kind of punishment for very long.

I stumbled and was forced to focus on keeping my footing. If I fell and she brought the car down on me I'd be finished. Unfortunately after another glancing blow I tripped and fell over a tiled area. Allie immediately took the opportunity to bring the car smashing down on top of me.

The sight of a two tonne car barrelling down onto you is one that tends to stick in your memory. I threw everything I had into my shield in the attempt to be able to at least survive the inevitable crater that her strike would create. The noise the collision made upon impact was stunning and sent ringing through my ears. The car, which was mostly wreckage at this stage, collided with my shield with stupendous force but the shield held! I was amazed, but it held!

I didn't have time to celebrate this fact that as I was just recovering when a second car came out of nowhere and smashed at me from my left side. This one was much heavier. It was one of those stupid four-wheel drive land rovers that city dwellers buy to prove that they have no Idea of what is an appropriate car to drive in the city.

The impact sent me flying across the pavement. I'd just regained my footing when the first wreck of a car collided with my shield again. I couldn't have defended myself even if I'd had the opportunity to try. I didn't even try – I simply attempted to throw myself out of the way. I almost made it too. Due to the angle of my leap both cars glanced off my shield rather than hitting me head on and smashed into the ground in front of me. The tiles shattered like wafers and exploded into tiny shards of gravel. A large rumbling echoed throughout the park as the ground beneath me churned under the impact.

Allie didn't let up in her attack and both cars were heading back towards me now. The first car looked more like a floating wreck of car parts as most of the external panels had been torn from the husk. The second car fared a little better and mostly resembled its original construction. How both cars hadn't exploded yet was beyond me. If this were a movie the car would have exploded into flames at the moment of first impact and then both car alarms would have gone off.

I was prepared for her follow up strike and deflected her shot causing it to hit the ground. Hers was an unusual way of fighting that I hadn't encountered before. By using a crushingly heavy object Allie had forced me onto the back foot and I was unable to go on the offensive. It was quite effective. I would have to remember this.

The second impact caused more rumbling beneath

my feet. The park looked relatively stable to me, but I was beginning to have my doubts. Was there an underground complex beneath the park?

Allie would have struck at me a third time, but unfortunately for her she was interrupted by a large crunching noise as the ground literally disappeared under my feet. I fell several metres and then slid along a large slice of concrete that had been unearthed beneath me.

I slid on my back with only rock and dirt for my companions until a savage thump indicated that I'd reached the bottom.

I couldn't see much as the air was filled with debris and dirt. If I hadn't had a shield around me I probably would be choking on the cloud of dust that surrounded me. I reached down and was able to determine that I'd landed on something metal and I was surrounded by broken glass. I think a car had broken my fall.

Sweeping the rubble away I concluded that I had indeed landed on a car, a red commodore by the looks of things. I'd sheered straight through the windscreen. Inside I could vaguely make out red leather seats. This seemed like an odd choice for interior upholstery. The bigger question was what the hell was a car doing down here anyway? Now that the dust had settled a little I noticed with some degree of alarm that I was in the worst possible place I could be. I'd fallen into a car park! I can't be in a car park! People try to kill me in car parks!

The fight had created a rift about ten metres in width in the roof above me. I suspected from the amount of debris that I may have dropped through two levels of car park. The only good thing about this was that the fall had created a forced interlude to the fight.

I used my powers to telekinetically leap through the rift and into the air. Allie had obviously been expecting this as she launched a thread at me. I was able to avoid this though, by leaping higher. I timed my jump to land just in front of her.

"Okay Allie, Enough crap!" I snarled as I landed, "You're coming with me."

"No, I'm not!" she hissed defiantly. "If you're going to kill me, you're going to have to do it here in front of all these people!"

I glanced around nervously. I hadn't realised until Allie had pointed it out just how many people had gathered around the scene. Three ambulances had arrived on as well as numerous police cars. A small team of police officers had mustered at the perimeter with guns aimed at us.

"I'm not going to kill you," I murmured. "Allie, please."

"My name isn't Allie anymore," she snarled, "its Alisha! Allie was a child and that child is dead!"

We were both very aware that we had an audience. A policeman was tentatively making his way towards us with his gun raised. He wasn't mucking about. Allie and I both glanced in his direction but neither of us were concerned. He couldn't hurt us. He was simply the first of many. I could see that there was a crowd quickly forming around us of police and emergency teams.

"Get down on the ground!" the cop called, "Now!"

"Allie," I pleaded.

"Stop calling me that!" she snarled, the Mana flaring across her shield in response.

The cop called for us to hit the ground again, both of us ignored him. A gunshot bounced off the shield surrounding my head. The bastard had shot me.

"I'll deal with you in a second!" I snarled at the cop as I turned to face Allie again.

Allie had used the distraction to strike at me again, her thread looped around and struck in full in the chest sending me tumbling across the ground. I got to my feet in rage and bolted towards her. This would end now! I would take her by force and make her listen to me!

I'm not sure how many cops shot me as I ran across the park. I'm not even sure that I heard the shots. The bullets ricocheted off my shield. I swung a thread at Allie and sent a second arcing out towards the police officer who had fired first. I intentionally aimed low taking his feet out from under him. I don't think he was seriously hurt, but he didn't get back up. I doubted he was dead though.

Allie easily blocked my attack and launched into an attack of her own. She had been well trained. Her attacks were short, sharp and effective. It was obvious however that she hadn't sparred as often as I had. My instincts were better.

Power wise she was my match. This was astounding! I had never met someone who could meet me head to head in that area. Even Marcus and Victor didn't attempt that, they use less power but a more effective thread to match me. They gained strength through skill rather than strength through sheer force.

Fighting against Allie was like two bulls going head to head in a narrow alley. They couldn't attack from the side and so they simply collided face to face. The impacts sent shockwaves rippling through the threads as our strikes collided. The gunshots hit us both as we fought, but both of us sent out stray threads to thin the ranks of the police. It didn't take too long before they fell back to the relative safety of the car line and left Allie and I to it. Unhindered Allie and I increased our assault on each other.

It took me a good few minutes before I realised the truth. I wasn't going to be able to overpower her. I could either kill her, or fall before her. Those were my options and neither option was appealing. I wasn't sure what was going through Allie's mind. Was she too enraged to think clearly about what was going to happen after this fight? Or was it that she simply didn't care?

The problem was that I did care. I had no intention of killing Allie. However I also knew from experience just how powerful the desire for revenge could be and I knew the white hot rage that can be induced as you watched your loved ones struck down.

I hadn't meant for the boy to be seriously hurt and in truth I didn't know if he had survived our encounter. His body was no longer on the ground where it had fallen. I assumed that it was currently in an ambulance heading for the hospital. I took this as a good sign, then again perhaps not. Allie would not stop her assault and would not stop to listen. There was nothing I could do now. I could not physically overpower her and I couldn't reason with her. This left only one viable solution – escape.

The trick was going to be to be able to escape without getting my molecules spread across a kilometre radius. That would take some doing. I wouldn't dare try to teleport whilst in the middle of combat and I couldn't incapacitate Allie long enough to make my escape.

In the end I used the rift that she had made into the car park below us. I launched an aggressive assault against my cousin and then leapt into the hole while she went on the defensive. The irony of fleeing into a car park for safety was not lost on me. The moment my feet touched the car park ground I sent out my Scry thread . I didn't care where it went, any solid ground away from the conflict would do. I knew that she would follow me so I put to good use the trick that I had learned from May in Paris.

The shading spell went off as soon as I began to teleport. Due to the static thrown up by the spell I couldn't see what Allie was up to. No doubt she had been preparing herself to descend into the car park. Once I had completed the first teleport, I teleported again, this time to my latest hotel room.

I needed time to think on how best to proceed. It might have been best had I simply admitted defeat and return to try to find Renee, but I wasn't prepared to admit that yet. I'm a fool sometimes, I really am. No, I can turn this around. Behold – the eternal optimist.

* * * * * *

My encounter with Allie kept going over and over in my head. The fact of the matter was that I had acted rashly and had mishandled things. This revelation didn't make it any easier to cope with. Who had that other guy been? He obviously hadn't been a bodyguard. He wouldn't have fallen so easily if he had been. That shield had been so badly constructed I was prepared to believe that he had been an apprentice. Why hadn't I seen that earlier? If he wasn't a bodyguard who was he? A friend? A classmate? Given Allie's reaction he was possibly even a boyfriend. Although of course Allie was far too young for that.

No, no she wasn't I reflected bitterly. She was eighteen. It was entirely possible that I had just killed her lover. The thought sent chills down my spine. She would never forgive me now. I had just killed my sister's lover.

That was the other thing that was haunting me. I was almost ready to believe that she was my sister. She certainly thought it was true. There was only one person who could confirm or deny this. There was only one person who was there, who could confirm my father's infidelity and Allie's parentage. Only one person I trusted enough to believe her unconditionally. My mother.

My palms were sweaty as I stood before the door. I

clenched my fingers several times before I was able to finally draw the courage to rap my knuckles against the doorframe.

It was late. It had taken quite a while for me to work up the nerve to come here. I heard the click of the security chain sliding into place, then the door opened slightly.

"Who's there?" A voice whispered through the gap. It had been a long time since I had heard that voice.

"Hi, Mum. It's me."

At first there was no response. I wasn't sure if she was even going to open the door. Nothing happened for several seconds then the door closed and the chain was released. The door slowly opened and my mother gestured for me to enter.

She didn't say anything as I walked into the corridor towards the lounge room. Everything was just as I remembered it. It was like I had just walked into my house after school. I could almost see my best friends Tony and Sarah lounging on the couch, laughing at some stupid joke I had made. It was so real it hurt.

Mum asked if I wanted anything to drink. I declined. The cat glanced at me before yawning and rolling over. He was looking a little greyer around the edges and a little more mottled than I remembered, but he was still essentially the same kitten that I had gotten on my 14th birthday.

"You're back," she stated as she settled herself into her chair. There was a half-finished glass of scotch on the table beside her.

"Yeah," I nodded lamely. There didn't seem to be much else to say.

"Why?"

"I need to ask you a question," I started hesitantly.

"Ask your question, then go." she said. "It's late."

Mum and I had never really gotten over the first time I had had to flee the country. I had visited her briefly the last time I had been in Melbourne and it hadn't gone well. She was still refusing to even look at me properly.

"Is Allie my sister?" I asked softly. "Did my father have an affair?"

She sighed softly and took a sip of her drink. She turned to face me, her eyes piercing me with her judging expression. I wasn't sure what she was looking for, but it was obvious that she hadn't found it.

"I don't know," she said eventually.

She was lying. I could see it in her face. She knew but just didn't want to tell me.

"Mum. It's important."

"What do you want from me?"

"I want the truth. Is Allie my sister?"

"Yes." The words came out so softly, yet they sounded so loud to my ears. In one word my mother had confirmed my worst fears. Allie was my sister and she had killed my father. She had killed my father because she had been unable to control her powers. She had been unable to control her powers because I had failed her. Victor was right – this was my fault.

I had been the cause of all of this. Every decision I

had made, no matter how right they had seemed at the time had led to this.

"How did you find out?" Mum whispered as she pulled another sip from her glass. A chunk of ice clinked in her drink.

"She told me." I replied casually.

"He wasn't a bad man, your father. He had his weaknesses like everyone does. I'm sure in his way he was able to justify it, but I could never forgive him."

"No, I don't imagine you could."

"To his credit, he never sought my forgiveness," Mum said quietly, "and never sought to hide his shame in lies."

"Allie's mother chose to raise Allie without knowing her father. It might have been better had she never known, especially now. It's sad that she'll never get a chance to know her true father."

My mother couldn't have been more right, but of course she didn't know that. It was sad but for reasons far beyond a daughter never knowing her father. My father's death had hit me hard, I couldn't imagine what that and the added guilt would have done to Allie.

"Do you have what you need now? Is there anything more I can do for you?" It wasn't a genuine offer.

This was obviously an unpleasant topic for my mother. I had no idea how she was coping with his death. I hadn't exactly been around after he had died. I knew that she had attended his funeral, but I knew little more than that. I hadn't exactly been in the best mental state myself.

I had attended the funeral under the cloak of an invisibility spell. I couldn't reveal myself to the world. I was wanted by the police for questioning in relation to my fight with Aaron Chen. There had been police in attendance, presumably waiting for me. My apparent lack of attendance had led to an argument between me and my friend Tony. He had been close with my father. My last words with Tony hadn't been good ones. It seemed that no matter where I turned I was souring my relationships with friends and family. Soon there would be no one left.

"No," I said softly in answer to her question. I had everything I needed.

There was no point in trying for reconciliation. I had hurt Mum too badly when I had left the last time. She hadn't known the reason of course, couldn't know the reason. It was better that she remain out of it. It was perhaps better that she should curse me rather than mourn me – that emotion might be easier for her to deal with, especially with what was about to happen.

I've never claimed to be able to predict the future, I had enough trouble figuring out what was going on with the present, but I could see trouble when I saw it. I'd seen it enough to recognise it. If Allie's boyfriend had died from my strike there would be nothing that would stop her from hunting for me. I knew this for fact. She would be like me – if someone struck Renee down I would move heaven and earth for vengeance. It would be better that when that judgment come that I be nowhere near anyone I loved.

"I'll go." I sighed as I got to my feet. I scratched the cat playfully around the ear, avoided it's half-hearted attempted to remove three of my fingers and left.

Mum didn't get up to see me out. It was strange leaving the home of my childhood like this, knowing that in all likelihood I would not be returning. This place that had played such an important part of my childhood was forever closed to me now.

Before I left, I leaned in and kissed Mum on the cheek. She flinched as my lips touched her flesh. I reached into my pocket and placed an object on the table beside her glass. It was the large diamond that Victor had created. Mum didn't appear to notice. It would do her more good than it would do me, should she find a way to sell it. I'd carried this thing around most of Europe and pretty much all of Asia. It seemed appropriate to leave it here. I'd have no need for it anyway. Once Allie tracked me down I'd have no need for anything.

You can't live in the past and my future was very quickly running out. I wasn't scared by the prospect of the end. In fact I can't say that the idea didn't have some appeal. I just wanted all this over. I should never have come back. I should have done as Renee had begged me to do and just disappeared into the unknown – leave everything behind. Renee had been right. That would have been the smart thing to do.

I wasn't sure what to do from here, so I went to the last place a man should go when they're suffering a mortality crisis. I went to a bar. The local pub hadn't changed much since I had last been here. Still filled with the usual riff raff doing the usual things. I ordered a beer and sat at the bar and tried not to think about what to do next.

This proved to be no small task. Fortunately the bar was crowded and noisy so there was plenty to occupy my attention. A TV was playing a selection of music videos. I don't get the music these days, but then again I guess I have actually very little in common with the rest of my generation.

"Authorities are still inquiring into the disturbance that took place today at Melbourne University." The TV blared expectantly over the noise. Someone must have changed the channel.

"Turn that off," one the bar jocks called.

"No, I want to watch this," was the reply. I agreed with the first guy. Turn it off.

"Fourteen Injured and four dead, including three police officers. No one seems to have any idea what occurred," the announcer continued as the vision flicked to aerial shots of our fight. They'd filmed it! I was able to make out Allie and me as we fought across the park. Fortunately at this distance it was impossible to make out our faces. We were moving too fast for the camera to frame us properly.

Between the wreckage of the cars and the collateral damage to the park, Allie and I had managed to make that place look like a war zone. I flinched as I saw the impact that had broken a rift in the ground beneath me. It looked all the more impressive from an aerial view.

It was funny but the impact looked all the more devastating when you couldn't see the Mana threads causing the damage. It looked more random and definitely more savage.

"That's gotta be fake!" one of the crowd called.

"Naw man, this is Channel 10, they wouldn't report it if it wasn't true," came the reply. "Besides it's on all the channels."

It took me several seconds to realise that the crowd had grown silent as they watched the coverage with varied expressions of disbelief and fear.

"The police would like anyone with more information about this tragic event to come forward." The reporter finished with her glossy smile. The news report was replaced by a series of advertisements. The silence remained for several minutes until eventually one of the sceptics called bullshit again.

"It's got to be some kind of marketing campaign for a movie. Cars don't just throw themselves at people."

"It's obviously fake!" another voice said. The TV channels are just in on it."

"I'd pay to see that movie," someone added, "looks awesome."

This was followed by a series of snickers from the crowd. It really is amazing at how quickly the human mind will leap to the most logical conclusion. Once someone had suggested a rational idea the tension in the room dissipated and the noise started up again.

I ordered another drink. It seemed that no matter

where I went the consequences of my actions would follow me. I wasn't worried about some bar flies in a local pub. What worried me was that one of our kind would see the report and trouble would follow. There would be those amongst my kind that would recognise me from the blurred images displayed on the TV screen. It's possible that this time I had gone too far.

* * * * * *

I was on my third drink before I realised that I was being watched. I didn't recognise the man doing the surveillance, but I could tell from his furtive glances that he recognised me. He seemed to be struggling with something, I could see him arguing silently with himself and wringing his hands together beneath the table.

I wondered briefly if I should approach him, but decided that I didn't care enough to investigate further. If and when he came to me, I'd deal with it.

About ten minutes later he made his way across the crowded bar and up to my seat. He was walking like he was walking to his death; his left hand shook slightly. It took him several seconds to work up the courage to speak.

"Do you want something?" I grunted irritably, without turning around. I could see him well enough through the reflection on the mirror behind the bar.

"No, no," he stammered quickly. I thought he was about to flee. He had visibly flinched when I spoke.

"You're... him… aren't you?" He eventually got out.

I turned around to face him. He went white as he finally got a good look at me.

"Holy shit, it is you," he whispered.

"Do I know you?"

"No, well, yes. We met a few years ago, right here in fact."

This raised an eyebrow. I didn't exactly frequent this bar much. I'd only just turned eighteen when I had killed Vin and had to go on the run. In fact there was only one person that I'd actually met in this bar...

I went cold. There had been a man whom I had met here. My friend, Tony and I had challenged him to a game of pool and I had used my powers to cheat. When it came time to pay he had threatened to bash my brains in with a tyre iron.

He had assumed that I was young and impressionable and hadn't expected me to stand up for myself. The unfortunate outcome was that not only did I stand up for myself, I lost control of my powers and seriously hurt him. He was older and greyer, but it was definitely the same man standing before me.

"What do you want?" I said cautiously.

If he was seeking revenge it was not going to go well for him. Previously when I had thought I had killed him I had felt guilty for my loss of control. I would feel no such guilt should I be forced to kill him now.

"I thought I dreamed you," the man whispered, "My boy said that I had been hit by a car."

He'd had his apprentice with him that night. Tony had instructed the boy to say that he'd been hit by a car in the car park. That hadn't been the case though; he'd been hit by a poorly constructed Mana thread wielded by a boy who should have known better.

"I knew though," the man continued, "I knew. I remembered you. I see them eyes of yours at night some time."

"So what do you want?" I muttered darkly.

"I needed to know. I was starting to think that perhaps I was crazy, but it's true. I saw you. If you're real, then those eyes are real," he reasoned.

What the hell do I do about this? Do I kill him now to preserve my secret? Is that what I'm supposed to do? Both Marcus and Victor would probably advise me yes, but I didn't want to do that. The man must have spotted the look of consideration on my face.

"I won't keep you," he said hastily, backing away from the bar, "I just needed to know... I needed to know."

I watched him depart hurriedly. It was probably safe to just let him go. Who was he going to tell? No one would believe him anyway.

A chill passed over the back of my neck as I watched him leave. I had to check the urge to throw a shield around myself. If I didn't know better I would have attributed that chill to Mana use in the area. What the hell? Was it possible that he was a Mage?

I had used Mana to bring him down, was it possible that this had triggered his capabilities? No – the odds of that were so astronomical that it defied belief. Fewer than one in one-hundred-thousand people have the capability to become a Mage and maybe one in ten of those ever develops full-blown Mana manipulation capabilities.

It wasn't until the door to the bar blew in, sending patrons scrambling for cover that I figured out just what had triggered the feeling of the threat. It hadn't been the man, I had been stupid for even entertaining the idea. I had felt a Scry thread passing over me. Someone had been searching for me and they had just found me.

The shockwave of the blast washed over me and sent a ringing through my ears. Instantly a shield sprang up around me to shelter me from the blast but no such protection had been afforded to the people beside me. They were thrown aside like drift wood in the path of a tornado. The thread hit one of the bars in full force and smashed a stack of glasses into shards, covering the floor and patrons in broken glass.

The bar room exploded into flame and I saw through the smoke my most tragic failure. She walked through the wreckage as a goddess would through a burning temple. Her face hard as stone. I saw death in her eyes and knew it to be my own. Allie had come for me.

CHAPTER EIGHT

Allie didn't say anything, she stood amongst the wreckage that she had created and stared at me, waiting for my move. Time seemed to move in slow motion as I watched as the surviving patrons of the bar struggle to get up and run for it. Allie ignored them, focussing her deadly gaze upon me. I carefully stood up. A cold feeling ran down the back of my spine.

"I don't want this," I called out to her. I knew it would be useless to talk her down. I had seen that look in another young Mage's face before and I knew just how futile it would have been to try to talk me out of getting my revenge. But I had to try.

"You killed him!" she snarled.

"I know." I whispered. My hushed voice sounded strangely loud in this inferno of a room.

"I'm going to kill you now," Allie announced.

I nodded as I prepared myself for her assault. This would be a vicious fight, there was a good chance that I would not survive it.

Allie began her attack predictably with a thread straight to me as she charged across the barroom floor. Her face was twisted into a mask of anger, loss and rage.

I almost considered letting her strike me down, but unfortunately the Mana had other ideas. With a savage crackle of sparks Allie's thread struck ineffectually against my shield.

All I could see in her face was the little girl that had been so eager to open presents on Christmas morning, the girl who had giggled with delight when she had been presented with a kitten. But the little girl that I had once known had been forever destroyed and I feared that I was the one responsible for her loss.

I took several steps back as the impacts struck me, my shield wavered dangerously but still held. Furious that her attacks had been repelled, Allie increased her assault. I couldn't do that again, I would be forced to defend myself.

"I don't want to do this!" I repeated as one of her threads passed overhead.

"I don't care!" Allie shrieked, "I hate you!"

As I deflected her attack I glanced at my sister, in the light of the fire now raging through the room. The inferno had now reached the roof and smouldering pieces of insulation and roof tile were falling down on us. Allie's eyes glowed in the fire of her Mana. Her irises glittered in the darkness of her face as she stared her hatred like daggers into me. Her stranger's face was harsh and her eyes were cold. I wondered if these were the eyes that my father had seen when he had been struck down or were they of a new devil created by my own hand.

"I'm not going to fight you," I announced.

Allie's next strike knocked out one of the supporting beams for the roof and brought a fair degree of the roof down upon me. My shield absorbed most of the fall, but I was forced to throw myself away from the rest by scrambling over the bar.

Ash was falling from the ceiling between us and it didn't look like there was much left to hold the roof up. Should that come down we'd have a hard time surviving. I'd already had to modulate my shield twice to reflect the heat of the burning building.

Allie attacked again, spinning and sending a thread my way, I easily dodged the thread but was caught unawares went she launched a volley of flame straight at me. My shield easily absorbed the impact of the flame.

It's actually rather ineffective to fight with flame in a Mage fight. There's a reason why we usually fight with Telekinesis. Flame is just too easily absorbed by our shields. Unfortunately I wasn't Allie's target. The alcohol rack behind me was. Her blast shattered dozens of bottles and set them on fire. Allie was certainly determined to bring this place down.

The subsequent explosion showered me in broken glass and alcohol, which then, just to add injury to insult, burst into flame across the surface of my shield. What the hell? Hiding behind the bar wasn't a very safe place to be and yet it's the first place that the hero jumps behind when there's some kind of fight scene in a bar. Is there nothing accurate in action movies?

The end result of Allie's attack was that a good

portion of the left side of my shield was now on fire. I could feel the heat through the shield and had to modulate it again to prevent being scalded. I knew that the flame wouldn't last that long once the alcohol had been consumed, but it was rather disconcerting being on fire. It wasn't a pleasant experience.

I flicked my arm twice to attempt to dislodge the flame but this only had the unfortunate effect of setting one of the miraculously untouched bar towels on fire as droplets of flame flicked from my wrist to the alcohol soaked towel.

Allie didn't let up her attack. Several threads impacted against me as I struggled to remove myself from the inferno that was now the bar. The threads knocked the wind out of me and sent me tumbling back into that raging inferno.

I grunted as I pulled myself back to my feet. I was pretty sure most of the surface of my shield was now on fire. It was certainly obscuring my vision enough so at least my head was. I winced as my side complained at the assault. Allie's last hit must have been harder than the others. Then I realised what had happened. I'd modulated my shield to protect myself more from the fire than a physical strike and her last hit and gotten through my shield.

The shield had been some protection, which was why my shoulder hadn't been shattered into a thousand pieces. I'd have to be careful now, I didn't dare risk changing the shield as burning to death didn't seem like a pleasant way to go either, but I wouldn't be able to absorb too many more direct strikes. Newly motivated, I blocked Allie's next three strikes and went on the offensive. If she was busy defending herself she couldn't attack.

Leaping out through the fire I struck at Allie again and again, keeping her off balance and on the defensive. It was the same tactic I had used with Victor, get up close and personal, keep them focused on the defence and not able to attack.

While it had worked on Victor, it didn't work on Allie. She simply let her shield absorb the strikes and countered. Her strike went straight through my shield and smashed into my shoulder again. Why was it always the same shoulder? I should have been grateful though, if her strike were a little higher and she would have taken my head off at the neck.

My shoulder throbbed painfully as I knocked Allie's threads aside and took her feet out from under her. My rage at being struck fuelled my fury and made me strong. Allie struck out as she pulled herself into a tight flip and landed on top of one of the pool tables on the far side of the room.

My shoulder hurt terribly, it was possible that she'd even broken my collar-bone. She lashed out at me from across the room, but at this distance it was easy to avoid her threads. I wasn't going to play that game, I moved closer. Wrapping two threads around several of the pool tables I launched them in her direction, but she was able to spin out of the way. The pool tables smashed against the far wall, knocking out several of the main supports for the building.

This building was going to come down. The longer we kept fighting here the more likely it was that it was going to collapse with us inside it. The only problem was that Allie wasn't going to let me get away and she had no sense of self-preservation to escape herself. This was going to come down to a race to see who could win this fight before the inferno took us both out.

Smoke and ash filled the room as more and more of the building caught alight. The fire that had previously been contained to the entryway and main bar had been renewed by the fire that Allie had started behind the bar. Thick smoke obscured everything. The only reason that we were still standing and not coughing our lungs out was that the shields around us were acting as impromptu air masks.

It was impossible to see anything clearly in the building. I had no idea where the closest window was, let alone the door. We could see each other though. The flare of our Mana signatures and shields was clearly visible through the smoke as we moved against each other. The crackle of wood burning and the impact of two Mana threads echoed throughout the room as we fought. There could be no hiding from each other in this fight.

Allie flipped over a burning column and smacked a Mana thread towards my head, I rolled under it and shot a return thread towards her, but unfortunately it went wide as Allie was able to somehow alter her flight to slide under it. She landed with grace and came out swinging, our two threads collided with sparks and we moved around.

Like two cats facing off against each other we circled, each trying to get the upper hand. We ignored the burning building around us and the ash and smoke that covered everything. Our shields flared as the waves of both hit them.

Allie struck again and again but was unable to land a solid blow. I could see the frustration on her face; I was just too good at being able to predict where her strike was going to come from. I was the survivor of far more Mage battles than her, so although we were matched in power, I was still her superior.

That would change in time though, my shoulder ached and the slightest movement sent waves of pain radiating throughout my side. I was unable to use my arm on that side properly, which gave me a huge disadvantage. Eventually I would make a mistake and she would have me.

I wasn't going to let that happen. I've fought dozens of battles in various states of pain and injury and knew how to accommodate for weakness. Allie, skilled though she was, just wasn't in the same calibre as me.

Finally I managed to sweep her threads from her and knock her down. Her shield fizzled as she hit the ground, it was up again in seconds, but it was weak – too weak. It was barely able to keep the heat at bay, let alone another attack. I loomed over her.

"This ends, now," I rumbled. "You're beaten! Submit!"

Allie stared up at me defiantly, but I could tell in her eyes that she knew she was defeated. This was probably a good thing too, because I didn't have that much left in me.

"Then kill me," she hissed.

"I'm not going to kill you!" I snarled, "I never wanted that!"

"Grandfather said you would! He said you would take your revenge for your dad!"

Grandfather? She was calling Victor grandfather now? The offense of that title from her lips sent waves of rage through me. Victor would pay for this. He had taken my only sister and turned her against me. I would find a way to end him for this.

"He's not your grandfather!"

We had to shout to be heard over the noise from the fire. The building was only moments from coming down upon us.

Allie didn't reply, she looked at me with her eyes hardened and her mouth set into a tight grimace. It was obvious from her stance that she had expected a coup de grace to come at any moment and was surprised when it didn't. I could have ended it, I could have ended it easily, but she was my sister. The only one I had.

"Devon…" she called.

"What?"

"Goodbye."

Before I could react Allie lanced out with everything she had. It wasn't a very well formed thread, but it was powerful. It was built of nothing more than sheer will and hatred and it hit the column next to me and brought it smashing down. Her final act had been to kill both of us, or at least I was sure that was her intention.

As the roof came down upon us my shield flared up in response. I saw Allie crawling from the wreckage. She hadn't been too far from the edge of the building and thus had avoided the worst of the roof that had crushed down upon us. Unfortunately I was not so lucky.

I had been standing right next to the column when it had fallen down upon me. The column had been made of a strong oak wood and the damned thing was heavy. It pinned me down as the rest of the roof collapsed. The weight smashed against my shield and I thought for a second that it was going to give. I threw every reserve I had into holding the shield together as the building slowly but inexorably crushed me.

Allie didn't look back as she made her escape. She used her powers to blow out what remained of the wall and escape into the cold night air. I didn't see her go, but I'm sure she would have gathered what remained of her powers and teleported to safety.

I would have liked to have done the same, but unfortunately most of my strength was being used to prevent myself from being turned into a fine red mist by the combined weight of the column and building rubble.

My shield was glowing red as I poured every ounce of power I had left into it. I was using every trick that I knew to enhance my shield and it still wasn't enough.

The collapsed beam pressed into my stomach and my shield could do nothing more than prevent me from being crushed. Even worse my shield, now optimised for strength, wasn't coping so well with the heat. Scalding waves of heat burned my left side as the fire burned closer.

It took me several minutes before I was able to gather the necessary reserves of power and summon a thread to pull me from the mess of fallen beams and roof. The cavity made by my body removed from the pile led to further rubble falling from the ceiling and more ash and smoke being kicked up. Once the smoke had cleared I was greeted by the sight that the whole left side of the building appeared to have fallen in on itself. I realised then just what a miracle it had been that I hadn't been immediately crushed in the collapse.

I staggered several steps and coughed as my mouth took in a lungful of smoke. Obviously my shield wasn't able to adequately protect me any longer. I had no idea how I'd survived this long, but I wasn't about to have it all end by passing out from smoke inhalation. I pulled my shirt over my nose and mouth and staggered out of the burning wreckage.

A fit of coughing brought bright lights to my eyes and I thought that I'd keep coughing until I choked. I crawled more than staggered from the bar with my shield fading fast. The sight of the streetlights outside was a relief and brought a resolve that allowed me to take the necessary last steps before collapsing outside on the cold hard concrete of the car park.

Several people rushed towards me and I felt someone gently roll me onto my side and place an air mask over my face. It could have been the rush of fresh air or it simply could have been a reaction from the adrenaline rushing through my body, but a wave of dizziness washed over me. I could hear voices arguing over me but I couldn't make out what they were saying. I think it was an argument over my apparent lack of serious burns. It certainly felt like I had burns, my skin was blistering in the cold night air, but the paramedics didn't look too concerned.

My shoulder had also stopped aching as much too. The impact mustn't have been as hard as I had originally thought. I weakly rolled my shoulder joint and cringed a little as it twinged in complaint. It hurt, but my collarbone certainly wasn't broken. That was a good thing at least.

My vision blurred and I thought I was about to pass out, but just when I thought the darkness was about to close in, my vision cleared and brought the world into stark clarity. I was lying on a gurney. Someone had placed a run into my arm and I could see a bag of something being held on a pole above my head.

I was still in the car park and had a yellow card wrapped around my neck. I had no idea what that meant. There were two paramedics nearby but they seemed more interested in the person on one of the other gurneys.

I supposed I could just get up and walk away without drawing too much attention to myself. A hand on my shoulder disabused me of this notion. A police officer was standing behind me and he didn't look like he was going anywhere.

He called over one of the paramedics.

"He's awake.".

"So it seems," the paramedic responded, "I'm not sure that changes anything though."

The paramedic came over. He took a blood pressure test and checked my eyes. He asked me basic questions for which I gave fake answers. I didn't particularly want them knowing my real name.

"He seems fine," The cop continued.

I wished they'd just get this over and done with. Being ferried from the site in an ambulance would be an ideal way of getting out of here. I was worried about Allie returning to ensure that she had finished the job. I had no wish to engage in a third encounter with her right now.

I had used the suppression technique to dull my powers, this would hide the visible aspect of my powers and make me seem normal to our kind. It would only work through a Scry spell, as if they saw me directly they would know me for what I was. It was possible that I might be physically recognised, but unlikely.

The cop and the paramedic seemed to be engaged in a not so subtle argument over who could take me. I think the cop wanted me for questioning, but at this point I didn't care who took me as long as they got me out of there. Eventually the paramedic relented, due to the fact that he could find no serious injury and that I genuinely seemed fine. I could tell it was bugging him though. People don't just emerge from burning buildings without a scratch on them. He made the cop sign a waiver anyway, but I think that was more about being antagonistic towards the police than any serious concern for my health.

* * * * * *

I'd never seen the inside of a police car before. It wasn't as interesting as I'd always thought it would be.

I was a little annoyed that they put handcuffs on me. It wasn't about the inconvenience – it was about taking liberties. I didn't appreciate it. It took me all of about three seconds to get out of them, but that wasn't the point. I left them on the seat next to me, snapped cleanly in two.

I wasn't quite sure where we were going. I had assumed that they would have taken me to the local police station, but we weren't heading in the right direction.

"Where am I?" I queried as they pulled into a car park.

They didn't answer; instead they exited the car. The cop glanced down at the empty handcuffs as he opened the door, and then back to me with a grimace on his face.

"Get out," he said in a deep voice. I wasn't sure if this was his normal voice or he was attempting to sound intimidating. I complied, but more out of actual curiosity than compliance. I could escape here at any point. My powers had returned sufficiently in the car trip that I felt I was now up to at least a small teleport jump. I was about to teleport away when I came to the realisation that no one would think to look for me in a police station. It was for now the perfect hiding place.

The cops turned me around and shoved me against the hood of the car with my arms behind me. I grinned slightly as they tried to place the handcuffs back on me. The one trying to cuff me cursed and threw them on the ground as he realised they were useless. A second set was quickly produced and these were placed on me. They weren't gentle about it either. I think I may have pissed them off.

They led me through a small double door at the back of the police station and into a long corridor. I glanced about as I passed through. I'd never really seen the insides of a police station, but it looked pretty mundane. It was mostly offices and desks. Obviously I wasn't moving fast enough for the cops as they grabbed me by the arm and propelled me forward.

They led me into a small cell and unceremoniously

threw me inside. The sound of the lock clinking on the gate as the door slammed shut echoed throughout the room. The click was almost louder than the sound of the door closing. I wondered if that was the point. If the click was a psychological trigger to the incarcerated that this was serious. It didn't matter much to me though.

They hadn't even bothered to take the handcuffs off. The location of the cuffs behind my back presented a little bit more of a difficulty, but soon they joined the first pair. This time however I'd managed to extricate myself without breaking them.

Once I was free I grabbed the cuffs from the floor where they had fallen and used them to link the door to the cell bars, preventing the door from opening. Now that I was secure, I grabbed a blanket and curled up on the bed. If they were going to make me wait, I'd use the time well – I was exhausted. Unfortunately they didn't give me enough time to fall asleep. This really was inconsiderate. I wondered who I should complain to.

The sound of metal clinking on metal and a loud curse drew my attention and made me glance at the cop standing by the door. It was one of the cops that had brought me here. He was glowering at the handcuffs locking the door shut as he fumbled around for the key. I could have told him that it would be useless. I'd broken the mechanism once I'd secured it to the door.

After several attempts he obviously came to the same conclusion and snarled at me. It was more a grunt of frustration than any real word, but it certainly would have contained some choice language had it contained words.

I grinned despite myself. I couldn't have stopped myself for all the world. I was going to have some fun with this. I waited until the cop had gone to get something to cut through the handcuffs and then I teleported into the empty cell on the far side of the room. The noise was extraordinarily loud in the cramped cell, but no one came to investigate. They were probably too busy looking for a set of bolt cutters or something.

It didn't take too long before three cops arrived with the aforementioned bolt cutters. They took one look into my empty cell and cursed loudly. They really weren't having a good day about this.

"Over here," I grunted, which caused all three cops to spin around. They looked like they were about ready to kill me.

One of them savagely opened the door and the other two stormed into the cell. I took the precaution of placing a shield around me in the event that they actually seriously threatened violence, but they managed to contain themselves. The first cop looked like he was having trouble doing it though, I didn't much blame him. I certainly knew how to rile people up when I wanted to.

I was led from the cell into a small room in the office area. On the far side of the room was a large mirror, which I assumed was a two-way mirror. I'd seen these rooms before in the movies.

One of the cops gestured towards a chair on the

facing the window. As the door was slammed behind me, I moved to the chair with its back to the window. After about ten minutes the door opened a new cop entered the room.

I assumed he was a cop. He wasn't wearing a uniform, but he did have that same gruff demeanour that cops seem to develop. He glanced at me in the wrong seat and a hint of a smile crossed his face. He shrugged, took the other seat and placed a manila folder on the table.

"Mr Devon Wills isn't it?" he began. I nodded, didn't seem to be much point in lying.

"That wasn't the name you gave the paramedics though."

"No, I used my maiden name," I murmured dryly.

He didn't seem overly impressed with that answer.

"This is serious, Mr Wills." I chose not to answer to that.

He opened the manila folder. Inside the folder were several pieces of paper, which I assumed were police reports, and several photos.

It was difficult to see from the angle, but the one on top had obviously been taken by one of the security cameras at the shopping centre where I had fought and killed Vin. I thought I could make out Vin in the background. It was hard to know for sure though, the photo wasn't that great a quality.

"This was taken about four years ago," The cop flicked the photo around, "during an incident at the Glen Waverley Shopping centre. The damage to the centre was extraordinary."

"How does this involve me?"

"Let's not play that game, Mister Wills." The Cop smiled dangerously as he laid out the rest of the photos. It was like a photo album of my greatest hits. There were numerous photos from the shopping centre and then some from Southern Cross station where I had been involved in a rather brutal fight with Aaron in front of most of the Victorian police force. I wasn't surprised that they had photos from that incident.

"You represent a very real threat to society, Mr Wills, and we want to know how. Everywhere you go property damage and deaths seem to follow you."

When I didn't comment the cop continued.

"We've attributed at least eight fatalities to you. This alone would be enough to put you away for good."

If he thought the threat of incarceration would be enough to cow me – it wasn't.

"Why am I here?"

"You're here because we want answers!"

Okay, that had been the wrong question to ask. That had just allowed him to play the TV show cop. If he'd slammed his fist down on the table as he said it he would have nailed the role perfectly. Amateur.

In fact the whole setup was like something from a TV show. I was only surprised that they hadn't tried to play bad cop, good cop with me. I should probably wait for that though, I was sure the good cop would be along shortly.

"Is there any chance of getting some food?" I queried

as my stomach grumbled. It had been some time since my last meal. I couldn't exactly remember when or what that had been, but it had been too long ago for my stomach

"In a minute," the cop grunted as he flicked through the folder. Eventually he found what he was looking for. It was a picture of Vin.

"Who is this man?"

"His name is not important," I shrugged, "He's dead."

"We know. We recovered his body, but that just raised further questions."

"His name was Vincent Lester."

"Nationality?"

"I don't actually know, I didn't know him very well."

"You just killed him huh?"

I didn't comment. I had no wish to be recorded on camera admitting to a murder. It had been a fair fight, more than fair actually – if anything it had been slanted in Vin's favour. It had been only luck and Vin's arrogance that had allowed me to win.

"Where did we land on that food?"

"I said in a minute!" the cop snapped as he looked for another photo. This one was of Renee.

"Who is this girl?"

"That, I'm not going to tell you."

"So you're withholding information from a police investigation?"

"Obviously."

"You're aware that there are stiff penalties for doing so."

"You're not in a position to penalise me for anything,"

I said finally losing patience. Why was I putting up with this? I could be out of here in a second with only a confused face and a burst of air to announce my exit.

"You could face prison time."

"Yes, you said that."

A buzzing noise came from his pocket. He pulled out his phone and glanced at it. His face screwed up in disgust as he read the message, then he got up to leave.

"Don't go anywhere," he grunted as he left the room.

He had meant it sarcastically, but I was happy to comply. Well, mostly happy – I'd need to get some food. There must be something in the police station to eat. I used a Scry thread to go looking.

It didn't take me long to go find what I was looking for. By the time the cop returned a packet of donuts was sitting on the table in front of me. They weren't very good, but in my hungry state they were really hitting the spot and had the additional bonus of giving me a sugar hit. His face fell as he saw the donuts.

"Where did you get those?"

"They were in the break room."

"How did you get out of this room?"

"I didn't," I grinned. I'd teleported the donuts carefully so that the three people in the observation room hadn't seen them teleport in. Given the size of the pack it hadn't made more than a dull thump as the donuts arrived.

He scowled at me and looked around the room looking for some explanation.

"Did you want one?" I smirked as I pushed the box over to him.

"Do you think this is a game?" he snarled, smacking the donuts from the table.

"More or less," I replied simply as I leaned back in the chair. "By the way – that's how you get ants." I gestured towards the fallen donuts on the floor.

"No, by God you're going to take this seriously." he blustered. His hand had reached down to his side where his side arm was holstered and for second I thought he was going to draw it on me. I didn't tell him how much of a spectacularly bad idea that would be.

I waited until he managed to get himself under control. I did feel some sympathy for the poor man. This situation was far from the norm, once they had someone in this chair the ball was well and truly in their court. They weren't used to someone for whom the rules just didn't matter. Even the most hardened criminals had some base fear of the law or at least the consequences of their actions, or at least fear of retribution.

I had none. These people couldn't harm me. I was completely beyond their power. It wasn't just that I didn't consider myself under their jurisdiction. It was that I didn't consider myself under anyone's jurisdiction and what was more no one had the strength to assert their power over me. I respected no law, no king, no government.

"Is now the right time to ask for a lawyer?" I asked lightly. This was the straw that broke the camel's back.

"Listen here," he hissed. "You're responsible for the deaths of several fine policemen. If you think I'm going to stand here and be mocked by you, you've got another thought coming."

The sound of a door opening interrupted his rant. The cop grimaced at me as he leaned over the table.

"I think that will be all," a stern voice intoned as a new comer entered the room. "You're dismissed."

The cop took one last look at me before crisply turning and leaving. The new comer was an older gentleman. He wasn't wearing a uniform, but he still looked like a cop.

"My apologies about that", he said as he gestured towards the departing cop.

"Unfortunately they decided to interrogate you before I arrived, "He cast a glance at the photos on the table. "My name is Agent Levenson and I'm here to have a little chat with you."

He briefly organised some of the photos on the table back into the manila folder, muttering under his breath as he flicked through them. He located a shot that had obviously been taken yesterday. It was of me and Allie. This shot, unlike the others, was clear. There was no mistaking my face. There was no way I was going to wiggle out of this one.

"Tell me, why is it that you're still here? You could obviously leave anytime you like. I was surprised when I received the call that they had detained you."

"I'm not sure of that myself." I said sourly. I had a

bad feeling about this. There was something odd about this man. He radiated a calm self-assurance that I'd only come to associate in people with true power. I was sure he wasn't a Mage, my Mana would have warned me of that. So who the hell was he?

"Would you like me to tell you why you're here Mr Wills?" the man continued, "You're here because you've reached the end.

"You're sitting here, right now because you feel sorry for yourself," he continued, "you're running away from a problem that you yourself created. And it's a doozy of a problem too. Few would judge you for running."

"What do you know?" I snarled, "you have no idea who I am."

"You're right. I don't. I'm simply following a script." The man continued showing surprising honesty. "I've been told how to talk to you. What to say and which topics to avoid."

"Why are you here?"

"I'm here because you're here."

"That's not an answer."

"You're right, as I said. The question you need to be asking yourself is why are YOU here?"

"I need help," I said softly.

"Indeed," Agent Levenson continued, "and you're seeking it in an odd place. You know very well that the police cannot help you."

He got to his feet and walked casually around the room. He walked behind me and I was sure he was staring into the two-way mirror. I'd taken the liberty of looking into that room when I had sent out my Scry thread in search of food. I wasn't sure if Levenson was lying about my being interrogated before he had arrived, but he hadn't been in the observation room before, so it was possible. I had to contain my nervous twitch as he approached me from behind. He leaned over and brought his lips to my ear.

"I was fourteen when I burned myself out."

Eight simple words, yet they explained everything. This man had been a Mage and now had the ability to order policemen out of an interrogation room. Who was this man?

"I know who and what you are, and I know what I'm looking at when I see photos like this," he said as he flicked at the photo of Allie and myself from yesterday.

"I'm also aware of who the other person in this photo is and we were under strict orders to leave her alone. I for one was very surprised when she started appearing on the nightly news."

A chill passed through my spine. I hadn't been the only person searching for Allie. In fact I hadn't been the one who had actually found her in the end. Marcus had told me where she could be found. How had he known? It seemed obvious in hindsight. He had had people looking for her.

But Marcus wasn't the only one who had known where she had been kept. This meant that it was possible that I was being questioned by someone who worked for either Marcus or Victor. Neither alternative was that appealing.

"Give me one good reason why I don't strike you down right now." I whispered darkly.

The man's lips pressed into a thin grimace. He walked around the table again and sat down.

"You could, but we have taken assurances that you won't."

"What assurances."

"You have three friends I believe – A Miss Sarah Benning, Miss Tina Higgins and Mr Tony Ward. You were involved in an unfortunate motor accident with them several years ago. This first brought them to our attention."

"Go on," I grunted. I didn't like where this was going.

"They were recovered this evening by a squad car. They are being held in a secure location right now."

I didn't answer, my fists slowly clenched and unclenched as I pondered my options. My face fell into a tight grimace as I realised I had none.

I had intentionally not visited my friends for fear of endangering them. My intention had been noble, I just hadn't counted on someone else dragging them into this for me.

"What location?" I snarled angrily. The Mana rose down my arms in response. I was seconds away from striking him down. It wouldn't have helped my situation any, but it would certainly have made me feel better.

"It's amazing how many people simply disappear

from police custody. Especially when there is no record of them ever being taken." He commented lightly as his eyes glittered dangerously.

"I get your point. You don't need to drill it in."

I needed some time to think. If they'd truly taken my friends they wouldn't have taken them to any old police station. I refused to believe that this guy was a normal cop. He knew too much for that. He'd be some kind of special division or something. They wouldn't want to involve too many people in on this.

I came to the conclusion that the only thing that really made any sense would be if they had taken them here. I hadn't seen them when I was Scrying before, but I hadn't really taken the effort to explore the station properly. It was possible that they were here. It was a large station.

This was going to be delicate. I'd need to use my powers without this man knowing what was happening. He claimed he'd once been of our kind so he would recognise when my eyes dilated through Mana use. I'd need to do this really carefully.

"Okay then. What do you want?" I sighed and I rested my head in my hands. Let him think he'd defeated me. I was only half listening to what he was saying. He was making some veiled threat about my friends' safety should I try to run for it. He needn't have worried – I had no intention of running until I had found them.

My Scry spell quickly found what I was looking for. They were in a cell in the other side of the complex. The question was what to do now. They weren't safe there, there were armed guards and security cameras in the room with them. There wasn't really much choice in the matter. They had to be removed from the room. The only trick would be to move them without getting them killed in the process.

I could attempt to fight my way to them, but that would probably result in them getting shot long before I got there, so that was out. Even if I teleported in it was possible that one of the guards would get a shot off before I was able to protect them. It would take me several seconds to get my bearings after I teleported – during which they would be vulnerable. Unacceptable.

"Are you listening to me," the agent interjected irritably.

"I'm listening," I grunted sourly not moving my hands, "Just don't expect me to be fucking happy about it."

This seemed to mollify him as he went back to talking. If going to them was out of the question then the only viable solution that remained was to bring them to me. Three teleports at once would be difficult, but not impossible. It wouldn't be a pleasant trip for them, but it was better than being shot on my behalf.

All three of them would need to leave the room at the exact same time. Any straggler left behind would risk being shot and that was unacceptable. The only upside was that I would be able to take as long as I needed to prepare myself for this as no one in the room would be able to detect the Mana until I was ready to use it. If one of my kind were in that room my plans would fail fast. Fortunately it was obvious that there weren't any of my kind involved in this. If there were, they would be here guarding me.

My only concern was that I couldn't take too long to activate the teleport spell. Once their molecules started disappearing I was sure that my friends would quite rightly get distressed and their noises would draw attention to what I was doing. I needed a finely tuned balance between power, speed and control.

Three bodies – none of them mine, all moved instantly to one location – it was a tough ask, but I believed I was up to the task. The last time I had teleported someone other than myself we had both been falling from an aeroplane, at least this time all three subjects were stationary.

I breathed out a sigh as my magic took hold. Sarah was the first one to notice something as she let out a shiver and her face went white. Tony was next and lastly Tina who had been sleeping on a couch. The guards in the room reacted with unanticipated speed, but fortunately due to Sarah's scream they had assumed some kind of external threat and had turned their attention to the doorway. By the time they realised their mistake my friends were gone.

My friends' arrival created a loud explosion that echoed throughout the confines of the room. My hands were torn from my head as Levenson stared into my

Mana enhanced eyes with a gun held firmly towards my forehead.

"You should have shot first," I whispered. It was too late now. A shield was protecting me. I kicked my chair back as I stood up and smiled at him. His gun followed my every movement, but I could tell from the resignation on his face that he knew it would be useless.

"What the fuck!" Tony shouted as he finally regained the power of speech. Sarah collapsed into Tony's arms with a look of complete and utter terror on her face. Tina appeared to have coped with the jump the best as she had been sleeping at the time. She must have awoken as the jump had taken hold, but probably wasn't totally aware of what had just happened. I felt sorry for doing that to my friends, but better they were with me.

"You'll never get out of this room," Levenson said as he lowered the gun.

I raised an eyebrow and grinned at Levenson.

"Wanna bet?"

"They won't, " he continued, gesturing towards my friends.

He might have had a point. I couldn't risk teleporting them to a new location one by one and I didn't have the strength to teleport all four of us in one trip. In the distraction of Scrying to a new location it was possible that I would be over powered.

"Then it looks like we'll do this the hard way, Tony grab the gun!"

Tony looked at me like I was mad. I could tell the

dilemma he was working through. As a society we are conditioned to respect and obey the police and our figures of authority. He hadn't made any move to retrieve the gun yet. What I'd ask him to do must have seemed to be crazy.

"Fine," I grunted, telekinetically ripping the gun from Levenson's fingers and breaking it in two. The gun crumbling into pieces seemed to finally jolt Tony into action.

"What's going on?" he asked angrily. "Why are we here?"

"These idiots thought they could get to me, through you." I said.

Tony's face hardened as he glanced between me and Levenson. I couldn't tell who he was more angry at. I didn't much blame him; I wouldn't have wanted to be put in that position either.

"Don't worry though, I've got your back," I tried.

He didn't look that impressed. In fact if anything that made him look angrier.

"What's your plan?"

"Stay close. I'll get us out of here."

"What about him?" Tony gestured towards Levenson.

"He's coming with us."

"You're going to kidnap a cop?" Sarah said, her eyes wide. It was the first thing she had said since the teleportation.

"He's no cop," I moved towards the door.

"I think we'll stay here," Tony said. "This doesn't seem like a good idea."

"Not going to happen, I'm not leaving you guys behind. I've got to keep you safe."

"It doesn't have to be this way," Levenson said.

"Listen to him Devon," Sarah urged.

"You don't want to take them out that door, Levenson continued, "my soldiers have orders to kill on sight."

"What? Why?" Sarah said. "That's not legal! We didn't do anything!"

Levenson didn't say anything, but his eyes flicked over to me. Tony and Sarah got the message.

"Won't they just pick us up again once we've escaped?" Tony asked.

"No, there's no record that you were ever here. Isn't that right Levenson?"

Levenson scowled but nodded.

"…and besides, I'm not going to leave you unprotected."

I tried the door. It was locked. This wasn't surprising. I looked at the two-way mirror and thought about going out that way. I assumed that the glass was bullet proof, which was why they hadn't already taken shots at us. They would have known that something was wrong. They would know I was coming. No, simply unlocking the door wasn't going to help.

Tina hadn't said a word the whole time, she was staring at me with a mixture of confusion and fear. She had visibly flinched at the words 'kill on sight'. She didn't know about the Mana, unless Sarah or Tony had told her. I suspected from her expression that they had not. This must have all been very confusing. I wish I had the time to explain it to her properly, but that wasn't going to happen.

"Devon," she whispered, "don't go out there."

I glanced at her and placed my hand on her shoulder. "It's going to be okay, stay close, I'll protect you."

I hit the door with the full force of my powers. I wanted the door to fly open with stunning force but I hadn't expected the door to fly from its hinges and hit several soldiers standing outside. I wasn't sure what they had been doing, but they weren't moving now.

Tina's eyes were as wide as saucers. This more than anything else confirmed the fact that she hadn't known about the Mana. Blowing the door off its hinges had been a fairly brutal introduction.

My shield was already in place as I stepped out into the hall. There were two teams of soldiers on each side. They were wearing police swat uniforms, but I was pretty sure that they weren't police officers. A small arsenal of assault rifles were pointed in my direction.

The sounds of bullets impacting with my shield reverberated throughout the narrow corridor. A casual thread took out the team of soldiers behind me and I turned to face the ones in front. The bullets were little more than an annoyance as they impacted against my shield, creating little more than little indents of sparks as the shield absorbed the shots. I reached into the interrogation room and grabbed Levenson and pulled him into the corridor. The bullets stopped immediately.

"Come on guys, get behind me." I called. I didn't blame them that it took them some time. Tony was the first, he gently led Sarah and then Tina out into the corridor and I extended my shield to surround them. The shield would be weaker, but unless they hit me with something really heavy it would suffice. At least I hoped it would. I'd never had to test how much damage my shield extended like this could take.

The soldiers backed down the corridor as I pushed Levenson towards them. I managed to get them to retreat all the way down before they showed any signs of slowing. Once they reached the office at the end they fanned out into a wide arc. There had been more soldiers waiting in the office. There were about twenty soldiers now. This would make it a little more difficult to take them out at once. These new soldiers were dressed differently. They didn't even try to look like cops – they were obviously military.

"Come on guys," I said, "don't make me take you all out. Weapons down."

That didn't work. I didn't think it would, but it was worth a shot. At least they hadn't fired at me. As that thought occurred to me a shot rang off my forehead. I had spoken too soon. My shield absorbed the shot easily, but it had hurt a little. A telekinetic thread quickly downed the soldier who had fired. I brought my hand sweeping back in a wide arc.

"Who's next?"

The only hope I had was for them not to all open up shooting at once. I'd already modified my shield so that all my strength was in the front arc, but I wasn't sure that it would be able to take a sustained fire burst without something getting through. With the shield this size I wasn't sure I'd be able to guarantee nothing getting through. The attempted headshot before that changed things dramatically. It had shown me that at this scope my shield would not long protect us. I was vulnerable here, my friends were vulnerable. If I wasn't careful someone was going to get killed.

"Tell them to stand down," I hissed into Levenson's ear.

"No."

"You're going to get everyone killed," I whispered grimly.

"No, I'm not. You are," was the reply. Levenson's eyes were cold. He was prepared to call my bluff.

"Okay, okay. I give in." I sighed.

Tony and Sarah looked almost relieved as I uttered the words. I wasn't going to risk my friends getting killed over this. It just wasn't worth it and the risk of failure was too high. I didn't resist as the soldiers closed in on me and forced me to my knees and placed me in handcuffs. To their credit they were at least gentle about it.

* * * * * *

I handed Levenson the broken handcuffs as we returned to the interrogation room. He glanced at them wryly and passed them over to a colleague. I didn't see where they had taken Tony and the others, they had been ushered further down the corridor when I had been directed back into the interrogation room. I would always have time to track them down later. A better opportunity for escape would arise shortly I was sure of it.

Even afterwards I didn't see the point of Levenson's interrogation. He asked me seemingly random questions, jumping quickly from topic to topic, then switching back to an earlier topic for more clarification. It was baffling. I gave him what answers he required. It didn't matter much anyway – he was more concerned with events that had already happened.

He was particularly interested in my fight with Aaron Chen that had taken place almost three years ago. This made sense, it had been less than subtle and I wasn't surprised that the authorities were interested in the specifics. The interrogation lasted about an hour and at the end I got the distinct impression that I hadn't told him anything he hadn't already known.

Once Levenson was satisfied I was led from the room and given a small cell under guard and camera. I was gruffly informed that my friends' good health depended upon my good conduct. I gritted my teeth as I entered the cell. The door was closed and locked behind me. It was more of a symbolic gesture than anything else. The door wouldn't last long should I choose to remove it. In fact Levenson knew that the door wasn't even necessary.

A quick Scry spell informed me that Tony and

Sarah were in a cell on the far side of the building, but I couldn't find Tina. This was worrying. Tony and Sarah were under heavy guard. There were three guards by the door and two inside the room with them. These weren't the cops either, these were the other sort.

The guard inside the room had a pistol in his hand. It didn't take me too long to confirm that the safety was off. This wasn't a joke. They'd at least get one shot off before I managed to teleport my friends away. There wouldn't be any repeats of my last trick.

I was wracking my brain trying to determine what their purpose here was. This couldn't be their long-term goal. Sooner or later they must realise they'd make a mistake and I'd have them. They were obviously either holding me for someone else, or had plans to take me to a more secure facility. Either way I wasn't about to give them the opportunity.

The Primea had warned me that human agencies had begun to search for me. I guess they had found me. I wasn't sure if it was a good thing or a bad thing yet. I couldn't imagine what they would want with me. If they were hoping to recruit me to their cause they were going to be in for a disappointment. I had no more intention of joining their cause than I did Marcus's or Victor's.

Our kind weren't allowed to reveal ourselves to norms. It was one of the rules. This was when I realised something. Both Victor and Marcus had done so at one point or another. Victor had even secured the services of a security company, revealing to them what Mages were capable of. Had that been some stretch of the rules or merely another instance of the powerful disregarding the laws to suit their own purposes?

I didn't know what it meant for sure, the only thing I knew for certain was that I had a bad feeling about this.

CHAPTER NINE

Not surprisingly, I didn't sleep well that night. I considered going to see my friends in their cell, but didn't want to risk it as it could have been interpreted as an escape attempt. When I did finally achieve sleep it was restless and I woke up tired and sore.

This bed was simply awful. I'd stayed in some bad beds during my travels. I'd often been forced to take respite in less than five star hotels, but this bed took the cake. It was almost as if someone had intentionally tried to design the world's most uncomfortable mattress. I'd complain, but they probably wouldn't care.

A knock on my cell door informed me that Levenson had arrived. He had brought me a tray of breakfast. I wasn't expecting it to be any good.

"Good Morning, Master Wills." He placed the tray on the table by the far wall.

"Morning," I grumbled as I moved over to the tray. I lifted the lid and was greeted by the delicious aroma of bacon and eggs. It had been some time since I'd last had bacon and eggs.

I breathed in the smell with delight. Bacon was perfect – even when it's bad it's still pretty good.

"Please eat," Levenson prompted, "don't mind me."

"Where are my friends?" I asked as I chewed a particularly crunchy piece of bacon. The rumours about prison food had been wrong. This was delicious.

"We had the food brought in for you." Levenson said, obviously noting my enjoyment. "We didn't think you'd like the usual fare here."

"My compliments to the chef. Now, what about my friends? Where have you taken Tina?"

"Miss Higgins was experiencing some distress at what she witnessed yesterday. Unlike your other two friends I understand she had no knowledge of your abilities?"

I nodded as I eyed off one of the eggs on the plate. Poached! It'd had been years since I had had poached eggs! My father had made divine poached eggs, but I had never mastered the skill.

"She's seeing a skilled counsellor. We have some experience in introducing people into your world."

"Thank you," I whispered, and to my everlasting surprise I found that I actually meant it.

"We are sorry for having to use your friends against you, but we were advised that it was the only way that you were going to co-operate."

"If you call this cooperation."

"You can be assured that we will not harm them should you continue this level of cooperation. Once this is all done, they can go on with their lives as if this had never happened."

"I'm sure that's true – right up until the moment that

you need something else from me."

Levenson didn't comment, but it was obvious that I'd hit upon a point that he wished to discuss.

"Your cousin – Alisha," he began.

"Sister," I corrected.

"Sister? Really? We didn't know that." Levenson murmured, "Anyway – she has become a dangerous threat. It's our job to make sure that your kind don't become the kind of threat that she now is."

"So go kidnap her friends," I suggested sarcastically between bites.

"We would have considered that – if she had any that we knew about. We don't believe that this particular tactic would have worked on her anyway."

"Our kind govern ourselves – let them deal with it."

"The Primea is currently unavailable," Levenson replied darkly."

My jaw dropped. How the hell had he known of the Primea? True he was a former Mage, but surely there were some secrets that we had kept from him. How many of our secrets did this man actually know?

Levenson went on, "If you believe that a secret organisation, no matter how powerful, has been able to keep itself completely separate from the rest of the world for hundreds of years, without anyone knowing of their existence, then you're more gullible than I thought."

Great it looked like he was gearing up for a lecture. Why did everyone over the age of forty feel the need to lecture me?

"MI7, or as it's simply known today as Division 7 has known about your kind since the Second World War."

"MI7? That was in a Bond film wasn't it?" I was sure I'd heard that name before. It had been one of the other agencies that Bond and MI6 worked with.

"Yes, surprisingly enough, but I doubt the producers of the movie realised that we had once been a real organisation. MI7 was officially shutdown after the Second World War. You'll occasionally find crack pot theories about us though, usually linked to UFO's or other equally crazy conspiracy theories."

"Officially," I prompted.

"That's right. During the war we discovered something unusual."

"Let me guess. Us."

He nodded. "The directors of MI7 at the time felt that it was better to appear to have shut down rather than face the consequences. The fear of reprisal from your kind was a constant threat."

"As the world changed I think your kind realised that they actually need us, which I'm sure came as a surprise at the time. We can clean up the messes that the renegades of your kind cause. We're getting awfully good at it. We've kept society blissfully unaware of your kind's existence for over sixty years."

"You were the ones who kept my fight with Vin in Glen Waverley hushed up,"

Levenson nodded. "We were well paid to do so. Although you certainly made us earn our money with your fight with Aaron Chen at Southern Cross Station."

"I'd often wondered why there wasn't a bigger fall out over that," I said sourly.

Levenson sighed. "People will believe what we tell them to, provided that the next day is much the same as the last. And of course, that the money keeps rolling in."

"Why are you telling me this?"

"Because sooner or later, you're going to have to make a choice and we would very much like to see you make the right one."

"What choice?"

"You know the choice. You've already been offered it numerous times now." Levenson's tone was curt. "Your preference to remain neutral is soon no longer going to be an option.

"Our Benefactor would like you to join us and is willing to pay you handsomely to obtain your skills."

"You couldn't pay me enough," I grunted angrily. The nerve of this man – I wasn't some thug for hire.

"Not in money, no," Levenson agreed. Your past shows that you have neither need nor care for money.

"Then how do you expect to entice me to join you?"

"With the one thing your kind always seeks – power."

I shook my head wearily, "I'm really not interested in power. You've got the wrong man."

This seemed to confuse him for a few seconds and he turned back to his papers. He shuffled through them and brought a new photo to the top. He flipped it round and faced it towards me.

"You know who this man is?"

The photo was of Victor.

"Yes."

"You'll join us for a chance at revenge then."

"I'm not interested in revenge either." I shook my head. This was going nowhere.

"He's a very dangerous man," Levenson continued, "and he's the most likely candidate to be the next Primea."

"He's already Primea, as far as I know," I grunted.

This seemed to give Levenson pause and he rechecked several papers, shuffling through them briskly to find the right page.

"We feel that his appointment would be catastrophic," he said, obviously unable to find the page he'd been looking for.

"There are no good contenders either way," I said.

"Not true. We feel that a more transparent leadership of your kind would be better in the long run."

"You're working for Marcus Devereaux." I said darkly.

It had been a shot in the dark, but it had made sense. Levenson didn't give me the satisfaction of confirming or denying my guess, but I could tell from his expression that I was right.

"Your kind can no longer remain in the shadows. They need to be recognised in a world environment. We cannot have our governments influenced by unknown factions any longer."

"You bring us out into the light and you're going to

have our boots at your necks." I said darkly.

"The sad fact is that your boots are already on our necks – but no one knows about it," Levenson finished softly.

He got to his feet. "I think I have given you enough to think about for the moment. I will leave you now with the knowledge that in a few weeks' time we're going to attempt to recover your sister and remove her from Victor."

"Why?"

"Do you have to ask after your display at the university?"

"Will she be harmed?"

"No more than is necessary to subdue her."

"Why her?"

"She is one of Victor's most prized agents and we suspect that when she is ready she will be a significant threat to both our organisation and to world stability."

"World stability?" I scoffed, "…and you're working with Marcus to achieve this end?"

"A hidden war is already being fought. It's just that no one outside of a select few have known how or why it's been fought."

"…and you're going to stop it?" I sneered, "Victor will crush you should you get in the way."

"Why would you assume that?"

"Holy Christ. I was right. You've sided with Marcus."

I knew that a war was coming between our kind, but I had foolishly never expected it to filter out into the real world and I never imagined for a second that it was already being fought. Now that it had been pointed out to me it seemed obvious what had happened. Marcus had begun it and Victor had retaliated.

This was just the most recent round of fire between the two Arch Mages. I had no doubt that they'd already exchanged shots, but I didn't know where the lines were drawn or even where the battlefield was.

"Any conflict between Marcus and Victor can only lead to war," I warned. "If you're seeking to directly stand against Victor there will be consequences."

"No one wants a war."

"I don't think that's possible to avoid now," I said.

"I agree," Levenson said softly, "but we have to try."

"What do you want from me then?"

"Isn't it obvious. We want you to help recover and neutralise your sister."

"Why?"

"Because she's dangerous," Levenson said, "and you don't want us to do the neutralising."

* * * * * *

Levenson left me alone to process his not so subtle threat. He'd made quite a case to sign up with him, making it seem almost like it was the only rational thing to do. I wasn't so sure though, I had no real wish to sign up with Marcus, I knew how manipulative and dangerous he could be. But I wasn't going to allow them to kill Allie, which was what they would undoubtedly do should I not help them. There really was only one choice. I'd have to do as they asked.

I often wonder if this decision was the one – the decision that damned me. Should I have chosen to remain neutral? But the end was coming regardless and my choices didn't count for much. Marcus and Victor had each arrayed a massive bloc of forces against the other. It was inevitable that eventually they would come into direct conflict.

But what would happen after we had recovered Allie? Could Levenson be trusted? Would Marcus keep his word? The whole thing felt like a game of chess between the two Arch Mages and I couldn't decide if I was a knight or pawn. I knew with certainty though, that I would be sacrificed instantly should it be required to achieve either of their ends.

When Levenson returned I grudgingly accepted his terms, but placed conditions upon my allegiance. One, my friends were to be set free. Two, Allie was to be kept alive afterwards. This was non-negotiable. Levenson readily agreed to this and Tony and Sarah were released. I didn't get a chance to talk to them before they left, but from the look that Tony had given me the last time we had met I was sure that this was a good thing. It might be best if I should not intrude in their lives any further.

Unfortunately Tina proved to be a little more difficult. She was refusing to leave until she spoke to me. I wasn't looking forward to that conversation. It took me several minutes to compose myself before I was able to knock on the door to her room.

"Come in." I slid the door open and walked in. Tina was sitting on her bed.

"What are you still doing here?" I said carefully as I pulled up a chair.

Tina didn't answer at first. She was staring at me like I was some form of monster. It was starting to get a little uncomfortable when she finally said, "Is it true?"

"I'm not sure what they told you, but probably."

"Why didn't you tell me?"

"It was dangerous for you to know."

Her eyes narrowed. "Tony and Sarah knew."

"That wasn't exactly planned and I didn't like telling them."

"You didn't trust me?"

"No, that's not it, by the time you needed to know it was already too late."

"They tell me the car accident during our final year was caused by someone called Vincent," Tina continued, her voice turning steely, "and that he was like you."

"Yes."

"I thought I had caused it," her voice was hard.

"I know," I sighed, "I did try to tell you it wasn't your fault."

"I thought you were dead."

"I had to run away, I thought that I would bring more danger onto you guys."

"You ruined my life."

Four simple words, yet they contained so much bitterness and anger. As much as I wanted to deny the truth of these words, I couldn't. She was right; I had ruined her life. I had taken an honours student with a bright and promising future and destroyed all that.

"I hate you," she whispered.

"You have every right." I sighed.

I'm not sure why Tina had held out to see me. She certainly hadn't seemed like she had wanted to talk. Perhaps she had simply wanted to see if what she had been told was truth, perhaps she had merely wished to tell me that she despised me. I didn't blame her. I despised myself.

* * * * * *

Later that day I was taken from the station and told we were going to an airport to meet someone. They didn't say whom, but I assumed they were bringing me because they were expecting trouble. Great, my duties as a hired thug had begun.

I had no idea where the airport was located; it took several hours to arrive there by car. I'd never spent much time in rural Victoria, with the notable exception of my stay in Omeo. Levenson had been unwilling to tell me where we were going. I could have used Scry to determine our exact location, but Levenson had been explicit – don't use your powers. He needn't have worried though, I knew how to remain off the grid.

It had been some time since I had done any notable distance travelling by car and by the second hour I was getting quite impatient. Had they told me where we were going, I could have arranged to meet them there, I suspect this might have been why he had refused to tell me the location in the first place.

After what seemed like a day of travel we arrived and were ushered through the main gates. The complex appeared to be a small, armed military camp. The perimeter was lined with barbed wire fences and watch-towers. This was obviously a military airstrip. That was an interesting development.

Our car turned into one of the hangers and pulled up next to a small passenger jet. I gripped the sides of the seat as I recognised the person standing next to the jet. The Mana unconsciously flared up along my arms and I had to clench my fingers into a fist to maintain control. The urge to strike was almost over powering. I wasn't here to protect someone I was here to meet someone.

Marcus.

A ghostly voice in the back of my head whispered "You will kill Marcus Devereaux". Victor's compulsion. It was still with me. I had hoped that it had been removed with the attempt on Marcus's life in Paris. Unfortunately, no such luck. The only upside was that it now seemed far weaker. Even so, it still took some effort to ignore it.

When I exited the car I could see a shield firmly around the Arch Mage. He was obviously expecting trouble, or more likely he had noticed my reaction in the car. I breathed out as I calmly walked over to the group. Victor's words echoed again throughout my head, but I was able to put it to the back of my mind.

Marcus nodded to me as I approached and let his shield down. It seemed that he had expected me to attack on sight or not at all. He smiled at me and moved over to shake my hand.

As I grasped his hand I vaguely wondered if I could end the whole conflict by striking Marcus down now. True that would leave Victor in control, but I had doubts that Marcus as Primea would be any less catastrophic.

The urge to strike was almost overpowering. The last time I had fought him I had been on the verge of complete physical and mental breakdown, this time I was in full control of my powers. It was possible that I could end this now. The problem was, I didn't know if that was a good thing or not. What would the consequences of killing Marcus be? I didn't know.

Marcus must have guessed what was going through my head as he gave me a wry smile and a nod. It was almost a challenge. "Try it," his eyes whispered to me. He seemed almost disappointed when I shrugged and forcibly brought the Mana under control.

"I wasn't sure if the compulsion had been removed," Marcus began in way of greeting, "hence why we're meeting in such a remote location – less collateral damage."

"You weren't worried about your jet being damaged?" I smirked.

"Never occurred to me actually," Marcus shrugged, "besides it's not mine."

"The jet belongs to Division 7," Levenson said. Marcus just shrugged as if this was inconsequential.

"I was glad to hear that you recovered from your burn out," Marcus continued, "I was confident that you would though."

I shrugged and didn't answer. I was trying to figure out the dynamic of the group. Levenson and Marcus weren't quite acting as henchman and Master. Some strange interplay of power was going on between them, but it was impossible as to who thought himself in control. If I had to bet I'd have guessed that they both thought they were the one running things.

"The compulsion is still intact," I said conversationally as I turned to walk towards the jet. I've always been amazed at how large these things seem when you're standing next to them.

"Indeed?" Marcus said lightly. I could tell that he was worried though, his Mana signature gave him away. It rose sharply in response to my words.

"Not as strong as before, but still there. I've got it under control."

"As long as you don't act on it," Marcus nodded crisply as he brought his own mana under control, "that's what's important."

"...Wouldn't dream of it." I assured him. Even to my ears I didn't sound sincere.

"James tells me that you've agreed to help us," Marcus

said, referring to Levenson.

"Hardly had a choice – if you're going to kidnap my friends," I said bitterly.

Marcus raised an eyebrow at Levenson. Perhaps Marcus hadn't been aware of that fact. I had assumed that Marcus had planned the whole thing and that Levenson was merely acting as the hatchet man. From Marcus's reaction that didn't seem to be the case.

Levenson shrugged, "Seemed the most appropriate way to ensure his co-operation."

"Well, it worked," I grunted.

"If you had joined me when you were first offered the chance," Marcus said, "none of this would have been necessary."

"I really don't understand why you need me so badly. It seems that you have all the tools necessary without me."

"Because up until very recently you were probably the only one who would be able to reign in your cousin."

"Sister," I corrected.

Marcus looked at me in amazement. He seemed less than impressed by this development. No doubt this new information made things more difficult for him. Good.

"Half-sister," I amended quickly. The correction didn't seem to help much. " Why recruit me now? I can tell you know that Allie won't listen to me."

"We assumed as much after all the property damage the two of you have been responsible for recently."

"Why does Allie factor so largely into your designs?"

"Because Victor will utilise her to take out his opposition. Neutralising her before he is established will allow us to take him on directly."

It made a strange sense. Victor would have turned her into an assassin. It was a role that he had planned for me, but when I had refused and had turned against him, he had turned to my sister. I remembered the speed with which Allie had launched into an attack when I had confronted her at the university campus. She had certainly shown no compunctions about killing me. I had originally attributed that to rage over her dead friend, but maybe that wasn't correct. Maybe she didn't have any doubts about killing me, because she had killed before. I breathed out slowly and clenched my fists. She could very well have become the monster that Victor had planned for me to be.

But something didn't ring true. "I still don't see why you can't handle Victor without getting Allie involved."

"Too risky," Levenson said. "She's too powerful and is known to associate with Mages aligned with Victor."

"Like that boy on campus when I first met her?" I asked, I wasn't sure I wanted to know, "I assumed he was a guard, but he was far too weak for that. Who was he?"

"We're not entirely sure," Levenson said, "His name was Justin Mitchell – he was a student at the university up until very recently. We didn't know for certain that he had Mana potential, but we suspected as much. We assumed that he was romantically linked with your sister."

"He was," I grunted sourly. I didn't much like this

subject. I had killed people before, but this one struck home. This one had been an unnecessary death. He had been no threat to me – had I been thinking more clearly or acted more quickly it could have been avoided.

"You are there to simply ensure that she is contained," Marcus said. "Once she's out of the equation we can deal with Victor."

"When do we do this?"

Levenson answered. "Not for a few days."

"Why not deal with her now? She's in Melbourne, we're in Melbourne. We could recover her now."

"We're not ready now." Levenson said. That seemed to settle that argument.

"Why aren't you doing this?" I asked Marcus.

"I assumed that you would prefer to handle this yourself," Marcus replied blandly. "If things get out of control. I will take steps." The threat hung in the air.

"Once your sister has been recovered, we will take you both to a remote location," Levenson said.

This made sense. Our fight had pretty much ruined any chance of Allie being able to live here undisturbed anyway. The only thing I wasn't sure about was whether Marcus trusted me enough to hold up my end of the deal once my sister was recovered. He may have had a point. I cared nothing for his war, I simply wanted Allie kept safe.

"I don't care what you do with her afterwards," Marcus said to Levenson angrily, "I only care that it happens soon, before Victor has a chance to spirit her out of here."

"She lives though. We take her alive," I said darkly. This was non-negotiable.

"Of course," Marcus nodded quickly, "our main priority is with her Master."

"…and have you figured out how you're going to deal with him, given he's practically immortal," I muttered snidely. I didn't like this. I didn't like this one bit.

"The magic sustaining him will only function while it is allowed to do so," Marcus said. "Any sort of disruption at the point of injury and the Mana will not be able to revive him."

"So we hit him with a disrupt spell and then kill him." I finished softly.

"It's a little more complicated than that. I haven't been idle since we last met. I'm confident I can end the regenerative effect."

I assumed he had come to this conclusion after reading the books I had taken from Victor's experimentation facility. This was at least good news for Karl, the prisoner I had met there. I hadn't thought about him for a long time and I felt a little guilty about that. If this worked, perhaps I could return and end his torment after this was done with. This assumed of course, that I was still alive to do so. I was so distracted by making my own plans that I nearly missed what Levenson said next.

"We know that Alisha isn't staying at her apartment. Your altercation has obviously spooked her. She's staying in university accommodation. We believe in Mr Mitchell's room. "

"So how do you plan on getting her out of there? I'd imagine those accommodation buildings are packed with students."

"We have arranged for a student event that will hopefully minimise the amount of student interference."

"What is this event?"

"A fund raiser for the university," Marcus said.

"How many people will be attending this… fund-raiser?"

"Many," Marcus grinned darkly. He found this amusing, the bastard.

"You don't see this as a problem."

"No, actually," Levenson interjected. "Your sister is unlikely to attend the event, but most of her fellow students probably will. Allowing us a chance to remove her from the dormitory without interruption."

Well, that made sense at least. I didn't like it though. It was dependent upon an awful lot of factors. This could go really badly, really quickly.

"You're only there if things get out of hand, to ensure a minimal amount of collateral damage." Levenson continued.

"Collateral damage?" I queried.

"If things should turn for the worse. You are to lead your sister away from the university grounds where she can be dealt with without onlookers."

"You're taking an awfully big chance here," I said.

Marcus nodded grimly. "You're right. I'd have just had her killed." I gritted my teeth as I glared at the man.

"It would be easier," Marcus continued, ignoring my death stare, "I don't particularly care for the girl. Removing her is merely one less weapon available to my enemy."

"Duly noted," I grunted unimpressed.

Marcus didn't comment further.

"The aim here isn't to create a disruption," Levenson repeated, but I wasn't sure who he was directing this to. "We go in with a team, recover the girl and get out."

"I'm going to be part of this team?" I queried curiously.

"Let's say you're just there to keep the team alive," Marcus interjected.

"In the event that things don't go to plan, you will be there to ensure that our team gets out intact," Levenson continued briskly.

"Why aren't you using drones for this?" Using live people sounded awfully risky. If things went sour people could get hurt.

"Drones?" Levenson said. I believe he thought I was referring to the American tactical jets. It was interesting to note that he didn't know about Marcus's forays into the realm of Necromancy.

"That's not a conversation for now," Marcus grunted. It was obvious that he was less than pleased with me for suggesting that. It did seem more practical though, a team of Drones could go in and take the fire. I'd seen just firsthand how effective they were at taking shots.

"Drones?" Levenson repeated angrily.

"Doesn't matter," I shrugged. I didn't particularly

want to explain the concept. Levenson's face squinted slightly as he glanced between us. I had no interest in explaining just what kind of monster that he had decided to do business with. At least until after he had helped me recover Allie.

I didn't like this. There were simply too many things that could wrong with sending armed soldiers into student accommodation. This wasn't filling me with confidence. There was no need to risk anyone else in this. I could go in, recover Allie and then get out via teleport.

"No," I said "I'll go alone."

"Like hell you will," Levenson snapped. "We're already very well aware of what happened the last time you tried to talk to your sister. If you think I'm letting you anywhere near the general public without some assurances you're very mistaken."

"And you think your 'team'" I said, twisting the word, "will help you should things go bad?"

"That's not the point," Levenson said. "She needs to be recovered and arrested by non-Mages. Anything else will bring the wrong kind of attention and there's already too much of that."

"How can you even be assured that she will be there? She's probably already on the run from the cops."

"She's not," Levenson replied blandly.

"Why not?"

"Because she's under orders from Victor to stay in Melbourne." Marcus said.

"Why?"

"Because he assumes that it's the one place that you won't go, I don't know," Marcus snapped angrily, "it's not important."

"Very well," I replied softly, "I've only got one question left. Why now?"

"The Primea has died."

Marcus's words were soft and factual. As if he were simply repeating a truth and not relating the fact that one of his parents had died.

"There was evidence to suggest that Victor may have been behind my mother's death." Marcus continued, "Perhaps even her sickness in the first place."

Marcus's eyes didn't reveal the pain that he must be feeling at relating his mother's death. The man's face was a mask that showed nothing. It could have been made out of bronze for all the emotion he revealed. This was typical of the man, he rarely showed any form of emotion, but I had to assume that he would grieve for the passing of his parents. This didn't seem to be the case.

The Primea's death was a little suspect. She had always seemed frail, so it was plausible that old age had been the cause of her death, but I knew from experience just how clever Victor was when it came to exploiting the human body. The kind of sickness that would keep her weak and malleable for years sounded just like the type of thing that he would do. It was a little also suspicious that she died shortly after Victor had thought that Marcus was killed.

"He is going to pay," Marcus finished softly, "Victor

thinks I am dead. He will be careless and won't see it when I come for him."

At last the mask broke and I could see the man behind. It hadn't been loss or grief that had broken the façade. It had been his talk of vengeance. Once the mask had fallen the hurt behind his words was almost palpable. For a few seconds I almost felt sorry for him. Until I realised that his quest for revenge could very well consume me, Allie, Renee or anyone that got swept up in its wake.

"You're planning something that could lead to an open fire fight in a very open and very crowded area. Non Mages are going to get hurt." I accused, I wasn't overly comfortable with this whole situation. Something was definitely off – It seemed too simple, too easy. The problem was that I couldn't figure out what I wasn't being told.

"Acceptable," Marcus grunted. I guess the matter was closed.

I often wonder if Marcus had any idea of just how many people were going to get hurt or if he simply didn't care. For all his claims of wanting to reintegrate into society Marcus was just as elitist as Victor about Mana. He didn't care any more about the common man any more than Victor did. I had no idea what was going on in Levenson's mind. Now that Marcus had ensured my allegiance he departed.

* * * * * *

He left a small team of soldiers had been left on side to cover my protection and any needs that I might have. I didn't spend much time associating with the soldiers though, they mostly wanted to keep to themselves. The only exception was a soldier named Marcellus. I couldn't tell if this was his first or his last name, but it was the only thing he would answer to.

Our conversations had been tense at first. I didn't particularly like the interruption and he was obviously nervous about being near one of our kind. I think his curiosity must have gotten the best of him though. It was half way through the first day after Marcus had left that Marcellus tentatively approached me. I'd taken to walking across the grounds periodically. I needed to do something, anything to break up the tedium of the day. There wasn't exactly that much to do on the army base. I was standing by the main gate when Marcellus walked over. I couldn't tell if he was on active duty or not, but I assumed not.

"You smoke?" he offered, as he gestured a pack towards me.

"No," I grunted, "Those things will kill you."

Marcellus grinned in reply, "Yeah, but it takes the years at the end – don't want those years anyway."

I was forced to grin as I tried that logic on for size. I could tell from the way that he'd stated it that he'd been joking, but it had been funny none the less.

"You might have a point there," I was grudgingly forced to concede.

"How old are you man?" Marcellus queried after a few seconds.

"I dunno, twenty two? Twenty three? I've lost track," I replied dryly, "Why?"

"You're just not what I expected," Marcellus continued.

"Oh?"

"No, when they tell us about you guys – they make it seem like you're not even human."

"We're not," I replied.

"You seem nice enough," He smirked.

I smiled and let my irises expand as I drew Mana forth. I didn't plan on doing anything with it, I just wanted the effect. It wouldn't be a good idea for this man to get the wrong impression about our kind. He seemed nice enough too. It would be a shame for him to make the mistake of trying to get friendly with the wrong Mage.

"Woah," Marcellus exclaimed as he took a step back, "that's freaky."

My performance didn't have the effect that I'd hoped. If anything he seemed more interested now. I didn't particularly want to get hammered with a bunch of stupid questions about Mana, but on the other hand there wasn't anything else productive around here to do. Marcus had been clear in his instructions - I was to stay on the grounds until he sent for me. He didn't want to let anyone know that I was in Melbourne or that I had survived my encounter with Allie. Let the world think I was dead.

"How do they recruit you guys?" I queried. I'd often wondered about this. Was there a recruitment company for this kind of work? Both Marcus and Victor had worked with soldiers that knew about our kind. I'd never thought to actually ask them how they learned about us. They'd seen us use our powers directly in front of them without comment. I assumed that they had been private security companies, but I was beginning to rethink that assessment.

"Mostly through regular services," Marcellus replied, "We get an offer for special training. During the training they assess us to see if we're what they're looking for."

"What are they looking for?"

"I've got no idea," Marcellus chuckled, "but obviously I have it."

I grinned back, "When do they tell you about us?"

"They don't do that until the end," Marcellus smirked, "they don't tell us anything. They take us in and show us videos. It's mostly security footage of you guys doing your thing. I remember first time I saw it I thought it was something from a movie. That shit just don't happen in real life."

I nodded sombrely. I would have thought the same thing in his place.

"Eventually though, you come to accept it," Marcellus continued, "Don't even really think about it after a while."

"So what do you guys think you're doing?"

"I dunno," Marcellus shrugged, "saving the world from you guys? Shit, I dunno."

"You haven't given it much thought?"

"Nope!" he grinned cheerily, "Not paid to think – I just shoot who they tell me to."

"I can tell you now," I murmured, "That gun of yours won't do you any good should things go bad."

"Heh? You guys can dodge bullets eh?" Marcellus joked.

"No," I shook my head, "We don't have to."

This didn't appear to be the answer that he was looking for and I could tell by the way that he waved me off that he didn't believe me. I didn't blame him, but on the other hand I didn't want him to have any illusions about the usefulness of the weapon against our kind.

* * * * * *

The other soldiers still didn't seem as inclined as Marcellus to talk to me, in fact I doubt that many of them knew who or what I actually was. Dinner was brought to me in a cursory manner by a closed mouthed soldier who simply placed a tray in front of me and grunted. If it weren't for the fact that the room I was in was well furnished and I could unlock the door at any point I would have been forced to come to the conclusion that I was in a prison cell.

I was actually rather relieved when Marcellus turned up with a rifle over his shoulder.

"Got a minute," he quipped as he poked his head in the doorway.

"Sure," I replied as I got to my feet and walked over.

"I wanted to show you something."

He led me through the base to a secluded area where there was a large field of sandbags that had been lined up. It was obvious that he'd taken me to a shooting range.

"I've set up this range with only one target," Marcellus grunted as we moved towards the firing lanes. I could see a human shaped object at the far end of the range. I couldn't exactly tell what it was made out of.

He unslung the rifle from his shoulder and presented it to me. I did find it rather amusing to note that he paused for several seconds as if allowing me to take the weapon. I had no intention of reaching for the gun.

"That's an M4 Carbine assault rifle," he announced, "It has an effective range of 300 metres. It's capable of a 700 to 950 RPM and has a standard ammunition capacity of 30 rounds."

I drifted off as he got into the more detailed specifics of the weapon. It just sounded like a range of numbers and details that I couldn't really understand. I nodded agreeably through most of the demonstration.

"It's capable of stopping someone in their tracks from half a block away." He finished softly.

"Understood," I replied briefly, "Was there somewhere you were going with this?"

"Have you ever fired a gun before?" he queried.

"Not successfully, no," I replied quickly.

I could tell that statement had confused him for a second but he recovered well.

"You're saying that you don't need to dodge a shot by one of these things?"

"Why is this so hard to believe? People use bullet proof vests all the time," I retorted.

"You weren't talking about a bullet proof vest."

"What do you want?" I sighed, "Do you want me to walk out onto that field so you can take a few pot shots at me?"

I could see the urge to say 'Yes' rising within him. It must have taken everything he had within him to shake his head and grunt 'of course not.'

"Then what do you want?"

"I just feel that you should have some idea of what a rifle like this is capable of and how hard it hits."

"I know what it's capable of," I disagreed, "I've been shot at numerous times."

I could tell he still didn't believe me. He couldn't believe me. He'd been trained to believe that these weapons were the ultimate expression of stopping power. To come across someone for whom the weapon meant less than nothing was a blow to everything he'd been raised to believe.

"Look," I replied wearily as I gestured towards the other end of the range, "Take aim at your target."

I held my hand out so that he could tell that I was doing something. I'd long learned that I didn't need to actively target an object like this, but I think he needed to see something showy to know that power was being applied. I flexed my fingers and sent out a shield field around the target. The distance involved made the whole process that much harder, but I was eventually able to complete the field at the required distance.

"Ready?" I prompted as he moved into a firing position.

He nodded.

"You will see a small blue arc and a spark as the bullet impacts with the shield."

The shot sounded abnormally loud, but then again I'd never been on this end of the rifle before. As predicted a small spark was clearly visible from the other end of the range. It was difficult to determine if the bullet had actually passed through the shield and hit the target at this range. The target looked intact though.

"Holy crap," Marcellus whispered. That pretty much confirmed it - the shield had soaked the bullet.

"Now you know what you're facing." I replied darkly.

I didn't have to tell him that this was the least of our powers, that most of our kind could put up a rudimentary shield easily enough. True there were many of our number for whom blocking a bullet with a shield would be out of their abilities, but I didn't need him to know that. All he needed to know was that if he was trying to take down one of my kind – the rifle alone wouldn't be enough.

"That's not right," Marcellus shook his head, "It's not human."

"No," I agreed readily. A stilted silence ensured between us.

"You want a shot? I could teach you how to shoot," Marcellus offered. I think he was mainly doing so to change the subject.

"No," I replied quickly, "I've never really liked guns."

Marcellus grunted and looked back at me, I could tell from his expression that he was looking at my irises as they slowly returned to normal. He expended several more shots and grimaced as the target sparked again as the bullets impacted against my shield. He scowled and began to check the rifle. I assumed he was looking for faults. I didn't have to tell him that there was nothing wrong with the rifle.

CHAPTER TEN

The click of a magazine sliding into a rifle caught my attention. I was sitting in a small van with a small troop of soldiers. I was being taken somewhere. I didn't know where. For someone who had supposedly recruited me into his service Marcus was being awfully close lipped about what he actually needed me to do. I wasn't surprised by this though, that was typical of the man.

I still didn't feel that comfortable in the presence of armed soldiers. This situation was a highly unusual occurrence for me as the soldiers weren't there to keep me prisoner, I was there to protect them. This was a novel feeling.

The van rocked backwards and forwards so much I felt like the back of my skull was slowly being turned into spaghetti as it slammed against the wall behind me. The soldier across the van from me was loading and unloading his rifle. I couldn't tell if this was a sign of nerves or if this was part of some unusual routine before battle. Either way it was starting to get to me.

My look of annoyance must have been noticed as the soldier scowled and leaned forward.

"I annoying you, boy?" he sneered. This didn't do

much to endear him to me.

"Yes," I replied politely, "please stop that."

His face darkened.

"What you gonna do about it?" he grunted angrily.

"Stop you if necessary," I murmured lightly as I leaned forward. I let my irises expand as I drew upon the Mana. I had no intention of doing anything, but just wanted the effect. I assumed that the man in front of me would know what it meant. He did.

"Oh shit," he whispered. "Sorry Sir, I didn't know."

He quickly finished loading his rifle and placed it by his side. Once I'd revealed my powers none of the soldiers seemed that interested in having much to do with me. Most wouldn't even look at me. I didn't much blame them.

Marcellus gave me a nod as he settled back down. I wondered how he had managed to look so calm. I wished that there were a window in this van, it would have been nice to see my home city one more time, but that wasn't to be, the windows had been blacked out. I assumed that they were also bullet-proof glass.

The truck eventually pulled up and we were ushered into a small underground loading bay. I was quickly directed into a storeroom that had been converted into a command room of sorts. The commanding officer was a man in his late forties, at least. He had a well-groomed moustache and a strong American accent. He nodded in my direction, but was distracted as one of the other soldiers called for his attention. Levenson had obviously been waiting for us to arrive and got up as we entered the room. He looked nervous.

He gestured me towards a small table at the far end of the room. On the table were a small earpiece and a sidearm in holster. He picked up the side arm first and offered it to me.

I shook my head. "Don't need that"

He didn't argue the point, but I could tell that he was slightly annoyed by the exchange. I don't really know what he had expected. He picked up the earpiece next and tried to fit it in my ear.

"Don't need that either."

"It's not for you," he cut me off, "it's if we need to contact you."

I relented with good grace and let him fit the earpiece. It was uncomfortable. I'd have to make sure that I lost it when the action started. He connected the earpiece to a unit that he slipped into my inside pocket.

"You know what you're supposed to do?" Levenson questioned gruffly.

I nodded. I knew what they wanted of me. What I wasn't sure of was what they expected me to do should things go wrong. It all sounded great on paper, but something about this all seemed wrong. I'd like to think in many ways that I'm a smart person, I can reason and use logical deduction to arrive at sensible conclusions. To this day I'm still wondering why the hell I just took what was being said at face value here. None of this made any sense. This was a university in a first world city. Why were armed soldiers being sent in? What could they possibly need this much firepower for?

This looked like something from one of those old World War II movies where they're going in to the fight a battalion of Nazis behind enemy lines. Something was definitely off here and yet for some reason I didn't see it. I could blame inexperience, I could blame nerves, I could even reason that maybe I had been affected by a compulsion to ignore common sense, but the truth was that deep in my heart I knew what I was doing and I didn't care. I was in this for one thing and one thing only. Regardless of what happened, I was going to free my sister from the influence of Victor. If only I'd known the costs of this decision. I might have re-thought it, for what little difference that would have made.

A voice in my earpiece asked me to confirm that I could hear them. I think it was Marcus, but it was hard to tell. I grunted the affirmative and I heard several other voices chime in as well.

"You should take that sidearm son," a crackly voice cut in from behind me.

"Master Wills, meet Colonel Stafford," Levenson nodded as the commanding officer approached from behind.

"Don't need it." Why was everyone determined to give me a gun? The one and only time I'd ever had to fire a gun I hadn't been very good. I'd had the safety lock on and nothing had happened. It didn't exactly fill me with confidence.

"Your choice," the colonel grunted. "You ready?"

I nodded briefly.

"Stay in formation," he said as he turned to survey the rest of his troops, "I'm not going to have this cock up because you took a wrong turn."

He seemed charming I thought sarcastically. It wasn't going to be overly pleasant working with him. Levenson gave me a curt nod and waved towards the corner.

"You understand what you're required to do here?" he asked again.

"Yeah. Hopefully nothing."

Levenson nodded in agreement, "That's right. Hopefully your sister will come quietly."

"When do we go in?"

"We've caught a break, Alisha either decided or was convinced to attend the event." Levenson grinned.

"This is good news? Surely that just means she's surrounded by more people."

"Yes, but it means that she will be travelling back to the apartment on foot. We're aiming to recover her during this time. Hopefully there'll be a minimum of witnesses. You are to remain out of sight until you're needed. We have people monitoring her, they'll let us know when she's on the move."

"Got it." I still didn't think that this was going to go how they expected.

"Thank you for this," Levenson murmured. I couldn't tell if he was being earnest or not.

"Answer me one thing," I turned to face him. "Why are you working for Marcus?"

"I'm not working for him. I'm working with him. And I do so because the directors of Division 7 believe that it's the right thing to do."

I scoffed softly. Although Levenson hadn't said it, I was sure that they planned to turn on Marcus should he be successful in displacing Victor. I felt no remorse over this. In some ways perhaps it would be better. With both of those Mages gone I would finally be free of their influence. Those directors at Division 7 were obviously feeling quite confident in their plans. Should this fail, I don't imagine that they would be able to escape Victor or Marcus's wrath should either discover that they were plotting against them.

I didn't care about this one way or the other. Regardless of their plans after this I would take my sister and find somewhere safe, somewhere remote. I could finally be free. Renee had once begged me to go with her. After I had saved my sister I would find Renee and we would all be free of this.

Colonel Stafford had obviously determined that we'd had enough time to chat. Two soldiers moved in on each side of me. This felt more familiar, just like I was being led into a prison. It's amazing how the little things can make you feel right at home.

"Keep them alive," Levenson said as we turned to leave.

I nodded back to him briefly as I headed out the door. Soldiers immediately flanked me on each side. It was an unusual experience, I was more used to being their prisoner than being protected by them, yet their entire demeanour was one of protection. It was almost humorous as the reality of the situation was that I was there to protect them.

"Target is on the move," a voice whispered in my ear. The earpiece was uncomfortably loud. "She's not alone."

"Does that change things?" I whispered more to myself than to anyone.

"Proceed," Levenson ordered down the line, "Ensure that civilians are not harmed."

I had wondered what they had meant by minimal casualties when they had said that earlier. I guess I was about to find out.

One of the soldiers directed me to follow him as he led me through the streets. This university appeared to be in dispersed with small houses, shops and industrial looking buildings. I didn't know if they were occupied or not. The whole place had the desolate look of a closed factory. It was strange contrast to the lights of the CBD that weren't that far away.

We held up in a small foyer that led out onto one of the main roads. Allie would have to come this way. From here we could monitor the situation without being too far from the action. It was important that I stay out of direct sight. If Allie saw me first, things would go badly very quickly.

"I'll wait here," I said. I hope that whoever was on the other end of the line heard me. I vaguely wondered if there was some sort of button I had to press like a walkie-talkie button.

"Team two is in position," another voice called down the line.

"Target sighted," the voice continued. I could tell they were nervous.

"If she shows any form of resistance, back off," I whispered into the line. I hope to god they heard me.

I could hear muffled talking through the earpiece but couldn't make out any exact words. The grim look on the soldiers' faces seemed to indicate that they were readying for something.

"Let's hope this works," I whispered quickly.

I could only hope that having her friends with her might convince Allie to co-operate rather than risk revealing herself. I found myself holding my breath in anticipation.

At any moment I expected to hear the short sharp staccato of gunfire that would indicate that Allie had chosen to fight. Nothing happened for several minutes. Just long enough for me to convince myself that this would all work out.

I almost didn't believe it when I heard it. It began so softly, a soldier simply swore into his headset and then the gunfire tore through the night. I didn't need the headset to hear it. The sound was quickly followed by several screams and then more gunfire.

The soldiers in front of me took off in high speed towards the fight. It took me several seconds to realise I was supposed to go with them. The sound of gunfire increased along with the muffled shouts and curses from the headset between blasts.

There was no way I was going to be able to keep pace with the soldiers, but fortunately I had other options available. I took to the air and vaulted over the building between us. From this vantage point I could see a team of soldiers fanning out to keep Allie within their sights. Four of their number had already fallen and Allie was about to deal with the others.

I was terrified that I would see the fallen bodies of Allie's friends that had been gunned down by the soldiers, but fortunately there didn't seem to be any sign of them. They must have been allowed to flee or had been collected once they had left the immediate vicinity. It wouldn't have surprised me if they had already been picked up by Levenson's team.

Allie had almost finished off the original soldiers before we arrived. The second team of soldiers opened fire. It was impressive how quickly they dropped into firing position. The shots ricocheted harmlessly off Allie's shield, but distracted her from finishing off the survivors of the first group of soldiers.

This wasn't going to end well for the soldiers, if things kept going this way. I had to stop her. The problem was how to without escalating things. This was the exact thing that I feared would happen. A disrupt spell would merely impact harmlessly against her shield now. I'd need to take down her shield first, but to do that I'd have to engage and that would lead to a fight. It wasn't a fight I was even sure I wanted to win anymore.

Voices were screaming into my earpiece, begging me to intercept. Two more soldiers had gone down before I managed to gather control of my wits. Allie had almost cut down the last of the soldiers who I had been supposed to be protecting when I leapt from the building and raised a shield around myself.

The impact created by my feet on the concrete behind her sent a wave of Mana pulsing in all directions. That got her attention. She turned around to face me and her eyes narrowed with hate. It took everything I had not to physically reel from her look.

There was no love in her eyes. There was no compassion, no recognition. I was dead to her now. It would have been so easy to simply turn around and walk away from her. I would have probably saved so many lives had I done so, had I accepted the fact that she wasn't mine to save any longer. But I didn't. I couldn't accept that.

* * * * * *

Allie's eyes narrowed as she summoned her powers and directed them against me. I let her flail at me as I summersaulted out of the way of her assault. Her attack was aggressive and powerful. If I hadn't been expecting such an attack I would have been downed immediately. Fortunately however I knew from our last encounter just what she was capable of.

"Why are you here?" she snarled, "You're dead! I killed you! Why didn't you stay dead?"

I didn't answer. Let her weaken herself as she expended her Mana ineffectually. She obviously wasn't thinking clearly as her rage took control of her. She increased her assault in an effort to end my life. Four threads sought out my destruction, but unfortunately for her I was always one step ahead.

This wasn't to say that I was always successful in avoiding her assault. She had managed to clip me several times, but I was moving too fast for her to secure a solid strike. The building behind me appeared to be taking the brunt of her fury as her threads were slowly and methodically tearing it to pieces in an effort to get to me.

I had leapt back onto the roof to create some distance between us, but unfortunately the roof collapsed under my feet as I landed. The damage to the building below had weakened the support structure for the roof and I slid into the chasm created by the collapsing tiles into what had previously been an internal room. I landed badly, but my shield absorbed most of the impact.

Allie didn't give me any time to recover from my fall as she attempted to bring more of the roof down upon me. The sound of gunfire distracted her; several of the soldiers had resumed firing at her.

It didn't take me long to clear myself of the rubble of the fallen building and break free. I sent shards of rubble flying in every direction as I emerged from the ruined building. I had thought that Allie might have turned to deal with the soldiers firing at her. Unfortunately she hadn't determined that she was done with me yet. If she hadn't been hit by some of the flying shrapnel caused by my escape she might have knocked me straight back down again. I couldn't allow her to corner me like that again. If she then did I was finished.

It had only been a fluke that the flying chunks of building had knocked against her shield and sent her back onto the defensive. Her distraction allowed me to clear myself from the ruin and leap up on top of the roof again. Allie soon followed me, leaping up onto the other side of the smashed building. She didn't attack immediately and I quickly realised my mistake.

From up here the soldiers couldn't get a clear shot. I was on my own and Allie was more enraged than ever. There was no way out of this, I had to subdue her without seriously hurting her.

"Allie! Please come quietly!" I called, "we don't have to do this! I don't want to hurt you!"

Allie's response was more of a cry of outrage and anger than any real response.

I engaged Allie tentatively, throwing a thread that I knew she could easily defend, to keep her on the back foot. She had already expended a serious amount of energy in her previous assault, but she didn't seem to be tiring. It was clear that this wouldn't be over quickly and certainly wouldn't be without cost to either of us.

"Why won't you just die?" Allie snarled as she launched a vicious attack at where I had previously been standing. "Leave me alone! I don't need you! Just leave me alone!"

The hatred in her words cut me to the core, but I knew that I could fix this. I could make this right. I could bring her back from whatever sick and twisted fate that Victor had planned for her. I had to. The alternative was too painful to consider.

I landed with several seconds before Allie brought her thread back around, and brought a thread of my own to block hers. Our threads collided in a shower of sparks and sound. Allie was relentless in her assault and I found that I had to use increasing levels of power to match her.

I grunted at the effort as I pumped more and more power into the thread. She was matching me! She was just as powerful as I was! That thought alone was staggering. I had never met anyone without the title Arch Mage attached to their name who could match me for sheer power!

Victor had trained her well, too well for me to simply exhaust her. I had to change tactics. Letting her thread sweep past me and smash the roof next to me into shards of tile, I threw everything I had at her. She wasn't able to bring her thread back in time and my thread caught her solidly on the hip and sent her flying.

She landed poorly against one of the buildings on the far side of the road. Her shield protected her as she barrelled through the wall and into the building beyond. I didn't give her any chance to recover from the blow as I knew that if I did so she would come after me with a vengeance.

I could hear soldiers screaming orders for updates in my ear, but I pulled the earpiece out in anger as I swept my thread down shattering the roof above Allie and bringing large chunks of wall down onto her.

This was exactly what she had done to me about two minutes ago and had much the same effect, our shields were simply too strong for kinetic damage to have much effect. I saw the tell-tale glimmer of her shield through the veritable vortex of dust and rubble that surrounded her. Beams were still falling from the ceiling, landing with a crescendo of noise. Allie appeared unhurt by her fall and was already launching her counter attack.

I had first thought that her target was me, but I was wrong. A powerful thread impacted against the building I was standing on and caused one of the few remaining walls to be reduced to rubble in a matter of seconds. Had I been able to predict her attack I may have been able to save myself, but as it was my footing was taken out from underneath me I fell into the ever-increasing void beneath.

I must have smacked my head on a beam on the way down as loud ringing noises reverberated throughout my head. I barely felt my landing even though I turned a bed of broken bricks and beams into rubble. My shield had held.

I leapt to my feet instantly and sent threads out towards Allie, literally tearing down walls to get to her. The sudden activity sent waves of dizziness washing over me, but I managed to hold things together. I pulled down the only remaining wall between us only to find that she had gone.

I quickly flicked the earpiece back into my ear.

"Spread out," I called into the earpiece. If I could distract Allie with the soldier's gunfire again we might be able to take her by surprise, "I've lost sight of the target."

There was a request for confirmation of the order, which was crisply given. It wasn't comforting to know that I wasn't the one directly in command here and that my orders would need to go through a third party. That could become a problem later. Especially if they kept seeking confirmation every time I needed them to do something.

Several soldiers emerged from around the corner and converged on the building where Allie had last been seen. It hadn't been hard for them to find, I was surprised that we weren't already inundated with cops and other emergency crew.

We had certainly created enough of a mess. It was lucky that this was a university campus and not general housing. At this time of night there unlikely to be anyone within the buildings. If there were people in those buildings then they had chosen the wrong day to work back late. There was little else that could be said really.

I emerged from the rubble to stand in the middle of the street. I hoped to provide her with an opportunity too tempting to resist and lure her back out into the open. The staccato of gunfire alerted me to her presence before I saw her.

She was on the roof of another one of the campus

buildings. By the time we were finished here there would be very little university left.

The gunfire did little more than annoy her as she leapt down to strike at me. I knew from experience just how devastating these attacks could be so it was critical that I didn't let it hit me. I rolled to the side at the last minute and recovered my footing just in time to see Allie's thread leave a massive gash in the tarmac.

"Allie…" I called again, "please…"

She didn't respond. It was obvious that she wasn't going to come quietly. This fight was like nothing I'd ever experienced before and I was well out of my depth. In all the fights I'd been in I'd never had to pull my punches like this. If truth be told I had become brutal and effective. I overpowered my foes through sheer strength and power. Whilst there was technique to my actions it was callous and without forethought. Any finesse was applied purely through instinct rather than design. Those traits would not serve me well here.

I deflected her follow up attack, sending her thread careening into a power pole and smashing it into splinters. The lines buckled as they absorbed the weight of the now useless pole. Amazingly enough they didn't snap.

The soldiers were still firing erratically at her. They knew that they weren't going to break through her shield through force alone and were obviously worried about wasting ammunition. They were right. The bullets were little more than an annoyance to her as she launched her next attack at me.

I countered with an attack of my own that swept past her assault and impacted solidly on her shield. The shriek she made as her shield buckled cut through me like a knife. Her temporary defeat seemed to bolster her as she launched yet another furious assault. Unfortunately for Allie she had let her rage get the better of her and her assault, while furious was mainly taking its toll on my surroundings once again.

Allie's attacks were getting increasingly erratic and I was able to make several decisive strikes to her side on her backswing. I was very conscious that although her attack was wild it was still very powerful. If she should connect my shield wouldn't be able to last for very long.

The more I struck her the angrier she got and the more aggressive she became. I couldn't see her face properly through her shield, but I could see her hate filled eyes. They pierced through me more devastating than any attack could ever have been.

I drew her in as I retreated before her. She was a whirlwind of aggression and power as she sought to catch me, but I was always just a step ahead. I ducked as a thread passed over me and leapt straight at her. She hadn't expected that.

This next part was going to be difficult. I needed to take out her shield without one of the soldiers shooting her. My thread impacted against her shield with shuddering force and sent cracks along the confines of her shield. Her shield held but only barely. It did not survive my next strike.

I moved in to point blank range as the final thread impacted against her shield at stomach level. I lunged at her hitting her seconds after my thread did. I pulled her into a tight spin and held her against me. I took several gunshots against my shield before the soldiers realised that it was over and held their fire.

Allie grunted and attempted to push me away, but I was too strong. Letting my thread dissipate I built up the power along my arms and formed the disrupt spell that would finish this. Allie's face took on a terrified expression as she realised that her end was near.

"No, no… no!" she whispered, "just… kill me… end this!"

The disrupt impacted at point blank range between us. It bounced harmlessly off my shield, but was absorbed by Allie. I felt her go rigid in my arms as her Mana field went crazy. I knew from experience just how much this hurt.

"I'm sorry," I whispered as I gently let her down. She was so light, so very, very light.

I glanced around to see soldiers closing in. Allie was convulsing slightly as the disrupt spell did its nasty work on her nervous system. She would be fine in time, but the experience was not going to be pleasant.

"Take the girl into custody," a distant voice said, at first I was confused, but quickly realised that it had come to the earpiece hanging from the wire on my chest. I quickly grabbed the earpiece and placed it back in my ear. This was the first time that this voice had interjected on the radio, but I recognised the American accent.

Colonel Stafford was certainly a man of few words.

"Gentle!" I scolded as one of the soldiers pulled her from me and began to bind her wrists with some form of wire tie.

The soldier looked in deference to me and did appear to treat her a little better. Allie's head tilted to the side as she looked down at me. A lonely tear slid down from her eyes across her cheek and down onto her shoulder. Her stare lasted only a few seconds, but her expression said everything she needed to. There was no coming back from this.

The soldiers pulled her roughly to her feet as a new voice cut into the earpiece. "Stand down and await new orders."

I recognised that voice too, it was Marcus's. What was going on? A van should have been sent to recover us and get us out of here. We were vulnerable here, if nothing else domestic forces would be closing in on us as we spoke. It was madness to remain behind.

"What's going on?" a third voice cut in. Levenson seemed almost as confused as I was.

There were several seconds of silence before Levenson thundered, "Get that van there now!"

"Belay that order," Marcus said calmly down the line.

I glanced at the soldiers to see which of the two instructions they seemed more inclined to take. They stared stonily back. They weren't exactly pointing weapons at me, but they had a sense of hostility about them. This was new.

"We should at least get off the street." I tried, but the soldiers didn't reply.

This wasn't right. Something was definitely off here. I looked around warily. I hadn't dropped my shield yet so it wasn't like I was in any danger, but I definitely didn't like what I was seeing. Several seconds passed before I realised how stupid this was.

"Give me the girl," I ordered as I stepped forward, "I'm getting out of here."

Immediately two soldiers raised their rifles at me and the third, who was holding Allie, stepped back protectively.

"This is stupid," I said as I let the Mana flow down my arms. "You can't stop me."

"No," the third soldier replied calmly, "but this will."

He placed the barrel of a pistol against Allie's head. My breath held in my throat. Time stopped. My eyes slowly panned between the barrel of the gun at Allie's head and the eyes of the soldier holding it.

"That is a death sentence," I said. "You pull that trigger and I will tear you to pieces."

"Step back Sir," one of the soldiers ordered as he gestured with his rifle.

"Levenson! What is the meaning of this?"

"Meaning of what?" Levenson's voice was agitated. "What the hell is going on?"

This left two options. Either Levenson was the greatest voice actor I'd ever met or these soldiers weren't operating under his orders any longer. Nothing led me to believe that Levenson was play-acting. That only left one real option – these soldiers worked for Marcus.

"Marcus," I hissed into the earpiece, "Don't do this. This is between you and me! Leave her out of this."

"This has nothing to do with either of you," Marcus replied darkly.

What? That made no sense. Of course it was about me. It was always about me.

"Execute the girl on my command," Marcus continued.

A shiver went down my spine and the Mana unconsciously rose in fury. This wasn't going to happen. This couldn't be allowed to take place. I was responsible for Allie. I was the one that had brought her down. I was the one who had disrupted her and left her defenceless. I was the reason she was standing there helpless whilst that mindless thug pointed a gun at her.

"You don't want to do this," I advised the soldiers, all three took several cautious steps back and their guns wavered slightly at the threat. I could almost see the soldier's finger twitch on the gun pointed at Allie.

Allie was staring at me with open eyes, her Mana field was still scrambled, but I could see her desperately trying to gain some control. It didn't look like she would be successful though, her Mana signature was still erratic.

"Put the gun down," I urged, "No one needs to die here. We can…."

I never got to finish. The sound of a loud explosion of Mana cut me off mid-sentence. The soldiers to each side were immediately swept away as threads wrapped around their necks and flung them down the street. It had happened so quickly. It was brutal in its efficiency. The thread tore through them as if they were no more than ragdolls.

The third soldier had obviously already pulled the trigger by the time the thread reached him, but for some reason the gun didn't appear to have fired. He must have had the safety on. I was glad that I wasn't the only one to make that mistake. The thread caught the gun pointed at my sister in a savage twist and most likely broke every bone in the soldier's wrist.

Allie stumbled forward a few steps as the man supporting her was swept away. Allie's head tilted to the side gently. She appeared to smile for a second and for a brief beautiful moment I thought everything was going to be okay.

The hatred and anger from her eyes fled before the smile and her face became young and beautiful again. Her smile lasted only a second but was reflected for all time in the light of her eyes. Then ever so slowly, her smile faded and her eyes swept upwards to look at the night sky.

At first I didn't notice her jaw slacken or the blood flush from her cheeks. I didn't notice the small but growing blood-stain on her shoulder from the bullet wound behind her head. I didn't see her steps falter as she weakened. I didn't see the Mana in her slowly begin to fade. Soldiers don't make mistakes about the safety lock.

My sight was locked firmly into my sister's eyes as they went dark. For that second in time her eyes were so beautiful, so clear and so pure. I wanted it to last forever. But it didn't. It couldn't.

Allie stumbled and fell forward. Unable to brace herself because of her bindings she crumpled against the hard concrete of the footpath. I would have done anything to have been able to catch her and lay her gently down, but I was too far away.

I was at her side in seconds, lifting her from the ground and cradling her in my arms. A fog of disbelief washed over me. There was so much blood, it covered her right shoulder and back. I pulled her to me and pressed my face against her forehead.

"He's here," a voice boomed through my head. The words were surreal and I didn't understand them. At first I thought the words were some figment of my imagination. Some horrid construct created by my mind unwilling to face the reality of my sister's death. I soon realised the words were coming from the earpiece in my ear.

It didn't matter where the voice had come from. It didn't matter what was said. I held my sister in my arms and turned her face towards mine. I desperately needed to see that light in her eyes again. I needed to see something, anything in her eyes that would let me know that she was going to be okay. But her eyes were cold now. The light had gone.

They say that in death, a person's face relaxes and their worries and cares seem to fade away. The hatred and anger they felt in life can no longer affect them. This is a lie. Allie's face in death was cold and her eyes reflected only the hatred and loss that I knew could be seen in my own.

Her eyes amplified my pain back at me tenfold. In her cold dead stare I felt every failure I had committed. Every injustice I had perpetrated against my sister. She had been young and she had been innocent. It was my actions that had turned her into something that should not have been. She had paid the price for my callousness and for my arrogance. This should have been my fate.

I should have left her in Omeo, I should have not begun her training. I should have tried harder to keep her from Victor. A thousand conflicting thoughts smashed through my mind as my world collapsed into no more than her two darkened and accusing eyes.

She was lying so still in my arms. Although she weighed almost nothing at all, her weight bore down upon me. I held her until I could stand her gaze no longer. With shaking hands I gently closed Allie's eyes. And just like that , she was gone.

I needed to be alone with my grief. Free for but a few moments before the world intruded again. I needed to say something, do something that would let her know how sorry I was. That I regretted the way things had turned out. That this wasn't the way things should have gone. But I wasn't alone.

Victor Whittlesea was standing behind me. He kept his distance, but eventually it dawned on me that he was there. He stood no more than a dozen steps away from me. His grief was clearly visible, as clear and as strong as my own. It was the first time I had seen loss or pain on his face and for a second it floored me. As with Marcus, emotion wasn't something that I attributed to Victor. I had seen annoyance and anger, but nothing like this. The mask that protected him from the world without wasn't just lowered, it had been shattered.

I had no words. For several seconds we were comrades in our grief. Shared companions in pain, then it dawned on me. Victor had studied Necromancy! He could bring her back!

"Save her" I croaked.

"I cannot," Victor said softly, "I can only reanimate the remains – and I will not do that to her."

The fury and rage threatened to overtake me once again. This was the man responsible, the man who had caused all this. He was just as guilty as I was for my sister's death. Once I would have leapt to my feet and struck at him with all the power that my frustration and pain would allow. I would have made him pay for making me feel this loss. Some unconscious part of my brain screamed at me to do so.

"Yes! Give in to your anger! Use it! Right the wrong! Make yourself strong!" my psyche whispered to me.

I would have loved to have risen to my feet to do as my psyche commanded, but the truth was I couldn't. Some wrongs can't be righted. I clasped my sister's body to mine and broke down. The walls that I had built around me came crashing down as the wave of grief overcame me. The power that I sought fled before my pain and for a moment in time I was nothing.

Victor for his part let me have my grief. He did not intrude, did not comment. I'm not sure how long I spent huddled on that sidewalk. The world without could go to hell for all I cared. It didn't exist for me any longer.

"Master Wills," Victor's voice pierced through the cloud of fog and pain. It was soft but filled with steel. I thought at first that his anger was directed at me, but it wasn't. It was a warning.

We weren't alone any longer. Six Mages stood on the rooftops surrounding us. At their centre was Marcus. He was staring down at us with disdain. This was the reason for all this. This had been nothing more than a trap for Victor. I recognised some of the Mages in Marcus's group, they were powerful supporters of Marcus. Victor would not walk away from this.

"Master Deveraux. You lured me here with the threat to a loved one." Victor intoned. "You are truly a monster."

This had obviously been the intent of Marcus's plan. He had been unable to draw Victor out and knew that he would respond if Allie were in danger. He also knew that I represented the biggest threat to Allie. He had used me.

This wasn't a surprising revelation to me. I had expected him to betray me. I just hadn't realised how far the man would go. The rage that I had been unable to summon at Victor surged through my very soul. The

Mana rose within me like wildfire as my anger finally found a target. Marcus was responsible. He is the one who would pay for my sister's life.

"You cannot escape," Marcus informed Victor, "and you must understand that you are horribly over-matched."

"I wonder if you are prepared for this?" Victor replied. "A direct confrontation between the two of us here can only end in disaster."

Marcus didn't answer.

"I suspected as much," Victor said. "This was your intention all along... "

Victor didn't get a chance to finish before they attempted to strike him down. They all struck at once, hoping to bring the Arch Mage down before he was adequately prepared. The magical shockwave that followed almost swept me away.

The street was smashed into pieces and the surrounding buildings were reduced to rubble. The flare of so much Mana being deployed at once was blinding. Once my vision returned there was only rubble where Victor had once stood. It didn't even remotely resemble an urban street any longer. It was now a war zone. If I had thought my fight with Allie had created collateral damage then this was taking it to a whole new realm.

Marcus has chosen his companions well, they were powerful and they were determined to end Victor's life. Had Victor remained where he had been standing he would have been immediately vaporised under that level of magical power. But somehow he wasn't standing there any longer.

It didn't take me long to figure out where Victor had gone. Two of Marcus's number fell immediately as Victor returned his attack. One was knocked unceremoniously from the rooftop and the other disembowelled as Victor's thread pierced through his shield and out his back. The remaining four Mages turned on him, but this time their attack wasn't co-ordinated. As inelegant as their attacks were, it looked like they still might overwhelm him through sheer strength. There were too many of them and Victor was quickly forced back onto the defensive. The end result appeared forgone. At least until I chose to intervene.

I don't think I interjected on a conscious level. I don't recall thinking that I was trying to save Victor's life. If I had been thinking clearly I probably should have let them end him. Everything that had happened to me, from the moment that I had met Renee had been the result of the feud between these two men. Aaron's death, Allie's death, my father's death – these could all be laid at the feet of these men. No, I wasn't thinking logically. My hurt and pain had taken over.

* * * * * *

There are few things more dangerous in this world than someone unwilling or unable to control their power. My attack was launched with a primal scream as I struck against Marcus. My thread wrapped around him and pulled him from the rooftop. Marcus shrieked as the thread drew him from the battle. I could see his shield straining under the pressure I was applying but it didn't look like it would fail. As I brought the Arch Mage before me I could see his face was a twisted mixture of outrage, fear and anger. I don't think he had expected me to survive the initial assault, let alone side against him with Victor. He should have.

"Devon! Let me go!" He snarled desperately. "He needs to die! We can finish this tonight! You know this!"

He was right – Victor did need to die, but Marcus would die before him. This was the man directly responsible for Allie's death. This was the man who had given the order. This was the man whose soldiers had shot her. He would be the first to suffer the consequences.

My grip tightened and I could see Marcus was sending everything he had into the shield to keep it intact. His eyes boggled at the level of power he had been forced to employ to keep me from cracking his shield like a melon.

Had I have been thinking more clearly I would have realised that this wasn't going to achieve the end that I wanted, that this was giving him too much of an opportunity to escape. But it had become a contest of wills, of who could exert the most power, who was the greater, and I was determined to prove myself his superior.

I was drawing upon reserves I didn't even know I had to end the man's life and it still wasn't enough. I could see it was costing him though, I could see it in his face. He was contemplating his own death and it was consuming him. Had I been allowed to continue, I suspect that I eventually would have cracked through his shield and ended him, but I wasn't allowed to continue.

My furious attention to the Arch Mage had blinded me to all other distractions, which proved to be a mistake. One of Marcus's companions swept through my shield with an attack and sent me reeling. My shield had been a flimsy shell anyway with all my power directed into my assault on Marcus. It crumbled around me and my breath was forced from me as the thread impacted on my side.

My shield must have at least softened the blow before caving because the thread didn't kill me instantly. Instead my entire left side went numb with shock at the impact. It may have broken some ribs, but I didn't think so. I could still breathe freely enough. The strike sent me reeling down the street. Before I struck the ground I raised another shield and flipped myself back around onto my feet to land.

I immediately launched several threads in response. My attacker seemed to be amazed that his strike hadn't killed me. Even from across the street I could see the wideness of his eyes as my thread launched towards him. I couldn't see where Marcus had gone, I assumed to take his fight to Victor, either that or the bastard had run from me.

In fact I couldn't even see where Victor and the other

Mages had gone, but I could hear them. The sound of destruction and of Mana clashing filled the air. I could also hear the sound of sirens. The local authorities had finally become involved.

My opponents threads arched over me as he launched a follow up attack. I savagely twisted my own thread to block his, leaving a vast chasm in the concrete road from the impact. He recovered with practiced ease and sent his threads weaving back to attempt to break through my defence. He didn't have a chance and he quickly realised it. He didn't have the skill or strength of Marcus and I had already proved that I was greater than he had been. This wretch couldn't stand against my might for long.

I was slowly but surely closing the distance between us and once I got close enough I would finish him. He was being pushed back down the street as I advanced upon him. I would kill this man and then go on to find and finish his Master.

I had almost reached point blank range when his thread just vanished mid strike. My thread swept through and destroyed the building behind him, but quickly rallied. Unfortunately that allowed him enough time for his next move. He should have used the opportunity to escape, but he did not. That mistake would cost him his life.

I had just about brought my threads around to finish him off when a volley of light assaulted me. I instinctively brought my hands up to protect my face as waves of fire rolled over me. The force of the blast hit my shield like a thunderbolt, but once it had passed it was like I was in the calm of a storm.

Fire surrounded me. It washed over me and drew me into itself. I could see the power that it contained; it was almost beautiful. The flame engulfed my shield, I must have looked like a human-shaped torch. I felt the power of the attack through the shield, but none of the heat. My shield more than adequately protected me from the inferno. This wasn't going to work that well for him.

Flame had been a desperate ploy on his part. He must have assumed that my shield wouldn't be finessed enough to absorb both direct assault and a more elemental strike. He had assumed that I was some mindless brute using mere force to exert my will, that my technical skills wouldn't have been sufficient to absorb new types of attack. He had hoped that a sudden change in tactics would slip through my defences and allow him victory. He had hoped wrong.

He must have known, when I kept approaching, that he was a dead man. He seemed almost resigned as my thread swept around and tore through his shield. The moment his shield fell the flames stopped. I glanced down at the crumpled figure at my feet. I could see the Mana leaving his body as his life fled him.

Now that the immediate battle had ended a stunned silence settled over the immediate vicinity. I could hear the sound of Mage battles in the distance, but it seemed to be coming from a long way away. It almost sounds like they had moved into the CBD directly.

That was the most stupid place they could have gone. The collateral damage would be extraordinary. I shook my head sadly as I realised that that was exactly the point. Marcus wanted the damage. He wanted to be seen by the norms. He wanted to bring our world into the light. Of course he would seek out the most heavily occupied area for the fight. The bastard wanted fatalities.

I gritted my teeth as I thought about it. I no longer cared if he was right or wrong. I no longer cared if our kind remained in the shadows or came into the main stream. I no longer even cared what damage our emergence would have on the world. There was only one thing I sought now and he was in my city tearing it to pieces.

I didn't take the time to think about my next move. I was about to interfere with one of the largest Mage battles in our known history, seek out one of the most powerful combatants and kill him. It might have been better if I had stopped for a moment to consider my actions, but then again I had never been known for that. I was reckless and foolhardy and I paid for it.

As I launched myself into the air and onto what remained of the building across the street I happened to glance down at the destruction that I had wrought. My eye kept picking out details that I didn't want to see. I saw my fallen opponent lying where I had struck him down, but further down the street I saw several other bodies amongst the rubble. These buildings had been inhabited.

I hadn't heard any shouts or calls for help during the fight, but that doesn't mean they weren't there. I was so focused in on my enemy it's possible that I may have missed things as our strikes struck the surrounding buildings. I couldn't imagine the fear they must have felt in their last moments. Peering from their windows at fight on the street and not understanding what was going on as a maelstrom of destruction and chaos overtook them.

I wondered how many more were even now peering at me through closed curtains or huddled behind walls and doors. Simple luck had been all that had spared them from the fate that had taken down their neighbours. It didn't seem fair.

It didn't take me too long to rationalise their deaths. The term – 'for the greater good' allows for all evil to be made acceptable. They were victims of Marcus and their sin had been nothing more than to be in the wrong place at the wrong time.

This kind of slaughter happened all the time in third world countries with petty warlords and gangs shooting up the place. Why was this any different? Just because this was a first world city suddenly it wasn't okay?

There was nothing that could be done for these people, but I could make sure that their deaths counted for something. I was becoming a master of deception. The only problem was that the only one I was deceiving was myself.

CHAPTER ELEVEN

It wasn't hard to find the other Mages. All I simply had to do was to follow the path of destruction that they had left for me. The closer I got to the city, the worse the damage. From the look of it the battle was still escalating. Cars, trucks even buildings were gutted as the other Mages had passed by. It looked like a tornado had torn through the place.

As I flew across the city I had grown up in, I realised that thousands of people must have been caught in their wake. This was one of the most populated parts of the city. There was no coming back from this. If Marcus had wanted to reveal himself to the world at large he could have chosen no greater feat with which to do so.

No one sought to intercept me as I passed across the devastation that used to be a city block. Police officers, firemen and survivors stared up at me. They all had the same expressions on their face – shock and disbelief.

It wasn't horror, it wasn't anger, it was simple disbelief. They simply couldn't comprehend what they were seeing. It must have looked so confusing without the ability to see the Mana. As the battle raged, it would have looked like the city was tearing itself apart at the command of mere man. You couldn't have done any more damage with a team of wrecking balls. My fellow Mages must have looked like Gods. At their gesture concrete and metal tore from their foundations and wreaked havoc. If I were capable of it, I would have pitied them. Their world was coming to an end and they couldn't even see the cause of it.

By the time I got into the CBD proper it looked like a war zone. It didn't take me long to find Victor. He was at the centre of a vortex of magical fury, both directed at him and from him. I was surprised that four Mages were now standing against him. I had thought that Victor had killed two of them in the initial assault, but that obviously wasn't the case. The one had he had knocked from the roof had obviously survived his fall.

It took me several seconds before I was able to understand what the hell was going on. Victor wasn't attempting to attack them directly, he was skirting away from them. He couldn't teleport out from the fight without making himself vulnerable and he obviously knew that he couldn't take them all on directly. His plan appeared to be attempting to keep the buildings between them all so that all four couldn't assault him at once. This didn't look good for Victor, eventually they would corner him.

I could tell that some serious power had already been expended in the fight. All five of the Mages' shields looked like they had taken some serious damage. However the damage done to their shields was nothing compared to the surrounding buildings. In their fury they weren't even trying to contain the collateral damage to each other. When Gods fight it is the mortals who suffer.

It looked like several Mages had gone through the skyscraper that Victor was perched on in an effort to get to him. Smashed glass and rubble fell from the sky like rain. This was a heavily inhabited area. The death toll must have been in the thousands from fallen debris alone. The city streets below looked like a wasteland of fallen masonry, glass and twisted metal. This was no longer a city street. This place was now nothing more than a battleground.

It seemed almost blasphemous as these people tore my city apart. I had memories of walking across that street as a child. There was nothing I could do about it though. If I interfered now I would only risk being drawn further into the conflict and that wasn't the plan.

As I watched as one of the Mages took out an entire corner of a skyscraper. The whole building shuddered from the impact and huge columns of concrete hit the ground. It threatened to topple, but it eventually stopped crumbling, leaving a gaping whole about half way up its length. This obviously wasn't the intended outcome as another swipe quickly finished the job, sending the top half of the building plummeting towards Victor.

The noise was terrifying as twenty stories of building tumbled down into the cityscape. It reverberated through the air and the very sound hit me like a shockwave. The building collected another skyscraper on the way down and sent more shards of concrete and shrapnel across the city. Victor only had one way to go to get out of the trap that they had set. He had no choice. He would have to attempt to make his way past the two Mages who were waiting for him.

They might have gotten him too, had I not chosen to intervene from below. I launched a thread upwards and wrapped around one of the Mages as he attempted to sweep in behind Victor. The thread impacted with a snap and sparks that were visible from here. It wouldn't have done much damage against his shield, but that wasn't the point. With a sharp tug I freed the Mage from the threads holding him in the air and sent him plummeting downwards. I could hear his shout of outrage as the threads holding him in place were torn free. Several large chunks of concrete were torn free with him.

He sought in vain to attach a thread to secure himself, but I quickly knocked his attempts loose. It didn't take him long to reach terminal velocity. Once that happened I doubted he would have enough strength to secure himself with a thread. He certainly wouldn't be able to pull himself out of his fall while projecting such a powerful shield around himself. I knew from experience just how much power was required for that in my own free fall above Germany several weeks ago. He would have to either teleport or lower his shield, and to teleport he would need to lower his shield anyway. He had no choice – he had to lower the shield. As soon as his shield was lowered I hit him with a disrupt spell. I watched impassively as his Mana aura went berserk and he fell to his death.

His death went all but unnoticed to the melee above, except for providing Victor with an escape route. I didn't care much for saving Victor, but I needed Victor alive to provide a necessary distraction while I pursued my real goal. I caught glimpses of Marcus through the now shattered top of the building and pulled myself up the sheer surface to meet him.

Marcus still hadn't noticed the death of another of his party by the time I reached the top of the building. I crouched on the side of a concrete column that had been sheered in two as I sought the Arch Mage. Victor had taken the opportunity to engage the now three-to-one battle in an attempt to even the odds a little further.

It wasn't going to work. There were still simply too many for him to handle. Fortunately for Victor he wouldn't have to struggle for long. I had lost sight of Marcus in the fighting and didn't get a visual again until the fighting had already resumed. This wasn't a bad thing, I didn't want to get caught in that brawl. If I was lucky I could get to Marcus and take him down without anyone being the wiser.

With an explosive burst of shattered glass and concrete the Marcus slammed another thread into the shield surrounding Victor. The impact sent shockwaves across Victor's shield and I could see it beginning to buckle. It wouldn't be able to take much more like that. I had to intervene and I had to do it now.

Marcus had leapt backward to avoid Victor's counter attack and he obviously hadn't noticed me crouching below him. He was in the process of getting back into position to launch another attack against Victor when I struck.

I waited just until he launched himself free from the building to swoop down onto Victor. I struck with everything I had and grimaced in satisfaction as my strike caught him by surprise and sent him careening back into the office block. I wasn't aiming to knock the Arch Mage out of the sky like his companion. No, that wouldn't do for Marcus. I needed to look him in the eyes as I ended him. He needed to know that I was the one who brought about his death.

The fury of my attack must have stunned him as he wasn't moving. I knew he wasn't out of it yet, as his shield was still intact. My attack had alerted the other two Mages to my presence but I wasn't concerned about them. They would be too busy fending off a very angry Victor now that I had evened the odds.

I grimaced slightly as I looked down upon the inert figure of the Arch Mage. This was too easy. He was definitely baiting me. There was no way I was going to enter the building. That was obviously what he was waiting for.

Fortunately I had other options. I launched everything I had at the building and watched with awe as my thread swept through, glass, concrete, metal and through the front side of the office. Another building toppling down in this mess of a city wasn't going to make much of a difference now. As I had suspected Marcus quickly regained his footing as the roof collapsed down upon him. I was pretty sure that this wouldn't kill him. Surely he had reinforced his shield enough to protect him from such a mundane attack.

A wave of debris and dust washed over me as I smashed my way into the building. The damage I had done previously had torn a large chunk from several levels of the building. I smashed my way through a large shelf of concrete that had fallen down onto the Arch Mage. As I had presumed Marcus was uninjured from the assault but had retreated further into the building. I sent several large chunks of concrete at him as I launched my attack, but wasn't surprised when he easily blocked them. That hadn't been the point. The point had been to force him deeper into the building.

I swept out the support columns holding up the far side of the building. My thread easily smashed through internal walls, cubicles and the hard concrete shell supporting the building. There was a horrendous crunching noise as the building began to collapse in on itself.

Adrenaline rushed through my veins as the building toppled over. It was like the gloves had finally come off. There was no need to remain hidden in the shadows. After today the world would see us as we were. When I had battled previously against others of my kind I had never completely restrained myself in the application of my powers. In that, the Primea was right to have judged me, but I had never intentionally sought out destruction for destruction's sake. I had never done anything like this before. This was different. This was new. It was exciting and terrifying all at once. Before me lay the golden apple and I was going to take that apple and bite it. It was as if I had finally thrown off that last nagging constraint and felt a freedom that can only come when you're doing something that you know you shouldn't be doing, but with the acceptance that whilst it may be a bad decision, it's your decision. Consequences be damned.

I was sure that I wasn't the only Mage that day to feel the same way. There was no other explanation for the carnage that surrounded me. It was as if as a people we had decided that we would no longer hide from the world any longer. Let them see us, let them see what we can do. It was intoxicating.

My threads pierced the brittle shell of the office block and centred in on Marcus. They tore through his defence and pinned him in place. I was a God, nothing could stand against me now. Marcus struggled to break free as my threads tightened further around him. Given enough time he could eventually smash through my threads, but I wasn't going to give him that time. I needed to keep him focusing on his shield so that he couldn't bring his powers to bear. With the majority of the concrete support structures taken out the building began an ominous rumbling noise. Concrete pillars exploded under the pressure of the floors above.

I threw Marcus against another pillar. The impact smashed it into shrapnel as the Arch Mage barrelled through it. His shield was weakened, but it wasn't weak enough yet. Perhaps dropping the building on him would do the trick. It wasn't the way that I had wanted this to happen, but perhaps it was for the best.

I had just thrown him through the second pillar when the building finally came down. The level that I was standing on and the two above it had already been opened to the air. I wasn't going to get caught in the fall. I wasn't in any danger or at least I had assumed that there wasn't. I was wrong.

The weight of the building as it collapsed sheered through both levels as gravity took hold of the structure. The gap that I had been standing in disintegrated into chunks of falling concrete and rubble. My last vision before the dust consumed me was a large sheet of concrete flooring from the level above bearing down onto me. I threw everything I had into my shield and struck upwards in an attempt to save my life. There was no way my shield would survive being hit with a dozen stories of building. I was a dead man. My only solace was that I would take Marcus with me.

I was amazed once the dust had settled to find that the building had sheared off to one side. It had slammed into one of its neighbours and now was resting at a precarious angle, hovering over the city. Rubble and debris from its interior rained down on the streets below. I hadn't known that the force directed by my thread, and presumably Marcus's, would alter the course of the building, yet the evidence seemed irrefutable. It seemed unlikely that two threads however powerful would have been able to move that much mass, yet they had. Truly I was a power to be feared.

I could see Marcus across the other side of the building through a vortex of dust and ash. He seemed to be yelling something at me, but I couldn't hear him over the grinding noise of concrete from the building bearing down on its neighbour, the sound of water gushing from broken water pipes and the hiss of sparking electrics. Not that it mattered, whatever he had to say I wouldn't listen anyway.

I launched my attack before he had finished, sending shards of concrete flying at my foe as I leapt towards him. Marcus easily deflected the projectiles and moved to block my attack. Our threads collided with staggering force as I moved closer to my target. The brief respite he'd had, had been enough for him to focus his powers and bring them to bear on me. Without the element of surprise this wasn't going to be an easy fight. In some ways though, perhaps that was better. I hadn't liked the idea of killing him by dropping a building on him. No, I needed something more personal. He needed to know that I was the one who had killed him. He needed to look into my eyes as he finally accepted the folly of his actions.

"This is stupid Devon!" Marcus yelled over the crescendo of noises that surrounded us.

I didn't answer him, but escalated my aggression in response. My threads hammered against his shield until I thought it could take no more. Marcus spun out of the way as my thread smashed into the remains of an office, sending a desk and filing cabinet spinning out into the city scape. Marcus landed several metres away his feet skidding along the uncertain surface of what remained of the office block.

"We're never going to get another chance at this," Marcus urged. He was still trying to get me to attack Victor. He must have known it was pointless by now, he must have known that I was never going to join him.

"Don't make me do this, Devon." He threatened as several droplets of rain hit my shield.

The rain started slowly at first, but quickly became more severe. It was as if the city were attempting to clean itself from the stain that we had inflicted upon it. The water pooled down the side of the building and into the artificial chasm that we had created in the side of the building. This was going to be the mother of all storms when it hit properly.

The deluge blanketed the city in a wave of water and cloud, covering over the hundred murders and evils that had been perpetrated this night. It would have to cover one more. One more man would die – Marcus Devereaux. His death wouldn't be a murder though. It would be an execution.

Victor's ghostly words echoed throughout my skull, "You will kill Marcus Deveraux."

It didn't matter that he was the father of my lover, it didn't matter if he was more powerful than I was. It didn't even matter there was a good chance he would kill me. If necessary I would take him down with me.

"You will kill Marcus Deveraux!" the compulsion howled. The words were getting stronger as my own will bent the compulsion towards my ends. I would kill Marcus Deveraux and I would do it today.

Marcus may have tried to talk again, but I didn't listen. I struck him. My strike had all the fury that I was able to summon. It sent him staggering. Several more strikes in quick succession struck against him before he was able to bring his powers to defend himself. The reality of this hit home immediately – I was faster than he was. The knowledge sent shivers of delight through my soul.

"Devon, wait!" he gasped as he ducked under another thread.

"Why? Why should I wait?" I snarled. "Did you wait before you murdered my sister?"

"There was no coming back for your sister, she was too broken. Victor had almost completely rewritten her personality. She was too broken! It was a kindness!"

"Lies!" I snarled as I struck again, "all you've told me is lies!"

Marcus let my strike pass harmlessly above him as he dropped from the side of the building. Cursing I ran forward to see him land gracefully onto a building below. The building he had landed on was still under construction; scaffolding and support beams surrounded the main structure. I launched myself down at him with all my fury, sending threads down to try to strike him from the face of the building and also to steady my landing.

I landed on a large concrete slab in the centre of the building. It cracked under the pressure of my assault and my shield complained at the abuse, but I didn't care. I immediately lashed out to strike at Marcus. It happened so quickly that Marcus was forced to throw himself from the concrete slab to avoid my attack. If I was going to win this I would need to utilise my speed against him.

Marcus had obviously realised this too and had leapt to the far side of the construction site. He was now perched on an awning. With a wave of his hand he tore several metal beams from the floor and sent them barrelling towards me. The beams would easily have knocked me from the concrete slab had they hit me and sent me tumbling down into the city below.

This couldn't be allowed. I simply reached out my hand and I stopped them. I saw his face blanch as I wrapped my power around the metal and brought it under my control.

He shuddered as I slowly and surely moved them to one side. The noise of them hitting the concrete echoed across the worksite. It took several seconds before we both came to the same realisation. I was not only faster; I was also stronger.

There was nothing standing against me now. This man had no power over me and he knew it. He cursed as he attempted to climb deeper into the construction structure of the building to flee. Seeking to hide himself amongst the scaffolding and nets that littered the site. That wasn't going to save him.

Fortunately for Marcus I was suddenly blinded by a harsh light from above. A helicopter hovered above the skyline level with a spotlight centred on the two of us. Where the hell had that come from? I had been so focused on my prey I hadn't paid attention to my surroundings.

"Get down on your knees" a voice blared from the helicopter. "We will fire upon you if you do not comply immediately."

That didn't bother me. I could take rifle fire. I ignored them. The helicopter swung around revealing a side-mounted machine gun hanging off the side. Oh shit, that was a little bit heavier than an assault rifle. This could be a problem.

I considered backing away when I heard the whine of the machine gun powering up. It was strange that I could hear it over the all the other noise, but I swear I heard the whine of the gun spinning before bullets flew in my direction.

I didn't have enough time to properly prepare myself. I threw everything I had into my shield as the concrete before me exploded into small shards of rubble and dust. I didn't even have time to leap out of the way it happened so fast. The impact knocked the wind out of me and sent me skidding across the ground. The sound through my shield was staggering and each blast felt like I was being hit with a sledgehammer. How was my shield absorbing this?

Unable to control myself under the constant stream of fire I found myself flung from the concrete slab and falling into the darkness below. I reached out to steady myself but the thread was too weak. I must have hit a dozen beams on the way down and I don't remember landing.

My shield must have failed when I had landed, but it had absorbed the worst of the damage. I blinked several times as I checked myself, looking for bullet holes. I seemed to have come through relatively intact if somewhat bruised.

I could see the floodlight from the helicopter searching for me, but I was too deep in the structure for it to reach me. The helicopter circled around several times then headed deeper into the city. I guess they assumed that I was dead.

"Don't do this Devon," a voice called out from the darkness, "Don't make me destroy you!"

I couldn't see him, but I recognised his voice. He must have been lurking behind the concrete deeper inside as I couldn't even see his Mana signature.

"You can't!" I snarled as I pulled myself to my feet. The effort was taxing, but no worse than once again raising a shield around myself. Pain echoed down my wrists as I drew upon the Mana to raise the shield. This was one of the first warning signs that I was attempting to use too much Mana. Despite the pain, I felt somewhat relieved now that I had a fresh shield around me. Marcus emerged from the tangle of concrete pillars and construction material. He too had taken the opportunity to refresh his shield.

"It doesn't have to be this way," he said. "We can still work together. Help me! Help me to take down Victor. He's the real danger here. We don't have to do this!"

I wasn't listening. The compulsion pounded through my head with fury at the sight of him. Marcus must have realised this too, as he flicked his wrists and his threads burst into the blue flame that indicated Mana Nova. He'd obviously decided that if he couldn't best me through strength or through speed, he would have to use technique. Mana Nova should be far beyond my abilities. There was only one problem with that assumption – it wasn't.

I flicked my wrists and staggered as my own threads burned into Nova. The sensation sent waves of pleasure coursing through me as the increased Mana use overtook me. I had figured out the technique after I had seen Victor use it when I had faced him in Poland. It had taken me several hours to locate the theories that Victor had utilised, they had been buried within one of the most fundamental of our books. Once I found the necessary passages it hadn't been that hard. I hadn't had the opportunity or the inclination to use it until now. I had studied it after I had burned myself out in Paris, it had been an exercise to keep my mind focused at the time. I didn't realise that the study would save my life.

The euphoria caused by the effect was staggering. The power was chewing through my reserves at a great rate but it was nothing like I'd ever experienced before. I had once thought that the rush given when you draw upon a Telekinesis thread had been the ultimate feeling of power. I was wrong. This was. Mana Nova is the ultimate expression of pure unadulterated power and I was now a master of that power.

Marcus's face fell as our threads collided in sparks, each thread seeking to consume the other in a spectacular shower of sparks and flame. The worksite fared the worst of our fight as we sheered metal beams from their mountings and sent them tumbling down. The noise was tremendous as beams smashed into concrete slabs below us and large sections of concrete were sheered in two. We couldn't hear each other over the echoing clang of the construction materials hitting the ground. It was amazing we didn't bring the whole damned building down on top of us.

We rose in fury as each sought the higher ground. Our shields were next to useless against Nova and the only real advantage was height and the limited protection of the concrete pillars. I was reluctant to emerge back into the night sky, but to remain below would give Marcus the advantage and I dared not do that.

I snarled with rage as I cut out the beam that Marcus was standing on and used his fall to leap across to him. He fell several metres before looping a telekinetic thread around a beam to save himself. He landed gracefully on one of the lower levels, but it was too late.

In saving himself he had lowered his Nova. He was vulnerable and I was all too ready to exploit that. With a savage strike my Mana Nova thread smashed against his shield. In seconds the shield was down and it was only luck that the angle of his landing had saved his life. Even so my Nova thread sheered across his left arm and it was obvious that he had been badly burned. His face contorted in pain and fury as he leapt away.

He used his telekinetic thread to send several more beams flying in my direction, I cut them in two with Nova and leapt to engage. Marcus snarled as his thread turned to a Nova again and we met for the third time.

The rain sizzled on our threads as I stared with hate into Marcus's eyes and blocked out all other noises. My world collapsed into two small pin-pricks of light reflected in the Arch Mage's eyes. This was the way it was supposed to be. This was my birthright.

Marcus was saying something to me, but I couldn't hear it. I didn't care anyway. He had nothing to say that was of any interest to me. His words disappeared into the howling vortex of commands issued by the compulsion. In a desperate gamble Marcus went on the offensive to recast his shield and I was unable to take advantage of his lapse.

With a new shield surrounding him he had hoped to regain some of the lost advantage in this fight. My shield had absorbed several strikes and although it was holding up pretty well, it wasn't a fresh shield. It didn't matter much anyway, with Mana Nova the shield only lasted seconds before it was consumed. I saw the truth on Marcus's face. He was desperate and needed to do something, anything that could save his life. He knew as

I did that he was going to die here tonight. It was only a matter of time.

I often wonder if he regretted his decisions. He certainly could have disposed of me when he'd had the chance. I wonder if he had known when he had first met me in that car in Singapore that I would be the one that would kill him. I suppose not. He had saved my life that night by sending me to Victor. Perhaps that alone was cause enough to warrant this execution. Sending me to Victor had been what had started this whole mess. It may have been best had he just let me die. Without me, Allie would never have been found by Victor and we would never be standing in this moment here.

I could tell from the weariness on his face and the flinches of pain as he was forced to move his left arm that his strength was fading fast. I wasn't experiencing the same fatigue, if anything I was growing stronger. My rage had lent me a new level of strength and it was terrifying just how quickly the Mana was responding to me.

Weary and injured though he was, Marcus was still a Master of our kind. He wasn't going to fall through sheer power alone. He summoned what remained of his reserves and went on the assault. As we fought our battle became a matter of prediction. There was no time to assess your opponent's strike and raise a counter. The melee was on an instinctive level and Marcus and I were both skilled combatants. I'd experienced this before in my fights with Victor, as if the Mana itself seemed to know where it needed to be to serve our interests best.

The flash of threads before my eyes blinded me as our wills contested. I had fought this way once before with Victor, but the difference was that now I wasn't the one who was over matched. Now, I was winning.

With a snarl of rage I snapped several Nova threads towards Marcus. He howled with fury as one of them tore through his shield and impacted against his left leg. His knee was taken out and he fell several levels to land gracelessly upon the concrete platform below. He wasn't moving.

It wasn't over though, I had seen him buffer his fall. He was alive, the only question was, for how long? He wasn't like Victor; he wouldn't heal. Should he survive my next attack he could still die from blood loss. He was bleeding quite badly from his destroyed knee. Death through loss of blood was a serious possibility. That wasn't what I wanted though. I must be the one to finish him.

I landed next to him and with a flick of my wrist blocked his strike. I had anticipated that he would try something like that. Feigning unconsciousness to strike when your opponent seeks to finish you off was one of the oldest tricks in the book. His attack had been weak, it was easily parried. He rolled onto his back and attempted to scramble away from me.

I'm not sure where he thought he was crawling to, there was nowhere to go and I would strike him down before he could teleport away. There was nowhere he could go that I couldn't follow him anyway.

"Devon," he gasped, "wait, you can't kill me."

"Yes," I whispered darkly, "I can."

"I'm the only one who can rally our kind together against Victor. They won't follow anyone else."

The words were barely from his lips when I ended him. A Nova thread through the chest; a look of outrage and surprise on his face. His eyes dulled and his head fell against his chest. He was gone. It had happened so fast.

"You will kill Marcus Deveraux." The ghostly words of the compulsion were still pounding in my head.

This brought me no joy. There was nothing to be proud of here. I had simply ended a monster who had thought to use me as his own. I had freed myself from the machinations of this man and I had avenged my sister. This wasn't an achievement. It had been inevitable from the moment he had plotted to use my sister against Victor.

"You will kill Marcus Deveraux". A last solitary whisper echoed through the confines of my mind before fading into silence. I know. I had already done it.

It hadn't been the compulsion that had prompted me in the end. I alone had made the decision to kill him. I didn't linger near his body. I had no desire to gloat over his death. He wasn't the first person to die tonight and he wouldn't be the last. At least one more would die tonight – Victor Whittlesea.

This was all going to end tonight. I would finish him tonight or die in the attempt. I doubted that either of us could live in a world where the other existed. If I was being honest I didn't much care about the other outcome. I had already destroyed my world and I had little interest in surviving the coming apocalypse that this night's actions would surely bring.

My only care was that if I was to die then Victor will die with me. Nothing else mattered. He was just as much culpable as Marcus in this. He would have to pay for his part in this too. Once he was gone, the only person who remained in guilt would be me. I would have to live with that. I think that given the outcome that death would have been preferable.

* * * * * *

Victor wasn't that hard to locate, In fact he was waiting for me. I found him surrounded by destruction and death. At his feet lay the still smoking bodies of the final two Mages who had attempted to bring him down. Had I been thinking clearly perhaps I would have seen this as a warning. But I didn't.

We were too far past that. Victor knew, as I did what needed to happen next. He knew that we were past words. He knew that there simply wasn't anything we could do to pull back from the brink. The only way forward now was through the ending of one or the other.

Victor's eyes passed across me with their usual disdain as I climbed to the top of the building. There was no gratitude for my earlier assistance in saving him from his attackers. He knew that my actions had been self-serving.

Vague hopes that Victor had been sufficiently

weakened by his own battles that I would be able to take him crossed through my mind. I quickly rejected them as unnecessary. After all, I had just defeated Marcus on my own merits in a fair fight. I could do this. The only difference between them was Victor's regenerative skills, but I could counter that. If Marcus has been able to then figure it out, then I could.

"I knew you would come," Victor said grimly, "I would have been disappointed in you had you run."

"This needs to end." I said.

"I agree. But do you think you're the one to accomplish the task?"

"Only one way to find out," I snarled as I launched my attack. As expected a shield sprung around him in response to my attack. My thread impacted with a solid thump and sent him reeling back several steps. His shield wavered uncertainly and for a second I thought it might fall. His eyes widened in shock at the strike.

"You have grown more powerful once again," he murmured grimly and I wondered if perhaps he was foreseeing his death in his words.

His counter strike sent me staggering as I slowly brought my defences up. I had been caught unawares at the sight of Victor's shield almost falling. I hadn't expected the strike to take such a toll and Victor quickly capitalised on my distraction. Three lightning fast strikes impacted against my shield in rapid succession and I was forced onto the back foot and closer towards the edge of the building.

"But you are still undisciplined! You could have finished me had you not stopped to admire your handiwork!" Victor snarled as he forced me from the side of the building.

I leapt backwards and threw a thread onto the building behind me, pulling myself into a tight ball. I shot through the window behind me like a wrecking ball. The glass on the side of the building shattered on impact with my shield and I was able to pull myself back onto my feet. My stunt had given me a break from Victor's attack and allowed me to regroup my resources. Taking his earlier advice I didn't hesitate in launching attacks back at him.

I had landed a level up on the building and this gave me a slight advantage, unfortunately the gap between us made combat difficult. Given the distances we were easily able to predict each other's strikes and it was quickly drawing to a stalemate. I knew from experience that this type of battle would not serve me well. I needed to get up and personal with the Arch Mage. He didn't cope well when his opponent was in his face. I needed to close the gap, but any attempt I made to cross the gap would result in me being swatted from the air like a fly.

Maybe I could lure him into making that mistake. I knew how out of control he got when he lost his temper. It wasn't an easy task to accomplish, but if I could make him angry enough his rage might unbalance him and give me the advantage.

My thoughts were disturbed by the familiar 'whop-whop-whop' noise of a chopper closing in on us. Harsh lights shone upon us and stern voices called for us to surrender. I had no intention of getting shot by that high calibre machine gun again and was contemplating disappearing into the building when the matter was taken out of my hands. With almost casual disdain Victor wrapped a thread around the helicopter and simply tore it in two. The explosion as the machine died was anti-climactic as the wreckage fell from the skies. Just a dull thump and screams as its inhabitants fell to their deaths.

Victor's face was grim as he surveyed his handiwork. "This is the first time in half a century that I have been responsible for the death of a non-mana user."

There was no possible way that I could have heard that statement from him. It wasn't said loud. It wasn't said with the aid of a whisper thread. Yet I had heard it as if he had been standing next to me. His dark eyes sought me out across the void between us. I knew in that moment that I wouldn't need to antagonise him to make him angry. He was already furious.

"Then let's end this now!" I snarled at him, "before anyone else gets dragged into this.

"I have the higher ground," I mocked, "come over and take me down, prove that you're the superior Mage! Prove it now or die by my hand!"

"Higher ground means nothing," Victor commented before launching a thread. I had at first thought that the thread was aimed at me. I had thought he had played right into my hands, but I was wrong.

Victor's thread took out the windows and support

structure of the level below me. There was a horrible rumbling noise as the floor I was standing on gave way and tipped me out into the air. Unprepared for this kind of attack I stumbled and attempted to grasp at something, anything to prevent what was about to happen. But of course, it was inevitable.

As I fell from the building Victor's threads sought me out and pulled me into the air before him. I heard a crunching noise as the thread wrapped around my shield and felt the pressure build as I had to pump more and more power into my shield to prevent it from being crushed like an egg.

Victor dragged me before him and held me in the vice like grip of his Mana. Threads stronger than steel wrapped around me and squeezed. My whole body arched with agony as I brought everything I had to bare against him, but it wasn't enough.

"Your shield is exceedingly well constructed," Victor commented casually, as if we were merely chatting during a morning class, "I would have liked to know where you learned to do this."

Shit, I don't know how I'd learned to craft my shield. It was possible that I had learned it from one of the numerous Mages that I had fought over the years. It was also equally possible that I had simply figured it out for myself. It didn't really matter in the end. Victor wasn't really asking the question seriously. I suppose he had just wanted to keep me talking until the end. I wasn't going to give him that satisfaction.

"You were always a most disappointing student," Victor continued, "but a talented one none the less. It seems such a waste for it to end like this."

The end – I had often wondered how I was going to die. I had never thought that it would be like this. I had survived things that I had no right to. I suppose I had thought that I was just lucky or blessed. That I couldn't fail like others. As Victor's threads wrapped themselves tighter around me I was forced to think about another Mage who had died in a similar way.

I had been the one crushing him though. Vin had died held up before his foe in bands of Mana just like these. I had barely been able to muster the strength to finish him back then and had limped away from the battle too wrecked to even remember the details properly. They had flooded back over the next few days as the guilt had taken me. His death had been the catalyst for my rise to power and my subsequent fall. It seemed almost fitting that I die in much the same way.

For a brief moment I contemplated just lowering my shield to embrace my death. It would be so simple, so quick – a moment of pain followed by nothing. The desire was almost overwhelming as I made my peace with my end. I kept promising myself just one more second, then I'll let the shield fall and then as that second passed I promised myself again. Soon this will be over. Soon. Then a hissing noise rose in my head as the pressure to keep going overtook me.

I couldn't hear Victor talking to me now. A ringing

in my ears had blocked out all external sound. It felt like I was being held underwater as the pressure came in on me from all sides. The crushing weight of it burned as it pressed me and I felt about ready to explode.

Conscious thought had almost left me by this stage as my primitive-self kicked into survival mode. My senses expanded as I sought anything, however remote, that could help me. But there was nothing.

"Allie," I thought desperately as my shield caved in, "I'm sorry. I failed you."

A loud explosion of air rocketed me as my shield imploded, there was a split second of immediate relief as the pressure released and I was washed in a breeze of cool air. It lasted less than a second before the pain overtook. As Victor's threads closed in on me I felt a wrench as my shoulder was first dislocated and then crushed into pieces.

The pain was more than I could bear. I would have given anything to have passed out, but the fates were not kind. The whole thing must have taken mere seconds but to me it felt like a lifetime. I swear I could feel every rib in my chest being crushed as my body was twisted between vicelike threads.

I could see blood dripping down across my eyes and in a brief second of delusion I had wondered who was bleeding before the reality kicked back in. I must have sustained a head wound. It was perhaps a blessing as the wave of nausea and dizziness blocked out the pain some. I felt Victor wrench me to one side and I glanced down and saw an alley below me. He was hanging me over the side of the building.

"I take no satisfaction in this," Victor intoned as he held me before him, "it is merely something that needs to be done."

I could barely hear him and for some reason I couldn't seem to lift my neck to look directly at him. I wondered briefly if my back had been broken. I couldn't feel anything. The last thing I heard was a loud crack followed by blinding pain and the brief sensation of falling. Then nothing.

"Renee," I gasped as the darkness overtook me, "... forgive me."

CHAPTER TWELVE

I was more amazed than relieved when the darkness relented and my vision became filled with light. I've heard stories from people who say that after they've had near death experiences that the only thing they remember is the light. They remember the light being welcoming and loving. They recall being anguished about not being able to go into it.

That's bullshit. The only light I recall was from the ceiling of an ambulance cabin and it wasn't comforting. It was hard and it was cold and it hurt my eyes. It definitely didn't envelope me in love.

I had no choice but to look at the light – it was my whole world. The light wavered uncertainly and for a second I thought the darkness might return. That would be good. I didn't like it here. The light returned with vengeance and my vision was torn to pieces by it. The light sought me out no matter where I chose to hide. It always found me. The light was bad – it brought pain.

"He's responding," a voice cut in. Who had said that? Did I say that? Why would I say that? What was happening?

Before I could ponder this further the light was

blissfully removed once more, but the pain remained. I couldn't for the life of me remember a time when there had been no pain.

I felt something painful jerk against my arm and it took me several seconds to realise that I even had an arm let alone where it was. Something was holding it down. I turned my head to see what it could be. All I could see was blurry light.

I tried to bring my other hand to my face, but it was pushed away. Grunting, I tried again. The feeling of my hand on my face sent shockwaves of pain lancing through me, though strangely, it felt that it was as if it was coming from a long way away.

The light blurred as it broke before me and I could see a hand. It looked familiar. It was my hand. I could recognise it. I could see it! I couldn't see much else, everything else looked like a blurred void. The Mana on my hand was going nuts. It took me several seconds to recognise what it was. I briefly tried to bring the Mana under control, but I must have blacked out. The effort must have been too much.

When I came to the hand was gone. The light had gone too. I was strapped to a gurney in the back of an ambulance. There were two paramedics in the ambulance with me. They had the look of soldiers. I'd know that look anywhere.

I attempted to rise, but my neck was in some kind of brace and I couldn't move. I brought my hand to my face to attempt to free myself, but one of the paramedics noticed me and brought my arm back down. He must have looped it into a fastening or something, because I wasn't able to move it again.

"You're okay kid" he murmured. "We'll be there soon."

I vaguely wondered which kid he was talking to and where this kid was hiding. I also wondered where "there" was but as I tried to open my mouth to speak no words came out. I glanced down at my body to see a tangled mess of blood and wires and tubes poking out from me.

That explained the pain. They were doing something to me. I should probably stop them, but I was so very tired. I let my head loll back into the brace again and closed my eyes. The darkness returned, but it wasn't the same. There was no comfort here.

* * * * * *

I opened my eyes. I was lying in a hospital bed in a very non-descript room. Hospital rooms are normally pretty sparse, but this one was completely empty. The sound of monitoring equipment behind my head slowly intruded into my consciousness. It was strange that I hadn't noticed it at first. Now it was all I could think about.

Beep. Beep. Beep.

I wasn't feeling any pain, but I was feeling fuzzy, kind of like when you've had too much to drink. This feeling wasn't anywhere near as pleasurable. They must have drugged me. I didn't know who they were, but it was the only explanation. I felt nauseous. If I was going to feel this bad I could at least do it without that god damned beeping noise from the machine.

The machine was too far out of reach for me to turn it off and my arms still appeared to be locked into some form of brace. I sat up as far as I could, which wasn't very far with the braces holding my arms and legs to the sides of the bed.

This wouldn't do.

A thread leapt from my fingers almost unbidden and unstrapped me from the bed. It happened so quickly that it took me several seconds for my mind to catch up. I had almost forgotten for a moment that I could do that.

In fact I only had very shaky memories of anything that had occurred. I knew who I was, but I had no idea where I was or how I had gotten here.

Then the fights with Marcus and Victor exploded back into my consciousness like a raging bull. Each memory struck me harder than the last. I gritted my teeth as I relived the pain of being crushed by Victor's threads. How was I even still alive? Had he somehow left me alive after that? That didn't seem likely. Had I died and this was some form of afterlife? That seemed even more far-fetched.

The only thing I knew for certain was that I couldn't stay here. I went to pull the brace from my neck and try to stand. Unfortunately this was made more difficult by the number of tubes connected to my nose and mouth. I couldn't seem to remove the neck brace without disconnecting myself from the tubes and wiring and I had no idea where to even start to do that.

My right shoulder and arm also appeared to be in a brace and most of my arm was in plaster. This more than anything else had been what was restricting my movement. I went to move my legs to the side of the bed and knew almost immediately that something was wrong. My legs weren't reacting the way they were supposed to. In fact, they weren't moving at all. I couldn't even feel them.

Just what kind of drugs had they given me? Had they sedated my legs? A hundred suspicions and theories rose in my mind until I finally settled on the horrible truth. My legs weren't moving because my back was broken. Victor had broken my back.

Had he meant to do that? I didn't think so. He had meant to kill me, but somehow had been unable to do so. That didn't seem right; by all rights I should be dead. Why wasn't I?

A chill settled over me. I didn't know how and I didn't know when, but he would pay for this. I would survive this somehow and I would find him and I would finish him. I gritted my teeth as the absurdity of that statement hit me. How the hell was I going to get revenge? I wouldn't even be able to get out of bed without assistance.

A particularly loud beep from the machine behind me drew my ire as it echoed throughout the room. Before I knew what had happened a thread had lanced out and smashed the machine. The impact sent the machine careening into the far corner of the room. There was a sharp tug as wires were unceremoniously pulled from my bed frame. The machine gave one last metallic squawk before it finally died with a small fizzing noise and a small exhale of smoke.

The door was almost immediately flung open and a white-coated man rushed into the room. He surveyed the scene. His eyes flicked from disbelief at the destroyed machine then through to annoyance at me.

"You shouldn't be sitting up," he growled as he came over.

"Where am I?"

He didn't answer. Instead he set about re-arranging the tubes and wires that I had knocked out of place earlier.

"Where am I?" I repeated darkly.

Again the man ignored me. I gritted my teeth as I pondered my next move. The inability to move my legs properly was only a minor inconvenience. With Telekinesis I didn't need my legs. I could kill him where he stood and there was nothing he could do about it.

"Answer me," I rumbled as I held out my good hand towards him. He gasped as a thread wrapped around his throat and pulled him from the floor.

"I didn't pull you from the ruins of Melbourne to let you torture doctors," a familiar voice said from the corner.

I dropped the doctor immediately as I turned to face the newcomer. Levenson was standing in the doorway.

Before I could think about it my thread lanced from the doctor to wrap around Levenson's neck. His eyes bulged as the thread squeezed around his throat.

"Were you working with Marcus?" I demanded.

Levenson couldn't answer with his throat constricted, but I could see him trying to shake his head from side to side. The doctor took the opportunity to scramble from the room. I was sure he was going to go get armed soldiers, but I didn't care. I'd deal with them when they got here too.

"Did you know what Marcus had planned?" I snarled.

Again, Levenson tried to frantically shake his head. He was going a horrible shade of purple before I loosened the thread. I wasn't sure I believed him, but I wasn't going to kill him. He fell back to the ground.

"Where am I," I snarled at Levenson as he got to his feet.

"You're in a secure military facility about 30 kilometres out of Melbourne." Levenson replied weakly. "We brought you here after we found you. You're lucky to be alive." There was a hint of reproach in his voice.

"I don't feel lucky."

"We were hoping you would be able to answer some questions." Levenson began.

"You dragged me all the way here, patched me up because you had questions?"

"Not as such." He looked like he was being completely honest with me. That was the problem though, he always looked like he was telling the truth.

"I can't feel my legs," I said.

Levenson nodded, "You have incurred some spinal damage. Your doctor wasn't sure you would even survive, let alone walk."

"You're saying I won't be able to walk again?"

"You are made of strong stuff," Levenson finished, cutting me off.

I didn't answer immediately, "What am I doing here?"

"That is up to you."

"No games, no lies," I snarled. "Tell me what you want."

Levenson gave a thin-lipped smile.

"We need your help." Levenson said softly, "but that can wait…"

"… until you're better." He trailed off as a small team of doctors entered the room. There were soldiers behind them. Levenson immediately waved the soldiers off, they didn't look happy, but they remained in the corridor.

The new doctor was an older gentleman though he still had the look of a soldier. All the men here did. That at least went some way towards validating Levenson's earlier statement about being on an army base. The doctor hesitated when he saw the ruins of the machine, then pulled the blanket from over one of my toes. I couldn't quite see properly as the brace didn't let me see that far down.

"Wiggle your toes," he ordered. The others behind him leaned forward to view my feet. It was a little off-putting. I could tell from their reactions that there wasn't good news to be had.

"Well, the good news is that there is some movement," the doctor said gruffly, "full mobility may return in time."

"May return?" I prompted.

He made several scratches on the chart. "There are no guarantees."

"You're saying I won't be able to walk?"

"Walk? You're lucky to be alive in the condition you were brought in."

I didn't want to hear it. I slumped back into the bed. I'd think I would have preferred it if Victor had killed me.

"Get out," I whispered.

"I have tests to run."

"Those can be done later," Levenson said smoothly as he gently but firmly guided the doctor from the room.

I nodded briefly to Levenson as he followed the doctor out. I contemplated tearing the braces from my body. What good had they done me? What good were they going to do? I was never going to walk again. What was the point though? Would it make me feel better? Possibly. Would it help me? No.

I'd never in the million years have thought that this would be my fate. I suppose I'd always just thought of myself as invulnerable. It wasn't that I thought that I couldn't be defeated, and it wasn't that I couldn't be hurt. I'd been horribly hurt before, but I'd always somehow come through it. I was young and I was invincible. Others had paid such a price; it was only my youthful arrogance to assume myself exempt.

What was the point of going on like this? I'd hardly be able to affect any kind of vengeance on Victor like this.

It took me sometime before I was able to get any sleep. In the end sleep found me, not as a gentle slumber, not as an exhausted collapse, because I could no longer bare to be alone with my thoughts any longer. A troubled mind can be a torturous place.

* * * * * *

I began a routine of physical therapy and exercise in an attempt to recover what I had lost. The sessions were long and they were painful. My legs were still pitifully weak and sensations came and went. Sometimes I felt pain, sometimes I felt nothing. What I felt most of all was simple exhaustion.

This place didn't seem to have any windows. My only measure of time was dinner, which seemed to arrive and pass with infrequent regularity. It was almost as if it was scheduled for different times in the day. But that doesn't make any sense. I could of course have teleported from the centre at any point, or used Scry to send my vision out into the world, but I had little interest in doing so as I had fear for what I would find.

I had little interest even looking in the mirror. The person that looked back was unfamiliar. There were several large scars across my face and upper torso. Although my shoulder had healed to allow free movement there were surgery scars clearly visible down my back.

I now moved about the complex via a wheelchair. I had at first rejected the idea, but the reality of the situation quickly became apparent. If I didn't want to be locked to my bed, I would need a chair to navigate around. Not that there was much to see. The complex consisted of a long corridor, with a series of offices and meeting rooms and a hall at one end that had been converted into a physical therapy room. I don't believe this building had originally been designed as a hospital.

Levenson visited infrequently and when he did I could sense that he was worried about something. This wasn't surprising. I couldn't even begin to imagine what the fallout from our battle over Melbourne had been. Marcus had claimed that his death would lead to a war. Was that the truth? I didn't know and I didn't care to find out.

I could tell that Levenson was disappointed with my improvement, although my doctors said my progress was nothing short of miraculous.

Miraculous indeed. I could stand for no more than a few seconds before my legs would fail and I would fall. The muscles were just too weak. The prospect of being able to walk again was quickly becoming more and more of a pipedream.

Eventually I came to terms with this, but with mixed emotions. You quickly learn to accommodate and the wheelchair wasn't so bad. But then again, I never had to travel very far. What I feared was that once it had become obvious that there was no more that could be done for me that I would be sent out into the world. I didn't want that. I wasn't ready. In fact the world could go to spit for all I cared. I was done. I was out. So I did my exercises and kept myself active. I did what the doctors asked of me. I did anything that would mean that I would be kept here.

I was careful to use Mana every day, the last thing I wanted was to go through a withdrawal whilst in this state. I used it for simple things, no more than parlour tricks, but it was enough.

I had no idea if the doctors and staff here knew who I was or what I was capable of and I didn't think it wise to reveal my powers to them. For all I knew they simply thought I was like everyone else.

My meetings with Levenson were a little tense. It was becoming more obvious with each visit that he was hoping to hear some good news about my recovery. No, that wasn't right. He was more than hopeful; he was desperate to hear some good news. Things must be going pretty badly out there. Sometimes after our meetings curiosity would get the better of me and I would wonder what was happening out there, but then I realised that I was no longer part of that world. I wanted nothing from it. It had nothing that appealed to me any longer. I wasn't happy here, but I was one hell of lot happier here than I had been out there. No, it was best to remain here.

Unfortunately after what must have been at least six months, that was no longer an option. I knew immediately upon entering the room that I was about to attend my last meeting with Levenson in this facility. Normally our meetings took place alone, this time there were doctors present.

"They tell me that you're not making much more progress," Levenson said.

I sat back in my wheelchair uncomfortably, "That's what they tell me."

"This isn't going to work. I need you mobile, I need you back to your full strength."

"Are you going to tell me why?"

Levenson twisted his lips together. "I'm sure you're aware of what's been going on outside these walls."

"No, actually I'm not."

Levenson looked surprised. He must have assumed that I was at least keeping myself current.

"There's nothing for me out there." I said sourly.

"No?" Tell me then, what do you know about this man?"

He passed a folio over to me. I flipped it open, it looked like a police dossier of a man named Killian Voll. That didn't mean anything to me.

I pushed the papers away, "Never heard of him. I'm assuming he's a Mage or you wouldn't be showing me this."

"He's creating quite a problem."

"And what do you want me to do? Roll over his foot?" I wiggled the chair a little in emphasis.

Levenson scowled, "If you're through being smart, I've prepared a short presentation for you."

"Oh?"

"This is a video of news clippings from the last few months." Levenson flicked on his laptop, which was connected to a screen on the wall. The TV flicked to the scenes of a firefight between armed soldiers and what I could only assume to have been a Mage. A crisp female voice over peppered the footage with comments about a catastrophic death toll and informed me that the film was taken in Paris. The shooting escalated to a maximum before the image of a small truck being thrown at the camera ended the transmission.

The next clip appeared to be of a press conference. The man I recognised as Killian from the folio I saw earlier was standing at the podium addressing a crowd of reporters. Standing behind him was a very nervous looking Levenson. He didn't look to be too thrilled to be there.

"We only want peace. We've lived amongst you all our lives. We don't want this. We never wanted this."

"What about the deaths?" one of the reporters interjected angrily.

"This is simply a result of a power struggle within our order," Killian responded.

"Singapore, Melbourne and Paris are in ruins. This is merely the result of a power struggle?" the reporter queried in disbelief.

"We as an organisation deeply regret the loss of life and damage caused by our internal struggle--" Killian was cut off by a barrage of shouted questions from the reporters. It was obvious that this had been rehearsed line and it wasn't delivered that well. Killian obviously wasn't the statesman that he thought he was. His reply sent shockwaves through the crowd with reporters shouting at him. Killian raised his hands to attempt to restore order, but was unable to do so.

Fortunately for Killian, and unfortunately for everyone else, Killian was cut off by a loud explosion of sound. I knew that sound. It was the sound of someone teleporting in. Cameras frantically swung around to catch the action. Three figures teleported into the back the hall.

"You don't speak for us!" a loud voice boomed across the chamber. People started screaming as the newcomers launched an attack at Killian. Chairs, tables and people were ground up as Killian was forced to defend himself. I couldn't see the Mana in the video footage but it wasn't difficult to imagine what was going on. It would have been carnage. There would have been nowhere for people to go and the Mages themselves didn't look like they even cared who got in their way.

Levenson paused the video at this point.

"Forty-three people were killed in that press conference. Voll survived and has been a thorn in our side ever since."

"Melbourne is in ruins?" I queried, "I didn't think we did that much damage."

"You did enough, but there have been three more battles there since. Let alone the damage caused by rioting and looting." Levenson said dryly as he hit play on the video again.

"Who was this compiled for?" I asked. He obviously hadn't gone to this effort for me.

"Some US General. He thought he could sort the situation out. He didn't."

I wasn't surprised.

"He took Los Angeles and Chicago down with him in an attempt to kill Voll." Levenson said grimly. "We are just ill equipped to deal with your kind."

I hadn't expected that, though I suppose I should have. Without the Primea to force order there would be nothing stopping us from turning on each other. It was inevitable that the rest of the world would be dragged into it.

"We currently have four small wars tearing across Europe with Mages being involved in all cases."

"Where is Victor in all this?" Even saying his name sent shivers of rage down my spine, "Surely that's his problem."

"We don't know. No one has seen him since Melbourne. The only spokesperson we have for the Mage community is Voll and you can see how well he's doing."

"What do you want from me?"

"In your current condition, nothing."

"Good."

"However there have been some doubts, that you're telling the truth as to the extent of your injuries." Levenson began.

"That would be a question for my doctors." .

The doctors looked uncomfortable. One of them eventually said, "Your leg muscles would have atrophied by now at your current level of injury."

"I'm not lying."

I didn't need this.

"Devon, we need help." Levenson pleaded. "This needs to end before it leads into another world war. That's the way it's heading."

I didn't reply.

"Devon… people are dying."

"I don't see what I can do."

"There are some options, machine supports, callipers. That could restore your mobility," Levenson said, "at least to a degree."

"Then what?"

"Then you work with us to restore order."

I scoffed.

"I'm not going to be a hired thug for you." I said darkly.

"Then there is very little left that we can do for you. Medically speaking." Levenson replied softly.

"I understand."

Levenson had diplomatically left the threat unsaid, but it was obvious what he meant. They would turn me out.

His arguments hadn't exactly fallen on deaf ears. It wasn't that I didn't care about what was going on outside these walls. It was that I didn't think that I could do anything about it. Arguments raged backwards and forwards through my mind as I pondered what to do.

If only I had listened to Renee. She had warned me that the path I had followed would lead to ruin. I was glad that she hadn't been around to see me like this. It was better that she never find out. No, I couldn't go back. Never go back. I'd have to find some other hole to crawl into.

* * * * * *

That night I ate a cold dinner in my room. I'd be leaving this complex within the week. I rolled from my room to the exercise chamber as I did after my meal every night. It was the closest thing I had to an afternoon walk. The scenery wasn't that exciting as I passed by meeting rooms and offices, but it was the best I could do at the moment.

I passed the open door of the meeting room that we'd occupied this afternoon and found to my surprise that Levenson's laptop was still hooked up to the television. In spite of myself I rolled into the room. The laptop was in power down mode, but didn't need a password to bring up the desktop. This was hardly secure. I was surprised.

The video was still loaded into the media player. With trembling hands I moved the touchpad and clicked play. The video started up again. I watched as a parade of news reports, surveillance camera and security footage detailed the rise of my kind into the 'real' world. It was sickening. We had turned on ourselves like animals.

I had done this. No, that's not right – Marcus had done this. He was the one that had started all this, but I had helped. Names and dates flashed up on the screen as more information became available. There was footage taken by surveillance drones of soldiers fighting side by side against Mages in war zones that used to be cities.

I was responsible for this. This wasn't the legacy that I had sought. All I had wanted to do was to save my sister. This was the stuff of nightmares. My lips tightened as I forced myself to watch the footage. My hands kept creeping towards the stop button, but I refused to actually click it. The footage went for an hour and I hated every minute of it. The video ended long before I turned away from the screen.

Each image on the screen haunted me. The news feeds in particular drew attention to the suffering of the innocents. A child's stuffed toy trampled in the dirt as booted heels trod over it, homes torn apart and families torn asunder.

I had to do something. But I seriously doubted that there was anything I could do in this condition. As soon as the thought entered my mind it was immediately assaulted.

What the hell was I thinking? I'm not a grunt soldier, I'm not an athlete whose entire world depends on their physical condition. I'm a Mage. My body matters not. I'd been thinking like some spoilt little child for too long.

If I was to go into battle, I'd go as a Mage, not as a

soldier. My Mana was still strong – that was all that ever really mattered. I spun my chair around and headed to the physical therapy room. If this was going to work I would need space.

I grunted as I pulled myself from the chair, supporting myself between two bars. My usual therapy involved attempting to move my feet into hesitant steps, supporting myself for seconds and only using the bars to prevent a fall. It was painful and it was tedious. The smallest of steps led to exhaustion and the only reward was more pain as the next step was required.

What if I didn't have to go down that path? What if I didn't need my muscles at all? What if I could control my own body with the one power I still had. The Mana.

It would take some doing, but it could be done. I focused and breathed out as the power flew into me. I formed a field around me and felt it clamp me into place. It was like a shield, except that it was keeping me upright.

I let go of the beams and stood there. This would normally result in screams of protest from my lower back and legs. Nothing. I was being supported by my magic. The concentration required was enormous, but I knew that with practice it would become second nature to me. This could be done.

A coughing sound caused me to spin about. Levenson was standing at the door watching me.

"I had wondered how long it would take." He commented.

"You left the laptop out for me to find?"

"Of course. I knew that you wouldn't be able to help yourself. I wondered how long it would take before you would think of using Mana."

"How did you know that I wasn't lying about my injuries."

"You think I don't know when someone is using Mana? Now of all times?"

"Fair point."

I took a few haltering steps through sheer force of will. I must have looked like an automaton as my footwork was clunky and robotic. It was difficult without any kind of response back from my legs, but I knew that I could learn to do this. Every day I would improve until I regained my mobility.

"So what happens now?" I grunted.

"Now?" Levenson smiled, "We get to work. I've taken the liberty of placing your friends and family in a safe location. You will be comforted to know that they at least are safe from all this. They think you're dead, but I can arrange for you to see them."

"No," I whispered, "Let them think me dead."

Levenson raised an eyebrow but didn't push the matter. He didn't understand. I couldn't afford the luxury of friends or family. I needed to cast myself free from them. It wasn't that I thought that they would be safer, although that was true. It was simply that I couldn't be who I needed to be while they were still a part of my life.

"Come, let's get to work." I said as I steeled my heart against the coming storm.

Over the next few months I learned to walk again without assistance. As I had predicted the effort of keeping myself mobile had dwindled into a negligible amount. Most of the time I didn't even think about keeping the field around me active, if I needed to walk somewhere the mana flowed to the required limb and I walked.

I would never be as graceful or as balanced as I had once been. I would never have the same control over myself that I had had as a boy. Those days were gone. That wasn't the point. I wasn't some boy attempting to take over the world in some damned fool quest. I was a Mage. I had been blooded and tested and broken. I had been remade anew in a crucible that would have broken most men. I refused to let my past actions dominate my future. I refused to let who I was dominate who I needed to be.

Our kind were sick. We had become irrevocably damaged. Perhaps we had always been a ticking time bomb – a time-bomb set to take out our species as a whole. For hundreds of years we had been quietly getting stronger and more arrogant. Our minds had been twisted with delight at our own power. We recognised nothing but strength and reacted only in anger when our will was thwarted.

I knew that Levenson wanted me to be a general, to lead troops into the battle, but that couldn't be my role. I could play at it, but in truth I was to be an assassin.

If mankind was to survive this war, then my kind could not. My hand had led to this war; my hand would end it. One by one my kind will fall before me. I could only hope that I was strong enough. There is no greater defeat in this world than to surrender to your hatred and I had finally let mine consume me.

To be continued

ABOUT THE AUTHOR

As an avid science fiction and fantasy reader
Christopher George has been immersing himself
in books from a young age. In 2004 Christopher
completed his Bachelor of Multimedia at Monash
University and has been working as an IT professional
ever since. He currently lives in Melbourne with his
partner, her daughter and three cats.

For more information about the book
and the series go to
www.christophergeorgenovels.com
or like him on Facebook.